God opposes the proud, but give

CW00458232

James 4 v 6

Best wishes

Al

Books by Alex Willis

DEATH ON THE CART

A DCI BUCHANAN MYSTERY

BY

ALEX WILLIS

Published by Mount Pleasant Publishing 11-11-2022

The story contained between the covers of this book is a work of fiction, sweat, and perseverance over many months. Characters, place names, locations, and incidents are either the product of the author's imagination or are used fictitiously. Any resemblance to actual persons, living or dead, or locals is entirely coincidental.

ISBN-13: 978-1-913471-25-5

All rights reserved
Copyright © ALEX WILLIS November 2022

No part of this book may be reproduced, stored in a retrieval system, modified by adding to – or subtracting from, or transmitted in any form or by any means without the prior written permission of the copyright holder.

Text set in Garamond 12 point.

Cover photo, river Cart, Busby. © Alex Willis
Cover Layout © Alex Willis 2022

Death on the Cart typeset

The River Cart at Busby

I lived in Busby during my early teens. The cover photo for this book is of the River Cart showing the bend in the river close to where we used to swim. Those of you with sharp eyes will see that I reversed the photo, this was done for cover layout requirements. I never knew this part of the river had a name; it was just where we would swim. I have since found out that it does have a name, Andy's Hole, thank you for Keith for this bit of information.

The history of the town dates back more than 700 years. The town's original name was Bushby.

Up until the 1780s, Busby village consisted of a few cottages spread out along a track leading from Carmunnock to Mearns. This route forded the River Cart at the end of Field Road by means of a hump backed stone bridge whose balustrades have since been removed and replaced by a post and mesh arrangement.

Over the years there have been cotton mills, meal mills, lint mills, and a commercial laundry alongside the river with power provided by a large water wheel situated beside the stone bridge. There have been other commercial operations, such as the print works and bleachfield. Most of these building still exist, but now being used for different functions.

Ch	Title	Page

1

Snakes and Scaffolds

For John McDermott, the job on Blackwater Road was to be just another window-painting job – so what was he doing lying below the hole in the garage roof where his body had passed on its downwards travel from the scaffolding seven floors above?

♦

For Detective Chief Inspector Jack Buchanan and his wife, Karen, today was special. Though it was early November, with the warmth of summer long gone over the horizon, this Saturday was to be their first BBQ with invited guests in their new home.

'Did you get the onions?' asked Karen.

'They're in the bag on the kitchen counter.'

'Parfait.'

'Parfait?'

'Sorry, it's having my sister here with us this weekend, we invariably end up speaking French to each other.'

'Hmm. I've put the beers in the chiller box in the garden,' said Buchanan. 'Tesco was out of ice, so I went to Sainsbury's.'

'Thanks. Can you put the steaks in the fridge? Oh, there's the bell, Jill said she'd come over early to help get things ready. Would you get the door?'

'Good morning, Jill.'

'Morning, Jack. Karen in the kitchen?' she asked, stepping into the front hallway holding two shopping bags.

'Yes, where's the car?' Buchanan asked, as the taxi drove away.

'In the garage, broken fan belt according to Stephen's diagnosis.'

'Oh, that sounds expensive. The ladies are preparing the food for the barbeque.'

'Ladies?'

'Poppy and Katherine, Andrew's wife.'

'Oh, good, I wanted to have a quiet chat with Katherine while they are here. Are Karen's sister and husband here yet?'

'They're in the sitting room, Armand is on the phone to their real estate agent in Paris and needed a quiet space. Here, let me carry those bags through to the kitchen for you.'

'They're not that heavy.'

'You're carrying enough already, wouldn't want you to overdo it.'

'Honestly, I'm fine, and in case it's slipped your attention, women have been having babies since day one.'

'Sorry, just being a concerned grandad to be. Where's Stephen?' said Buchanan, reaching for the heavier of the two bags.

'He didn't get in till gone three this morning. There was a break-in at the jewellers in the Beacon Centre and he had a lot of paperwork to take care of before he went off shift. He's sleeping late. He'll be here as soon as he wakes.'

'Lucky him.'

'Are Nathan and Susan coming?'

'Yes.'

'Hello, Jill,' said Poppy.

'Well, if you ladies have things under control, I'll put out the chairs and start the barbeque.'

Buchanan stepped out onto the patio and stopped in beautiful sunshine. He looked over the back garden, whose borders sported the remains of the magnificent display of Karen's horticultural excellence. Off into the distance to the west of Eastbourne he could make out the outline of Beachy Head.

He smiled as he walked over to the stack of garden chairs. He was thinking about Karen's recent comment about having many days like this if he retired. But could he retire, spend weekends pottering around the garden? He shook his head, no way, he couldn't tell the difference between a pansy and a daisy. Besides, every time the phone rang, he'd be on it in a flash wondering where the next body or jewel robbery was.

Of course, there was the imminent arrival of Jill and Stephen's baby, his grandson, according to the latest scans. As a mark of respect towards Buchanan, the baby was to be called Jack. Now there was a reason for retiring. As he mused about one day taking young Jack Hunter fishing, Karen's sister and husband stepped out on to the patio.

'Bonjour, Jack.'

'Bonjour, Eloise.'

'Comment allez vous?'

'Bien, merci. Et tu?'

'Comme ci, comme ça.'

When she saw the look of indecision on Buchanan's face she asked, 'Es-tu sur que tout va bien?'

Buchanan thought before answering and realised everything was just fine. He smiled and said, 'Parfait, simplement parfait.'

Eloise grinned, 'I see your French is as good as ever.'

'It's just high school stuff.'

'You could improve it if you came over and visited with mother more often.'

He shrugged, 'If only I wasn't so busy.'

'You'd have plenty of time if you retired.'

'What's this, a conspiracy? Are you and Karen working together?'

'No, of course not. She's told me many times about how much you love your job and how the country would soon be overrun by criminals if you ever did retire.'

'Now you're making fun of me.'

'Of course, she is,' said Armand, 'and for your information I visit mother as often as you do.'

'Who does what often?' asked Andrew Mansell, passing Eloise as she went back into the kitchen.

'Hello, Andrew,' said Buchanan. 'Just chatting about visiting in-laws. Have you met Armand, Karen's brother-in-law?'

'No, we haven't met. Nice to meet you, Armand,' said Mansell, as he shook Armand's hand. 'Andrew Mansell. I understand you've been in France these last few years?'

'Yes, I was sent over to setup a branch office in Paris for our European sales team. What was supposed to be a six-month tour ended up being two years. You're a doctor?'

'He's my doctor,' said Buchanan.

'What he means, Armand,' said Mansell, 'Jack tells me the what and where, I tell him when and how, then it's up to Jack to tell the who and why.'

'Sound like a children's game.'

'What they are not telling you?' said Nathan Greyspear, who'd just joined them. 'Doctor Mansell is a police pathologist.'

'Oh, you're that doctor,' said Armand. 'Jack has mentioned you many times.'

'Nice to be remembered.'

'Seen anyone interesting lately?'

'I'd rather not say, don't want to spoil the party with gruesome details of someone's innards.'

'Jack,' said Karen, from the kitchen door, 'sorry for interrupting – is the barbeque ready?'

'Should be, I lit it twenty minutes ago.'

'Good, would you start the chicken? They're in the foil-covered dish on the kitchen counter. I've already cooked them in the oven, they just need flavouring up on the grill. I'll bring the steaks and burgers out when you've done the chicken'

'Your wish is my command.'

♦

'How are you finding university here in England, Poppy?' asked Eloise.

'It's not that much different from the one I was attending in Dallas, though I found some of the accents take a bit of getting used to.'

'I hear you are off on holiday next week, Jack,' said Armand, helping himself to salad.

'Yes, Poppy has invited us to go with her and Harry to spend the Thanksgiving weekend with her parents in Dallas, Texas.'

'Just the weekend?' said Armand. 'Dallas is a long way to go for just the weekend.'

'It will be a long weekend. We fly out on the Wednesday morning and return early the following Wednesday morning.'

'Harry, I hear you are leaving Castlewood stables to take up a position in Dallas?' said Stephen, who'd not long arrived.

'Yes, I'm going to be the new stable manager at the Webb Ranch.'

'Nathan, have you found a new manager to replace Harry?' asked Andrew.

'Not yet. I'm still waiting for Jack to apply for the position.'

'Very funny,' said Buchanan. 'Why is everyone offering me jobs around stables?'

'Who else has been offering you a job at their stables?' asked Nathan. 'Whatever they have offered, I'll double it.'

'Cynthia McCall offered me a job at her stables.'

'Ah, the fair Cynthia, who could forget her? Did she really offer you a job?'

'Not really, she was just kidding – at least, I think she was just kidding.'

Greyspear laughed, 'I can just see you, six in the morning, pushing a wheelbarrow full of steaming horse manure across the yard and Cynthia telling you to get a move on.'

'That's an image I'd rather not dwell on,' said Buchanan.

'When are you Harry getting married?' asked Katherine.

'Not till next spring,' said Poppy. 'We felt it would be better for me to complete university and for Harry to get settled in his new job.'

'Is Thanksgiving like our Harvest Festival, Poppy?

'I'm not sure what your Harvest Festival is.'

'It is a celebration of the harvest and food grown during the year,' said Jill. 'It is also about giving thanks for all the good and positive things in our lives, such as family and friendships. The festival is an old tradition, usually held in churches but also in schools and even sometimes in pubs. In times gone past, country estates and farms would celebrate the festival in the estate barn. Where there is more than one church in a village or town, the celebrations are usually staged so as not to coincide with each other.'

'What sort of food is involved?' asked Poppy.

'Mostly homegrown food from gardens and allotments, sometimes the local farmer will provide hay bales and food such as potatoes, turnips, kale, cabbages, and eggs, all produced on the farm. As part of the celebration there sometimes is a meal made from the donations with the surplus given to local charities.'

'In the States, Thanksgiving is more than just a weekend,' said Poppy. 'It's the beginning of the holiday season and begins on the last Thursday in November. There's the Macy's Thanksgiving Day Parade. That's held on Thanksgiving Day in New York and is televised all over the country. Thanksgiving Day is seen as the beginning of the Christmas season.'

'What's the weather like in Dallas during Thanksgiving weekend?' asked Karen, I want to make sure I pack the correct clothes for Jack and I?

'Dallas, Fort Worth in November will be cool, temperature ranges between forty-eight- and seventy-degrees Fahrenheit.'

'Is there much sport during the weekend?' asked Stephen.

'You can watch football, American football that is, non-stop from Thursday morning till Sunday evening. Watching football on Thanksgiving Day is a Texas tradition and, in Dallas, it's all about the Cowboys. On Thursday this year they will be playing the Las Vegas Raiders at AT&T Stadium. But, if that's not to your liking there's shopping and Christmas markets.'

'What about clothing?' asked Karen. 'Will we need coats and scarves?'

'Because Texas is one of the southernmost states, it's not nearly as cold as some other places in the U.S. in November. As a result, you may not need to bring a coat, but you will want to pack long-sleeved shirts and sweaters, sunscreen is a must, even when it isn't hot.'

'Sounds like you and Jack are in for a busy time,' said Susan Greyspear.

'It will be nice to have a change of scenery,' said Karen. 'Anyone for coffee?'

♦

'Thanks for the lovely day, Jack,' said Andrew, 'I expect I'll see you around before you head off to Texas.'

'You'll probably see him at the next body,' said Armand.

'Stephen,' said Karen, holding the house phone in her hand. 'You have a phone call.'

'For me? How do they know I'm here?'

Karen shrugged and handed him the phone.

'I'm not on duty till four, that's why I turned my mobile off. Hunter. Where? OK, I'll be right there.'

'What is it, Stephen?' asked Jill.

'Industrial accident. A man has fallen seven floors from scaffolding, gone headfirst through the garage roof, and ended up in the driver's seat of a 1956 Jaguar XK120 convertible.'

'On a Sunday afternoon?'

'Didn't realise weekends were off limits for accidents.'

'Stephen, can you get a lift?' said Jill. 'I came by taxi and Katherine promised she would stop by the flat on her way home.'

'I could drive you, Stephen,' said Buchanan.

'Why don't you go with Jack, Stephen?' said Jill. 'I'll see you this evening.'

'Jack, if Katherine is going to take Jill home, could you drop me off at the house after you take Stephen?' asked Andrew.

'No problem.'

'In that case, I need to get my bag out of our car, I'll only be a moment.'

♦

'You carry your bag with you, Andrew?' asked Stephen.

'Just the basic tools of the trade.'

'We were here a couple of years ago on a case,' said Buchanan, as he parked on Blackwater Road behind a patrol car and an ambulance.

'What was that? I don't remember being called here,' said Mansell.

'You weren't, but you were still involved in the case. It was called *The Case of the Laminated Man,* by Tony Miasma of the *Herald.*'

'Ah, a gruesome case out by Gardner's books,' replied Mansell. 'Wasn't there also a body by the castle – nailed to a tree if I remember correctly?'

'That's the one,' said Buchanan. 'Eastbourne's been quiet since then.'

'All except for a hanging off the pier. Surely you can't forget that one?'

'If we are counting,' said Stephen, 'let's not forget the recent stabbing in Kent,'

'Surely you can't count that. It was under Kent's jurisdiction,' said Mansell.

'Still part of an ongoing case here in Sussex,' said Buchanan.

'There is still another, the body parts found in the village of Westham, your backyard if I may be so bold in pointing out.'

'Yes, Andrew, and we did resolve that case.'

'Do you two want to come in?' said Stephen, as he opened the car door.'

'Why not?'

'Hi, Stephen,' said a uniformed constable. 'The paramedics are just inside the garage, it's not a pretty sight.'

'Hello, Morris. How's the baby?'

'Grace is finally sleeping through the night, thankfully.'

'Good to hear.'

'Ever seen what happens to a body after falling seven floors and through a garage roof, Jack?' asked Mansell, as they approached the open doors of the garage.

'No, I haven't had that dubious honour.'

All that could be seen of the green Jaguar XJ120 was its boot, which was spattered with splashes of white paint. Blocking the view of the unfortunate painter were the remains of the car's convertible roof and the timber from the garage roof. A green-trousered paramedic was leaning into the car's interior. The sound of approaching voices made the paramedic raise up to see who was arriving.

'Afternoon, Doctor.'

'Afternoon, Ray, surprised to see you out and about.'

'Well, you know what it's like, can't spend too much time in the office with your feet under a desk, got to get out every now and again and see how the other half live.'

'How is the injured party?'

'He was dead when we got here, body still warm. The face damaged beyond recognition by the impact it made going through the roof. Pity about his last meal.'

'Why is that, Ray?'

'He's swallowed the gear knob.'

'Morris,' said Buchanan, 'does everything look OK to you, anything suspicious?'

'I had a look up on the scaffolding where he was working. Something doesn't look quite right, but I can't quite put my finger on it.'

'Do you know when he died, Morris?' asked Buchanan.

'The call came in at 15:48., so probably ten, fifteen minutes before that.'

'Thanks. Do you and Andrew want to have a look around before the body is removed to the mortuary, Jack?' asked Stephen.

'Sure. Morris's comment has got me curious.'

Buchanan walked into the garage and looked at the remains, then up to the roof where the body had come through.

'Does he have an ID?' he asked Ray.

'His driving licence says he's called Stan Hendricks,' replied Ray.

'How old was he?'

'Birth date 23rd August 1980.'

'What a shame, such a waste of life. What's his address?'

'Ah, what's this?' said Ray, 'he has two driving licences in his wallet, the second one hidden behind a flap at the back.'

'I've been there on that one,' said Buchanan. 'I remember thinking I had lost my driving licence and applying for a replacement only to find the original in the back of my wallet.'

'Not this one,' said Ray. 'Both photos are the same, just different names, here have a look,' he said, passing the wallet containing the two driving licences to Buchanan.

'Now, this is interesting,' said Buchanan. 'I've never heard of anyone calling themselves Stan Hendricks, but I knew a John McDermott once. I wonder if this was him, and if so, what's he doing down here in Eastbourne living under an assumed name?'

'You escaped from Glasgow,' said Mansell, 'you're probably not the only one.'

'Very funny, Andrew. The John McDermott I remember was a troublemaker. I put him behind bars more than once.'

'Well, he'll now be spending eternity six feet under.'

'Do you know where he fell from, Ray?' asked Buchanan.

'I don't. But the constable might, he was first one here.'

'Morris?'

'As I said, Jack. I had a quick shin up the scaffolding, and that was when something didn't seem right. There are some paint pots and brushes lying on the scaffold boards on the seventh level. The brushes were scattered on the boards and the paint tin was open, with a skin forming on the top of the paint.'

'So, what was he doing up the scaffolding at four on a Saturday afternoon?' asked Buchanan.

'The lady in Flat 1 on the ground floor said they'd been painting the windows.'

'They?'

'Yes. She said there were two of them.'

'Where's the other chap?'

'I asked the lady the same question.'

'And?'

'She said the painter started work at nine o'clock this morning and when she returned from shopping at twelve-thirty he was sitting in the van talking to a young man.'

'Did she see, or hear, what happened?'

'No. The first she knew of it was when the young man knocked on her door to say there had been an accident.'

'Where's she now?'

'She's in her apartment. It's on the ground floor, Number 1, the one with the green door.'

'Is she alone?'

'No, one of the ambulance paramedics is with her.'

'Did you get her name?'

'Elizabeth Solomon.'

'Thanks, I'll go and talk to her.'

Buchanan knocked on the open door and entered. He could hear voices from the room at the end of the hallway. When he entered, he saw the paramedic standing beside Elizabeth Solomon.

'Excuse me, sorry to intrude, Mrs Solomon. I'm Detective Chief Inspector Buchanan, Sussex Police. I was wondering if you could tell me what you know about the unfortunate accident?'

'It's Miss Solomon and, no, I can't tell you anything other than what I told the other policeman.'

'Would you mind retelling me, please?'

'All I know is I went shopping this morning and the painter was up on the scaffolding painting my kitchen window, he'd been working on the windows all week. When I returned, he was sitting in his van eating lunch and chatting to the young man. Just before three o'clock there was a knock at the door and the young man said there had been an awful accident. He said his friend had fallen off the scaffolding and was very badly injured, his mobile was dead and would I call for an ambulance.'

'What did you do?'

'I dialled 999 and asked for an ambulance.'

'Did you go outside to see what had happened?'

She shook her head. 'The young man said there was nothing I could do, and it wasn't a pleasant sight.'

'Do you know where the young man went?'

'No. I supposed he's out there somewhere, helping.'

'Thank you, Miss Solomon. I will have someone come and take a statement from you.'

'Why? I've just told you what happened.'

'It's just for the records. Oh, before I go, could you describe the young man?'

'Quite pleasant.'

'How about his height? How tall was he?'

'You suspect something's not right about the accident?'

'Not at this point. It's being a policeman for thirty plus years I tend to look for crime everywhere.'

'Well, if that's the case, I'd say he was about five feet ten, slim build, dark brown hair, blue eyes, and a scar on his left cheek and another across his nose.'

'How about an accent? We have many European young men working in the country these days.'

'That's easy, I'd say he was from Glasgow.'

'Thanks, that's an excellent description.'

'You recognise him, don't you?'

'In my work I come across lots of young men that fit that description.'

'Oh.'

'Would you recognise him again?'

'Most certainly.'

'Thank you for your time, Miss Solomon. If we have any further questions, we'll get in touch.'

When Buchanan returned to the garage, he saw the ambulance crew had extracted the deceased from the garage and were loading the body-bag into the private ambulance.

'You weren't able to do anything for him I suppose, Andrew?' said Buchanan.

'No, unfortunately not. His neck's broken and who knows what internal injuries he suffered on the way through the roof. Do you think it's an accident?'

'I'm not sure, something Morris said has me wondering. Something's not right, my niggler is niggling.'

'Where are you going? No, don't tell me, you're going up there to look at where he fell from?'

'Why don't you join me? Bet there's a good view of the town from the seventh floor,' said Buchanan, as he started up the ladder to the first level of the scaffolding.

♦

'You were right about the view,' said Mansell, as he looked out across the rooftops.

'This must have been where he was working from,' said Buchanan, as he looked down at the unopened tins of paint, scattered paint brushes and spilled paint. 'Miss Solomon said he'd just finished painting her kitchen window.'

Buchanan stood up, grabbed at the guardrail, and gave it a good shake. 'Nothing wrong with the guardrail.

'Something bothering you?' asked Mansell.

'Just wondering how a fit man, probably used to working from heights, could just fall off this perfectly safe scaffolding? Could he perhaps have been drinking? It was just afternoon, and he had stopped for lunch. That will be up to you to determine when you have a look at his innards.'

'He could have simply tripped and gone over the rail.'

'I wonder,' said Buchanan, stepping back a couple of steps.

'Do you see something?'

'Just wondering. I'm looking at the window, the brushes laying on the boards, the tins of unopened paint and the paint splatters. If he'd been painting the window and stepped back one step too many to admire his work, yes, maybe he could have fallen backwards over the guardrail.'

'But you're not convinced?'

Buchanan shook his head. 'Look at the brush and paint rag, imagine he's just brushed the last lick of paint. He takes two steps back to view his masterpiece. He backs against the guardrail, loses his balance and over he goes. My question to you is, where would the brush and paint rag drop?'

'Probably over the rail along with him,' said Mansell.

'So, what are they doing on the boards directly under the window?'

Buchanan walked over to one of the unopened tins of paint, got down on his knees and peered at the paint tin, 'I think I am going to require the services of a CSI team. I can see what looks like blood and human hairs on the corner of this paint tin.'

'Are you saying what I'm thinking?' said Mansell. 'That he was hit over the head with the paint tin, then his unconscious body was chucked over the guard rail hoping the fall would cover the injury?'

'Andrew, do you remember the carpenter who fell off his ladder a few weeks ago and stabbed himself with his chisel?'

'Yes, but that was deemed an accident by the coroner.'

'You didn't believe that any more than I did.'

'What did your boss say about it?'

'She didn't, told me to take up a hobby.'

'It happens.'

'Talking of the dead carpenter – you know, there are striking similarities to the two deaths. Both involved tradesmen with names I find worryingly familiar. Both fell to their deaths, and both had been seen with young men who happened to have Scottish accents. I think we are just witnessing the aftermath of a second similar killing, let's hope there isn't a third.'

'I'll give him the once over when I get him back to the lab.'

'Would you do me a favour, Andrew? When you give him the once over, would you take his fingerprints, a blood sample and have forensics get his DNA profile for me?'

'Will do, but why?'

'My suspicious nature tells me there's more to this than just a simple fall from scaffolding.'

2
A Suspicious Death

Buchanan stopped at the Pevensey Starbucks for his coffee and almond croissant, the garage for his copy of the *Herald*, then drove on to the office. The barbeque had been a great success albeit for the excitement at the end of the day with the dead painter, and that had caused him a near sleepless night. What was it, what was going on in his subconscious?

As he sat behind his desk, coffee in one hand, croissant in the other, he realised he'd become a creature of habit. He browsed through the *Herald* realising that with it coming out on Friday it wouldn't have any news on the death of the painter.

He'd just finished his read through when his phone rang. He pressed the speaker button.

'Buchanan.'

'Jack, it's Sam Richmond, HSE, how are you?'

'Fine, how can I help?'

'Did you attend a death from a scaffolding accident Saturday afternoon?'

'Yes, I did, why?'

'What were your thoughts?'

'Initially it looked like an unfortunate accident.'

'That's what I thought. Did you go up the scaffolding to look where he fell from?'

'Yes.'

'See anything sinister?'

'The scaffolding all looked fine to me, no missing or loose handrails, all scaffold boards clipped down, ladder to every lift clipped and gated.'

'That's what I saw as well. So, with that in mind did you come to any conclusions?'

'The police pathologist and I concluded that the painter was hit over the head with an unopened paint tin. Then his unconscious body was chucked headfirst over the guardrail. I'm waiting for the CSI report and pathology report before I can be definite about both deaths.'

'Sorry, not following you on that?'

'Do you remember back a few weeks ago to the incident where the carpenter fell from a ladder in a barn out on the Pevensey Marshes?'

'Yes, fell on his chisel and bled to death. An accident the coroner said?'

'I wasn't convinced then, and now we have the dead painter, I'm even less convinced.'

'What's got you stirred up?'

'Well, it all begins with the death of the carpenter. He and his mate were working on a barn restoration.'

'I remember.'

'According to the emergency call, the mate said he'd been outside having a cigarette and heard his boss call for help. When he went into the barn, he saw his boss had fallen from the ladder and landed on his chisel.'

'That's the story as I know it.'

'Well, directly after he called in the accident, he went to his digs, paid his bill the following morning and disappeared. He was next seen in Westham High Street doing at least sixty in his Golf. If it wasn't for my allotment friend, Dave, I wouldn't be on the phone to you now.'

'Did he get caught?'

'No. He was next seen on the A27 by a traffic patrol car, they clocked him doing upwards of ninety. In their attempt to stop him he crashed and ran off; he hasn't been seen since.'

'Did you get the reg on the car?'

'Yes, turns out the plates were cloned from a car registered in Glasgow that had been written off. The car itself had been stolen from a carpark in Glasgow.'

'What happened to the car?'

'Taken to the scrap yard where it was sold for parts.'

'No trace of the lad at all?'

'None. We talked to the landlady of the B&B where he was staying. She said she thought he and his boss were from Glasgow.'

'That's not so unusual these days.'

'I saw the body and he was the dead ringer for someone I put away on more than one occasion. When I ran that information past my contact in Glasgow, he said I must have been mistaken, the name I gave him was for a stiff lying in Cathcart cemetery.'

'Supposedly we all have a double somewhere.'

'You misunderstand. The boss gave his name as Jackson Hardcastle when he checked in to the B&B, but when I looked at the body, I was sure it was a Jamie Gallagher, yet according to my source Gallagher died in a car crash on the M8 about five years ago. On top of that, the painter who died on Saturday was supposed to have died in the same car crash that killed Gallagher.'

'Is there a Jackson Hardcastle?'

'None in the PNC. The only one I could find online was a sixty-five-year-old Jamaican singer doing cabaret acts on a Viking cruise ship.'

'How about the mate?'

'He went by the name of Steve Jameson.'

'Anything on file?'

'When checked, we did find a record for a Steve Jameson on the police national computer. Mostly for minor incidents such as shoplifting and being in possession of small amounts of marijuana. His mugshot was taken several years ago so isn't much use to us currently. Incidentally, he's the son of Andy Jameson, an enforcer for one of Glasgow's most notorious gangs.'

'So, nothing on him being a killer?'

'Not yet anyway, and since we only have a sketchy description and an out-of-date police mugshot of the lad, we are stymied at this point.'

'Did you do a DNA check on the carpenter's body to check if he was who you thought he might be?'

'Not for the want of trying. I called the morgue and asked for a blood sample to be taken but the body had already been claimed by a sister. It was given a quick service then cremated. Strange bit was, when we checked the address for the sister, it was a phoney address.'

'So, you have nothing tangible from the accident to identify who the dead carpenter was?'

'Absolutely nothing.'

'What about the tools, where are they?'

'The lad's tools that were in the car were claimed by the person who purchased the wreck.'

'Have you managed to talk to that person?'

'Not yet, I'm still waiting for the details of the sale to come through.'

'What about the carpenter's tools, what happened to them?'

'Disappeared without a trace.'

'So, you have nothing with which to unwrap the mystery?'

'Looks like that.'

'Do you have a description of the lad working with the painter?'

'Five feet ten, slim build, dark brown hair, blue eyes and a scar on his left cheek and nose. He had a Glasgow accent, similar description to that of the lad working with the carpenter.'

'Will that get you anywhere?'

'As soon as we hang up, I'll give my contact in Glasgow a call. Maybe with that description Gus will be lucky this time.'

'Fine, keep me posted on what you find.'

'Will do, bye.'

'Keep who posted?' said Street, who'd just come into the office.

'That was Sam Richmond from the Health and Safety Executive, he wanted to know about Saturday's accident in town.'

'That the one about the painter who fell off the scaffolding?'

'Yes.'

'It was an accident, wasn't it?'

'I'm not so sure.'

'Why do you say that?'

'If it was just one suspicious death, I might accept the incident as an accident but with the description of the lad who was working with both men matching, I'm bound to say there is the distinct possibility of foul play.'

'What will you do?'

'I'm going to go back to the beginning and in the light of my suspicions look at all the facts as I know them.'

'Can I help with anything?'

'Yes, you certainly can. Would you get out the file or whatever you can find on the carpenter who managed to impale himself on his chisel a few weeks ago?'

'Will do.'

'I've got some questions for Dr Mansell that would be better asked in person. While you are checking on the dead carpenter, I'll go and see Dr Mansell at the hospital.'

◆

'Good morning, Andrew,' said Buchanan, as he closed Mansell's office door behind him.

'Jack, what brings you here?'

'I've been thinking about the painter who fell from the scaffolding. Have you done the autopsy yet?'

'Yes, just finished an hour ago. He was stone cold sober and free from any intoxicating chemicals.'

'And the cause of death?'

'Death from respiratory failure as result of his neck being broken and rupturing the spinal cord at the fourth cervical vertebra. I sent a blood and hair sample to forensics, perfect match for the hair and blood found on the edge of the paint tin.'

'So, it looks like our suspicions about him being hit over the head then chucked over the guard rail are correct.'

'No doubt in my mind.'

'Humour me for a moment, suppose he'd deliberately jumped off, would the injuries he sustained be commensurate with what you saw?'

'If he climbed over the rail and jumped feet first, I would have expected to see lower limb injuries, not the neck and facial injuries he incurred.'

'It's a pity you couldn't get blood samples for a DNA profile from the dead carpenter.

'Ah, but I think I can help you with that,' said Mansell, as he opened a glass-fronted cabinet. 'We both know the carpenter's body was claimed by the family and subsequently cremated, but what they didn't remove, is this.' said Mansell lifting a plastic bag and showing it and its contents to Buchanan.

'What is it?'

'This is the chisel I removed from the carpenter's body.'

'Where's it been these last few weeks?'

'One of my lab assistants, who knew my liking for unusual tools, which in this case looked to him innocuous, stored it away to await my return on Monday. He went off on holiday forgetting to tell me what he had done. I came across it this morning when looking for a special scalpel and saw the chisel in the bag, see,' he said, holding out the bagged implement. 'It's an all-steel chisel, sometimes favoured by carpenters when working on hardwoods. It looks just like the ones we use here in the morgue.'

'Is it clean?'

'Thankfully not. My lab assistants are trained not to clean anything unless I specifically tell them to.'

'Hmm, they've finally made their first mistake.'

'Who's made a mistake?'

'Whoever has been sweeping up the evidence in this case. Ever since I got involved there has been someone going ahead and behind me tidying things up.'

'Such as?'

'Such as when you said the carpenter's sister showed up with a death certificate for the carpenter Jackson Hardcastle. You told me he and his effects have been incinerated.'

'Yes, just as well I sent you a copy of the release statement.'

'You did? I never received it.'

'My, this is turning into a bit of a farce. I'll send you another copy, although the original may have gone astray, I should still have a copy of the email attachment.'

'The lad driving the stolen Golf with cloned plates has also disappeared.'

'Sorry, can't help you on that front.'

'O'Shea went through the holdall and found his wallet. According to his driving licence he is called Steve Jameson. Unfortunately, the photo on his licence is useless for identification purpose, almost like he deliberately didn't want to be identified.'

'So, no point in contacting the DVLA for a replacement?' said Mansell. 'Do you have his age?'

'Twenty-seven. The Golf GTi was sold for parts to someone calling themselves Jason Locke, as was the tool bag found in the car.'

'So, the carpenter has been cremated along with his effects, there is no body or materials for DNA testing, the young driver has disappeared, and the car and tools have been sold for cash to someone. In my book that equals case closed,' said Mansell.

'That's what I was beginning to believe, except for one thing.'

'What's that?'

'This chisel that killed the carpenter,' said Buchanan, holding up the plastic bag containing the chisel. 'His blood and DNA will still be on it. With that I can cut into this cadaver of a case. Will you make sure it goes to forensics for DNA and fingerprinting?'

'Do you have a case reference number for it?'

'No. Tell you what, mark it as, DI Jill Hunter, exhibit 3, DGH, and the date.'

'Why not your name?'

'Because, if someone is trying to make evidence go away, this should fox them. I'll let Jill know to watch out for the results.'

♦

'You look pleased,' said Street. 'Was Dr Mansell able to help?'

'Yes, we now have the deaths of two individuals to investigate.'

'Two individuals? Which ones are you referring to?'

'You remember the carpenter who fell off his ladder and impaled himself on his chisel?'

'Yes, the coroner said that was an accident, and the other?'

'The painter who fell, or I should say, was pushed off the scaffolding on Saturday afternoon.'

'You know he was pushed off?'

'Not yet, but all the evidence points to it. Talking of evidence, the chisel that killed the carpenter has turned up. I've asked Dr Mansell to send it off to forensics and have the results sent to you.'

'Why didn't you have it sent to yourself?'

'Because I think I'm being watched.'

'What do you mean, watched?'

'Nothing definite, it's just a feeling I have that someone doesn't want me investigating the death of the carpenter.'

'I think Karen's right, you do need a holiday.'

3

Pevensey Levels

'You won't be late home, will you?' asked Karen.

'No, there's not much happening other than chasing up on the death of the painter who fell from the scaffolding on Blackwater Road Saturday afternoon. Should be home by four. By the time we pack the car and get on the road, most of the evening commuter traffic should be gone from the M25.'

'Do you really think he was pushed off the scaffolding?'

'The evidence points to it, but unless we can catch up with the lad who was working with him, we're stymied.'

'It's not going to prevent us going to Dallas tomorrow, is it?'

'No, definitely not, Jill can handle the case for the time being. We're just waiting for information to come through from forensics, plus Andrew Mansell has some paperwork to email. I asked him to send it to Jill.'

'Good, I'll have the suitcase ready for when you get home.'

Buchanan left the house and drove to Starbucks for his morning coffee. Being such a popular stop for morning commuters, the carpark was quite full. He parked between a white transit van displaying an Amazon logo and a grey van with the word 'Koly' in large gold lettering painted on its side. Interesting, thought Buchanan, wonder if the driver is inside?

'Good morning. Jack, your usual coffee?' asked the barista.

'Yes please, Alicia, and to celebrate my wife and I going to Dallas tomorrow, I think a cinnamon roll to go with it would be appropriate. Also, instead of taking it with me, I think I'll drink it in."

'Would you like the cinnamon swirl warmed up?'

'No, thanks, I'll have it as it is. Alicia, do you know who drives the little grey van with the word Koly on the side?'

'Yes, that's Tom. He's at the end of the counter waiting for Michelle to make his coffee.'

'Thanks.'

Buchanan paid for his drink and walked to the end of the counter to wait for his coffee and say hello to Tom.

'Tom?'

'Yes ?'

'Jack Buchanan, Sussex Police.'

'Oh.'

'Nothing to worry about. I noticed your company supplied scaffolding to a barn restoration job out on the Pevensey Levels.'

'Yes, and the carpenter dying didn't have anything to do with our scaffolding.'

'We know that. He fell off his own ladder while working inside.'

'Phew, you had me worried for a minute.'

'Are you a local company?'

'Yes, Westham.'

'What sort of jobs do you do?'

'Why, do you need some scaffolding?'

'No, just wondering.'

'We specialise in all aspects of residential and commercial scaffolding, such as building developments, extensions, schools, colleges, temporary roofs, high street scaffolds and much more. We can easily travel anywhere in Sussex. We are always happy to travel, provide free quotes, estimates and consultation to make sure our clients receive the best possible service.'

'You sound like an advertisement for your company.'

'It just what's on our website.'

'Did you or your men notice anything odd while erecting or dismantling the scaffolding at the barn?'

'I only visited the site once, while it was being erected. None of the lads said anything to me before or after, why?'

'Just wondering. How about the scaffolding job on Blackwater Road in Eastbourne?'

'Just another job, pity about the painter falling over the rail. Do you know anything about the investigation? The HSE won't tell me anything, and I don't get paid till the job is complete.'

'I'm not sure if their investigation is complete. But what I do know is, they haven't found any faults with the scaffolding.'

'I never thought they would, we don't mess around when we erect scaffolding.'

'Thanks, Tom, it's been nice chatting, I learned something today.'

'Anytime.'

Instead of driving straight to the office Buchanan turned right out of the garage then left onto Rickney Lane. He was curious to see if the barn where the carpenter died had been sold.

He stopped by the gate and looked across the field to the barn. Gone was the scaffolding and any sign of the barn being worked on. Over to the left of the barn door, in a small, fenced enclosure, were a group of cows grazing peacefully. Beside the gate was a large green Range Rover with its engine idling, the driver standing beside the front wheels talking on his phone.

Buchanan turned off his engine, got out of the car and walked over to the gate. As he did, the driver of the Range Rover said something to the person he was talking to on the phone and hung up.

'Morning,' said Buchanan. 'Looks good, they did a nice job of the restoration.'

'You're the agent?'

'No, just passing and thought I'd look at the barn. First time I've seen it without the scaffolding.'

'Oh, it's just a barn, lots of them around here.'

'But not with the history this one has.'

'What history?'

'The accident, you must have heard about it? It was in all the local papers.'

'No, tell me.'

'The one where the carpenter fell off his ladder.'

'Really? Never heard of it.'

'You didn't hear about his falling off the ladder he was working on, and landing on his chisel?'

'It's news to me. I'm with the National Rivers Authority, we're just checking the slews. With the onset of winter, the rivers can back up causing floods. What's got you interested in the barn?'

'Nothing particular. I sometimes take the detour along Rickney Lane on my way to work from Starbucks. After many years of commuting to and working in the city, it's a joy to be able to be just drive slowly through the countryside.'

'Know what you mean. I've been watching a couple of buzzards wheel in the sky. The crows aren't as happy about it though. I get the impression they don't like the buzzards invading their territory.

Something clicked in Buchanan's brain. Was he being warned off? Was the mention of the crows not wanting the buzzards intruding into their territory a veiled attempt to get him to move on? He decided to push the envelope.

'Yes. I suppose to some, protecting territory is important,' he said, as he looked at the man. Buchanan smiled; he'd hit a nerve. Something he said had elicited a reaction. 'Do you get to spend much of the time out here on the Pevensey Levels, watching birds?'

The man visibly relaxed. 'Yes, it's one of the perks of the job. Better than any day working in an office.'

Buchanan decided to keep the banter going, something was niggling his niggler.

'Have you worked for the National Rivers Authority long?'

'The NRA? No, I used to have a day job in London.'

'I know what you mean about getting away from the rat race. Prior to coming down here, I worked in Glasgow for many years.

27

One day I was in Glasgow, the next here in Eastbourne. For several years my family worked in the yards on the Clyde; but when my father saw the decline in the shipbuilding, he told me to stay at school and get a job with a future.'

'Sound like good advice. Are your parents still alive?'

'Yes, the whole family still live in Glasgow.'

'Any brothers, sisters?'

'Just a brother. He's a lawyer.'

'That's handy if you need legal advice.'

'Not really. We tend to argue a lot.'

'Just like me and my brother. He's a Liverpool supporter and I support Man U.'

Buchanan chuckled. 'I'm a Rangers supporter, my brother supports Celtic.'

'Ah, the old firm Derby, sounds a little like the battle between the brothers Cain and Abel.'

'Not quite that bad. I love my brother even though we see life through different lenses.'

'What do you do for a living?'

'Me, I'm a policeman and have been for last 35 years. Close to retirement, my boss keeps reminding me.'

'Is that why you've moved down to Eastbourne?'

Must let out just a bit more line, thought Buchanan, the fish is still nibbling at the bait.

'You could say that. Sometimes my superiors say different.'

'You've been a bad boy, put out to pasture, that it?'

A dim light came on, a distant memory going back to Buchanan's last day at the police HQ in Glasgow. The young cadet with the beer mug collecting for Buchanan's departure had used those exact words. The light in Buchanan's brain became much brighter.'

'Bad boy? That's funny. I've never known that word to be associated with me. I just do my job. I get on with looking up or locking up the bad guys who think they can get the better of me, and those who tried, living many years in jail, regretting trying it on with me.'

'What about your brother, what did he think of your way of giving out justice?'

'Sometimes he didn't appreciate my methods, and that usually led to the arguments we had.

'Sounds like me and my brother, we're close though.'

'Well, it's been nice chatting,' said Buchanan, 'but I do need to get to work, or the boss will assume I've retired.'

'That bad, eh?'

'If it's not the boss, it's the wife.'

Buchanan was wondering if he'd been on the losing end of the verbal tennis match. This supposed NRA workman was getting more information out of him than he was getting out of the worker.

'Look, it's been nice chatting about our families, but I do need to get to work. See you around sometime.'

As Buchanan opened his car door, he glanced at the Range Rover to see if the workman was watching. When the workman looked down at the Rover door lock, Buchanan took a photo of the open door plainly showing the NRA logo and its registration, then climbed back in his car.

♦

Instead of driving straight to the office he returned to the A259 and turned left onto the road to Hastings and the police garage.

'Excuse me, Jim,' said Buchanan, looking at the name tag on the overalls. 'I need to talk to someone about a Range Rover.'

'Sorry, sir. This is a police garage.'

'DCI Buchanan,' he replied, taking out his warrant card. 'Jim, you work here?'

'Yes, I'm the workshop manager.'

'Good. Jim, I was wondering if you recognise this vehicle and reg,' said Buchanan, showing Jim the photo of the Range Rover.

Jim looked at the photo of the Range Rover on Buchanan's phone. 'Yes, it's one of ours. It's kept here when not in use. It's used as a surveillance vehicle, but I'm not supposed to tell you that.'

'Thanks, Jim.'

'Is there something wrong with the Rover?'

'No, just wanted to make sure about its pedigree, wanted to make sure it was one of ours, and not some rascal up to no good.'

'Yeah, fine, whatever. Do you need anything else, because I've got a BMW bike to get back out on the road?'

'No, I'm happy knowing all is well with the Range Rover.'

Buchanan smiled to himself and got back in his car wondering what the National Crime Agency was doing in the Pevensey Levels disguised as the National River Authority.

♦

Street was at her desk when he got to the office.

'He's just come in, I'll tell him.'

'What are you going to tell me?'

'That was Doctor Mansell. He called to say he's just sent through the information you requested.'

'Oh good, I asked him to send it to you.'

'He did, I've just opened the email, want me to forward it to you?'

'No, don't do that, print it will you?'

'Still think someone is spying on you?'

'That sounds a bit weird when you put it that way, but yes I do.'

'What's happened to make you think that?'

'This morning, I went to Starbucks for coffee and afterwards instead of returning directly to the office I took a detour over the Pevensey Levels. I wanted to have a quick look at the barn where the carpenter died.?

'Such a natural thing to do considering your suspicions.'

'When I got to the entrance to the property there was a Range Rover blocking the entrance with NRA painted on the door. I got chatting to the driver and ended up playing verbal tennis about family for the best part of an hour.'

'That happens when I get to the antenatal classes, we all do the same.'

'I got suspicious about the vehicle, so I went to the police garage in Hastings and talked to a very helpful mechanic called Jim. He informed me that the Range Rover was being used as a surveillance vehicle. So, I'm now wondering what the National Crime Agency are doing on our patch.'

'We do live in an Alice in Wonderland world, don't we? Maybe they were looking for sheep rustlers? The marshes are in quite a secluded place.'

'That's a possibility.'

'But why would the National Crime Agency be involved? I thought it would have been dealt with on a more local level?'

'Sheep rustling is just the tip of the crime iceberg,' said Street,

'It's one possibility,' said Buchanan, getting up from his chair to collect the printout of Dr Mansell's report from the printer.

'Something caught your interest?' asked Street, looking at the intensity on Buchanan's face. 'Do the fingerprints and DNA connect the two deaths?'

'Yes, and I have the blood type of the dead carpenter, plus two sets of fingerprints.

'I suppose one will be Dr Mansell's, wonder who the other belongs to? Probably those of the carpenter,' said Street.

'Dr Mansell always wears gloves when doing his autopsies. One of the tasks he does during an autopsy is to take the fingerprints of the deceased. From this report, I'm assuming one of the two sets found on the chisel belonged to the deceased, the other will be from the person who stabbed the carpenter.'

'You're still convinced that carpenter was murdered?'

'Absolutely.'

'And now with this,' said Street, 'I can get busy chasing down Steve Jameson.'

'Jill, do you have the CSI's report from the scene where the painter died?'

'Yes, I put it in your in-tray.'

Buchanan shuffled through the papers in his in-tray and found the results of the CSI investigation. He stopped at the page that showed the copies of the fingerprints lifted from the paint brushes.

'Eureka!'

'What? What have you found?'

Buchanan, slowly shaking his head and grinning said, 'We've got him, Jill.'

'Got who?'

'I'm looking at one of the two sets of prints from the carpenter's chisel. I'd say they were the dead ringer for the prints on one of the paint tins found on the scaffolding.'

'So, if I understand you correctly, both the carpenter and the painter were killed by the same person?'

'Got it in one.'

'If what you say is the case, after stabbing the carpenter he couldn't have gone home to Glasgow, he must have been staying somewhere else in Eastbourne. But where, and more importantly, how could he have been working with both men?'

'How about this for a scenario? said Buchanan. 'The carpenter and the painter knew each other; they also knew the one they were calling Jameson. They may have not required a full-time helper, so they took Jameson along and shared him as and when needed.'

'Nothing wrong with that, as a scenario it does work. 'So, what do we do next since he's probably gone back into hiding? Though matching prints from two murder scenes is always a good beginning.'

'Do tell me. If you were SIO in this situation, what would you do next?'

'I'd take a leaf out of my mentor's book and go for a coffee, but since it's almost five, and you have to get up to Heathrow to fly to Dallas tomorrow, I'd go home and think while sipping on a glass of prosecco.'

'Whisky, if it were me. Seriously, what will you do while I'm away?'

'I've been thinking about that. I will begin by finding out all I can about the barn in the Pevensey Levels, you said it was Koly Scaffolding who provided the scaffolding?'

'Yes.'

'Do we know who handled the sale of the barn?'

'There was no sign of an estate agent.'

'Pity, it would have been helpful. I'll start with Koly Scaffolding; they must have information on who engaged them. Do you know where their office is located?'

'Their boss just said they are local, and I do know he is quite often in Starbucks when I go in for my morning coffee, He drives a grey van with Koly on the side, and his name is Tom.'

'Thanks. After I've run that lead into the ground, I'll see what I can find out about the painting job on Blackwater Road.'

'If things get too busy for you, don't forget you have Morris and Stephen available for the leg work, and …'

'And what?'

'Listen, there's something going on, something I can't quite put my finger on, my knower knows it, but won't tell me. If things get out of hand, or you're not sure, please call me, any time of day or night.'

'Jack, you're supposed to be going away on holiday for a long weekend, you said you needed time away, take it and leave the worrying to me and the boys.'

'I realise that, but with two unsolved murders with a similar MO, I don't want it to blow up in our faces. I'd rather you interrupt my time away with your thoughts and questions about what is going on, than return to WW3 having broken out.'

'It already has.'

'Ah, Ukraine.'

'Yes.'

'What I'd like to do with that shit Putin.'

'I rather think Mr Zelensky and the Ukrainian army are well ahead of you on that.'

'You're right on that.'

'We'll be fine while you are gone, Putin or no Putin.'

'In that case, I will leave you to unravel the mystery. I'm off to Dallas for a rest; although I doubt my services will be of any use to the citizens of Dallas.'

'Are Poppy and Harry on the same flight as you and Karen?'

'Yes, her dad knows someone who works for the airline and has got us all upgrades to business class.'

'Lucky you.'

4

Flying to Dallas

Buchanan looked in the mirror at his foam-covered face and for a fleeting moment wondered should he grow a beard. Of course, he already knew the answer to that question. He tipped the razor in the hot water in the sink and began the once-a-day habit of scraping his face, though today being special was one of the few occasions when he was going to shave again in the evening.

His mind was in a quandary, here he was staying in a luxury hotel getting ready for dinner before a restful night's sleep. Tomorrow they would be flying to Dallas for an American Thanksgiving weekend celebration. The Verso was to stay at home and solve the mystery of the dead carpenter and painter.

In his mind he should have said no to Travis's invitation to attend Thanksgiving in Dallas and spend the next however many days investigating the double murder. He shrugged, completed shaving, and letting the water out of the sink, returned to the bedroom to get dressed for dinner.

'I'm glad we decided to stay overnight at Heathrow,' said Karen, as she did her makeup, 'makes for such a more relaxed beginning to our holiday.

'I agree, and of course, the free parking and shuttle bus both ways between the terminal and the hotel is a bit of a bit of a bonus.'

'And let's not forget the upgrade, makes me feel like royalty.'

'You are, you're the queen of my heart.'

'Flattery will get you everywhere! Are you ready? Our table is booked for seven-thirty.'

'Lead on Mrs B.'

'Mrs B, where are you?'

'Staying in a four-star hotel, about to go down to the restaurant for a gourmet dinner with the most desirable woman in the world.'

'Oh, really? When are you going to introduce me to this wonder woman?'

'Look in the mirror.'

'Jack Buchanan, you flatterer! Oh, I just talked to Poppy, they're already in the bar.'

'I wonder what her parents would think of their daughter drinking in a bar.'

'Her father might make a fuss, but Shelly might see it as a sign their daughter is growing up.'

'Remember the argument she had with Travis at the Castlewood ball?'

'About how at eighteen it was lawful for her to drink alcohol in the UK?'

'Yes. But I think the real issue was her father had difficulty seeing his little girl becoming a woman. Remember, Castlewood was where Poppy met Harry and fell hopelessly in love.'

'How could I forget? Ready?'

'You know,' said Karen, as they walked along the corridor towards the lift, it's been a long time since we were away for a holiday, I'm really looking forward to our trip to Dallas.'

'What about our Dutch canal cruise, surely you haven't forgotten that?'

'I might have been on holiday, but if I remember correctly, you spent most of the time working. Remember Irene? You arrested her husband for her murder?'

'Ah, but he didn't kill her, did he?'

'Enough shop talk, Mr Buchanan, whisk me away on your magic carpet for a fantastic time in Dallas.'

'Do you remember that television show, *Dallas*?'

'Yes, of course, it was all about who shot JR.'

'It was also famous for another shooting, the shooting of John Kennedy.'

'Enough of that, Jack, we're on holiday. Remember, it's an early rise in the morning, so don't drink too much at dinner. You know how difficult it is for you to rise early when you've had a skinful the night before.'

♦

Buchanan opened his eyes and looked out the window, then turned to Karen who was sitting beside him. 'Are we here already?'

'Yes.'

'Boy, I sure was tired, I can't remember the last time I was able to sleep on a plane.'

'Might it have had something to do with how much you and Harry had to drink at dinner last night?'

'Oh, that.'

'Yes, that. Remember, when we get to Travis and Shelly's, they don't drink like you do.'

'I admire that in them. But I suppose that living in a state where it is near impossible to buy alcohol helps. Did you know that during weekdays, stores can only sell beer and wine from seven a.m. until midnight?'

'No, I did not know that.'

Buchanan returned to staring out the window as the plane continued its descent into Dallas Fort Worth airport. It was all so different to that of landing at Heathrow or Gatwick. Landing at either London airport you were treated to a patchwork display of green fields and occasional, red-roofed buildings interspersed by tendrils of grey tarmac and the occasional ribbons of sparkling rivers. Here, over Texas under a brilliant, cloudless blue sky, was a dead flat landscape with lattice work of tan-coloured roads dividing row upon row of ranch-style houses.

♦

'I just talked to Dad,' said Poppy, as they stood in line to clear immigration. 'They're waiting outside for us. Dad has brought the new Yukon.'

Flying to Dallas

'What's a Yukon?' asked Karen.

'It's Dad's new truck, seats seven comfortably plus plenty of room for luggage.'

'Your Dad needs a truck for what he does at church?'

'No, we have a sedan for everyday use. He uses it when working with the help-at-home team. It's a sort of thing with Dad, he and some of the men help with yard work and home repairs for those at church who aren't able to do repairs themselves.'

Ranking number four in the list of the world's busiest airports, it took the party almost an hour to transit through immigration and customs. As they exited the final gate, there was a roar of excited voices from the waiting crowds. Not only were Travis and Shelly waiting for them, but a good slice of the Grant family and friends were there to welcome Poppy and Harry home. Jack and Karen stood and smiled as the travellers were welcomed back into the arms of the family

When the hugs were relaxed, tear-filled eyes were dried, waves and see-you-later salutations had been said, the party headed for the garage and the drive to the Grant family home.

As they left the airport behind, Poppy said, 'Dad, could we stop by the ranch? It's on the way.'

'I'm sorry, Poppy. Your grandmother is waiting at the house for you. How about we go over on Friday morning instead?'

'Grandma Burge is at the house? I thought she and Gramps were in Hawaii?'

'They few back yesterday, they will be with us for Thanksgiving.'

'Oh, wonderful, can't wait to tell her about my stay in England!'

'How about it, Jack and Karen?' suggested Travis. 'We can go over Friday to see where Poppy and Harry will be setting up home?'

'Fine by me,' said Buchanan.

'I'd love to see it,' said Karen.

'OK, Friday to the ranch it is,' said Travis.

♦

'This will be your room while you are here,' said Shelly, as she showed Karen and Jack their bedroom. 'It has its own dressing room and bathroom.'

'This room is simply lovely, Shelly; we could get our whole downstairs in here,' said Karen.

'Thank you. There are fresh towels in the bathroom. Would either of you like something to eat? I'm not sure what food you had on the plane.'

'I'm fine,' said Karen.

'Jack?'

'I'm not really hungry.'

'We had lunch at twelve. We usually have dinner at seven, but seeing how you'll probably want an early night, how about I rustle up some eggs and bacon for you?' asked Shelly.

Buchanan looked at the time on his watch. 'Five-thirty here in Dallas, that makes it ten-thirty back home, I hadn't realised what time it is. Bacon and eggs sound perfect any time of the day.'

'How would you like your eggs?'

'Cooked?'

'Sorry, what I meant was, do you want them sunny side up or over easy?'

'Whatever, sunny side up.'

'Hash browns, toast?'

'I'll take the lot.'

'Coffee with?'

'Black, no sugar, please.'

'Karen?'

'Just one egg and a piece of toast, with coffee, please.'

'Fine, come on down when you are ready.'

'OK,' said Karen, 'we'll just freshen up a bit first.'

She turned to Jack. 'This is quite some house. That staircase could have come out of a Hollywood movie. Couldn't you just see

Barbara Streisand making a grand entrance as she slowly descends to the waiting crowds below?'

'It would be Dolly Parton for me.'

'I wonder why?'

'I like her singing.'

'I'll bet. How many rooms does it have?'

'Poppy said the house has six bedrooms with eight bathrooms.'

'Eight bathrooms?'

'I think each room has an en-suite bathroom and there is a guest bathroom on the ground and first floors.'

'Goodness, can you imagine how many towels you need for that many bathrooms!'

'How about shopping for toilet rolls?'

'No need to be so crude.'

'The master bedroom has its own staircase,' said Buchanan, as he looked out the bedroom window. 'You'll like this – I can see a huge pool with a jacuzzi in the back yard.'

'The pool will have to keep for later. I'm ready, which way is the kitchen?'

♦

'No Poppy or Harry?' asked Karen, as Shelly cleared their dishes from the table.

'They've gone to see Poppy's grandfather; they're going to have dinner there. You'll see them tomorrow at Thanksgiving.'

'I'm looking forward to that,' said Karen. 'Can I help with the preparations? I hear the Thanksgiving meal is quite a production.'

'Are you sure? You're our guests.'

'No, really, I'd love to help.'

'Fine, consider yourself part of the team.'

'What can I do to help?' asked Buchanan.

'Thanks for offering, but I think we're OK here in the kitchen. You could go and exercise in the gym if you want. Travis has all sorts of equipment.'

'I think Jack would rather sit and read, Shelly,' said Karen, seeing the awkward look on Buchanan's face.

'No problem,' said Shelly. 'There's plenty of coffee in the pot, Jack. You'll find the TV remote on the armrest of Travis's recliner.'

'Thanks,' said Buchanan. He got up from the table and yawned.

'Early night for you, Jack,' said Shelly.

'Probably. I'm not good at adapting to time changes. Right now, it's nine o'clock in the evening,' he said, looking at the time on his phone.

'I understand. Travis should be home soon, and we can have an early dinner.'

5

Beginnings

Thursday morning in Eastbourne

'Where are you working today, Jill?' asked Stephen, as he put the breakfast dishes in the dishwasher.

'I told Jack I'd check with the company that supplied the scaffolding for the barn restoration job on Pevensey Levels and after that the flats on Blackwater Road. And you?'

'Who knows? Depends on what's come in during the day.'

'Off to bed then?'

'I was hoping to get some time to do some studying for my sergeant's exam. Remember, it's in three weeks' time and I don't want to muck it up.'

'You'll fly through it; I've seen how determined you are to succeed.'

'Thanks.'

'OK, will I see you before you go on shift?'

'Only if you come home early.'

♦

Street drove into the Starbucks carpark and was pleased to see a small grey van parked in the far corner with the word Koly painted on the side. She parked beside it and saw that the driver was on his phone. She got out and walked round to his door and stood waiting for him to complete his call. He hung up and wound his window down.

'Yes, can I help?'

'I hope so. Are you Tom, Koly Scaffolding?'

'Yes.'

'Are you going in for coffee?'

'Yes.'

'Good, my boss said to buy you one – cappuccino, isn't it?' asked Street, as Tom opened the door.

'Yes, who's your boss?'

'DCI Buchanan.'

'Oh,' he said, nodding.

'What can I get you?' asked the barista.

'A cappuccino for Tom, Alecia,' said Street, looking at the barista's name badge, 'and I'll have a medium latte, please.'

As they moved to the end of the counter to collect their drinks, she explained, 'I'm DS Street, Sussex CID, My boss said your company recently supplied scaffolding to a barn out on the Pevensey Levels?'

'Yes, we did.'

'Can you tell me who ordered and paid for the job?'

'Is that the one where the carpenter fell off the ladder and landed on his chisel?'

'Yes, that's the one.'

'It was an estate agency in Eastbourne.'

'Do you remember the name of the agency and the person you talked to?'

'Just a minute, let me check.' Tom scrolled through the display on his phone. 'It was a James Hoskins from Newfords Estate Agents.'

'Thanks. How about a job in Eastbourne at a block of flats on Blackwater Road?'

'Same agency and contact.'

'Did you get paid for the barn job?'

'Yes, we always do.'

'What do you do if someone is slow to pay?'

'The scaffolding stays up, can really hold back completion on a job.'

'Thanks, Tom. If we ever need scaffolding, we'll give you a call.'

Street got back in her car and looked up the number for Newfords Estate Agency. As the phone rang out on her speaker, she sipped on her coffee and wondered what Buchanan would do next. Go and talk to them, she reasoned.

'Good morning, Newfords Estate Agency.'

'Good morning. DS Street, Sussex CID. Could I talk to James Hoskins, please?'

'Can I ask what it's about?'

'About a property on the Pevensey Levels.'

'I'm sorry to say he's not in the office yet.'

'When will he be in the office?'

'He's usually here by ten.'

Street looked at the time on the dashboard. 'Tell him I'm coming in to see him at ten, will you?'

'He already has an appointment at ten.'

'Then tell him I'll be there at nine forty-five. I won't keep him long.'

'I'll call him and let him know you'll be here at nine forty-five.'

'Thank you.'

Street smiled to herself and thought Buchanan couldn't have done that any better. She finished her coffee and drove off towards the office. Buchanan always checked the overnight incident report when he got into the office in the morning.

Street drove to the office and parked beside an empty slot where Buchanan's car usually sat.

'Morning, Jill,' said the desk sergeant, 'no Jack this morning?'

'No. He's taking it easy in Dallas for a few days.'

'Nice for some.'

'At least some of us are still working.'

Street checked her emails and the overnight incident report then left to interview Hoskins.

♦

Street was shown into Hoskins's office. He didn't look pleased to be forced to come to work early.

'Is this about the house in Litlington, Detective? If it is, I must inform you it has been sold and the new owners are completely redecorating the interior.'

'It's got nothing to do with a house in Litlington, Mr Hoskins. I'm here to ask you about the barn restoration job on the Pevensey Levels. I understand your agency handled the sale.'

'Oh, is that where the carpenter had the accident?'

'We're still investigating if it was an accident.'

'Oh dear, what can I say?'

'You can say who owns the barn and which company was contracted to do the work.'

'I believe it was a company called Pace who were the main contractors. As far as who owns the building, I'm not sure who currently owns it. It was being sold by an overseas owner who wanted to sell up, but since the accident, no one seems to be interested in the property.'

'What about the flats on Blackwater Road?'

'Although we manage the letting on the non-private flats, the Homeowners' Association asked us to engage a suitable local company to renovate the windows. Once again, we chose Pace to do the work.'

'Thank you for your time, Mr Hoskins. Who should I talk to at Pace about the work at the barn and the flats?'

'You could ask for a Mr Pace. I believe he runs the company.'

'Do you have their address?'

'I think their office and workshop is on Finmere Road. Want directions?'

'Thanks, I know my way, good day.'

♦

Street drove to Finmere Road and the workshop of Pace Decorators. Two men were standing beside a large VW transporter van, talking. She parked beside the van and got out.

'Excuse me, I'm looking for the owner of the company.'

'That's me, can I help?'

'I hope so. DS Street, Sussex CID. Do you recall a job out on Pevensey Levels, this would be a few weeks ago?'

'Sure I do, shame about the carpenter.'

'Was he working for your company?'

'Not directly, he was a subby.'

'What is a subby?'

'Sub-contractor. He worked for himself.'

'Had he worked for you long?'

'No. The barn job was the first, did a real good job, pity he wasn't able to complete it.'

'Did he give any references?'

'No. We were stuck for a carpenter so initially he went out with Nigel.'

'That's me,' said the other person, 'It soon became obvious that he knew what he was about, so we just let him get on with the job.'

'You left him alone?'

'No, he had a mate with him.'

'Did the mate have a name?'

'Not sure, I think he was called Steve.'

'Do you have a description of the mate?'

'About five-foot-ten, black wavy hair and a scar on his left cheek and across his nose.'

'What about the painter who fell off the scaffolding? Was he also a subby?'

'Strange that, yes, he was. I think he and the carpenter worked together and the lad Steve helped either of them depending on which of them needed help.'

'How about an address for them? They must have invoiced you for the work.'

'You'll need to ask in the office for that, I don't do the paperwork.'

'Upstairs?' asked Street, pointing to the open door in front of a staircase.

'Yes, Julie should be at her desk.'

'Thanks.'

As Street climbed the steps to the office, she wondered how much longer she would be working in the field. Eventually the inevitability of her pregnancy would have her working from the office. She stepped off the stairs and entered the office. In front of her were two back-to-back desks. The one on the right was empty, on the left a young girl was busy typing.

'Hello, can I help?'

'Yes, I hope so. DS Street. I was just talking to Mr Pace, and he said you could provide me with an address for the carpenter, painter, and mate, who were working for your company.'

'Such a shame them both having accidents like they did.'

'What can you tell me about the young lad who was working with them?'

'Not much, he hardly ever came up here to the office. Mr McDermott took care of their invoices.'

'Do you still have one of those invoices?'

'Should do, let me have a look.'

She got up from her desk and went over to filing cabinet, opened the second drawer, flicked through the folders, and said, 'Here you are, would you like a copy?'

'Yes, please.'

Street looked at the copy of the invoice and the company name, McDermott Services. The address for the company was Sandyford Road in Paisley.

'Is that what you are looking for?'

'Yes, thanks, it is exactly what I am looking for,' replied Street, thinking Buchanan would be pleased. They finally had a lead on McDermott, Gallagher, and Jameson, though where it would take them was anyone's guess.

6

Dallas, Thanksgiving Day

Buchanan woke and for a moment wondered where he was, the room was in complete darkness, then it dawned on him. They were in Texas at the home of Travis and Shelly Grant, parents of Poppy, who'd been living with them these past few months.

'Can't sleep?' asked Karen.

'No. How long have you been awake?'

'Just since you started snoring.'

'Oh, sorry, didn't mean to wake you.'

'You're forgiven.'

'What do we do now?' said Buchanan, looking at the display on his phone, 'It's only two in the morning.'

'I'm going to try and go back to sleep.'

'I can't. I think I'll get dressed and go downstairs and read.'

'OK, don't make a noise.'

Buchanan turned off the light in the dressing room and made his way downstairs.

The hallway was lit from a light coming from the kitchen. Buchanan walked through the archway and saw Harry sitting at the counter reading from his laptop.

'Couldn't sleep either?' he asked.

'Tried but I'm so used to getting up at six to begin morning stables. Coffee's hot, just made a pot.'

'Thanks, need a refill?'

'Yes, please.'

'Been up long?' asked Buchanan, as he sat down on a bar stool beside Harry.

'An hour. By now we'd be halfway through cleaning the stalls, and you?'

'At eight o'clock,' he said, looking at his watch, 'I'd be sipping on my first coffee of the day while reading through the previous night's incident report.'

'Been working on anything interesting?'

'There's been two peculiar deaths that officially are accidents, but I'm not so sure.'

'What's got you so unsure?'

'After thirty-plus years as a policeman, I just know when something is not right.'

'I know what you mean, all I have to do is to watch a horse walk and I can tell when something's not quite right with it.'

'The police surgeon and I worked through some scenarios, though quite comedic to an observer. Unfortunately, they were not quite good enough for court. But they are good enough to convince me.'

'Do you have a suspect?'

'Yes, but we're not quite sure where he's gone to earth.'

'You have a description, don't you?'

'What I mean is, the name of the suspect is that of a young man, Steve Jameson, the son of someone I put behind bars on many occasions.'

'What's he thought to have done?'

'Stabbed a carpenter with his own chisel and then a few days later, pushed a painter off a seven-story scaffolding.'

'Sounds like a nasty piece of work, and you say he's following in his father's footsteps?'

'Yes, unfortunately.'

'How bad was the father?'

Buchanan picked up his cup and sipped slowly from it while thinking back to the look on Tommy Findlay's face and the night he'd been chased up on to the roof of the MacSween bar in Glasgow by McDermott, Gallagher, and Jameson senior.

'This happened just after I'd been made up to Inspector. A week before the incident, we'd been following up on a robbery in a convenience shop. Unfortunately, the assistant hadn't been aware that the owner had agreed to pay protection money each week to prevent anything happening to the store.'

'Protection money?'

'Precisely.'

'I thought that sort of thing only happened in the movies.'

Buchanan shook his head. 'It's never called that; it's usually described as an insurance policy against vandalism and stock loss due to fire or theft. When the assistant refused to pay up, he was shot as an example to the other shopkeepers not to mess with the Busby Gang.'

'Shot? I thought gun ownership was illegal in the UK?'

'It is unless you are criminally minded. One of the gang, Tommy Findley, had been giving information to his handler about the robbery.'

'Handler, what's one of those?'

'Sometimes it is necessary for the police to pay for information about upcoming crimes. This usually is the result of a criminal offering information in exchange to an officer, called a handler, for a lenient sentence. Or in the case of an infamous Glasgow thug, one Tam McGraw, he had an unofficial licence to continue as a gangster involved in organised crime which included but was not limited to extortion and drug trafficking. He was usually referred to as the licensee.'

'Sounds like a nasty piece of work.'

'The worst kind.'

'What happened to him?'

'He died a few years ago at the age of fifty-five from a suspected heart attack.'

'Do you know who's behind the gang that Andy Jameson is a member of?'

Buchanan smiled, 'Oh yes, I certainly do. His name is Robert Anthony Maxwell, son of an immigrant Italian family.'

'Did you suspect a Mafia connection?'

'No. The Busby Gang is strictly a homegrown form of evil, a fiefdom in its own right. Though I don't think many of the gang actually live in the Busby area. Only Rab Maxwell lives in the town; that is, when he's trying to avoid jail.'

'Do you know if he's still alive?'

'Yes, very much so. The last I heard he'd only served three months of a two-year sentence for money laundering. He'd been let out following a successful appeal against his sentence. Instead of serving out his sentence in an eight by six-foot cell, he's able to luxuriate in his mansion beside the River Cart.'

'Did you catch the person who shot the shop assistant?'

'No, unfortunately. We had been working on infiltrating the gang and had found one of them willing to provide us with not only the name of the gunman, and the names of two others who had been involved in a vicious beating of an armoured car driver in an attempted robbery.'

'Was that Tommy Findley?'

'Yes. According to what Findley told his handler, he'd decided he'd had enough of gang life and wanted to go straight. The agreement was he would hand over the names of the killers, and the guns that were used, complete with the users' DNA and prints. He said all he needed was some cash to help him start a new life in Spain.'

'What happened?'

'We'd arranged to meet him at the back of quiet bar. But before we got there the gang, which included Andy Jameson, got wind of the meeting, got there before us, spooked Tommy and gave chase. I and two of my men went up to the roof of the building next door to cut off his escape. Tommy, realising he was faced with a certain fatal beating or a long jump between buildings, decided his only option was to leap across to the adjoining building and the safety of a fire escape to the street below. I can still see Jameson senior's face as he laughed at us from the adjoining roof. The sound of Tommy's scream as he fell five floors to his death still haunts my dreams.'

'You saw him fall?'

Buchanan nodded.

'I can see why you are so interested in catching young Steve Jameson. And you think he is responsible for the deaths of the carpenter and the painter?'

'Yes, and it really gets up my nose that he's loose and running around out there possibly with other names on his list, including mine.'

'You? Why would you be on his list?'

'I put his old man, and a bunch of the gang, in jail on more than one occasion.'

'You make him sound like he's a mob hit-man.'

'That is one possibility, Harry.'

'Did you ever recover the guns that were used in the killing of the store clerk?'

'No, can we change the subject? I'm supposed to be on holiday, be it only for a few days. Are you looking forward to working over here in the US?'

'Absolutely.'

'Any word on your visa?'

'Tentative, I've heard it has been approved, just waiting for the paperwork to come through.'

'Good. Now, if you'll excuse me, I'm going to see if I can get back to sleep. See you at breakfast.'

Buchanan made his way back up to the bedroom and saw Karen had managed to get back to sleep. He climbed back into bed and as his head touched the pillow, he fell asleep.

♦

Buchanan woke to an empty bedroom, Karen had already dressed and gone downstairs. He dressed, went down for breakfast, and found a very busy kitchen.

'Ah, there you are, I'm afraid you'll have to fend for yourself with breakfast,' said Shelly, 'we're a bit busy with preparing the Thanksgiving meal.

'That's fine, I just need a cup of coffee. I can help myself; I found the coffee last night.'

'I've diced the carrots, Shelly. What can I do now?' asked Karen.

'Would you dice the fruit for the ambrosia?'

'You need to explain that?'

'You don't have ambrosia in the UK?'

'Yes, it comes in a tin; it's a rice pudding dish.'

'Ah, proper ambrosia is chopped fruit, usually oranges mixed with shredded coconut. Variations to the recipe add chopped walnuts, whipped cream with a mini marshmallow.

'Jack will love that; he's got a real sweet tooth.'

'What's that?' asked Buchanan.

'Fruit salad with cream,' replied Karen.

'How are you, Jack? Sorry, we're a bit busy with the meal,' said Shelly. 'Plane travel not your thing? You looked tired when you came out of arrivals.'

'Work has been heavy; we've been chasing someone who's murdered two people.'

'Well, I'm sure they aren't here in this kitchen.'

'I'm glad to hear that,' said Buchanan. He poured himself a coffee then left the frenetic activity of the kitchen for the sitting room. On his way there he passed through the dining room and noted that the table was set for nine.

'Morning, Jack, sleep well?' asked Travis.

'As soon as my head hit the pillow the second time, I was asleep and dreaming a crazy dream.'

'What was it?'

'I was in a small rowing boat, no oars, going down a river. Ahead were rapids and beyond the rapids the river went under a bridge then flowed out into a still area just before a bend. I could hear a voice shouting but couldn't make out what they were saying. That was when I woke and saw it was only two o'clock. I think the voice was Karen telling me to stop snoring. I got out of bed and went downstairs to the kitchen where I had a coffee with Harry and then went back to bed.'

'Jet lag takes me at least a week to recover from when I travel to Europe,' said Travis.

'I don't travel that much.'

'What do you think, Jack?' asked Travis. 'You like football?'

'Football, yes, what we call soccer. The American football game – sorry, I've never seen one.'

'Come join us, Harry and I are watching replays of the previous week's games. We'll explain the rules as the games go on.'

'Thanks.'

'We'll have the Dallas game on after lunch, it starts at four-thirty.'

Buchanan sat through the recaps of some of the playoff games and thought the game was similar to that of rugby, except it kept stopping every few minutes for player changes and commercial breaks for the television broadcast.

At one o'clock Poppy's aunt and grandparents arrived, and Buchanan and Karen were duly introduced. Shortly after, the women went off to the kitchen while Poppy's grandfather joined the men in the lounge to watch football highlights till dinner was announced.

'Travis,' said Shelly, 'turkey's ready, would you bring it through and put it on the table?'

'Hungry, Jack?

'Yes.'

'Well, follow me, and I'll introduce you to what makes America great.'

Buchanan followed Travis and Harry through to the kitchen, and the turkey. He stopped at the entrance and stared at the table and shook his head. Centrepiece was the largest turkey he'd ever seen and covering the rest of the table was a selection of foods that wouldn't look out of place on one of the photo-plates in Mrs Beeton's cookbook. Buchanan was especially pleased to see the one item that he had been looking forward to trying - the ambrosia.

Tummies full to bursting, desserts consumed with glee and the table cleared, the whole family retired to the lounge to watch the Thanksgiving football match between Dallas and the Raiders.

'Well, Jack, what do you think?' asked Travis, when it ended.

'Reminds me of rugby a bit, but a bit more brutal. I'd say the Cowboys lost the game due to the fact they had so many penalties called against them at critical moments. You say it's a sixty-minute game?'

'Yes, with a few breaks for commercials and league games updates. The actual playing time of the game is one hour, divided into four 15-minute sections. Each round is spaced 12 minutes apart. However, this only tells part of the story. When you include commercial breaks, and incidentals, the game can take an average of just over 3 hours to complete.'

'The game actually stops for commercial breaks?'

'Someone's got to pay for the players' salaries.'

'That would never go down well back home in the UK. But I suppose it is a different type of football played here in America.'

'I suppose you've got a point there. You look all in, Jack?' said Travis.

'Jack isn't used to sitting and relaxing,' said Karen.

'There's the gym if you want to exercise,' said Travis.

Buchanan smiled and said, 'If you'll excuse me, I think I'll just go have a nap.'

7

Jameson

Succumbing to the habits of her boss, Street stopped in at Starbucks for a coffee.

'Where's Jack?' asked Magda, as she made Street's latte.

'Still in Dallas. He'll be back early next Wednesday morning.'

'Nice for him. Here you are.'

'Thanks.'

♦

Street parked in Buchanan's parking slot and smiled. As an acting SIO, she would play the part.

She sat at her desk and decided to begin with calling Buchanan's former partner in Glasgow.

'Is this DI Fergusson?'

'Yes, who's calling?'

'DI Street, I work with Jack Buchanan here in Eastbourne.'

'Oh, how is he, keeping out of trouble?'

'Not sure, he's only been gone a couple of days.'

'Where's he gone to?'

'Dallas for a long weekend.'

'That's plenty for Jack. How can I help?'

'I'm trying to trace someone you might know.'

'What's the name?'

'Steve Jameson.'

'The same Jameson Jack called about?'

'Yes. We think he's been following in his father's footsteps.'

'What's that?'

'We think he chucked a painter off a seven-story scaffolding.'

'What do you have on Jameson?'

'Just an address in Glasgow.'

'OK, what is it?'

'It's an address McDermott had on the invoice he gave the landlady where they were staying.'

'McDermott is dead?'

'Jack isn't convinced.'

'OK, shoot.'

'Sandyford Road, Paisley.'

'OK, let me check, I'll have to put you on hold, this may take a few minutes – are you sure about the address on the invoice?'

'Yes.'

'OK, talk to you in a minute.'

'Jill?'

'Yes, what did you find?'

'Well, I'm sorry to say I think it's a fake address.'

'Why is that?'

'It's an industrial area beside the M8, with a sewage works beside the White Cart River. Sandyford Road has a couple of abattoirs, a scaffolding company, a scrapyard, and other various businesses, but no residences. Someone has a weird sense of humour.'

'Any chance you might have a photo of Steve Jameson?'

'As a matter of fact, I do. I told Jack there wasn't one, but he got me interested so after his phone call I did some digging and found one. It was taken at a gangland funeral two years ago; he was part of the crowd of mourners at the funeral for one of the members of a rival gang.

'When a gang figure dies, the opposing gangs like to show up for the funeral to make sure the person being buried is really dead. The photo's in black and white, but quite a good one. Be careful if you cross his path, he's not called Sneaky Steve for no reason. His MO is to use a knife to settle arguments. I'll email the photo to you, what's your email address?'

'Thanks, I'll watch for it. I'll get back to you if anything comes up.'

Street looked at the image on her screen and smiled. She was looking at the face of Steve Jameson, complete with scar on the face. She printed a copy and left the office with the photo to see if the landlady at the Wisely B&B and the tenant on the ground floor flat on Blackwater Road could identify Steve Jameson.

♦

Friday morning in Dallas.

'How did you sleep?' asked Karen.

'Did I snore?'

'Not till about five o'clock.'

'Sorry, did I wake you?'

'No, I was already awake. I was thinking about Jill and Stephen - who will look after young Jack while they are at work?'

'I think you already know the answer to that one.'

'You won't mind if I volunteer?'

'As long as you don't expect me to come home and change poopy nappies, I don't mind in the least.'

'It won't be every day. I'm sure Stephen's parents will want to be involved as well.'

'I imagine they will.'

'Just thinking, we should get together with them. We haven't seen them since Jill and Stephen's wedding.'

'I hadn't realised it had been that long. I suppose that is what happens when you have a job like mine. What time is it?'

'Six forty-eight.'

'I think I'm getting adjusted to the time difference, I really feel rested. That sure was some meal yesterday, I can see why it's such a popular event. I don't think I've eaten that much since I was a teenager.'

'Well, I hope you're rested. Remember, we're going to see Poppy and Harry's ranch after breakfast.'

'I haven't forgotten.'

'Right, I'm for a shower before breakfast.'

'You go ahead, I had mine last night before I came to bed. I'll see you downstairs, I need coffee.'

As Buchanan poured his coffee, his mobile rang. 'Buchanan, Oh, hi Jill, hang-on, I've just poured coffee on the counter, I'll put you on speaker.'

'You're drinking coffee from the counter?'

'No, I was in the middle of pouring when my phone rang, made me jump.'

'Well, I hope you will jump with joy at my news.'

'You're not…'

'No, I'm not in labour, that's still months away, you can relax. I have a photo of Steve Jameson. It's black and white, but very clear.'

'Where did you get it?'

'I called your oppo, Gus, in Glasgow and he managed to find a photo taken at a gangland funeral. Jameson senior was a pallbearer, Jameson junior was a face in the crowd.'

'Well done. What are you planning to do with it?'

'I've been over to the B&B where the carpenter and mate were staying, positive identification, as was with the resident of the flat on Blackwater Road.

'I don't want to spook him by circulating the photo. So, what I will do is have Stephen and Morris go out on patrol in civvies round the town and see if they can spot him, though I suspect after two deaths he will not be out in the daytime and with that in mind they will try the clubs later this evening.'

'What about the railway station?'

'I'll have them check with the station staff. I'll have them say we are trying to find him as he was a possible witness to an accident.'

'That should work. You will make sure the station staff contact you at first sighting and don't try to apprehend him?'

'Yes, we'll make it clear. Also, we'll do the rounds of the taxi and bus ranks.'

'Are you sure he's still in the Eastbourne area?'

'As sure as I can be. So, what's on the agenda for today for you?'

'A visit to Poppy and Harry's new home, then out to dinner and for me, probably an early night.'

'OK, talk to you when I have any more news for you, bye.'

♦

'Webb Ranch was recently purchased by the Bar3 Ranch,' said Harry, as they took the exit from the interstate. 'It's the property over there beyond the lake,' he said, pointing.

'It's called Webb Ranch,' said Poppy. 'It's been set up to be a world-class equestrian breeding facility.'

'Is that what you'll be doing, breeding horses?' asked Karen, as Travis stopped the car in front of a large building, reminiscent of a traditional Dutch barn house.

'No. The breeding of horses is a specialised job for horse people,' said Harry. 'My job will be to manage the running of the stables. Such as making sure there is always food and bedding, for the horses. On top of that I'll be responsible for the day to day running of the ranch and surrounding grounds, the ranch sits on 87 acres.'

'This where you two will be living?' asked Karen.

'Yes, our first home together,' said Poppy, while hugging Harry's arm.

'Lovely, isn't it?' said Shelly. 'Travis and I started out in married life living with his folks.'

'The lake looks like it could be fun,' said Karen.

'Yes. It has all sorts of recreational features such as fishing, kayaking, swimming, and boating,' said Harry.

'There is a lakeside picnic area with firepit for those late evening family barbeques,' said Poppy.

'What about the house?' asked Karen. 'Is the inside as magnificent as the exterior?'

'The house sits above the horse barn,' said Poppy. 'It was built in 2017 and has 4,998 square feet of living space. It has two en-suite bedrooms and two smaller bedrooms suitable for children.' She looked up at Harry with a grin on her face. 'There are also two separate bathrooms. The kitchen is wonderful, it has two ovens, a side-by-side fridge-freezer and dishwasher. We will have to supply our own dishes and cutlery.'

'What about the horse facilities?' asked Buchanan.

'The house was designed as a breeding facility for horses on the ground floor, and upstairs will be where we live. Out here in Texas this type of building is called a barndominium, based on traditional farm barns found in the Netherlands,' said Harry.

'The Webb Ranch features a world class 7,200 square foot horse barn designed with the centre aisle running southwest to northeast to optimize the natural breezeways. The barn features eight oversized stalls, each 16 feet by 16 feet. It also has a large tack room, break room and a storage room. The walls are twenty inches thick, perfect for temperature control here in this part of Texas.

'There is a 5,000 square foot hay barn. It also has 2,150 square feet of shed space, providing covered space for feed, hay, tractors and implements. The barn also features two interior heated and air-conditioned rooms, one of which I will use as my office, the other probably as a maintenance workshop.'

'What about shopping, schools, and doctor's surgery, should one be required?' asked Karen.

'The ranch is forty-five minutes from downtown Dallas, and only a twenty-minute drive along the interstate from Mom and Dad's,' said Poppy. 'There's an excellent shopping market about a ten-minute drive from the ranch. It's also within a highly acclaimed school district.'

'Sounds like you two are well fixed,' said Buchanan.

'Who's hungry?' asked Travis, 'How about we stop off at One90 Smoked Meats on the way home and show Jack what a real barbeque restaurant is like?'

'I'm up for that,' said Buchanan.

'Good, I'm sure you won't be disappointed. They are well-known as a boutique purveyor of smoked meats. I think we'll let them do the serving and washing up. There's a solid menu of dine-in and take-out options, including pulled pork sandwiches, brisket tacos, and salads. They serve whole briskets, turkey breasts, and pork loins, all vacuum sealed and ready to prepare at home if desired.'

'Lead on,' said Buchanan.

♦

'Well, what did you think, Jack?' asked Travis, as he parked the Yukon in the driveway.

'I don't know how I managed to eat so much; the ribs followed by the steak then dessert was more than I've eaten in a long while, and all that after the huge meal we had yesterday, you Texans sure know how to eat.'

'I guess we do. Fancy watching some college football?' asked Travis, as he opened the front door to the house.'

'Yes, if you don't mind me snoring through the game.'

'No problem.'

8

Lazarus

'How are you feeling this morning, Stephen?' asked Street.

'I must be getting old, or the music in the Cameo is getting louder?'

'No comment.'

'After last night I could do with a quiet day just pottering around the house.'

'What happened?'

'There was a fight outside the Cameo. Some chap tried to pick up someone's girl. What he didn't realise was, she was part of the travellers' group camped out on Five-Acre Field, and her boyfriend and brother didn't appreciate her getting the attention. It was mostly fists and feet, but it took hours to book them all in.'

'Any sight of Steve Jameson?'

'Nothing. Morris and I will go out again this evening. Saturdays are usually busier, and you?'

'I need to think things over and decide what we are going to do next now we've identified Steve Jameson.'

'How about I drive?'

'That sounds good to me. Coffee first?'

'Starbucks?'

'Where else? After we're done, we could go on to Croydon and look for baby clothes in John Lewis. We will eventually need a car seat and pram, so it would be wise to see what's available.'

Saturday morning Dallas

'Good morning.'

'Morning, did you sleep well, you didn't snore?'

'I think I'm getting used to the time difference and this bed is the most comfortable one I've ever slept in while away from home.'

'Last night, after you went to bed, Shelly invited me to go shopping with her today. She said it's a great time to get some bargains, how about you?'

'Travis wants to introduce me to the help-at-home team at church.'

'Will you go?'

'Of course, I will. I'm looking forward to it.'

♦

'How did you sleep, Jack?' asked Travis as Buchanan entered the kitchen.

'Better, but still miss my own bed.'

'I know what that's like. Still want to go meet my friends at church?' asked Travis.

'Definitely.'

'Good. I'll introduce you to the guys on the help-at-home project. I think Shelly and Karen are going shopping this morning?'

'Karen just mentioned it.'

'Good, I'll just take Shelly her coffee, see you in a minute.'

On cue, as Buchanan poured his coffee, his phone rang.

'Hi Jill, any developments?'

'No, not yet. Yesterday, Stephen and Morris did the rounds of the station, taxi, and bus ranks, but no sightings of our boy. I've put in a call to CCTV to see if they can spot him. This evening we will have another go at the night clubs and see what we can find.'

'You're not going to the night clubs, are you?'

'No. of course not, I'd be too conspicuous. No, for me tonight it's a hot bath, manicure, mug of Horlicks, a girly movie and early bed. What about you?'

'Travis is taking me to church to meet with the help-at-home team.'

♦

'What do you think of our roads, Jack?' asked Travis, as they sped along the freeway.

'We could do with some of them at home. Though with Texas being more than twice the size of the UK with half the population and being so flat, it is easier for you to build the roads you have.'

'Agreed. But we don't have the public transportation you have, it's all a bit of a trade-off. You can go anywhere on the train, while we use the car.'

'Or a truck. What's that?' said Buchanan, pointing to a large black 4x4 truck.

'That's a GMC truck. There are a lot of farmers in this part of Texas, and they mostly drive trucks.'

'They'd have trouble driving those in the UK, our roads aren't big enough. This is your church? It looks like one of our shopping malls.'

'The church is a Bible-based, evangelistic, spirit-empowered church. It was founded in 1997 by my predecessor, Pastor Dave Andrews. Today we meet as one church in many locations with more than 80,000 people attending each weekend.'

'Eighty thousand! That's almost as many people live in my home town.'

'We're all about people because God is all about people. One of the ways we express our love for Him is by helping people to grow in their relationship with the Lord.'

Travis parked in the church carpark beside a bright red corvette and ushered Buchanan into the reception hall. He scanned his ID card and said, 'This way, Jack. 'Saturdays we meet in the Jefferson Room upstairs.'

On the right in the reception hall was a café with a Starbucks counter. There were groups of people sitting, drinking coffee, and chatting. Several of the occupants waved a hello to Travis as they crossed the floor towards the lift and rode it to the upper floor.

Buchanan followed Travis along the carpeted hallway to the Jefferson Room. The door was open and, as he entered, Buchanan saw a large group of men milling around with doughnuts in one hand and large coffee cups in the other. He smiled; he was at home.

'Help yourself to coffee, Jack,' said Travis. 'I need to have a quick word with the Dean of admissions.'

Buchanan walked over to the table and saw three large Starbucks insulated coffee urns marked: House, Espresso and Decaf. The man in front turned to see who had joined the line and said, 'Hi, you must be Jack Buchanan, Travis said you might be here. Lazarus Washington.' He reached out to shake Buchanan's hand. 'Welcome to Dallas.'

Buchanan nodded and looked at Lazarus and his hands; they were big enough to single-handedly crush a large melon.

'Travis says you're a cop?'

'Yes.'

'Me too, detective, and you?'

'Also a detective.'

'I like to be out there on the street keeping order. You carry?'

'If you mean do I carry a gun, no, I don't. We have a special division for that.'

'You just here for the Thanksgiving weekend?'

'Yes.'

'Well, you sure chose one of the best. To my mind, Thanksgiving is what America is all about.'

'I can see why you think that.'

'When do you go home?'

'We fly home next Tuesday morning and arrive early Wednesday morning.'

'How about coming out with on Monday, see how the other half live?'

'Sure, I'd love that.'

'I'll need to clear it with the boss first. What rank are you?'

'Detective Chief Inspector.'

'Over here, that, I believe would make you a Captain.'

'Sounds impressive.'

'Will you be coming to church tomorrow?'

'Yes, as guests of Travis and Shelly.'

'Great, I'll catch you then, see you later.'

'I see you've met Lazarus,' said Travis.

'Yes, he's invited me out on patrol with him on Monday.'

'Good, you'll get to see how we keep order in this country.'

♦

Later back at the house

'With tomorrow being Sunday,' said Travis, 'we tend to go out for breakfast before church,'

'The church membership being so large,' said Shelly, 'it is sometimes difficult to catch up with our friends. So, we get together before the church meeting instead.'

'Oh, that sounds perfect,' said Karen, 'Jack will love that, won't you, Jack?' She nudged him in the ribs.

'Uh, yes, sounds like a perfect way to start the day.'

'Then, after the service, we are going to have a bring-and-share family barbeque.'

'On top of just having a Thanksgiving meal on Thursday and dinner out last night?' said Karen.

'Not everyone can afford to have a traditional family Thanksgiving meal,' said Shelly, 'so the church organises a bring-and-share meal. That way the spirit of Thanksgiving can be shared by everyone, irrespective of their financial situation.'

'Are you still coming to church with us, Jack?' asked Travis.

'Yes, I'm interested in seeing how church is done in the US. When I was still living at home, I used to go with my parents to church, a very sedate experience.'

Travis smiled, 'I think you'll find us a rather enthusiastic bunch of worshippers.'

'Good, I'm looking forward to experiencing that and hearing you preach,' said Karen.

'I'm not there to entertain, Karen. I just proclaim the good news of Jesus and Him risen from the dead.'

9

Breakfast at Denny's

'You still want to go to church this morning?' asked Stephen, standing beside the bed with Street's morning mug of coffee.

'Yes, how about you?' she said, adjusting her pillows and sitting up in bed.

'Yes.'

'What time did you get home?'

'Just gone four-thirty.'

'Poor you, what happened?'

'I was going to wake you but thought you could use the sleep.'

'Why would you want to wake me at that unearthly hour?'

'I thought the news was important, but when I saw you looked so comfy tucked up in bed, I decided to just let you sleep. Besides, Steve Jameson wasn't going anywhere.'

'You found him? Did you arrest him?'

'No, nothing as dramatic as that, but we do know where he is holed up though.'

'Do tell all.'

'We went out early, about eleven, to see who was on the streets. There were just the usual shopfront beggars. Next, we tried the bars, just in case, but still nothing. It wasn't till about two-thirty in the Cameo that Morris spotted Steve Jameson. He's quite a dancer and impressed a few of the local ladies, thought he didn't seem to latch on to any of them. At closing time, we followed him outside and round the corner to the taxi rank. He was so drunk, he was completely oblivious of Morris standing behind him as he booked a taxi.'

'Did you get an address?'

'We certainly did, a big house on Prideaux Road.

'What did you do?'

'We went outside and while Morris kept an eye on Jameson, I called control and got one of the guys in the station to bring an unmarked car round to give us a lift.'

'Smart thinking.'

'Thanks.

'We told our driver to wait out of sight till Jameson got in his cab. From there it was an easy job to follow him to his lair.'

'You said Prideaux Road?'

'Yes, and that is where the story gets interesting. The house is for sale and by looking at the state of the garden I'd say it's been on the market for quite some time.'

'Did you get the estate agent's name and number?'

'Yes, and you will like this: the estate agent is Newfords Agency, the same agency that handled Du Marchon's house in Litlington, the barn on Pevensey Levels and the flat on Blackwater Road.'

'Great news, Jack will be pleased,' she said, looking at the time on her phone. 'I think I'll wait for him to wake and then call him with the news.'

'Wasn't he going to church with the Grant family?'

'Yes, so he said. In that case, I'll call him later on this evening.'

♦

Sunday morning in Dallas

Buchanan stared at his phone as he poured his second coffee of the morning, willing it to ring. Where was Jill? What was going on, surely, they had to be up by now? But it was Sunday afternoon back in the UK, maybe she and Stephen had gone out for lunch after church, just like he and Karen were about to do. The question of had they found Steve Jameson would just have to wait.

'Ready to go to church, Jack?' asked Shelly.

'Ah, yes.'

'What's up?'

'Nothing, at least I hope it's nothing.'

'Are you OK?'

'Yes. It's just I've been getting daily updates on an important case from my partner in England.'

'But nothing today?'

He nodded.

'It's Sunday, do they go to church?'

'Yes, I think they do, and they probably have gone out for lunch after.'

'There then, problem solved. Shall we go, everyone is waiting in the Yukon.'

'Where are Poppy and Harry?' asked Karen. 'Aren't they coming with us?'

'They've gone on ahead to see some of Poppy's friends,' said Shelly. 'They'll join us at church later.'

♦

Denny's carpark was almost full, as was the restaurant. As soon as Travis entered, he was met by a waitress.

'Good morning, Pastor, your group is already seated.'

'Thanks, Jaz.'

They were shown to their table where two other couples were already seated.

'Good morning, Pastor,' said one of the guests.

'Morning, Dale. Jack, let me introduce you. Jack and Karen, these are my friends, Dale and her husband, Roy, Harriet and her fiancé, Rod.'

'Good to meet you all,' said Buchanan, as he moved into the booth beside Karen.

'Hi, Karen, what do you think of Dallas?' asked Dale.

'If there had been time, it would have been nice to see more of the country while we were here. But with the country being so big, sightseeing will have to wait till we return next year for the wedding of Pastor Grant's daughter, Poppy.'

'Ah yes, Poppy's wedding to Harry. We're all excited about that,' said Dale. 'They look so suited to each other, and Harry is such a gentleman. Did you know he will be managing a stud farm?'

'Yes, we are aware.'

'I take it you already know Harry?' asked Rod.

'Yes, we met at the stables where he's currently working,' said Karen. 'My husband is a close friend of the owner of the stables.'

'Poppy said someone tried to kill Harry.'

Karen nodded, 'I had heard that story as well, Roy, but all's well now.'

'Good, glad it's sorted,' said Roy. 'We all like Harry. It would be a shame for anything to happen to him, now he's almost one of us.'

'All finished, Pastor?' asked the waitress.

'Yes thanks, Jaz. Could we have the bill, please?'

'Be right over.'

Breakfast paid for; they all went off to church.

♦

'How could you, Jack?' said Karen, as they filed out of the church hall.

'How could I what?'

'Sleep through Travis's sermon.'

'I was tired.'

'Well, at least you didn't snore.'

Instead of going for coffee, they followed the crowd out to the field for the bring and share barbeque.

'What do you think, Karen?' asked Buchanan. 'Do you think your church could put on a spread like this? Just smell those barbeques and there must be at least a couple of hundred tables set up.'

'We do the same, just not this many people, remember we are a much smaller church.'

'But look at that marquee with no sides, those trestle tables are heaving with food.'

'Impressive, isn't it?' said Karen.

'Where are we supposed to be?' asked Buchanan.

'Over there,' she said, pointing to a group of young men throwing a football to each other, 'Don't you recognise Harry?'

'Not with that Dallas football T shirt he's wearing.'

'Fits right in, doesn't he?'

'You like tablet, Jack?' asked Travis, as he put his arm on Buchanan's shoulder.

'Traditional Scottish tablet I do.'

'Then let me introduce you to Mrs McGoo. She's our expert on traditional Scottish candy.'

'I'm intrigued.'

'Sharon, this is Jack Buchanan. He's over visiting for Thanksgiving.'

'Hi Jack, you like tablet?'

'Certainly, my dad used to make it, and he got the recipe from my grandmother.'

'Would you like to try some of mine?'

'Yes, please.'

'Here you go,' she said, passing Buchanan a small bag. 'I hope mine is as good as your gran's.'

'I'm sure it will be,' said Buchanan, putting a large chunk of tablet in his mouth.

♦

They had just returned to the house when Street called.

'Not interrupting anything, I hope?' said Street.

'No, just about to watch a football game, American football that is.'

'Well, you'll like this news, we've found him.'

'Steve Jameson?'

'The very same.'

'Where?'

'He's been hiding out in a house on Prideaux Road. It has a for sale sign outside and looks like it's been empty for several months.'

'Well done.'

'Not sure what to do next, I believe you wanted to see if he had accomplices?'

'Yes, that's correct. What time is it there?'

'Just gone eight pm.'

'Is anyone watching the house?'

'Yes, Stephen and Morris are taking turns, they've borrowed one of the surveillance vans, just another white van amongst many.'

'Smart thinking. I suppose it's a bit late to do anything now, but would you make enquiries with the estate agent first thing in the morning and come back to me as soon as you find out anything?'

'Not sure if I should.'

'Why is that?'

'It's the same estate agent that was involved with the barn and the painting job on Blackwater Road.'

'Hmm, something's not right, why would Jameson be hiding out in an empty house – unless he's got another victim in mind?'

'How about yourself? You did say he tried to run you over on Westham High Street.'

'That's possible. Keep the surveillance on the house going. Do you need more people for the job?'

'Not at the moment. I think Stephen and Morris can handle it between them till you get back.'

'Good, when I get back we can discuss how to take this forward.'

'OK. I'll check in with you tomorrow, enjoy your football, goodnight.'

10
Out on Patrol

'Any developments?' Street asked Stephen, as he came in from his night surveillance duty.

'No, all is quiet.'

'Good. Do you want breakfast before I go to work?'

'No thanks, I just need a shower and bed. I'll make something when I wake.'

'Fine, I'll see you in the office later.'

♦

Monday morning in Dallas

Buchanan was wondering if Street would call, or maybe he should call her, he reasoned. looking at the time. Seven-thirty in Dallas would make it twelve-thirty in Eastbourne. But before he could decide, the doorbell rang.

'I'll get it,' said Shelly.

'Hi Lazarus. Jack, your ride is here,' said Shelly. from the hallway.

'Be right there,' said Buchanan, draining his cup of coffee. 'Good morning, Lazarus.'

'Morning boss, ready to rock and roll?'

'Yes, sir!'

'We're going to be cruising in my backyard,' said Lazarus, as he unlocked the patrol car's boot to extract a stab vest for Buchanan. 'It's where I grew up as a police officer.'

'Is it a rough area?' asked Buchanan, as he put the vest on.

'Not really. It's much like any other area here in Dallas. It's a mix of mostly residential with shopping markets and some light industrial units scattered throughout. This is the area I was assigned to when I came out of the academy as a rookie.

'Prayer before the patrol – you don't mind if I pray before we go out?'

'No, especially if it helps.'

'Gracious Lord, we are about to go into the lion's den, would You give us the faith to know You are ever present with us and the conviction to do Your work? That no works of the evil one will prosper against us and if this day we are called upon to pass through the valley of the shadow of the death we are assured by Your word that You are there in the midst of us. Amen.'

'I've never started the day like this before, that was some prayer, thanks.'

'You don't have to thank me, it's all down to the Lord.'

'So how long have you been in the police?'

'Just celebrated twenty-seven years.'

'You're a detective, yet you are in uniform.'

'While working the streets in a patrol car it works better, no confusion as to what we are. You wear a uniform?'

'No, not since I became a detective. In fact, I don't even own a uniform. Do you do this sort of work often?'

'Today there's a programme, where we as detectives are required to go back on patrol for two weeks every six months. It's been just over eight years since I've been doing any kind of full-time patrol work.'

'This is your car for your time on patrol?

'Yes.'

'Do all patrol cars have this much technology built in?'

'They've installed cameras and listening devices in squad cars and all this fancy equipment is related to the video system. I don't know how to use it, and don't plan on touching it. Shall we get going?' he said, closing the boot.'

'Do you just go where you want, or is there a prescribed beat?'

'I've been assigned to two beats where they're having a ton of residential burglaries. They used to be quiet beats but now, with drugs, it's all changed.'

'Where are we going first?' asked Buchanan, as Lazarus turned right out of the police compound.

'We need fuel.'

'I thought you did that in the yard?'

'Not that kind of fuel. You drink coffee?'

'Never start the day without at least one cup. I usually stop in at my local Starbucks just after they open on the way to work. As soon as they see me park, the barista begins my coffee.

'Now that's what I call service. What about doughnuts?'

'Starbucks in my area don't sell doughnuts, I buy mine in the garage first, then go into Starbucks for my coffee.'

'Where I'm taking you opens at five am.'

'People are around at five to buy doughnuts?'

'Ted starts baking around two in the morning, then opens at five and is usually sold out by two in the afternoon. He told me he stops baking about ten in the morning. Pity you weren't here a couple of weeks ago.'

'Why?'

'The 5th of November is National Doughnut Day. It was created in 1938 to honour the Salvation Army "doughnut lassies" who served the treats to soldiers during World War I.'

'I didn't know that fact,' said Buchanan, reading the sign over the shop. 'Lucky Doughnuts, quite original. People really like their doughnuts,' he said, looking at the queue of people standing outside the shop waiting to enter and be served. 'Is it always this busy?'

'Most mornings, c'mon, let's join the line.'

The queue moved forward quickly, and Buchanan was soon standing in front of a long glass-fronted display case.

'Five shelves in each of the six display cases, and each with different shaped and coloured iced doughnuts. You Americans certainly know how to enjoy doughnuts.'

On top of the final display case by the cash register was a sign that said, "Happiness is a doughnut in each hand."

'What do you want, Jack?' asked Lazarus.

'How can I choose? There's such a choice. Whatever you're having, I'll have the same.'

'OK, what about coffee?'

'Just black, no sugar.'

'Sorry, what I meant was, would you like espresso, vanilla, regular or decaf?'

'I suppose espresso will do, please.'

'Fine, cups are beside the coffee pots, I'll have espresso, grab a table by the back of the shop.'

Buchanan walked to the rear of the shop and placed their coffees on the table. While he waited for Lazarus to pay for their coffees and doughnuts, he picked up the discarded newspaper lying on the adjacent table.

The headline in the *Dallas Observer* grabbed his attention.

'Dallas cops aren't issuing tickets like they used to'.

'Interesting one that,' said Lazarus, as he put Buchanan's doughnuts in front of him.'

'Four doughnuts?'

'My doctor said eating a doughnut regularly is one activity that contributes more to weight gain than almost anything else.'

'So, you have two?'

'Who counts?'

'Has this article in the *Dallas Observer* got something to do with you guys doing occasional patrol duty?'

'Got it in one. Dallas used to have thirty to forty patrol units doing traffic duty, now we're lucky if we can field fifteen. Revenue is hit hard as well. In the 2013 revenue year, drivers were issued with just over two-hundred thousand tickets. Last year ticket numbers didn't even reach a hundred and fifty thousand. To give you an idea of where it should be, back in 2006-7 a total of four-hundred and eighty thousand tickets were issued.'

'That must have put a dent in the municipal revenue stream.'

'It certainly does. During the 2016-17 fiscal year the courts took in almost nineteen million dollars, the following year that sum dropped to just over sixteen million dollars.'

'All I can say to that is, you either have a very efficient police force or a community of very bad drivers.'

'Finished your doughnuts?'

'Yes.'

'Good, coffee refills are free, you can finish in the car.'

Buchanan fastened his seat belt and was about to ask a question when the computer display on the dashboard lit up.

'Ah, wondered how long it would be before we got our first assignment.'

'What is it?'

'A resident reported a group of teenagers congregating in an alley behind their house. Two with red hoodies and a third wearing a black hoodie, let's go.'

'Lights and siren?'

'Not for this, I want to talk to them, not scare them away, but there's no reason to go slow.'

♦

Lazarus turned into the alley and drove slowly past rickety wooden fences, garage doors scrawled with graffiti, and overfull garbage cans.

'There they are,' said Lazarus, 'there's no reason why they're creeping around like that. See they are just aimlessly wandering, looking over the fences and likely up to no good. You sit here, I'll go talk to them,' he said. as he burped the patrol car's siren.

The one wearing the black hoodie turned to see where the siren emanated from, his shoulders dropped when he saw Lazarus getting out of the car and unclipping the safety strap on his sidearm. He beckoned them to come over to the patrol car. Buchanan wound down his window to hear what was said.

'You have ID? ID with your name and your picture?' Lazarus asked the youth wearing the black hoodie. 'You two stand in front of the car. All of you, hands on the hood where I can see them.'

Buchanan watched as Lazarus went from youth to youth, patting them down and collecting their IDs. He returned to the patrol car and ran the IDs through the on-board computer.

'Well. That's OK, no records or outstanding warrants.'

Lazarus got back out of the patrol car. 'Don't go hanging around in alleyways,' he warned the youths as he returned their IDs, 'now, go on your way.'

'Quite a sophisticated system you have,' said Buchanan, as Lazarus climbed back in the car.

'So, what do you guys have?'

'Nothing like this, but we do have ANPR.'

'What's that?'

'Automatic Number Plate Recognition. If a car is uninsured or untaxed the scanner immediately tells the patrol car driver. The patrolman has access by radio to up-to-date criminal records through the control room.'

'So, not that much different to what we have here.'

'I suppose so. Those lads were in the clear?'

'Yeah, I guess we caught them green. Hopefully we turned them from doing anything today, but we got them identified. If we come up with something in this area this afternoon, we know who to look for. I think we're going to watch this area real good.'

'That sounds like a good method of crime prevention.'

'As a patrolman you need to learn how to answer calls, put butts in jail, communicate with people – all the time realising that most people are lying to you. You do all this in order to set the foundation for later on in your career as a detective.'

'Is today typical of what it's like to be a patrolman?'

'Pretty much. Tomorrow morning I'll start over again and see what happens. You never know what can happen. It can be nice and quiet and then we go home a little early or it could be total chaos and we are stuck in the middle of a situation till the early hours.'

'How often do you have to draw your sidearm?'

'Whenever it's necessary, it helps to show that you are serious and shows who's in charge of the situation. You Brits don't carry?'

'We have specialist firearms teams that respond as necessary.'

'Sort of like our Swat teams?'

'Yes, that's a fair comparison.'

'So, what does the average bobby do when he's confronted by someone with a firearm?'

'Thankfully since the UK is mainly weapon free, that situation rarely happens. But if it does, depending on where the incident is, an armed response team is on site within minutes of the call coming into control.'

'Been any recently where they were required?'

'Back in 2019, there was a case of a young man who went on a killing spree in London with a knife at a venue called Fishmonger's Hall. He was actively attacking people when he was shot twenty times by armed police. During the stabbing spree he killed two young people; this was after he shouted that he had a bomb.'

'Did he have a bomb?'

'No, there was none found. After the initial shooting, while he'd been lying prone on the ground, he started to get up. He was shouted at to lie still but ignored the instructions and yelled, *No allahu akbar* before rolling over and sitting up. He was shot a further nine times. In all, twenty shots were fired, as well as him being tasered by sixteen officers. He stopped moving about fifteen minutes after he began his knife attack.'

'So, he kept moving while being wounded?'

'Not really. He simply didn't know he was already dead.'

'Fifteen minutes total from report to dispatch, not bad. I guess we would react in a similar manner, though we might bring in a Swat team to deal with it, but you said he was actively attacking the public?'

'Yes, there was no time to plan a response. Our officers are trained to think and react on the spot.'

'Was that a standard response to a knife attack?'

'No, usually we try and contain the person, and when contained, disarm them. There's a video on YouTube where a deranged man is standing in the street, wielding a machete.'

'Was he shot, like the other guy you mentioned?'

'No. Initially the first responder engaged him by shouting at him to put his machete down. As that was going on, more units arrived who kept the guy busy while a supply of riot shields were brought to the scene. When each of the officers had a shield, they advanced on him and forced him to the ground where he was immobilised and fully restrained.'

'He wouldn't survive here. If we were confronted by a knife-wielding person, we'd just shoot them.'

'What's that on the display?' said Buchanan, pointing to the computer screen.

'Detectives over by the South Dallas district are working on the murder of 33-year-old Samson Pierre. Their chance of solving the murder is cut in half if they don't get there within the first 48 hours. They need to know if the surviving victim can ID the gunman.'

'Is that common to have the victim ID the suspect?'

'It does sometimes happen. The report says a Latin male shot his friend then stole his bicycle. The witness described the dude that had the gun as having little dreads braided across his head. We've been asked to go collect the witness; he'll be waiting for us at a crossroads. It is an open area with trees on the corner of Coleman and Parnell, that way he can see who's approaching before they can see him. We'll pick him up and head to where the gunman supposedly lives and hand him over to the detectives working the case. If the survivor can ID the suspect, they will be arrested and charged.'

♦

'He looked scared,' said Buchanan, as they left the unfortunate witness with the detectives.

'He should be. If word gets out, he'd ID'd the suspect, he won't last a week.'

'So, where do we go next?' asked Buchanan.

'Back on the beat, we have a quota to meet.'

'Quota? You mean you have to arrest so many criminals in a shift?'

'There isn't officially a quota. The city has a recorded number of crimes a day, everything from murder to jaywalking. The city fathers say with so many crimes and so many officers out on patrol we should all be doing our bit. So, what they say is, for example, there are five thousand crimes reported in South Dallas and there are one hundred cops on the beat, there should be a minimum of fifty citations issued by each police officer every shift.'

'Is this a typical patrol?' asked Buchanan.

'Yes, it can be a quiet one, sometimes.'

'Does that happen very often?'

'Not for a long time. Most days we are busy dashing to one crime or another, a traffic incident, or a domestic disturbance, it's quite a circus working the beat here in Dallas.'

'Sounds a bit like how my old hometown was.'

'One bad incident I remember was back in 06 when a crazy guy bought a used armoured car off the internet. He then climbed in with an automatic rifle, loads of ammo and a bomb. He parked it outside the police station and proceeded to shoot the shit out of the building. When he'd had enough, he broke the cordon and sped off. Eventually he was trapped and instead of giving up, he blew himself up.'

'How many died?'

'None, thank God. But that's not the worst shooting that's happened in Dallas.'

'JFK?'

'Now that was a tragedy, and Oswald paid dearly for his moment of infamy. No, what I'm referring to happened back in July 2016 when an angry young Army Reserve veteran of the Afghan War, Micha Xavier Jonson, ambushed a group of police officers. When he was done shooting, five policemen lay dead with nine others injured. Two civilians were also wounded.'

'Sounds like the bad old days of gangsters, gun runners and prohibition.'

'That's not all. Following the shooting, he fled inside a building on the campus of El Centro College. Police followed him there, and a standoff ensued. The negotiator tried to get him to give up, but instead, the gunman tried to enlist those who were there to arrest him – he had the nerve to tell them to turn their guns on each other.'

'A black on white revolution?'

'Precisely. He was angry over police shootings of African American men, which had occurred in the preceding days.'

'How did it end?'

'In the early hours of July 8th police killed Johnson with a bomb attached to a remote control bomb disposal robot. It was the first time U.S. law enforcement had used a robot to kill a suspect.'

'Cowboys never grew up in Texas.'

'Seems that way, doesn't it?'

'Where to next?'

'Back on the beat.'

As Lazarus turned out into the busy flow of traffic, the computer lit up with a call about an attempted robbery at a local 7-11 shop.

'Will you respond?' asked Buchanan.

'Absolutely, hold tight,' said Lazarus, as he turned on the lights and siren. 'It's only five minutes from here.'

As a passenger, Buchanan tried to remember that he was in a police car with an experienced driver, but it didn't stop him from bracing himself with his hand against the dashboard. They were the first patrol car on the scene.

The shops were a typical suburban arrangement of businesses made up from the 7-11 where the robbery was underway: a dry-cleaner, coffee shop that according to the sign in the window made fresh sandwiches every day, a tax preparation office and finally a hardware store.

There was ample parking in front and the shops were protected from the weather by a canopy supported by pillars running the full length of the shops. Over to the left, lying on the ground, was an elderly woman trying to crawl away from the shop to the safety of a row of parked cars.

'Wait here,' said Lazarus, as he got out of the car.

Buchanan watched as Lazarus, once again and probably by instinct, undid the safety strap on his sidearm and removed his gun from its holster. He looked at the shop front then back to the figure on the ground. His mind made up, Lazarus walked crouched, while holding his gun with both hands in front of him, across the car park towards the individual lying there..

When he reached her he looked back at the shop front then down at the individual. He knelt, said something, then helped her to her feet and escorted her the short distance to the safety of a second police car which had just arrived.

When the person was safe, Lazarus had a short conversation with the now growing number of officers about tactics. Having decided what to do, they fanned out and walked slowly forward, guns at the ready, to the door of the shop.

Lazarus got ten feet from the door when the robber ran out. Seeing Lazarus and the other officers approaching, the robber pulled the trigger on his own gun and fired several shots. Lazarus fell, and the robber ran off along the front of the shops towards what he assumed was an empty police car.

Without thinking of the consequences, Buchanan stepped out of the car and stood behind one of the pillars and waited for the robber. As the robber passed the pillar, Buchanan grabbed him by his gun hand and spun him headfirst against the door of the police car. The robber crumpled to the ground, blood pouring from his face.

Buchanan left the unconscious robber to the arriving police officers and ran over to the prone Lazarus, who was being attended to by two of his colleagues.

'Hang on a minute, I'm all right, just winded,' said Lazarus, as he rolled onto his side.'

'You were shot, I heard the gun go off and saw you fall,' said Buchanan.

'Just like going down in the spirit.'

'Sorry, I'm not following you.'

'Here, let me up and I'll show you.'

Buchanan stood up and watched Lazarus get to his feet. He reached into a shirt pocket inside his flak jacket and removed a small book. 'This is what I meant, it's my daily reader,' he said, opening it at the page where the bullet had stopped.

'Well, I'll be –,' said Lazarus, bursting out with laughter.

'What is it, what's made you laugh at nearly dying?'

'Look,' he said, showing Buchanan the page, 'it's today's reading, November 26. Psalm 118 verse 24, *rejoice and be glad, this is the day the Lord has made.*'

'I'm glad for you, truly I'm glad.'

'This mess is going to take some time to sort out. When was the last time you were a witness to an attempted cop killing?'

'This will be the first.'

'I was about to get one of the other guys to run you back to Travis's, but now?' he shrugged.

'What happens next?'

'Witness statements, crime scene investigation, that sort of thing, probably something you do all the time.'

'Like you guys, we also have crime scene investigators that do that. It would be interesting to see how they go about their job.'

'We're not going anywhere.'

'You're sure you're not injured?'

'Take more of a bullet than that to stop me, I'm fine, really. I'll put it in my report and will probably have to go to the hospital to get checked out. It's all part of the procedure when an officer is injured on the job. The report will be forwarded to the DA's office for consideration as evidence to be used against the defendant when he is charged.'

'You'll want me to make a statement?'

'Yep. It won't be me though, I'm also a witness. It might mean a court appearance as a witness for you.'

'That won't be the first, though it would be the first overseas one.'

'It may not come to that; it will be down to the DA's office to decide. We need to get a cordon up quick; a cop shooting will have the news media here quicker than flies on a fresh cow pat and we don't want them trashing the crime scene with their big feet and satellite broadcast trucks.'

'You the Limey riding with Lazarus?' asked a uniformed officer.

'Yes.'

'Sergeant Ross. My duty is to take statements, and I don't mind telling you I just hate it when civilians ride with the cops, causes all sorts of troubles, especially when they get involved with the action. What on earth made you pull such a stupid stunt as to grab a fleeing gunman who's just tried to kill a cop? Oh, never mind answering, probably get an equally stupid answer. What's your name?'

'Jack Buchanan.'

'Occupation?'

'Cop.'

'Oh, a wise ass. Let me tell you this is no joking matter. Now tell me, what is your real occupation?'

'I'm Detective Chief Inspector Jack Buchanan, Sussex Criminal Investigation Department. This is my warrant card and badge,' said Buchanan, removing his wallet from his jacket pocket and showing his credentials to Ross.

'That rank makes you a chief. My apologies, sir. It's just sometimes cops like to take friends and family out for a bit of a joy ride, something the department wholly disagrees with and discourages.'

'An honest mistake, especially since you guys are undermanned and having to deal with the Defund the Police brigade.'

'You've heard about that?'

'Been watching Fox TV News.'

'Brainless morons the DTP people, what will be their cry when they call 911and find there's no cops available to respond when their person, house, business or property is violated?'

'Sorry, I'm just a visitor to your country. You want a statement of what I saw and did?'

'Yes, please.'

♦

'Thanks for today, Lazarus. It certainly has been an eye-opener,
said Buchanan, as Lazarus dropped him off at Travis and Shelly's
house.'

'You're welcome, and thanks for your card, I'll let you know if
anything comes of today.'

'OK, bye.'

♦

'Quiet day?' asked Karen, as Buchanan entered the living room.

'Not quite. Managed to stop someone who tried to kill a
policeman.'

'Jack, you're supposed to be on holiday! What happened?'

'It sounds more that it was. While riding in the car with Lazarus,
he got a call to attend a convenience store robbery. Someone took
a shot at him and ran away; I managed to grab the robber and
subdue him till the other police arrested him.'

'Oh, the way you said it, I thought you'd been involved in a
shootout.'

'Really, you should know me better than that.'

'That's just the point, I do know you only too well.'

11
The Visitor

'It's been great having you here for Thanksgiving,' said Travis, as he helped Buchanan get their suitcases out of the Yukon.

'It's certainly been an adventure; you will keep me posted on Lazarus? He said he was uninjured, but I think he was just trying to put a brave face on his assault.'

'I will. Have a safe flight and see you next spring for Harry and Poppy's wedding?'

'Looking forward to it, bye,' said Buchanan, as he stood for a moment and waited for Karen to say goodbye to Shelly, Poppy and Harry.

♦

Wednesday Morning, early
The Visitor
'That was quite a meal,' said Karen, as she passed the remains of her chicken lunch to the flight attendant.

'I thought the chicken was a bit dry,' said Buchanan.

'Not the on-board meal, I was talking about the Thanksgiving meal we had with Travis and Shelly, reminded me a bit of our wedding meal.'

'Now that was a feast to remember.'

♦

'No matter how enjoyable a holiday is,' said Karen, as Buchanan parked the car in front of their house, 'it's always nice to come home.'

'I totally agree with you, but…'

'But what, Jack, what is it?'

'Stay here, I'll just check something.'

Karen stood beside the car watching as Buchanan walked up to the front door and, instead of using his key to open the door, pushed it open with his finger.

'Oh, Jack, we've been burgled!'

Buchanan turned to face Karen, put his finger to his lips and gestured to her to stay where she was.

He pushed the front door fully open then peered into the entrance hallway. There was someone standing outside the kitchen at the far end of the hall holding a steaming coffee cup in his right hand.

'Good holiday?' asked the intruder.

'Yes, but who the hell are you? And what do you mean by breaking into my house?'

'It's not really breaking in if you have the door key,' he said, holding out a Yale key.

'Where did you get that from?'

'Archery Locks, same place you got your keys from, they were ever so helpful.'

'So, smartass, what are you doing here in my home?'

The intruder handed Buchanan a collection of pennies and five-pence pieces.

'What's this?'

'You said to make sure you got them back, don't you remember?'

'You remember me after all this time?'

'You have quite a reputation, sir.'

'All bad, I hope.'

'Yes, sir, some are not repeatable in polite company.'

'So, the last time I saw you, you were just a cadet, what are you now?'

'Detective Constable Bull.'

'My suspicious mind detects something going on here.'

'You may remember my uncle, Sergeant Bull? He recently retired.'

'Bull by name, bull by nature, certainly, I remember him. He was my sergeant when I was still wet behind the ears. His favourite saying was, *never polish your arse in a chair*. How is he?'

'Enjoying his spare time growing vegetables on his allotment.'

'Something we have in common.'

'Yes, he took retirement not long after you transferred down here to Sussex.'

'Transferred? I had no choice in the matter. Retired you say, does he enjoy being retired? My wife keeps hinting I should do the same.'

'He did retire, not long after you left. But since we are short on beat staff, he came back on contract. He now does part-time on the front desk.

So, why are you here?'

'I've been sent to deliver you.'

'Deliver?'

'Yes, and I'd leave that coat on if I were you, sir, we'll be going back out as soon as you've explained things to Mrs Buchanan.'

'Well, you're not me, young man, and before I go anywhere at all, I shall change out of these clothes that I've been wearing for the last many hours. Also, I think I'd like a coffee and to tell my wife it is safe for her to enter her own house. Stay there and I'll bring the cases in.'

'Can I do that for you, sir? The cases that is, not bring Mrs Buchanan into the house, that I'll leave to you.'

'At least you have manners. You go and make me a coffee; I see you've discovered where the kitchen is.'

'Black?'

'Yes, no sugar.'

'And Mrs Buchanan, do you think she would she like a coffee?'

'She'll have a tea, strong, with milk, no sugar.'

'What is it, Jack?' asked Karen, 'what's that young man doing in our house?'

'Apparently, I'm needed.'

'Needed? Just what does that mean? Oh, you're not in some sort of trouble are you, something you forgot to tell me? You can tell me; we can find a way to work it out.'

'No, I'm not in any kind of trouble, at least I don't think I am.'

'Could it have something to do with the robber you knocked unconscious in Dallas? Oh dear, Jack, suppose he died of his injuries, and they have sent this young man to arrest you?'

Buchanan shook his head, 'The last I saw of the robber was of him struggling to get away while the police were putting handcuffs on him, he certainly was alive at that point.'

'Your tea ma'am, your coffee, sir. Sorry to have startled both of you with being here when you returned, but it is urgent.'

'You're not here to arrest my husband, are you?'

'No, certainly not.'

'Then what is it all about?'

'It's a security issue. I am only at liberty to tell Chief Inspector Buchanan.'

'Well, in that case, Jack, will you take the cases upstairs for me, then you two can talk about whatever security issues you like.'

'Certainly. I'll be back with you in a minute.'

'Yes, sir.'

Buchanan returned to the room, shut the door and went over to the armchair beside the fireplace. 'Why don't you sit down? You make the room look untidy. Now, what's your first name, I already know your surname.'

'Most of my friends just call me Gray, it's short for Graham.'

'Then I will add myself to your friends list and call you Gray.'

'Thanks.'

'Gray, I've been reviewing my situation during the last twelve hours while sitting strapped into a seat at thirty thousand feet above the Atlantic Ocean. I've surprised myself into realising, that after a lifetime of fighting a never-ending onslaught of criminals, I shall give myself up full time to the profession of growing vegetables. I've taken on an allotment, and I intend to devote my time to the cultivation of the freshest, most nutritious vegetables known to man. I will also get a dog, a police dog probably, and that, my young friend, will be my only compromise to ridding myself of the wasted years of my life. I'm going to put an end to dashing to the phone each time it rings. In fact, I may never answer another phone call in my life.'

'That's a bit drastic, sir.'

'Gray, this house, here in this charming village of Westham, will be where I drop anchor. I will furl the sails one last time and let this old hulk rot on the beach till one day an insignificant tide will come in and wash it off over a distant horizon.

'Here, in this idyllic village, I shall establish myself as just another elderly gentleman who coos at the babies in their prams. Mothers will warn their young sons that unless they work hard in life, they will end up being just like old Jack. I will forget to shave every day, wear the same shirt several days in succession. I shall become a gnarled old elm tree in the middle of the graveyard.'

'Why were you chosen for this odious task?'

'I came top in my sergeant's exam, I just happened to be outside the boss's office when a volunteer was required, take your pick, because I have no idea as to why I was asked.'

'As an answer, that is an answer.'

'You're quite poetic.'

'Will I need overnight things?'

'It's not that far.'

'Where are we going?'

'Castlewood Country Club, just off Arlington Road. I believe you're known there.'

'Fine, I'll meet you outside, I just need to let Mrs Buchanan know where I'm going, I can tell her that much at least, can't I?'

'Oh, yes, sir, certainly you can tell her that much.'

♦

'You even know where it is,' said Buchanan, as they turned off Arlington Road onto the driveway up to Castlewood Country Club.

'Yes. It helps to have good directions. The golf is great here, one of the best courses I've played on.'

'So, I hear.'

'Do you play?'

'Me, chase a wee ball round the green? No way.'

'That's right, I heard you prefer riding horses, came fourth in the inaugural Castlewood Cup race.'

'My, you are well informed, you have been doing your homework.'

'I came first in the class with my sergeant's exam.'

'Somehow that doesn't surprise me.'

'So, who am I going to have this clandestine meeting with? Who is it that required the presence of this old Glasgow cop?'

'I don't know everyone who will be there, I was just asked to deliver you. Oh, I do know that James Anderson will be there.'

'Chief Constable Anderson, I thought he'd retired?'

'He has, from day-to-day policing, but he now works as a consultant.'

'Don't tell me, he's a consulting detective?'

'Like Poirot, or Sherlock Holmes? I'm sure he will find that idea amusing. No, he just consults on matters pertaining to domestic security.'

♦

Gray opened the door to the club for Buchanan and followed him in.

'They're waiting for you in the library.'

'Decent of them to wait.'

The reserved for a private function label was showing on the door to the library. Once again Gray opened the door for Buchanan and waited for him to enter. Standing in front of the blazing fire, was Sir Nathan Greyspear. Beside him was a white-haired individual who stood almost four inches taller than Greyspear. Chief Constable James Anderson was deep in conversation with ACC Helen Markham.

At the sound of the library door being closed Markham turned and smiled at Buchanan as he crossed the thick carpeted floor.

'Ah, Jack, how was Dallas?' she asked.

'We enjoyed it immensely, even got to go out on patrol with one of the squad cars. Karen went shopping, at least we only had two suitcases to fill for the return journey.'

'Good to see you again, Jack,' said Greyspear. 'Dallas is quite a city, been there a couple of times on business. You know James?'

'Yes, we have met. How's retirement, sir?'

'Oh, we can dispense with those formalities now, just call me James, like Nathan does, and yes, retirement suits me fine.'

'OK, James it will be.'

'Let's sit and be more comfortable,' said Greyspear. 'Would you like something to drink, Jack?'

'Coffee, black, no sugar.'

'How are you, Jack?' asked Markham.

'Fine, been thinking about retiring and growing vegetables.'

'I'll believe that when you bake me an apple and rhubarb crumble.'

'Settle for strawberry and rhubarb?'

'Either will do.'

'So, Jack, I bet you are wondering why you have been dragged away from your holiday so soon after landing,' said Anderson.

'Yes, it has crossed my mind.'

'Well, to a certain extent, it is your fault.'

'My fault?'

'Well, maybe I should rephrase that. Because of your due diligence and tenacity in following up clues, you've brought to the surface an issue we didn't realise we had.'

'I just do my job.'

'You may see it that way, yet to some you are an anachronism, you're like — like one of those Russian Van'ka-Vstan'ka dolls.'

'Roly-Poly dolls in case you don't understand Russian, Jack,' interrupted Greyspear.

'Are you saying I'm fat, James?'

'No, certainly not. What I mean is no matter which way, or how hard you're pushed; you just pop back up again. And we're glad you do, despite how it sometimes rubs the wrong way.'

'Talking of the wrong way, why have you had young Gray break into my house, drag me away from my wife – just to tell me I'm needed? And why are you telling me what I should be doing, when you're retired? I'm an active police officer, I should arrest you for inciting the crime of breaking and entering.'

'I'm sorry, Jack, I'll explain, but first would you be so good as to bring us up to date on what you've been working on?'

'I shall, but, before I do, what's brought you down here? You could have just as easily phoned.'

'My brother's granddaughter lives in Eastbourne, and she's just given birth to triplets, that reason enough? That and the fact you've been stirring up the dust of history.'

'My, retirement has certainly made you more lyrical in your use of words.'

'Shall we drop the wordplay?'

'Fine with me. A few weeks ago, Saturday, I was nearly rundown on Westham High Street by a Golf GTi bearing the plates we later found were cloned. On the following Monday I met with Sam Richmond at the Pevensey Starbucks; he's an investigator for the Health and Safety Executive.'

'Do you hold many meetings at your local Starbucks?' asked Anderson.

'If you've ever tried the station coffee you wouldn't have to ask that question. Sam was investigating an industrial accident on the previous Saturday; I'd dropped in for a coffee on the way to work. Sam gave me details about a carpenter who had fallen off his ladder and accidentally stabbed himself with his chisel. He and his mate were working on a barn restoration on Pevensey Levels when the accident happened.'

'Did you talk to the mate?'

'Unfortunately, not. He'd done a runner by the time we got to the B&B where they had been staying. In fact, I believe it was he who almost ran me down on the Saturday morning.'

'Where did you get the B&B address from?'

'I got the address from Sam Richmond; it is a local address in Pevensey.'

'So, you connected the carpenter's death with the disappearance of the mate?'

'No, not then, I thought it could simply be a case of the lad went into shock seeing his boss die in such a way; and being in the possession of a car with cloned plates, he simply got scared and did a runner.'

'Did the HSE investigator think the death was suspicious?'

'No. He said it was a simple case of an accident brought about by the ladder the carpenter was working from not being secured properly and, unless there was any further evidence, that would be the way he would report the incident.'

'Hmm. What did you think?'

'At first I couldn't make up my mind, it wasn't till Doctor Mansell gave me his sandwich and banana that I saw what really happened.'

'I know you can be circumspect when being quizzed by the press, but that answer deserves an explanation,' said Anderson.

'Shortly after the body had been brought to the morgue and after Dr Mansell had performed the autopsy, I paid the morgue a visit to get a first-hand explanation from the doctor. Since there wasn't a high ceiling in the morgue, or a tall ladder to hand, he had me re-enact three different scenarios pertaining to the possible cause of death. From that I was sure there was no way the carpenter could accidentally have stabbed himself. I was further convinced when I saw the deceased's face, I was sure it was Jamie Gallagher, though his ID said he was Jackson Hardcastle, and the only Jackson Hardcastle I could find was a night club singer working on a cruise ship.'

'Are you sure about that? Because Jamie Gallagher died in a fiery car crash on the M8 a few years ago, body now residing in Cathcart cemetery.'

'That's what Gus said.'

'Gus?'

'DI Michael Fergusson, I used to work with him.'

'So, you believe the lad killed the carpenter?'

'The lad has a name.'

'Oh.'

'Yes, Steve Jameson.'

'Are you sure about that?'

'No doubt in my mind.'

'What makes you so sure it's Steve Jameson?'

'We've made a positive identification using the mugshot being shown to witnesses. We also know where he is hiding.'

'Why haven't you arrested him, especially since you have witnesses?'

'We're waiting to see if he has any accomplices, he's under a 24-hour watch and can't leave where he is hiding without being seen and apprehended.'

'And the car?'

'The plates were from a Golf that had been written off. The car had been stolen from King Street NCP carpark, Glasgow.'

'That the one in the East End?

'Yes.'

'What about the painter who fell off the scaffolding?'

'That happened two weeks ago. We were having a barbeque at home with some friends when our son-in-law Stephen received a phone call to say there had been an accident in town.'

'Why would your son-in-law get that phone call?'

'He's a PC and the only one available to take the call.'

'I see.'

'I drove Stephen and Dr Mansell to the scene.'

'Why would Doctor Mansell come along?'

'Doctor Andrew Mansell, our local police pathologist.'

'Thanks.'

'When the paramedics got there, the painter was dead, with the body still warm. The face was damaged beyond recognition by the impact it made going through the garage roof. The victim ended face down on the gear knob.'

'Did he have an ID?'

'His driving licence said he was called Stan Hendricks, but the second driving licence tucked in the back of his wallet gave his name as John McDermott, address had him living on Sandyford Road in Paisley.'

'How sad,' said Anderson, shaking his head. 'How old was he?'

'Birth date 23rd August 1960.'

'And, only a few more years till retirement and he does this. I knew a John McDermott once,' said Anderson. 'But he's dead, died in the same car crash that Gallagher did.

'The John McDermott I remember was a troublemaker,' said Buchanan. 'I put him behind bars more than once.'

'So, you're certain it was McDermott and Gallagher's bodies you saw in the morgue?'

'Yes.'

'Were there any witnesses to the painter's death?'

'No. The first indication of trouble was when the other painter knocked the door one of the ground floor tenants and said there had been an accident.'

'Did you interview her?'

'Yes, but she didn't actually see the accident or the dead painter, she's the one who called for the ambulance.'

'Was she able to give a description of the one who knocked on her door?'

'Yes, a very good one, which matched the description of Steve Jameson, the lad who we think killed the carpenter.'

'Do you think she might be able to recognise him in a line-up?'

'When I asked her that same question she said yes.'

'Good, do you recognise him?' said Anderson, passing Buchanan an A5 mugshot of a man in his mid-thirties.

'Looks familiar.'

'Do you have someone who could go and check to see if your witness recognises this chap?'

'Give me a chance, I'm just in the door, and to answer your question, yes, there is someone who may be available, please wait.'

Buchanan took his phone out of his pocket and called Street.

'Hi, Jack, how was Dallas?'

'Dallas was fine. Are you anywhere near town?'

'I'm in the office, and I've got good news for you?'

'Can that wait for a moment? I need you to do me a favour.'

'OK, what is it?'

'If I WhatsApp you a mugshot, would you have a look at it?'

'Certainly, send it – got it, yep, I recognise him, that's Steve Jameson.'

'How do you know who he is?'

'I got a mugshot from Fergusson in Glasgow. Took a bit of looking for him, but Gus eventually came up trumps.'

'Well done. Is our quarry still laying low?'

'Yep, hasn't stirred from his lair.'

'Good, let's hope he stays put till we get a handle on what's going on. I'll see you in the office when I'm done here.'

'OK, see you after lunch.'

'I suppose your sergeant had good news for you, Jack?' said Anderson, as Buchanan hung up on Street.

'Yes, she positively identified Steve Jameson. She asked the landlady at the B&B, also the resident of the flat. She's also been able to run Steve Jameson to earth, he's hiding in an empty house in town.'

'Was he arrested?'

'No, we want to see if he's got company.'

'I don't like the sound of this. What else has your team found?'

'They've discovered that Steve Jameson is hiding in an empty house in Eastbourne. The house is located in an exclusive area of town, and has a sold, subject to contract, sign outside. The asking price for the house is 1.3 million.'

'Surely that's going to be beyond the reach of someone like Jameson? Have you asked the estate agent who the buyer is?'

'We haven't asked yet.'

'Why? I thought that would be one of the first things you would do.'

'The reason is simple, it's the same estate agent that handled the sale of the barn where Gallagher died. It is also the same agency that handled the barn restoration on the Pevensey Levels, and the leases for the block of flats where McDermott died.'

'Ah, I can see why you are reticent to arrest Jameson.'

'There's more.'

'What's that?'

'That estate agent was also involved in the sale of Du Marchon's house at Litlington.'

'The chap who used to deal in drugs, and ended up dying when his plane crashed in the Channel?'

'That's him.'

'Jameson could be babysitting for someone till the sale goes through.'

'In that case, who's the buyer? I wonder if – no, that's too far-fetched.'

'What's too far-fetched?'

'Nothing,' said Buchanan, shaking his head, 'I'm tired and my imagination is running riot.'

'Well, if it comes to you, let me know. I've been hearing good things about you, Jack. Pity we lost you,' said Anderson, as Buchanan put his phone away.

'Lost me? That's not what I remember.'

'Well, anyway, that's water down the Clyde now. All settled here in Eastbourne?'

'It's the village of Westham where we live, the office is on Hammonds Drive in Hampden Park. The Eastbourne shop was closed for development.'

'Sounds like what's happening in Glasgow with listed buildings. Developers see a chance to make a quick profit, get stuck with acquiring planning permission, then mysteriously the listed building burns to the ground and hey presto, planning approved.'

'Pity so much of Glasgow's heritage is being ripped up in the name of progress; for example, how many times has the Macintosh building caught fire?'

'That might be stretching things a bit, but I have read several reports in the *Glasgow Herald* recently about mysterious building fires. Shall we have a walk? I hear the greens here at Castlewood are something to behold.'

'I am sensing a bit of déjà-vu coming up.'

'We'll be back shortly. Nathan, Helen. Gray, keep our friends amused while Jack and I have a private chat.'

'This way to the green, James.'

Buchanan let the door close behind them as they stepped out onto the path that circumscribed the eighteenth hole.

As they stepped off the patio, Buchanan asked, 'So, what do you want to say that can't be said in front of company?'

'When you and I last had a chat, you wanted to sort out the mess with Randal and Shelton, I'm afraid I dismissed your offer out of hand. Unfortunately, I've lived to regret that decision.'

'You instructed me to abandon my enquiries because you had a team ready to make arrests.'

'Oh, was that what I said? How very pompous of me.'

Buchanan shook his head and smiled. 'You play with the cards life deals you.'

'You never had any, did you?'

'What?'

'Children, you and Karen?'

'Not then.'

'You've adopted?'

'Sort of. My partner, Jill, she lost her parents when she was very young, we've sort of ended up adopting each other. She's married to one of our constables, Stephen Hunter, though at work she prefers to be to be referred to by her maiden's name, Jill Street.'

Anderson chuckled. 'Buchanan and Street, the dynamic duo of Sussex CID.'

'Let's not forget Buchanan Street, the main shopping district in Glasgow.'

'Quite true, one of my wife's favourite haunts.'

'Same goes for Karen.'

'Jack, I must admit, I didn't absolutely trust your motives. As you were lying in bed recovering from your altercation in Porters toilet, I thought you were just thinking about looking after yourself and avoiding a possible disciplinary hearing with the resulting forced resignation. I have since lived to regret that moment and my decision to send you south. Our loss was Sussex's gain.'

Anderson stopped to watch a tall blonde in white slacks pot a fifteen-yard shot then nodded graciously to her male partner who'd obviously lost the round.

'I remember when women could only play golf on ladies' days.'

'Times change.'

'Gallagher and McDermott didn't die in the car crash on the M8.'

'I figured that was the case.'

'The two bodies you recently saw in the morgue were in fact Gallagher and McDermott, they'd turned State's evidence in exchange for clemency. They've been living quietly in Eastbourne with new identities for the last eleven months. The lad who was helping them was, as you deduced, Steve Jameson. The last we heard of him he was working as the enforcer for Rab Maxwell. You need to watch him, don't get too close. His MO is to pretend to give you a hug, then slip the knife lowdown into the belly or genitals, just in case you are wearing a stab vest.'

'Thanks, I'll keep that in mind.'

'You do.'

'I've been away for several years and have lost touch with the goings on in Glasgow.'

'There were three of them altogether.'

'Three? Who's the third?'

'Agnes Morrison, she was Andy Jameson's former wife and bookkeeper for the gang, and Steve Jameson's mother?'

'Yes.'

'So, she's also in danger?'

'Possibly.'

'What's the status on Maxwell?'

'Up to the demise of Gallagher and McDermott, the Procurator Fiscal said with the three witnesses in line to testify against Maxwell the case against him was as watertight as could be. The local police were about to put a move on Maxwell and arrest him, but now that two of the star witnesses are dead, things have gone on hold awaiting further developments.'

'What about Agnes Morrison, is she being looked after?'

'Yes, she's safe, for the moment.'

'Suppose I need to talk to her?'

'Call me first and I'll see what can be arranged.'

'You know where she is?'

'I'm one of a small group.'

'Sounds like Agnes is in good hands.'

'She is.'

'So, with Gallagher and McDermott both dead, are you saying Maxwell is off the hook for the present?'

'It was looking that way, till you started digging for information on them.'

'Really?'

'Your reputation for getting things done has raised the hopes of those who are sick and tired of Maxwell and his criminal activities.'

'I see, but where do I come in? Glasgow is a long way from Eastbourne.'

'I was coming to that.'

'Hang on, are you about to ask Karen and I to return to Glasgow?'

'No, not that. What I, and those I represent would like you to do, is to return to Glasgow, on a temporary basis, and put this case to bed, once and for all.'

'Like I said before, I'm not rolling up my trouser leg for anyone.'

'We're not asking you to do any trousering. This will all have to be done above-board and legal.'

'So, what are you proposing?'

'What we are proposing is, for you to come up to Glasgow, set up an office, and run a full background check on Maxwell, his methods, and his operatives. No door will be closed to you, and of course, you will have a suitable budget to enable you to complete the task. What do you say?'

'You want me to run a covert operation in Glasgow? That doesn't make sense. Surely you must realise murder detectives never go undercover. Detectives chosen for those types of roles are specialist in what they do and use specialist tactics. They never share what, or how they go about their operations, except, of course, with those who need to know.'

'No, of course not, I realise that. Those things only happen in bad Hollywood movies. What I want is for Maxwell to know that someone is looking over his shoulder, has a hand in his wallet, even listening in on his pillow talk.'

'You really want him that bad?'

'Yes, I do.'

'What's he done to you to make you this angry?'

'Never mind what he's done, I just want him, and his operation put out of action once and for all, do you understand? I want him to feel that someone is there in his thoughts as he goes to sleep and is still there when he wakes in the morning. I want him to be so rattled that he cracks.'

'I'm just to pack up and head back to Glasgow. What happened to the team you told me were just about to make arrests?'

'I'd rather not go into that. Suffice it to say, they couldn't take the investigation any further.'

'Witnesses got sudden amnesia, evidence got mislaid, threats of violence, is that what you mean?'

Anderson nodded.

'And what makes you think I can do any better?'

'I don't, but things are getting desperate.'

'At least you're being honest. Right, I'll come up to Glasgow and sort out your mess, but nothing else, do you understand me?'

'I told them you'd say that.'

'And what was their reply?'

'I'd rather not repeat it.'

'So, where do you want me to begin this probably pointless endeavour?'

'Pick up from where Randal and Shelton died, work backwards, or go forwards if you feel it will get you anywhere, be a Hercules and clean the stables for us.'

'That's quite a task. If I remember correctly, the stables contained thousands of cattle and it hadn't been cleared in thirty years.'

'An apt appraisal of the situation.'

'Is Maxwell still in control of his empire?'

'Yes. This is a list of the key players with their photographs. You might recognise some of them.'

'Well, Maxwell I certainly recognise, and I see Andy Jameson is out of jail. What's his position in the game?'

'He took over from Randal as banker.'

'Randal as banker – what a decision that was. That was like asking the fox to guard the chickens. Who took over from Shelton as lawyer?'

'The one standing beside Andy Jameson. The face on the far right of the picture is Toni Benatti, he's the lawyer, and he apparently knows his stuff. The female is Agnes Morrison. You recognise the two in the middle?'

'The curly-haired one looks familiar, no idea who the bearded one beside him is, who are they?'

'The one on the left's name is Jason Wardlow, the other is Tam Laidlow.'

'Wardlow and Laidlow, with names like that they should be related. I seem to remember something about those two. They did time for ABH, sexual assault, and didn't they hold up a branch of Ladbrokes?'

'You have a good memory, yes they did.'

'Are they out on the street?'

'We're not sure. They seem to be keeping a low profile, they haven't been seen for several weeks.'

'Maxwell's aged a bit since I last saw him, Gallagher and MacDermott I can discount, they're currently residing in the Eastbourne morgue.'

'There's a turf war brewing. You remember young Tam Beckerman?'

'Maxwell's nephew, his sister's boy?'

'That's the one. He was found in a squat above the Governor bar, loaded to the gills with smack and a syringe full of the stuff sticking out his arm.'

'That happens, drugs are no respecter of family.'

'Beckerman, as far as can be determined, was clean, not known to take drugs.'

'Suicide?'

'It was made to look that way.'

'What's known?'

'Beckerman and Steve Jameson went to school together.'

'And?'

'Talk on the street is Beckerman wanted to take over the running of the firm from his uncle. You may not know this, but Maxwell currently runs a very profitable construction company. Young Beckerman was rumoured to think he could run it more profitably than his uncle'

'Are you saying Maxwell has become respectable?'

'In some ways, yes.'

'There must be more to this than you've said so far.'

'Beckerman was his mother's carer. She died from a heroin overdose when he was eleven. From that day on he swore to never touch drugs of any type.'

'A most admirable commitment.'

'He worked hard at school and graduated from Glasgow University with a First in Business Administration.'

'How did he end up working for Maxwell?'

'Maxwell's company mainly do property renovations. I'm sure you know there are a lot of properties in Glasgow that require modernising.'

Buchanan nodded. 'I remember my gran's flat shared a toilet with three other families.'

'Thankfully that sort of accommodation is now a distant memory.'

'So, where does Maxwell come into the story?'

'You remember the Governor bar?'

'How could I not?'

'Do you know who owns it?'

'Wasn't it one of the Glasgow bars run by the Jim Donaldson clan?'

'The very same. When Donaldson died, under mysterious circumstances I might add, it fell into disrepair and was a money loser. It was put up for sale by the widow.'

'When did Maxwell get his hands on it?'

'Officially about three years ago. As you will probably remember, it is on the corner of a row of old tenements on Hope Street. They've been slated for demolition for several years, but someone decided that they were one of the few remaining examples of 18th century Glasgow and should be preserved.'

'So why was Maxwell involved?'

'The location is close to one of the M8 junctions and with city apartment prices rising the way they are, the area is ripe for redevelopment. The Governor bar was still operating but trade was bad, and, with the owner dead, Maxwell's company purchased the bar and said they were going to refurbish it and turn it into a bistro bar.'

'That doesn't make sense. Why would he buy a rundown bar – unless he had other ideas?'

'You're quick. Yes, not three months after Maxwell's company purchased the bar, one Saturday morning it caught fire and before the fire department could get to the scene, not only was the bar in flames, but the old apartments above were also on fire. By late Saturday morning a large section of the block was a burnt-out ruin.'

'And I suppose Maxwell's company has the contract to rebuild the apartments, and turn the old Governor into a modern bistro bar?'

'Exactly. There was a secondary reason why the Governor bar had to catch fire. The flat above the bar is where Beckerman was found. It was also the suspected location where Maxwell stored his drugs for distribution. The police and forensics were going to raid it and we think Maxwell decided to kill two birds with one stone.'

'Maxwell was tipped off about the raid?'

'Looks that way. The raid was supposed to be a secret only known to a few that needed to know.'

'I'll need somewhere to work from, and someone to do the legwork.'

'Your parents, they are still alive, aren't they?'

'I will visit them, but I don't want them to get involved in what I may stir up.'

'In that case, I'm sure we can find an office at headquarters, and there will be many DC's only too willing to work with the legend that is DCI Jack Buchanan.'

'You're making me sound like some sort of superhero.'

'Well, to some you are a bit of a hero.'

'I think in this case, the less I'm seen around headquarters the better things will be.'

'OK, that makes sense. Where will you stay?'

'The Busby Hotel on Field Road. It's a peaceful hotel just off the East Kilbride Road and just round the corner from the railway station.'

'Hmm, an interesting choice. Doesn't Maxwell live at the end of Field Road?'

'Yes, or at least he did when I was living in Busby.'

'I'll get the office to make the reservation for you.'

'If you don't mind, I think it would be better if I do that.'

'Why? It's no problem for us to make the reservation - the room, meals, and bar tab will get charged directly back to headquarters.'

'I think it would be prudent for me to make the reservation myself. I'd like to remain incommunicado for as long as possible.'

'If you wish, it's your operation.'

'I'll submit my expenses when I successfully bring this case to its conclusion.'

'And if you fail?'

'If I fail – my life insurance policy will take care of my bill and all of Karen's needs.'

'You're not joking, are you?'

'Not in the least. So far, we have a dead carpenter, a dead painter, a missing killer, and my name on the shopping list, what's to stop the trail of death there?'

'How will you work if you don't come into the station?'

'I have DI Fergusson for that.'

'Anyone else?'

'My old sergeant, George Bull.'

'Young Gray's uncle?'

'Yes. According to young Gray, his Uncle George works the front desk, he's in a perfect place to dig through whatever records I need looking at.'

'And if he is unable to access the files you require?'

'You still have access to the station, don't you?'

'You want me to do your snooping for you?'

'You said clean the stables, I'll use whichever broom and shovel I can get my hands on.'

'When can you start?'

'I've just got back from Dallas, my team will need to know what is going on, and probably do some groundwork first, so how about Saturday morning? That way, if I'm seen arriving in Glasgow, it will be assumed I've come up to visit my parents.'

'That works. Come, let us return to the warmth of the club.'

♦

'All well, Jack?' asked Greyspear.

'Yes, all is well.'

'Did you say yes?' asked Markham.'

'Yes indeed, but with provisos.'

'Dare I ask,' said Markham, 'what are these provisos?'

'My departure depends on who will watch the shop while I'm gone.'

'Who do you suggest? DI Hanbury?'

'No, while I'm gone, I'd like DS Street to stand in for me as SIO.'

'But I heard she's pregnant,' said Gray.

'Gray,' said Markham, 'you've obviously never met DS Street.'

'Yes, Jack, an admirable choice,' said Markham. 'Oh, she'll need a partner, who do you suggest?'

'How about PC Hunter? They work well together.'

'How did I know you'd suggest that?' said Markham. 'How soon can you go?'

'My bags are still packed from Dallas,' he said, shaking his head. 'Saturday, how about I go this Saturday? Hopefully I should be done with the investigation by Christmas.'

'Good,' said Anderson.

'Give me a call when you feel it's safe to do so,' said Markham.

'Will do.'

'In that case,' said Markham, 'I believe we've concluded this meeting.'

'I'll drive you home,' said Gray

♦

'Jack,' said Karen, as she opened the front door to let him in, 'what's going on? Who was that young man, and what was he doing in our house?'

'Let me in the door first, then I'll explain.'

'I certainly hope so. Do you want something to drink?'

'Coffee, please.'

'You go through to the sitting room; I'm doing laundry in the kitchen. I'll bring you your coffee and then you owe me an explanation.'

'Thanks.'

'Here you are, one coffee, black no sugar. Now, I know you too well, you have that look on your face. What's up?'

'Do you remember Chief Constable Anderson?'

'Yes, it was he who managed to get us down here to Eastbourne.'

'Well, I just had a meeting with him, up at Castlewood.'

'What was he doing at Castlewood?'

'His brother's granddaughter just had triplets; she lives in Eastbourne.'

'But why did he want to talk to you?'

'It seems my services are needed in Glasgow.'

'But we've just got settled here in Eastbourne.'

'Relax, it's only me they want. Initially it should only be for a few days. If I'm successful, it should be all over by Christmas.'

'That's what the troops were told in WW1 and look what a mess that turned out to be.'

'I should only be gone Monday to Friday. I could be home by next weekend. I'm only going up there to collect enough evidence for the Procurator Fiscal to charge and get a conviction against Maxwell.'

'But why must you go?'

'The two deaths in Eastbourne, it's possible Rab Maxwell and his gang are behind them.'

'But why you? Surely there must be someone in Glasgow who could sort it out? You're just one man, what can you do? How can they expect you to take on the whole of Glasgow's crime scene?'

'According to Anderson, Maxwell's influence on gangland operations and the drug world is causing great concern to one and all. I have been asked to gather evidence for the Procurator Fiscal so they can bring a case against Maxwell.'

'What about Anderson, where does he fit in?'

'I'm not quite sure at this point. There may be a need for someone to go behind the scenes and access certain files that I would not have access to.'

'Are you sure you should be getting involved in this? Cloak and dagger stuff isn't what you are trained for.'

'Anderson says I am uniquely equipped to deal with Maxwell.'

'Isn't that what he said when he sent you down here?'

'Yes, I seem to remember him saying those exact words. But don't worry, I'll have George Bull, DI Michael Fergusson, and young Gray, on my team in Glasgow, and I will also have Jill and Stephen here in Eastbourne.'

'I thought Anderson was retired?'

'He is, but is retained as a consultant.'

'When will you go?'

'Saturday morning.'

'That doesn't give me much time to get you ready.'

'I'm sure you'll manage.'

'Will you be home for dinner tonight? It's already quite late.'

Buchanan looked the time on his phone, 'Hmm, five-thirty. Jill will have gone home by now, I expect I will be late, sorry.'

'I was going to make a salad for dinner, I'll put yours in the fridge.'

'Thanks. After what I've been eating these last few days, a fresh salad sounds just perfect, I'll try and not be too late.'

♦

Buchanan walked into his office, and as he expected, Street had already gone home for the day. He looked at the time and realised Lazarus had probably stopped for lunch. He turned on his computer and began the task of finding temporary office space for rent in Glasgow. He chuckled to himself as after an hour of searching he found a recently refurbished office to rent on Buchanan Street, a short walk from Central Station and only a few minutes from the nearby Starbucks.

He took the fact he would be close to a Starbucks as a good omen and happily filled in the on-line application form, realising as he did that, at this rate, he might have to call the bank and get an extension to his credit limit.

Next, he looked up the Busby Hotel and booked a single room for the week. The following weeks he'd book as and when required. A car – would he need one? Why not? Of course, he could quite easily avail himself of a pool car, but they would probably all be known to his adversary, no, that wouldn't do, he would choose the moment he would become visible to his quarry.

He returned to Google and looked up the Avis rental site and looked at renting himself a Mercedes, then realised with public transportation being so good in Glasgow, he didn't need a car, rental, or pool.

12
Game Plan

'Morning, Jack. How was Dallas?' asked Street.

'Wild is how I would best describe it.'

'How about we have a meeting, and you can tell me all about it?'

'Sounds fine to me.'

'And I can bring you up to date with Steve Jameson.'

'Ah, I was going to talk to you about that.'

'Coffee? Starbucks?'

'You drive, my head is still on the right-hand lane.'

♦

'Morning, Jack, what's it to be?' asked Michelle, holding an empty cup.

'Could I have a large Americano, and what would you like, Jill?'

'Medium latte, thanks. I'll grab a seat in the corner.'

Buchanan paid with his loyalty card then sauntered along the counter to collect their drinks.

'Been away?' asked Alicia, as she passed Buchanan the coffees.

'Yes, went to Dallas for the weekend.'

'Nice.'

Buchanan picked up the coffees and walked carefully over to the corner table where Street was waiting.

'So, how was Dallas?'

'Not quite what I expected. It is a busy city not unlike London, but much smaller. Driving in the city seemed to me to be easier than London, but then I was a passenger in a police car.'

'How did you manage that?'

'It was a police friend of Travis; he took me out on patrol on Monday.'

'What was that like?'

'Like being on patrol with one of our armed units.'

'That sounds interesting.'

'Oh, it was, I even helped stop a robbery of a convenience store.'

'Trust you to get involved! Were you collected from the airport?'

'Yes, Travis met us at immigration and drove us home in the Yukon.'

'What is a Yukon?'

'A large SUV that Travis uses for church business. It's a seven-seat minibus.'

'Is it a big church?'

'I think I heard the auditorium seats about five-thousand per service.'

'That's a lot of people. Did you go to church?'

'On Saturday Travis took me to meet the help-at-home group. Sunday, we all went to the service, then a bring-and-share barbeque after church.'

'How was it?'

'Lively, intelligent, it's similar to Karen's church, I slept through most of it.'

'Karen's church?'

'You know what I mean, I just go along to keep her company.'

'What about Poppy and Harry?'

'Poppy and Harry have stayed on for an extra month. Poppy wanted to discuss wedding arrangements and Harry had meetings with the ranch owners. But tell me, how far have you got with the Jameson case?'

'Well, thanks to your friend Gus in Glasgow we have positive identification on Jameson as the person at the scene of both the carpenter and the painter deaths.'

'That's what I like to hear.'

'Then Stephen and Morris located Jameson in the Cameo club and followed him back to the house on Prideaux Road.'

'Is he still in situ?'

'As of twenty minutes ago. He hasn't left the house.'

'Has he had any visitors?'

'Only a parcel delivery.'

'Post Office?'

'We assume it was a private delivery company. There were no markings on the van.'

'Did Jameson come to the door to accept the delivery?'

'Yes, and that is the strange bit. The delivery driver followed Jameson into the house. He was in there for about thirty minutes.'

'Long enough to discuss something?'

'That's what we thought.'

'Did you get a description of the driver?'

'Yes, and a photograph of him as he left the house. We also got the registration number of his van.'

'What did you find out about the van?' said Buchanan. as he looked at the photograph of the delivery driver.

'It's all legal, tax, MOT, and insurance. Registered to a delivery company based in Glasgow.'

'Why am I not surprised about that? Name of the company?'

'Castle Deliveries. Registered address, 60 Wellington Street, Glasgow.'

'Did you check the PNC for the driver?'

'Nothing on the PNC,' she said, passing Buchanan a printout.

'So, what's this?'

'I did a reverse image search on Google and landed on a back issue of the *Glasgow Herald*. Apparently, there was an issue about him being sent to Barlinnie Prison. Someone has had his record flushed.'

'Well done on getting what information you have.' Buchanan shook his head and read the limited information Street had transcribed from the newspaper. 'Dino Volente. He's new to me, and not exactly a big-time player. Three years in a young offender institution for persistent shop lifting, fighting and two cases of taking without permission. Two years in Barlinnie for breaking and entering, then appears to be clean from his late teens.' He passed the rap sheet back to Street. 'You did well to get that information; these records are usually sealed after seven and a half years from the age of eighteen.'

'Thanks.'

'I wonder where he's been since he got out of Barlinnie? This sort of MO is usually the precursor to a life of crime.'

'I can tell you. With his name and photo, I did a check with the passport agency, then immigration. For the last fifteen years he's been living in the Spanish city of Bilbao. I put in a request for information on Volente to the Spanish police. The reply came back saying Volente was chucked out of Spain for being an undesirable and suspected Mafia operative. According to the Spanish police, Volente was dealing in drugs and was suspected of at least two shootings.'

'A real nasty piece of humanity. Now, there is something important I need to tell you.'

'What's that?'

'Well, first, Senior Investigating Office Detective Sergeant Street. I'm leaving you in charge here in Eastbourne while I pursue the case up to Glasgow.'

'You're appointing me the SIO in this case?'

'Yes, and on one condition.'

'Just one?'

'Yes.'

'And it is?'

'That you take your pregnancy seriously. From now on, till you go on maternity leave, it will be light duties for you, understood?'

'Yes, Dad!'

'Stop that, you'll make me cry.'

'Right, what's going on?'

'Remember your promotion is just till I get back from the little job that apparently I am the only one suitable to undertake.'

'So, what is going on?'

'Do you recall me talking about the Busby gang and a character named Rab Maxwell?'

'Not recently, you've only talked about Steve Jameson, Gallagher and McDermott.'

'Gallagher and McDermott were on the witness protection programme, how Jameson found out about them, I have yet to discover.'

'Someone trying to get even, someone leaked the information?'

'That would be my guess. Rab Maxwell has ruled Glasgow's criminal underworld with an iron fist for the last twenty or so years.'

'What's he like?'

'Maxwell, boss of the Busby gang, is a very violent, ruthless, clever criminal, a real nasty piece of work. His organisation is responsible for sixty percent of all the cases of money laundering, extortion, insurance fraud, drugs distribution and phony insurance policies in and around Glasgow. Oh, and the occasional shootings and frequent knifings. When I worked in Glasgow, the Busby gang was one of several gangs vying for dominance.'

'Not someone I'd like to meet in a dark alley, how would you describe him?'

'Maxwell is powerfully built with a chilling stare. It is said that one look from him would have people cross the street or leave the room in fear of coming too close to him.'

'What's his main source of income?'

'The last I heard it was drugs, smuggling, and providing protection to bar, clubs and restaurants.'

'I thought you had to be authorised by the FCA to offer insurance?'

'For traditional insurance you do, and the same goes for security, for that you require an SIA licence, and this is where Maxwell was clever. He would never say he provided insurance; the paperwork always described it in the guise of loss prevention for property damage and loss of income due to unforeseen circumstances.'

'I wonder what the unforeseen circumstances could be?'

'Buildings catching fire in the middle of the night, business owners mysteriously falling down flights of stairs and breaking legs, coffee machines in cafés breaking down. There is an unproven case, where the owner had a road-side food wagon blown up when he told Maxwell to get lost. Those who paid were given a notice to hang in a prominent position saying *This property is protected by Maxwell Security Services.*'

'That's a bit brazen of him.'

'He doesn't really care who knows.'

'So, where does he make the core of his money? The illegal money that is.'

'Mainly the supply of drugs, alcohol and/or tobacco products, all items must be paid for in cash.'

'How does the money change hands?'

'He has his thugs, or agents as he calls them, collect. They are instructed to only accept cash for the illicit side of the business. Invoices for security services are issued by Maxwell's office.'

'He has an office?'

'Oh, yes. To cover his criminal activities, he runs several legitimate businesses. Everything from domestic cleaning all the way to building construction. His thugs are all employed in his various businesses, thus providing them with a legitimate income to pay taxes on and to cover their extravagant lifestyles, though I doubt if any of them ever show up for work.'

'So, unlike Al Capone, they can all pay their fair share of taxes and stay out of jail?'

'Yes, he's clever that way.'

'How does he prevent trouble or stop other gangs encroaching on his territory?'

'To stop trouble or fend off unwanted solicitations, all the business owner or bar manager needs to say is, "This establishment is protected by Maxwell Security Services".'

'Just like that?'

'As I said, he is the most feared criminal in all of Glasgow.'

'So, should I deduce you are going to return to Glasgow and deal with him and his gang?'

'Yes, I've been tasked to clean the stables.'

'Stables? Are you going to be working in stables? I'm confused.'

'Ah, now why didn't I think of that?'

'What, what have I said?'

'When I lived in Busby I used to help-out at a local stable. They are beside the River Cart, a stone's throw from where Maxwell lives. I'll go and see my old friend Jock, he runs the stables, maybe he can give me a fresh angle on Maxwell's coming and goings.'

'So, in the meantime, what shall we be getting on with?'

'Who's watching the property on Prideaux Road?'

'Stephen has just come off duty, Morris has the afternoon shift. Shall I call Stephen?'

'No, I'd like to talk to him in person.'

'He's gone to collect a package from the post office for me, then he'll drop in here.'

'Good, I'd like to hear what, if anything, is going on at Prideaux Road.'

'He shouldn't be long.'

'Have you had lunch?'

'An hour ago.'

'Oh. In that case I'll just pop over to the Poppy Seed bakery, hopefully it's not too late for them to make me a sandwich.'

◆

'Hi, Jack,' said Stephen, as Buchanan returned with his late lunch sandwich, 'Jill said you wanted to talk to me?'

'Yes, Prideaux Road, what's going on there?'

'Not much.'

'How about you tell me what the *not much*, is?'

'As soon as you asked for surveillance on the house, we parked one of the vans on the street next to the house where Jameson is staying.'

'Isn't that being a bit obvious?'

'The house next door is having an extension added, there are already several white vans parked outside, I just added ours to the collection.'

'That makes sense.'

'I went on watch at four this morning. Nothing stirred till ten-fifteen when a Tesco delivery showed up.'

'Could you see what was delivered?'

'I stepped out of our van and casually walked past as the driver removed the delivery boxes. I had a quick glance and I'd say there were only enough groceries for one person for a week.'

'Could you see what was in the delivery?'

'A loaf of white bread – thick sliced, butter, cheese, bacon, ground beef, some baking potatoes, a 4-pint milk carton, and six four-packs of McEwen's export.'

'Well remembered.'

'I have a Boy Scout badge for that.'

'Not quite a gourmet list of ingredients, more like someone who is camping out.'

'That's what I thought.'

'What about the visitor, has he been back?'

'No, just that one visit.'

'Sounds like Jameson's babysitting the house.'

'That's what we thought, but for who?'

'That is a question that requires an answer. None of you have approached the estate agent handling the sale of the house on Prideaux Road?'

'I did approach the agent last week,' said Street.

'What did he have to say?'

'He told me that they handled the leases on the flats and the barn restoration had been at the request of the owner.'

'Did you ask about the house on Prideaux Road?'

'No, I thought that you would want to follow up on that.'

'If that's all,' said Stephen, 'I'm off home to bed.'

'See you tonight,' said Street.

'I think now would be an ideal time to go and talk to Mr James Hoskins about the house on Prideaux Road,' said Buchanan.

'Want me to drive?'

'Yes, please.'

'Shall I call to see if he's in first?'

'Good idea.'

Buchanan stood by the door and waited while Street called the number for the Ramsdens Property Management.

'He's in, and expecting us,' Street said, hanging up the phone.

♦

'Ah, Inspector, how nice to see you again,' said Hoskins, looking up from his desk. 'Not sure what I can do to help. As I told your young friend here, the house in Litlington has been sold and the new owners have moved in and are in the process of having the house redecorated.'

'Oh, that's a pity, I had hoped to have a viewing.'

'I am sorry. Oh, any news on the accident involving the painter?'

'No, sorry. The Health and Safety Executive haven't completed their investigation yet, but I suppose that is just a formality in this case. Why do you ask?'

'The scaffolding company have been on to me, they want to take down the scaffolding, but since they haven't been paid yet, they are refusing to dismantle it.'

'Why haven't they been paid?'

'The job is not complete, there are still three flats to be painted.'

'Have you called the contractors to find out why they haven't finished the painting?'

'Same story as the scaffold company: waiting to be paid.'

'Why would they be expecting to be paid if the job hasn't been completed?'

'It was a floor-by-floor contract, as each floor was completed, they were to invoice. But since they haven't been allowed back on the scaffolding, they are unable to do so.'

'That would be the painter's death. As I said, the HSE are still investigating the accident and won't reopen the worksite till they are satisfied that it is safe to work from the scaffolding.'

'How long will that take?'

'Sorry, the HSE is a law unto its own, you'd need to contact them direct and ask.'

'That is not good enough. I come into my office every morning to this,' he said, holding up a stack of post-it notes. 'Complaints from residents wanting to know when the scaffolding will be removed. I spend more of my time fielding complaints from residents than I do selling houses.'

Buchanan shook his head. 'I am sorry that you are being so inconvenienced. I know the HSE investigator who is dealing with the case, would you like me to have an informal chat with him and ask how the investigation is progressing?'

'Oh, that would be so helpful, I'll be forever in your debt if you could have a discrete word with the investigator.'

'No problem.'

'Are you saying you are not selling any houses?' asked Street. 'I thought Eastbourne is one of the few high-demand towns on the South Coast, especially for the higher-priced properties in town?'

'No, no. It's not quite that bad. In fact, we just sold a very nice property on Prideaux Road.'

'I'm new in town,' said Buchanan, 'I don't know where Prideaux Road is located.'

Hoskins smiled. 'Inspector, you surprise me. You a local policeman, and you don't know the roads in Eastbourne? Let me elucidate you, Prideaux Road, is located in an excellent area of iconic Eastbourne. It is close to schools, shops, the main railway station, and should you require it, there is the excellent District General Hospital nearby.'

'That sounds like a perfect location for some London stockbroker to retire to.'

'I'll have you know Ramsdens Property Management is not just selling properties to those retiring from a busy life in London. The house on Prideaux Road has been sold to a businessman from your part of the world.'

'A Glasgow businessman?'

'Yes, you might have heard of him, you coming from Glasgow.'

'Lots of people have come to live in Eastbourne from Glasgow, myself included,' said Buchanan.

'Of course, they have. Maybe you know the purchaser, Mr Robert Maxwell? I understand he is big in property and other businesses.'

'No, sorry, the name doesn't sound familiar. You must realise Glasgow has a population of over one and a half million souls. Other than my friends and family, I only know a handful of Glasgow residents.'

'Do you get many home purchasers from Glasgow?' asked Street.

'A few, but not many as Mr Maxwell.'

'You've met him?'

'Not directly. He sent one of his agents to look after the purchase of the house. I understand he's been staying at the property while the sale is going through.'

'Isn't that a bit strange?'

'What?'

'To have someone living in a property while the sale is being processed?'

'Not in this case.'

'I thought a house being sold is the seller's property till the sale is complete and the money has changed hands?'

'Yes, normally it is, but Mr Maxwell is a cash buyer, and the property is in all respects already his.'

'Lucky him, my husband and I are still saving up for a deposit.'

'Oh, I'm sure we could help you and your husband with that. These days there are many methods of financing the purchase of a house, including the raising of a suitable deposit.'

'Oh, I wasn't aware of that, could I have one of your cards? I will discuss the possibility with my husband.'

'Certainly, I'd be pleased to assist. As you leave, if you tell my receptionist you have talked to me about our Easy in the Door programme, she'll take your details and we can then get in touch and assist you and your husband onto the house-buying ladder.'

'Thank you, I will.'

♦

'Well done, Jill.'

'About what?'

'When you got him to talk about the fact, he knew Jameson was living in the house.'

'Was that what you wanted to hear?' asked Street, as they drove back to the office.

'Yes, and no. The yes is we now know a great deal more about what is going on here in Eastbourne, and the no is the last thing

East Sussex, and Eastbourne in particular, need is for Maxwell to setup camp here in town on Prideaux Road.'

'What will you do about it?'

'When we get back to the office, I'll give Gus in Glasgow a call and ask him if he's heard anything about Maxwell's recent activities.'

◆

Instead of using his office phone, Buchanan made a WhatsApp video call on his mobile. 'I'll put the call on the speaker,' he said.

'DI Fergusson. Jack – a video call, must be important?'

'Gus, I've got Jill listening in, so watch your language.'

'Me swear?'

'When you going to make chief?'

'You are kidding? Promotions are as scarce as hens' teeth around here, how can I help?'

'It's about Maxwell and his little helper, Jameson. Do you know what Maxwell is up to these days?'

'Rumour has it that all is not well in Palace Maxwell, it seems some of the knights in armour are getting restless.'

'A palace coup?'

'Not quite sure what's going on. A few weeks ago, a couple of his henchmen went missing. The talk on the street is they were getting above their station and were attempting to set up a fiefdom of their own within the Maxwell empire.'

'Names?'

'Laidlow and Wardlow.'

'I don't know the names. What happened to them?'

'No one knows. You know we keep an eye on Porters bar?'

'I'm not surprised, that's Maxwell's HQ.'

'Well, the two of them were seen drinking with an unidentified individual, then observed going out the back for a smoke. They never returned. Our man went out back to check on them, but when he got there, he found no sight of them.'

'This individual, did you get a description?'

'A discrete mobile photo.'

'Is he known?'

'No.'

'Gus, if I send you a photo, would you check to see if you recognise him?'

'Sure, send away.'

'Done.'

'Oh, this is interesting, he looks very much like the individual I was just talking about. Does he have a name?'

'Dino Volente.'

'Never heard of him.'

'He was a bad boy in his teens, then as far as we're concerned, he's been clean.'

'So, why the interest?'

'Jill has managed to unearth his past. For the last fifteen years he's been living in Bilbao, Spain. He's been dealing and is a suspect in at least two shootings and has Mafia connections.'

'What will you do?'

'There's not much we can do at the moment; especially since we have no idea where he is.'

'How about Maxwell, what are you going to do about him?'

'What can we do? He's dug himself so deep in the Glasgow scene I wouldn't know where to begin.'

'Jack, sorry to cut you short, but I have a lunch date in ten minutes with the missus.'

'That's fine, what I wanted to say can wait for another day,' said Buchanan. holding up a hastily scribbled note that said: *Call Jill on your wife's mobile when we hang up.*

'That suits me, Maxwell is not going anywhere, and Jack, don't be a stranger, call again soon, bye.'

'What's all that cloak and dagger stuff about?' asked Street, as Buchanan put his mobile back on its charging stand.

'Just being careful, you never know who's listening in on your phone call.'

'You are becoming neurotic.'

'No, I'm not, I'm just being careful,' said Buchanan, as Jill's mobile rang.

'I believe this call is for you,' she said, passing her mobile to Buchanan.

Buchanan pressed the answer button then the speaker button.

'Jack, what's all this secrecy about?'

'I have been tasked to come up to Glasgow and put an end to Maxwell's criminal empire.'

'On your own?'

'No. I'll be working behind the scenes.'

'Who with? No one's asked me to help.'

'Don't feel hurt, your invitation is in the post. You remember Sergeant George Bull?'

'Absolutely, who could forget old Bull? I was on the same rugby team as him and pity anyone who got in his way!'

'Yes, at six foot four, and being an ex-marine commando, he certainly knew how to take care of himself in a tight spot. Dislocated a few shoulders when removing weapons from criminals if I remember correctly.'

'He's been a fixture of the station for years, supposedly retired a few months ago. Though I've seen him around the station on the booking-in desk when they are short on staff. He must be back on a temporary contract.'

'He was my sergeant when I started with the force. Taught me how to keep out of trouble when I was still wet behind the ears.'

'He was mine as well. So, Jack, tell me just what's going on?'

'Steve Jameson is what is going on.'

'How? I thought you said you had him corralled in a house in Eastbourne?'

'We do, but I want to find out more about what he's up to before bringing him in.'

'Where does Dino Volente come into the picture?'

'We're not sure at this point. Volente has made a connection with Jameson under the guise of a delivery person, and as I just said, in Spain he is known to have Mafia connections and is a suspect in at least two gangland shootings.'

'You think he and Jameson are up to something, a palace coup maybe? Or it could simply be that Maxwell is retiring and is handing the reins over to Jameson and Volente?'

'Who knows? With Maxwell it could be either of those things, or any of a dozen others. Has Maxwell given any indication he is about to retire?'

'None that I'm aware of. With Maxwell being such a prominent, public figure, the *Daily Record* publishes every scrap of tittle-tattle that oozes out of the swamp he calls his city. Are you really going to bring him down?'

'That's what Anderson and his backroom boys want.'

'You mean Chief Constable Anderson? I thought he'd retired.'

'He has. He's now working as a security consultant.'

'That's a new one on me. His pension not enough he's got to keep milking the sacred cow?'

'It's the way things are these days. I think it's become a case of not what you know, more a case of who you know.'

'Ah, the old boys' club. You will be careful, won't you? Anderson may be the retired Chief Constable, but…'

'But what?'

'Anderson is such a vain toff; he could be being played by those standing in the shadows behind him.'

'That thought had crossed my mind.'

'But, if that was the case, what would Anderson's cronies have to gain over the demise of Maxwell?'

'For a start, control of one of the most profitable drug distribution networks in Scotland.'

Fergusson shook his head, 'I canna see that, Jack. I know most of Anderson's cronies, some are local city councillors and business owners and supporters of our local youth charities.'

'I know those who you are referring to, and I know who they owe their allegiance to.'

'What about an office, where will you set up?'

'Are you ready for this? I've booked a temporary office on Buchanan Street.'

'Buchanan Street, you're joking – aren't you?'

'No, I'm not joking. It's a recently refurbished office on Buchanan Street, just off Argyle Street and close to Central Station. The paperwork says it has excellent meeting facilities and super-fast broadband.'

'Sounds perfect for you.'

'It even has showers and a kitchen.'

'You don't plan on dossing down there, do you?'

'No.'

'So, where will you be staying when you're up here?'

'I'm going to book in at the Busby Hotel.'

'Not with your parents?'

'No. If things turn nasty, I don't want them involved.'

'Makes sense. I expect you'll see your brother?'

'Yes, I suppose so.'

'You two still not seeing eye to eye? You know he's making quite a name for himself as a public defender lawyer?'

'No, I haven't heard, been busy taking care of business down here in Sussex.'

'Well, you'll find out for yourself when you get here.'

'I'm looking forward to that, I think.'

'Have you talked to Bull yet?'

'No, not yet. I'll do that myself later.'

'You think you're being played as piggy in the middle?'

'Not sure what to think at this stage, it's early days.'

'Hang on, this may sound crazy to you, but could it be possible that Anderson and his cronies want to take over Maxwell's empire and he's using you to get rid of Maxwell?'

'That is stretching things quite a bit, but it did cross my mind.'

'Boy, that would be the end of the world as we know it. Jack, you really need to be strong and full of courage if you are going up against Maxwell.'

'What did you just say?'

'You need to be careful; Maxwell doesn't play games.'

'Oh, don't I know it. I will be careful.'

'Good, see you are. I've been to too many funerals of those who chose to stand up to Maxwell.'

'Fine, I'll call you on your mobile when I get to Glasgow, it's probably best I don't come in the station.'

'OK, Jack, talk to you later.'

'Are you sure you should be going to Glasgow on your own?' asked Street. 'This Maxwell character sounds like real bad news, makes me think of a previous gangster.'

'Do you mean Arthur Thompson, the godfather of crime in Glasgow?'

'Yes, him and all the others who have followed in his slime trail. When doing my studies for my sergeant's exam, I read up on him and his antecedents.'

'Such as?'

'The one called the Licensee, Tam McGraw.'

'Oh him. He was suspected of ordering the killing of the Doyle family in a dispute during the ice cream wars. Two men, T C Campbell and Joe Steele were convicted of murdering the six members of the Doyle family in 1984. After many appeals they were finally had their convictions quashed in 2004.'

'Twenty wasted years, where is justice when it's needed.'

'Interesting that that should come up,' said Buchanan. 'Campbell, Steele and two others were arrested in a police raid on the Busby Hotel, the hotel where I am going to be staying.'

'Lucky you.'

'Did you read up about the killing of Thompson's son, Arthur junior?'

'Yes, and the subsequent trial of Paul Ferris. He was accused of shooting young Arthur. Did you know the cost of the court case was put at four million pounds with more than three hundred witnesses being called to give evidence during a 54-day trial? It was the most expensive trial in Scottish history.'

'Yes, it was, and unfortunately it didn't paint a very good picture of the police at the time, and to top it off, after all that expense, Ferris was found not guilty.'

'Well, I suppose if there weren't any witnesses or evidence, he deserved to be acquitted. Do you remember the case?'

'Vaguely, I'd only been in the force a few years when the shooting happened.'

'Must have caused quite a sensation?'

'Oh, it did.'

'What happened to Ferris?'

'Retired from crime, became a family man and took up writing and giving interviews.'

'Lucky him. So, why aren't you worried about going up against Maxwell and his associates?'

'I know I should be, that's common sense, but I'm not,' said Buchanan, as he took his mobile from its charging stand and put it in his pocket. 'I realise I need to watch what I'm doing, but this is what I'm paid and trained to do.'

'You will be careful, won't you? Young Jack will need a grandpa.'

'Yes, I will be careful, but in the meantime, I think we've done enough work for one day. I will see you here tomorrow morning.'

'Are you going home?'

'Not yet. I've been thinking.'

'Sometimes an asset, what have you been thinking?'

'I've been wondering if I should just call Anderson and tell him I'm not taking on this job. I could say I'm getting too old for this sort of work. I could say this should be handled by someone more suited to clandestine type of work.'

'Who would you suggest?'

'The NCA, they have covert capabilities. Their officers work at the forefront of law enforcement, building the best intelligence picture of all serious and organised crime threats; relentlessly pursuing the most serious and dangerous offenders; and developing and delivering specialist capabilities on behalf of law enforcement and other partners.'

'You sound like their poster boy.'

'I'm reading it off my computer screen.'

'Could they do the job?'

'Probably, but at what cost?'

'What do you mean?'

'Well, what you get with the NCA is a dedicated organisation with a management, research, legal, procurement, enforcement, welfare, and who knows what else, and at what cost to the public purse?'

'And with you?'

'You get me, Gus, George, Gray, and my expense account, saving the taxpayer a heap of cash.'

'You're forgetting Anderson.'

'I suppose I am, though I'm still not sure whose team he is playing for.'

'You will be careful, won't you?'

'Yes, I will be careful.'

13
Basher Bull

'Good morning.'

'Morning, Jill.'

'How did you sleep last night?'

'Fine.'

'Glad to hear that, I was concerned you'd end up worrying about whether you should take the job or not.'

'I'm fine, in fact I'm really looking forward to getting back out on the streets of Glasgow and having a go at Maxwell.'

'In that case, what shall I get on with?'

'Would you call Sam Richmond at the HSE and ask if he's come to any conclusions? Say that the residents of Blackwater Road are unhappy about the scaffolding and the painting not being completed. While you do that, I'm going to call Glasgow and see if I can make contact with Bull.'

'OK.'

♦

'Police Scotland, Cumberland Street. How may I direct your call?'

'Yes, I wonder if you could you put me through to my uncle, Sergeant George Bull?'

'Which department is he in?'

'Booking-in desk.'

'Wait one.'

'Desk.'

'Good morning. Can I talk to my uncle, Sergeant George Bull? It's a family matter?'

'Sorry, he's not available to take your call.'

'Oh, I understand. If I give you my mobile number, would you ask my uncle to give me a call? Please, it is urgent family business.'

'Certainly, what is your number, and your name?'

'07976 73971, and my name is Jack.'

'OK, Jack. As soon as your uncle comes in, I'll pass the message on.'

Buchanan hung up from calling the Glasgow police station thinking that they were either very security conscious, or old Bull really wasn't there. He didn't have long to wait for the answer, within ten minutes his mobile rang.

'Buchanan.'

'Is this my nephew Jack, whose snotty nose I used to wipe?'

'I see you've never lost your sense of humour. How are you, George?'

'I was fine till I saw your message. Since when did I become your uncle? What's up?'

'Maxwell, that's what's up.'

'That shithead, why are you interested in him?'

'I've been tasked with the job of taking him down.'

'You and whose army?'

'I was sort of hoping you'd like to enlist for that position?'

'Are you serious about this, it's not some sort of windup?'

'I'm deadly serious.'

'Dead might be the operative word, Jack.'

'Don't I know it! So, will you help?'

'Do I have a choice?'

'Yes, of course you have, but my gut feeling is you'll jump at the chance to get even with Maxwell.'

'You know I still miss her.'

'How could you not?'

'The memory of that day when Helen was injured and the carnage that followed has stayed with me all these years. It fair broke Maggy's heart, you know she's never really got over it.'

'I can imagine.'

'Yes, of course I'd love to help you take down Maxwell. Want me to break his neck?'

'No, not just yet. This must be above board, no neck-breaking, or talking to in dark alleyways.'

'Pity. So, how can I help?'

'I need someone to do the legwork for me, someone who works on the inside, someone who can wander the streets of Glasgow and not be noticed. Could you be that person?'

'Jack, as far as anyone is concerned, I retired four years ago, no one notices me. I'm just an old duffer who sits quietly in his local supping on his beer.'

'I thought you'd say that.'

'So, what's the plan of action?'

'I'm coming up to Glasgow on Saturday to get things rolling.'

'Won't your appearance on the scene attract unwanted attention?'

'If anyone asks what I'm doing there, I'll say I've come up to see my parents and have a look around the old places where I lived.'

'I suppose that includes Busby?'

'Yes.'

'You realise Maxwell still lives in Busby?'

'I was counting on that.'

'Where do you want to meet up?'

'Are you still living in East Kilbride?'

'Yes.'

'I'm staying at the Busby Hotel, how about we meet in the bar Sunday evening, say about seven?'

'Seven in the Busby Hotel bar it will be. Anything else?'

'No, that's all for now, see you Sunday.'

'Who are you seeing Sunday?' asked Street, who'd just come into the office.

'My old sergeant, George Bull.'

'Your old sergeant? You make him sound ancient.'

'Sorry, a slip of the tongue. I think he's only a few years older than I am, but probably twice as fit.'

'So, what are you two cooking up?'

'Maxwell.'

'So, George Bull is your army?'

'If you'd ever seen him take on a drunken, rowdy, Saturday-night crowd, you'd understand why I would feel safe with him by my side.'

'I still don't like you going up to Glasgow, even if you have your Basher Bull at your side.'

'Basher Bull, that's a good one, he'll get a laugh out of that, but, please, don't worry about us - we know how to take care of ourselves.'

'I don't know how Karen manages being married to a policeman.'

'You're married to a policeman, you manage.'

'I suppose I do. So, Sir Galahad, it's Thursday and will soon be lunchtime, what shall I get on with seeing how I'm confined to barracks?'

'Who's keeping an eye on Jameson?'

'Morris – Stephen's just come off duty.'

'Has there been any change to the situation?'

'According to Stephen, it's all quiet as of thirty minutes ago.'

'Probably a good idea on his part. No sign of Volente?'

'None.'

'I wonder where he's gone to earth?'

'We could circulate his picture.'

'No, the fewer people who know we are looking for him, the better, but…'

'But – you've just thought of something?'

'Yes. Have you ever heard of the Eastern Screen Owl?'

'No, should I?'

'Not particularly. It has one particular trick that puts it above many other birds.'

'What's that?'

'Like many owls it can sit on a branch of a tree, and, because of its plumage, it is almost invisible to the naked eye.'

'So, you think Dino Volente is sitting naked on a branch of a tree?'

'Amusing, Jill, but no.'

'So, where would you choose in a public place if you wanted to be unseen?'

'I can think of lots of places, for instance, he could be a night-time shelf-stacker at a supermarket or work as an office cleaner. But no matter where he worked, or what hours he worked at night, he would still have to find somewhere to sleep during the day.'

'I've got it. Where could you sleep during the day and work during the night and get paid to sleep and not have to commute to work?'

'Nothing comes to mind. What are you thinking?'

'I bet he's working as a night porter at one of the Eastbourne hotels. He's free during the day to sleep or go wandering round town, and no one would notice him at night. But which hotel, and how will we find out without spooking him into doing a disappearing act?'

'We could try booking in late and see if we recognise him?'

'That's an idea, but I don't think it's a practical one, there must be hundreds of hotels in Eastbourne that have night porters.'

Further discussion was prevented by Street's desk phone ringing.

'DI Street … He has? … Can you follow him? … No, I suppose that wouldn't work …. Good idea, I'll get on it right away.'

'What's a good idea?' asked Buchanan, as Street hung up.

'That was Morris, Volente just pulled up outside the house on Prideaux Road and Jameson got in. Morris said it would look too suspicious if he started following.'

'Makes sense. What will you do?'

'I'll get a trace put on the vehicle reg using ANPR. I'll also post full descriptions and mugshots of the two, plus put out a bulletin saying not to stop them or the vehicle, just to observe as we want to know where they end up. Did I miss anything?'

'No, that's exactly what I would do.'

'Good, I'll get right on it.'

'They're most likely heading for Glasgow,' said Buchanan, looking at the time. 'Three forty-five, yes, I'll bet that's what they are up to. They have chosen this time of day so they can be inconspicuous in the evening commuter traffic. I'll give Gus a call and let him know what's going on, can I borrow your phone?'

Street nodded and passed her mobile to Buchanan.

'You really think your phone calls are being monitored?' she asked, as Buchanan called Gus.

'It's possible. Gus, it's Jack, just a head's-up call to let you know that the chickens have flown the coop … yes, I know that chickens can't fly … yes, I wanted you to know that they are on the road and probably headed your way. Where? Who knows at this point? Jill is putting out an APW to be on the lookout for them, but not to apprehend. Yes, I'll call you as soon as we hear anything … Saturday … I'm coming up by train … I'm staying at the Busby Hotel … I'm having a meeting with George Bull to discuss a plan of action … Good, I was hoping you might join us … Sunday evening in the hotel bar … OK, I'll see you Sunday.'

'So, what's happening Sunday?'

'I've asked Gus to join Bull and me for a strategy meeting Sunday evening in the bar of the Busby Hotel.'

'If what you fear is true, won't that look suspicious?'

'Unlikely. Everyone knows that Gus and Bull are old friends, what could be more natural than three old friends get together for a drink?'

'That sounds logical.'

'And while we are there, what's not so unusual about three policemen talking shop?'

'I'll give you that point.'

'How did you do on the All Ports Watch request?'

'It's running. I said the occupants of the van are suspects in an injury hit and run incident in Eastbourne, but not to apprehend, just to report location.'

'Anything yet?'

'Yes, vehicle just reported as passing Beddingham roundabout heading west on the A27.'

'Excellent news. How did you get on with Sam Richmond?'

'Good news for the residents. He said the Health and Safety Executive are happy to leave the investigation to us, and as such he's no longer interested in the site. We are free to make decisions as to when work can recommence on painting the windows on the apartments.'

'In that case I think we can allow technology to do its work, and we can go home for the day.'

14
Tracking Jameson

Buchanan stopped in at the garage for his copy of the *Herald*, and a bag of fruit gums. He also purchased two bags of jam, plus one bag of chocolate doughnuts for his barista friends in Starbucks. Since he was going to be in Glasgow the following day, he decided this morning he would sit-in and eat two of the jam doughnuts as he leisurely drank his coffee and read his paper.

Page six had him shake his head. A recent crackdown on drug dealing had seen several drug dealers arrested and sent to trial at Lewes Crown Court. Several were given various sentences, ranging up to forty-five months, while others were remanded in custody awaiting sentencing on a date yet to be determined.

Page seven made him smile. He read with interest that the Police and Crime Commissioner had been awarded 1.5 million pounds from the Home Office under the latest round of Safer Streets funding. Good luck to her, he thought, raising his coffee for a sip.

Page fourteen was a completely different matter. He read that the firearms officers were sent to more than six hundred incidents in the year 2021/22. At least no shots had been fired and weapons had only been pointed at individuals twenty-six times.

Page sixteen had him shaking his head again. The article gave details from a meeting of the roads policing group that drivers were becoming less tolerant and more impatient since the end of the outbreak of the Chinese bat virus pandemic. An appeal to the driving public was made asking them to think twice about how they reacted to those around them. Some other items causing bad driving were put down to drivers still ignoring the rule of not using phones while driving, being under the influence of alcohol or drugs and just not being aware of other road conditions.

Coffee and newspaper consumed, he said goodbye and drove on into the police station and the office.

Street was already at her desk and staring at her computer screen.

'Morning, anything of interest on our two?' asked Buchanan.

'I'm just reading the report. At Cobham services they stopped for thirty minutes. At Oxford services on the M40, they were seen eating in McDonalds, CCTV picked them up buying petrol then they re-joined the M40. They were next observed at Keel services on the M6 buying coffee in Starbucks. Then they were observed on the East Kilbride Road heading into Busby.'

'Excellent.'

'You know where they are heading?'

'Yes. I'm assuming they are heading for Maxwell's house, it's beside the River Cart in Busby, right at the end of Field Road.'

'If you're so concerned that your phone calls are being listened to, how are we going to keep in touch?'

'Easy,' he said, pulling a mobile phone from his pocket, 'I grabbed this from the exhibits room. Don't worry, it's not a piece of evidence. It's one of three that were headed for the recycle bin. I'll call you, then you will have my number ready.'

'Go ahead – got it. I'll save it to my contacts. Now, have you given thought to how we are going to run this investigation?'

'Not quite sure what you are asking?'

'Surely you don't think you are going to hightail it up to Glasgow and leave one of your main assets sitting here in Hampden Park twiddling her fingers and wondering if I'm going to need to send Doctor Mansell up to Glasgow to do an autopsy on an old Glasgow cop, do you?'

'Ah, I now see I was correct when I recommended you take on the role of SIO in this case. I was going to discuss tactics with you later, but since you have brought it up, there's no time like the present.'

Street smiled and said, 'Sorry, just wanted to make sure you realise I am part of this case, even though I will be stuck here behind a desk.'

'Sitting in the nerve centre, what could be more important?'

'You've told me a bit about Maxwell and his empire, are all gangs like his?'

'A good question. OK, a potted history of gangs in Glasgow. Gang presence in Glasgow is recorded as far back as the eighteenth century. By the middle of the nineteenth century, an influx of Irish immigration brought over those from traditional fighting gangs. By the nineteen twenties, most Glasgow gangs were referred to as fighting gangs.'

'So, Maxwell's outfit is not really a gang in the true Glasgow gang sense?'

'Quite correct. His activities should be more correctly labelled a criminal enterprise. With Maxwell, violence is only a means to an end, though some of his henchmen take a delight in inflicting pain on their victims. Maxwell's main driving force is to make money, a great deal of it and pay very little taxes.'

'You know we discussed the idea that Anderson might be acting on behalf of others who wish to take over Maxwell's operation?'

'Yes, I do remember us discussing that.'

'Well, I've been thinking about that. Suppose it's something quite simple: he just wants you to do the dirty work of getting rid of Maxwell, that way you take all the risk, and he takes all the glory.'

'All hail Anderson, thou shalt be king hereafter?'

'I think Charles might have something to say about that.'

'I'm sure he would. That was a quote from *Macbeth*, prophecy of the third witch.'

'I never could get my mind around Shakespeare. Though at school, I remember watching Ian McKellen recite something from *Macbeth*, he was very good.'

'Did you see him as Gandalf in *Lord of the Rings*?'

'Yes. Stephen is a great fan of Tolkien, reads *Lord of the Rings* every year.'

'Really?'

'No, that was from a Netflix video Stephen likes to watch. In the video Ian McKellen is on stage talking about his role as Gandalf, really very funny for such a serious actor. I do know Stephen has read *Lord of the Rings* several times, he does read a great deal.'

'Do you read much?'

'No, probably should read more, but at the end of the day, my mind is too tired to concentrate. I do read on holiday though.'

'What do you read?'

'You'll find this amusing, I read crime stories.'

'Any particular author?'

'Dick Francis and his son, Felix, write some great stories.'

'You've obviously been giving this case a great deal of thought. What are your ideas, seeing as how you are the SIO?'

'For a start, I would like us to stay in contact. Daily to begin with, probably first thing in the morning, that way if you need anything from my end, I can get on it right away. Also, with us making contact first thing in the day, that way I know you are not in some sort of trouble.'

'I appreciate that, and agree, what's the second item on your list?'

'Until those around you prove themselves personally, trust none of them, not even your friend Gus, and that also goes for your old friend, Sergeant Bull.'

'That's a bit rough, isn't it?'

'Maybe, but it's your neck you are sticking out, I wouldn't want to see it getting chopped off.'

'I'll be careful. Any other thoughts?'

'To be an efficient and responsible SIO, I would like a complete list of the players you are going up against. I want their names, dates of birth, criminal record if they have any, known associates, friends, family, and addresses where possible.'

'I'll put a list together for you, shouldn't take too long, anything else?'

'No, that should be fine for the moment.'

'Great, I'll get on with the list.'

'While you are doing that, I need to collect a prescription from Tesco.'

♦

'That was quick.'

'Should be, I put the prescription in a week ago.'

'I have your list for you. I've done it as an Excel file and saved the file as Maxwell Dead End Street on HOLMES. That way you and I can make changes as we go along; I've emailed you a copy.'

'Thanks. Maxwell Dead End Street, as a file name it will do, even sounds a bit prophetic, to my mind sounds like Maxwell is on a dead-end street.'

'Let's hope Maxwell is on a dead-end street.'

'There's not much more we can do from this end, so with that in mind we may as well have an early night, besides, I need to get ready for my trip to Glasgow tomorrow.'

'Are you flying?'

'No, I've reserved a first-class seat on the train, and I intend to take full advantage of it and enjoy the journey.'

'Sounds nice. I will think of you as I sit at my desk writing reports.'

'Thanks, I'll think of you too.'

'What are you two doing this evening?'

'I'm taking Karen out to dinner.'

'Where are you taking her?'

'A restaurant in Herstmonceux called the Sundial.'

'Oh, she'll love that. Stephen's parents took us there a few months ago. You do like French food, don't you?'

'Yes.'

'Then you'll have a wonderful evening. Talk to you Monday, goodnight.'

15
Busby

'What time is your train?' asked Karen.

'Seven thirty-two, it's non-stop to Victoria,' replied Buchanan.

'Are you sure you shouldn't be flying? It's only an hour flight to Glasgow.'

'Two reasons. First, it's an hour and a half's drive to Gatwick, two-hour check-in, thirty minutes to board. You are right when you say it's an hour's flight, but add the time to taxi to the gate, time to wait for the luggage, then a bus ride into Glasgow, walk to the station and catch the train to Busby. Add that all up and you are close to eight hours of traveling.'

'And secondly, the train?'

'Door to door service and only seven hours travelling, and if you book ahead, it's half the price. Plus, on the train you can get up, walk around, and if you travel first class like I am, drinks and meals are served at your seat and are included in the ticket price. No contest, the train wins every time.'

'Will you have time to go and see your mum and dad?'

'Hope so, it's been a while.'

'And Matthew, your brother, you do remember you have a brother?'

'Yes, of course I do. I'll give him a call.'

'And you're sure you don't want me to drive you to the station?'

'I was about to say there's not much point, it's only a short walk but then I remembered Starbucks opens at seven.'

'Then you need to get your skates on, it's six-forty. After I drop you off at the station, I will pop round to the allotment and check the greenhouse, I want to make sure all vents and the door are securely shut.'

'Thanks, I should have done that yesterday.'

'You had a lot on your mind, greenhouses probably weren't one of them. Are you sure you should have left Jill in charge? It's quite a responsibility.'

'I have my orders; I have to check in with her every morning.'

'Really? She's bossing you around?'

'If you'd heard how she took charge, you wouldn't be so concerned.'

'I'm pleased to hear that. Just imagine, Jack Buchanan being bossed around by a woman half his age. You have your coat, scarf, and hat? Remember it's Glasgow you are going to, not the Riviera.'

'Yes, thanks, I don't know what I'd do without you women in my life.'

'I suppose you would just muddle on somehow. You will be careful, won't you?'

'Aren't I always?'

'You're forgetting you are going up against Maxwell and his thugs, and he's probably not forgotten how your last encounter went.'

'I only did my duty and presented the evidence as we found it. It was the Procurator Fiscal who decided to prosecute Maxwell.'

'Well, please make sure you take care, I wouldn't trust him to take out the rubbish.'

'I promise, I will look after myself.'

'You do that, if you get killed, I'll never speak to you again. C'mon, if you want your coffee, we better be going, while you're in there would you get me a medium late, please?'

◆

'You're here early, Jack,' said Alicia. 'Sitting in or taking away?'

'It's taking away today. Could I have a medium Americano, black, please?'

'And Mrs Buchanan?'

'She would like a medium latte, please.'

'OK.'

♦

'Thanks for the coffee,' said Karen.

'You're welcome.'

'Now I see your train arriving. Let me hold your coffee for you while you board, you need two hands for your suitcase. Which end is your seat?'

'I think the first-class compartment is behind the driver's cab.'

Karen waited with Buchanan's coffee as he manhandled his suitcase onto the train.

'Here's your coffee,' she said, passing him his cup. 'Take care, I love you.' She kissed him.

'And I love you, too. Don't worry, nothing is going to happen to me, I'll probably be back in a few days with things all resolved.'

♦

Being early on a Saturday morning; there were no issues about getting a seat, and since today was going to be a long one, he was pleased he had chosen first-class. The ride from London to Glasgow was also sorted as he had a confirmed reservation.

The doors closed and Buchanan took his seat in the first-class compartment and as the train slid out of the station he waved goodbye to Karen, wondering if he would really be home by next weekend.

The Victoria underground line to Euston was a different matter. He struggled onto the train and stood beside his case, along with travellers of all descriptions. It seemed that half the population of London were all trying to get from Victoria to Euston. Thankfully the escalators were working. Buchanan made his way up from the underground platform to the Euston concourse and the first-class lounge.

He showed his ticked to the receptionist and was shown to a seat in the lounge while he waited for time to board his train to Glasgow.

'Can I get you something to drink?' asked an attendant.

'Coffee, black no sugar, please.'

'Would you like a pastry to go with your coffee?'

'Yes, please.'

While he waited, he looked at his fellow travellers. One he recognised as having been interviewed on the six o'clock news the previous evening spouting words of praise for his party-political leader. Seated beside him were a group of American businessmen, laughing and joking about a recent Thanksgiving football match, which he himself had watched the previous week with Travis and family. There was another face that looked familiar, but hard as he tried, he couldn't quite place it.

He finished his coffee and looked up at the clock: it was time to board. He stood, picked up his computer bag, draped it over his shoulder then, taking his suitcase by the handle, walked out of the lounge and down the escalator. On his way he glanced up at the departure board and saw his train would be waiting for him on platform one.

He followed the crowd down the ramp making its way towards the entrance. As he passed through the gate, he saw the front end of the sleek Pendolino train, capable of speeds in excess of 120 miles per hour.

Looking at the train, dressed in its yellow and white livery, his mind went back to his childhood when the livery of the trains was just plain blue. Then, seeing a train or just the mere thought of a train journey. would fill him with excitement. Today, even though it was many years later and a business trip, he was still just as excited.

His reservation was for a single seat with table, facing forward. He looked at his seat reservation ticket and saw he was in carriage H. The doors at the end of the carriages were already open, waiting for the passengers. He climbed on board, placed his suitcase in the storage area and walked back along the brightly lit carriage looking for his seat.

He relaxed back into his seat and was about to reach for the seatbelt, when he realised, he wasn't in his car.

'Good morning, sir, will you require breakfast this morning?'

'Yes, I think I will.'

'Would you like something to drink in the meantime?'

'Could I have a black coffee, no sugar?'

'Certainly, I'll be back shortly to take your order, in the meantime this is what's available,' the attendant said, passing a breakfast menu to Buchanan. He was back in five minutes. 'Here is your coffee. Have you decided on what you would like?'

'Yes, could I have the Classic bacon sandwich?'

'And juice to go with it?'

'Could I have orange juice, please?'

'Certainly.'

Buchanan glanced back at the now empty platform and realised the train had imperceptibly begun its journey of almost three hundred and fifty miles to the city of his past.

As the train passed under the M25, he finished his bacon sandwich and was on his second cup of coffee. Sitting with his laptop open on the seat-tray he looked at the table he had drawn up for Street.

Looking at the list, he'd put Maxwell at the top. He was sixty-eight years old, with his wife, Sheila, next at fifty-seven. She was listed as a nightclub entertainer. Following the parents' entry were their two grown children: Harold, thirty-two years old, married, occupation listed as advisor for fruit exporter, and living in Brazil, while Angela, thirty years old, single, worked as an entertainer on cruise ships, current location somewhere in the Pacific Ocean.

The rest of the list consisted of the known members of Maxwell's entourage, locally known as the Busby Gang. Shelton and Randal, both deceased several years prior, died under a police car after an altercation with Buchanan in Porters bar. Gallagher, deceased, fell off ladder, and died landing on his chisel.

McDermott, deceased, fell seven stories from scaffolding while painting windows. Jameson senior, now employed by Maxwell as the banker, Jameson junior, alive, suspected of stabbing Gallagher with his chisel, hitting McDermott over the head with a paint pot and then pushing his body off the seventh floor of the scaffolding, Steve Jameson's location assumed to be in hiding somewhere on the Maxwell estate in Busby along with Dino Volente, assumed to be an enforcer and have possible Mafia connections. Laidlow and Wardlow, Maxwell's enforcers, unaccounted for. Benatti, alive and working as Maxwell's lawyer.

Maxwell's company was currently legitimately involved in the renovation of a block of tenements, previously damaged by fire. The illegal activities such as extortion, protection rackets, drug dealing, money lending and extortion appear to be continuing as before.

Buchanan looked up from his laptop and realised the train had just arrived in Penrith. He decided this was as good a time as any to order lunch. He picked up the on-board food menu and saw he was too early for the afternoon tea, so ordered a Charcuterie Grazing Plate with a glass of prosecco and a pot of tea.

As he grazed his way through his lunch, he did some on-line digging into the background of the tenements that Maxwell's company was refurbishing. The ground floor level consisted of a newsagent, a laundry, a twenty-four-hour mini market, the Governor bar, and a betting office. All that is required to supply the needs of a local community. His search also brought up the story about the fire in the bar that had spread to the adjacent betting office, and on to the mini market. The *Daily Record* had interviewed Maxwell and had asked him about his plans to redevelop the 1950's tenements.

A check about the fire in the *Daily Record* newspaper gave Buchanan further insight as to the cause. The story the newspaper printed said the Governor was a local watering hole for Tam

McGlinchey. Buchanan remembered the bitter rivalry between Maxwell and McGlinchey over control of the protection racket in the area. The newspaper had interviewed one of the mini-market employees who spoke on condition their identity would not be revealed. He said that they had seen two men earlier in the evening, about eleven pm, acting suspiciously at the rear of the bar. This was about thirty minutes before the fire started, and the alarm raised.

The fire brigade spokesman said in a later interview that the fire had apparently begun in a rubbish bin that had been improperly secured at the back of the bar.

One local tenant had said there had been trouble in the bar the previous night. A fight broke out in the bar between four men, two men had been injured and taken to the infirmary with serious injuries. One man had been released into police custody, and the other retained for wounds that required surgery.

By the time the train arrived in Glasgow, Buchanan had brought himself up to date on the latest comings and goings of Maxwell and his not so merry band of thieves, cut-throats and bully boys.

He reluctantly stepped down from the Pendolino onto the platform and looked at the time, a few minutes past two – the train had arrived exactly on time at two o'clock. He looked along the platform to the station concourse and saw that it was quite quiet, then realised that being just after two on a December afternoon, Scotland's busiest railway station was resting in readiness for the evening commute. Having not long finished his lunch, Buchanan decided he could wait for dinner.

The train to East Kilbride, stopping at Busby on the way, was on an adjacent platform. He opened the carriage door at the end, climbed in, found a space inside to place his suitcase, then went forward to find a window seat.

Within ten minutes of joining the East Kilbride train, the train growled, rumbled, and shook its way out of Glasgow Central and into the early December drizzle.

As the train rumbled past where the Pollokshaws Baths once stood he saw, instead of the elegant Victorian building of his childhood, there was now nothing but an empty wasteland. It was at the baths on Sunday mornings that his dad took him and his brother, Matthew, swimming. He shook his head and wondered why so many of Glasgow's classic buildings were being turned into carparks or flats. Surely there must be other sites that could be used to house the residents of that fair city.

Not for the first time that day he wondered why he was doing this – going to Glasgow to deal with a problem that should be tackled by someone else. Something just wasn't right. Why couldn't they find someone local? He'd lost count of the number of times he'd pondered the question; was he in fact being used to feather the political nest of Chief Constable James Anderson, retired, or was there something far more sinister going on behind the scenes?

The train crossed the Busby viaduct on its approach to the station and came to a screeching halt. Buchanan picked up his suitcase, climbed down from the train and walked towards the exit. Being such a quiet station there was no-one waiting to check his ticket, though there were a few people looking in the window of one of the station buildings. It only took Buchanan a few minutes to realise they were looking at the menu of Ming's Express Chinese Takeaway. That pleased him, Asian food of any kind suited him, and the fact it was also takeaway was perfect.

The last time he'd walked this journey was six years previously. He'd come to visit Jock and to tell him that he had been seconded to Sussex CID. Jock had questioned why that was happening, especially since Buchanan was held in such high regard in Glasgow. Buchanan had pondered that very question many times over the following years and was still pondering it now as he dragged his suitcase down East Kilbride Road. At least the walk to Field Road, the hotel and his room for the night, and he knew not how many more, was downhill.

Just before the bridge over the River Cart, he turned left and walked the final few yards to the Busby Hotel

'Good afternoon,' said the receptionist. 'How can I help?'

'I have a reservation, Jack Buchanan.'

'Ah, here it is. Would you like a paper in the morning?'

'Yes, please, could I have copies of the *Herald* and the *Record*.'

'I hope you have a pleasant stay,' said the receptionist, handing Buchanan his room key.

'I'm sure I will, thank you.'

Buchanan rode the lift to his floor and walked the final steps to his room. He entered the brightly lit room and sighed as the door closed softly behind him, this would do just perfectly. It wasn't a huge room, but it certainly was a comfortable one. A double bed on his left with a dressing table against the opposite wall. The bathroom, just on the left as he entered, was in keeping with modern hotel standards. It had no bathtub but instead a spacious walk-in shower.

He took off his coat and hung it in the wardrobe, put his jacket on the back of the chair that was tucked under the dresser, placed his suitcase on the bed and proceeded to empty its contents into the drawers.

Content he knew where everything was in the room, he walked over to the window and drew back the curtains. Below was Field Road and the roofs of what looked like brand-new houses. Beyond that flowed the River Cart. He looked at the time and thought it was a suitable moment to go down and sample a single malt before dinner, but before he did, he decided to call his parents and let them know he was in Busby.

Why was it always so difficult to call his parents, he wondered, as he dialled their home number. The ringing stopped and he was about to say hello when the recorded voice of his mother announced, 'The Buchanans can't come to the phone at the moment, we are either in the loo or swinging from the dining-room chandelier. Please leave an intelligent and interesting message and we will call you back.'

'Mum, Dad, it's Jack. I'm up in Glasgow on business for a few days. I'm staying at the Busby Hotel; I'll call you when you get off the chandelier. In the meantime, I'm going down to the restaurant for dinner.'

Always the comedian, his mother. How his dad put up with her he didn't know, but of course he really did know – they loved each other. What else could it be?

He walked across the lobby to the restaurant and stood by the door, waiting to be shown to a table by one of the young servers. Looking round the room he realised there had been some serious money expended on the décor, it all looked like it had just been refurbished and he was one of the first customers.

The bar looked impressive, situated right in the middle of the room, and wouldn't have looked out of place in any five-star establishment. Being on his own he was shown to a secluded table away from the cosy night-club styled dining booths.

'Chef's special this evening is sea bass. Can I get you something from the bar while you decide?' asked the waitress.

'Yes, could I have a double Lagavulin, with a splash of water, please?'

'Certainly.'

He looked at the bar and heard rather than saw, a group of patrons excitedly discussing the comments made recently by a report in one of the Glasgow newspapers.

'Am telling you, I'm no happy to see the game in Australia being abandoned, because you know why? It brings to the fore the real issue across the Glasgow divide. Look at the Manchester United and Liverpool's planned game in Bangkok and compare it with the Old Firm friendly. You know why those two teams are doing it? I'll tell you, it's because they respect one another, why can't we do the same?'

Looking away from the bar, Buchanan could see the kitchen and the staff in their whites working diligently preparing food. He was getting hungry.

'Your drink, sir. Have you decided what you'd like to order?'

'Yes, I'd like to start with the squid and tiger prawn, and follow with your recommendation of the sea bass, and could I have some water please?'

'Tap water do?'

'Perfect.'

'Thanks, I'll get your food order started and bring your water.'

Dinner over, Buchanan declined to end the evening sitting in the bar and returned to his room; he had two phone calls to make. One to his parents and the other to Karen. He chose his parents first, wondering if they were still swinging on the chandelier.

'Buchanan residence.'

'Dad, it's Jack.'

'Oh, it's Jack! Wait, I'll get your mother.'

Nothing ever changed he thought. one day he would get to talk to his dad without first being passed immediately to his mum.

'Jack, how nice of you to call. Your message said you are staying at the Busby Hotel; you know you always have a bed here at home?'

'Yes, I know that, but this is strictly business.'

'Are you coming back to Glasgow?'

'No, I'll only be here for a few days, then I'll be going back down south.'

'You'll come to dinner tomorrow?'

'Sorry, I've got a meeting tomorrow morning and another tomorrow evening.'

'During the week?'

'I'm sorry, Mum. I have no idea how my week is going to work out. How about if I have, I'll come to lunch next Saturday?'

'Good. I'll call Matthew and let him know you will be here for lunch. How is Karen?'

'She's fine.'

'And Jill and the baby?'

'Both mother and child are fine.'

'She is taking it easy, isn't she?'

'Yes. She's on light duties till she goes off on maternity leave.'

'You mean she's still working?'

'Of course, she's not due for another couple of months.'

'Oh, I thought it was closer than that.'

'Mum, I've got to go, I need a good night's sleep to be awake for tomorrow's meetings.'

'OK, son, give us a call if you get time.'

'Will do, love you both, goodnight,' he said, hanging up, thinking even though he loved his brother, he could do without the inevitable argument that would ensue when they met.

Lastly, but not the least, was to call Karen.

'How are you, how was the train ride?'

'Pure luxury, I don't know why anyone would fly anywhere.'

'Do you know of any train lines to New York?'

'You have a point there.'

'Are you settled in?'

'Yes.'

'Call your parents?'

'I just hung up from talking to them. I'm invited to dinner next Saturday if I'm still here.'

'What's the hotel like?'

'Very nice, it's had a makeover, food's great though the restaurant and bar are together. Gets a bit noisy if there are a lot of people drinking. My room is quiet and well laid out. I can work from here if needed, but won't,' he said, yawning.

'Well, you sound a bit tired, how about I let you go to bed, and we'll talk again tomorrow?'

'OK, love you much, good night.'

'I love you too, have a good night's sleep, I'll be praying for you.'

When didn't she, he thought? As his head touched the pillow he thought about Karen's comment as she hung up, *I'll be praying for you.* How he loved her, she never stopped caring for him, or apparently praying for him. Did it really make a difference, prayer, was there really a God who listened? The pastor who'd married Cynthia, Stanley Adebayo, had said all Buchanan needed to do was to ask God if he was real, to reveal himself. Stanley had also said that prayer was nothing other than having a chat with God. Well, if it was true, he'd have a go, after all, nothing ventured, nothing gained.

'God if you can hear me, I don't know what is going on. I don't know if I'm being taken for a fool, being used for someone else's profit and my loss. Would you reveal yourself to me in a way that I know you are there and listening, and that believing in you is not just some sort of crutch that weak people use? Goodnight.

16
Council of War

Buchanan was swimming in a river. The river was wide and muddy with winter rain washing debris into its flow. He sensed the river was very deep and, as he reached the middle, something grabbed his ankle and tried to pull him under. He was trying to reach the surface while desperately holding his breath.

He woke with a start; the corner of his pillow was in his mouth. He'd had the nightmare again, the one about being in a swimming pool and sinking to the bottom while desperately trying to reach the surface.

For a moment he wondered where he was. Then, as sleep departed with its hidden memories, the present memory of the conversation he'd had with Anderson surfaced and the realisation of the enormity of the task he'd readily accepted fully dawned on him.

He looked at the time on his watch, seven-thirty, time to get up and start the day. He threw the blankets back, rolled out of bed and dressed. He hastily made up the bed, tidied the room as best as he could, pulled back the curtains and glanced through the window. Even though it was cold outside, it wasn't raining. He crossed the room and opened the bedroom door. The newspapers he ordered were lying on the carpet in front of his door.

He picked them up and glanced at the headlines. The *Herald* was intelligent. The headlines emblazoned the plight of the Scottish homeowner, already in energy debt long before the winter rises in energy prices were applied to their bill. Not so different a situation to those who lived south of the border. The *Record* read like Glasgow had been taken over with hordes of knife and gun-wielding thugs. He shook his head, tucked the papers under his arm and went down for breakfast.

He thought about ordering porridge but since this was day one, he ordered the full Scottish breakfast of bacon, sausages, haggis, grilled tomatoes and beans. He left off the black pudding and potato scone in favour of two slices of toast and marmalade with fresh coffee.

Breakfast over, he returned to his room for his coat and hat. It was time to go outside for some fresh air and take a walk along Field Road and say hello to his old friend, Jock.

He stepped out of the warmth of the hotel lobby and realised it was three degrees and overcast, but at least the sun was rising, and he could almost see along Field Road. He buttoned up his coat, turned left and headed off along the road.

When he was young, the property on the left of Field Road was just fields, hence its name. Now, as he made his way along the path, he realised just how built-up the area had become. Was that the reason Maxwell had purchased a house in Eastbourne? Buchanan remembered from looking on Google Earth the size of the Maxwell estate and figured that if the old house was demolished and the trees cleared, a savvy developer could get somewhere in the region of twenty houses on the plot.

As he pondered on the pros and cons of modern development, it began to drizzle. He pulled his collar up about his neck and the brim of his hat down to let the rain drip off. He continued with his walk and wondered how he would go about dealing with Maxwell. Buchanan was just one man; Maxwell had a whole army of cut-throats eager to do his bidding. As Buchanan pondered the problem, a high-school history lesson came back to him. It was the story of Sir Francis Drake and how he, with smaller more mobile ships, managed to defeat the Spanish Armada. The result was the population of England today spoke English and not Spanish.

Yes, Buchanan would be a Francis Drake. Where Maxwell may have unlimited finances and muscle at his disposal, Buchanan would match Maxwell's brawn power with brain power.

Like the beginning of the television show *Mission Impossible*, where the leader, Jim Phelps, went through his list of agents, photo by photo, Buchanan went through in his mind his list of agents. First and foremost, there was Jill and, though she was six months pregnant and based in the Hampden Park Police Station office, she had access to all the legal tools he would need. Then there was PC Stephen Hunter, Jill's husband. Someone who would go far in his career. As a reserve there was PC Morris Dexter, another competent constable who worked well with Stephen.

In Glasgow there was DI Ferguson, Gus to his friends, one who Jack had worked with for years, next was Sergeant George Bull, retired, though now working the desk as a civilian under contract. At six foot four, and built like the proverbial barn door, he would be the muscle in the team. Finally, there was young Gray, an as yet an unknown factor, and nephew to George Bull. What could go wrong with a team like that backing him up?

As he continued along Field Road, he realised that houses had been built all the way up to the entrance of the industrial estate. As he approached the entrance to the estate where Maxwell lived, Buchanan saw things had changed since his last visit to Busby. Gone were the stone gatepost columns with the Victorian wooden gates that hung languidly back against the shrubbery. The entrance to the estate was now guarded by eight-foot-tall mesh-covered steel gates. On top of each of the steel gate posts were two modern CCTV cameras that tracked Buchanan as he walked past.

At the entrance to the industrial estate the road dipped down to reveal a row of brick-built industrial buildings on the right with several cars parked close. The first building was a single-story affair with a plaque fastened to the wall saying this was the old forge. That was news to Buchanan as he remembered it being a small workshop that used to repair kettles, coffeemakers and toasters. In his mind, it was never a forge, but then the building was a great deal older than he was.

He continued past the first building, then stopped and shivered. In front of him was a three-story building painted red. He realised it was a cold and damp day, but he was fortified by a huge breakfast and was well wrapped up, so why did he shiver? Need more sleep, he told himself, and continued past the parked cars in front of the old forge.

Another childhood memory came to him. It was the smell of dry-cleaning fluid that would emanate from the main door of the building, which used to be a laundry. The area in front of the old laundry building used to be gravel, it now sported a paved road with a solid white line along the building fronts, kerb stones, painted lines for car parking and even a lone lamppost.

He walked on past the three-story building that over the years had been used for many purposes. He remembered another story from his childhood. Many years before electricity had been brought to the end of the road, the building had been powered by a huge water wheel that had been fed from a dam and water channel further up the river. Of course, with time all traces of the wheel were now long gone and the location of where it would have been had been filled in. A small one-story brick building stood in its place.

He continued towards the end of the office building and turned to cross over the little hump-backed bridge. Something else had changed, the original stone balustrade had been replaced by a steel post and fence. Progress? He doubted it, what local council was going to pay for a stone balustrade renovation when a few galvanised fence posts and some wire netting would do?

The river run hurriedly under the bridge and even though it was now December, due to a long dry summer, it was not running hard like he remembered it could.

Looking straight down he could see water cascading over the larger rocks, creating small streams of bubbles that were carried away by the swift-moving water. At the edges the water gurgled in and out of the long grass and straggling brambles and today it was a steady flow. He remembered one year in early spring how the river had almost burst its banks.

Of course, that was before Jock filled in the reservoir ponds and raised the ground to create a flat wide area to build his stables.

Did young Busby boys and girls still swim in the river? As he thought back to his childhood and the time she spent messing around in the river, he remembered finding an adult salmon resting in a small pool upriver just before the old weir. It seemed remarkable to a young mind that an ocean-going fish could swim all the way up the Clyde from the Atlantic, then struggle its way up the Cart to lay its eggs.

Another memory was of the time he and a friend found a stick of gelignite in the river. He ran home and told his dad, who then informed the police. They never did hear the results of his find, and for many years after that incident he mused that the gelignite was from some bank robbery that went wrong, and the crooks, who were being chased by the police, threw the gelignite into the river to get rid of the evidence.

His memory was on a roll. About 200 yards further up the river was a wide, flat, sandbank from when the river was in full flow from winter storms. On this sandbank, men used to stand in a circle and play Pitch and Toss, a gambling game where three old pennies would be tossed in the air and the men would bet on whether it was three heads, three tails, two heads and a tail or two tails and a head. This of course being illegal, the police would regularly raid the game and arrest all the gamblers.

Further up the river where the old sandstone block weir stretched across there was just enough depth in the water to swim, as long as you didn't kick your legs too vigorously. Unfortunately, when the angling club took over the management of the river, the remaining sandstone blocks were dislodged, thus allowing fish to swim more easily up the river.

On the other side of the river, just a few yards upriver from the old weir was the confluence of the Cart and Thorntonhall Burn. One of young Jack's adventures consisted of walking up the burn to the hillock called Black Rock, just a natural outcropping of rock. This was where he would pretend to be a mountaineer and climb the rock-face to the top. As a child, the rock-face seemed to be very high.

He shook his head and closed the door to his past. He reminded himself that the past was the past, the present was here and now, and he was here to resolve the issue that was Maxwell. But first, this morning's business was to go and see his friend Jock at the stables.

He stood back from the bridge railing, taking one last look at the river and the building. As he did so, another memory surfaced. It was the advice that Stanley, the Pastor who had recently married his friend Cynthia, said to him after the ceremony.

Stanley had asked him if he was working on a case that had something to do with a river. Buchanan replied no, and this was the part that was causing the most discomfort. Stanley then went on to describe what Buchanan was at that moment looking at. A large building painted red and directly beside a river with trees on the opposite bank. Stanley went on to say that there was something in the river, something of great danger, and for Buchanan to be strong and of good courage, not to be afraid nor be dismayed, for the Lord would be with him wherever he went. Was this momentary revelation the way God would speak to him?

Could there actually be something in what Stanley said? Could it even be possible that there is a God? This was too much to contemplate for a Sunday morning, then the irony of it all sunk into his head: this was Sunday, the day of rest, the Lord's Day.

Buchanan shook his head, he was tired, he'd spent the previous day travelling, ate late last night and slept in a strange bed, albeit a comfortable one. He left the bridge behind and turned right to walk the track to Jock's stables.

Before he could go far, he was stopped by a rickety five-bar farm gate. Buchanan looked at it and saw the bottom two rails were missing, and the gate was obviously barely hanging on its hinges. There was a groove worn in the dirt showing where it had dragged as it was opened. Buchanan lifted the latch and pushed the gate far enough to get past, then closed it behind him.

In the distance, in the small car park, he could see an old Land Rover with a sun-bleached canvas top. That was good, Jock was at the stables, but where was anyone else? The last time Buchanan had visited the stables, the carpark would be full at this time of day on a Sunday. Then he noticed the bushes on each side of the gravel track were unkempt.

Jock's stables were nestled in the crook of the bend in the river. If the gate, bushes, track and empty carpark were anything to go by, something wasn't what it should be

He walked along the track beside the riverbank avoiding the puddles. In the distance he could see the exercise ring in front of the long row of horse stalls. At the end of the row of stalls, was the small canteen and next, the office.

There was a solitary horse standing in the exercise ring by the fence, eating from a loose pile of hay.

'Jock, you in there?'

'Who's that?' came the reply.

'Jock, it's me, Jack Buchanan.'

'Hang on.'

There followed the sound of a squeaky wheelbarrow as it exited the stall.

'Well, look what the wind blew in! How are you, Jack?'

'I'm fine, and you?'

'Look, I'm done here, just have to dump this stuff, be right with you.'

Buchanan watched as his friend pushed the steaming wheelbarrow over to the midden and dumped its contents.

'Come on into the office and we can chat there.'

Buchanan followed Jock into the small office and sat in the chair in the corner and watched while he filled the kettle and plugged it in.

'It seems quiet, Jock, where are all the horses?'

'I'm closing down the stables, Jack.'

'Closing down? I don't believe it!'

'It happens to all of us. Even you, one day, will hang up your handcuffs.'

'I think there's more to your retiring than what you are saying.'

'Ever the policeman, aren't you? I've had an offer; one I've found very difficult to refuse.'

'What's that?'

'The decision was taken out of my hands, really. The land has been compulsory purchased for houses.'

'After all these years. I remember when you first came here. The land was nothing more than four empty, overgrown, reservoir ponds.'

'Times change, Jack. People need somewhere to live.'

'But here, these stables? I watched you build them up from nothing more than holes in the ground to what they are today.'

'Jack, the stables are too small. Look at the exercise ring, barely enough room for a couple of horses, and talking of horses, I could do with something more like Nathan has.'

'Where will you go?'

'You see where they built William Wood School?'

'On Eaglesham Road?'

'I've bought a couple of the fields further up the road.'

'How will you get planning permission? That's prime farmland.'

'Already have it. It was part of the deal to get me to sell up here.'

'I smell a rat, and the rat's name is Maxwell. Does he still live across the river in Busby House?'

'Yes, we are still neighbours separated by the Cart. But not for long, I hear Busby House has been sold.'

'That makes sense, sort of.'

'What do you mean?'

'Just something I heard.'

'He's moving out of Busby is what I heard, and his house and land is going to be part of the riverside development.'

'No guessing who will be handling the building contract.'

'You think it will be Maxwell's company?'

'Probably.'

'So, Jack, to what do I owe the honour of your visit?'

'It's been a while since I visited with my parents.'

'You want to pull the other one?'

'No, I really will be visiting my parents. But since you asked, while I am here, I've been tasked to see what Maxwell is up to.'

'He's moving, that's what he's up to, though I've no idea as to where he is moving to.'

'I think we have that sorted.'

'So, you and who else is working on this business?'

'Gus Fergusson, a DI I used to work with, and my old sergeant George Bull and his nephew.'

'That's it, no one else?'

'I'm only supposed to gather the evidence of Maxwell's criminal operations, then turn what we have found over to the Procurator Fiscal. It will then be up to him what happens next.'

'Either way, you need to be careful, Andy's Hole is deep enough to hide all sorts of unwanted secrets.'

'Andy's Hole?'

'The pool in the river behind the stables, that's its name.'

'Oh, that's what it's called, I never realised it had a name. We just used to swim in it.'

'There's a story that goes around about the swimming hole,' said Jock.

'You mean the one about it being haunted? I remember that from childhood.'

'Did you know the story behind it?'

'No, just thought it was one of those fact-less tales that children tell each other.'

'The tale is the pool was haunted by someone called Andy, who had spent the day delivering coal. On the way back to the coal-yard, the wagon broke a wheel, so he left it at the side of the road and rode his horse towards home. On the way Andy passed the bar. So, being thirsty after a hard day's work, he stopped off for a quick pint. Well, one turned into two, turned into three, turned into an all-night booze-up. Thankfully this was in the days before most people had cars. His route home took him along Field Road and over the bridge. His horse, having worked hard all day and being thirsty, turned right at the bridge and wandered, with Andy too sozzled to know what was happening, along the path where it proceeded to step into the river for a drink. All that was found the next morning by the search party were the horse tracks leading into the river. Neither Andy nor the horse were ever seen again.'

'I bet that's just a story put about by the owners of Busby House. Shame it's going to be demolished for housing. Another bit of Glasgow history trampled by the bulldozer of progress.'

'I just told you one story about Andy's Hole, that probably was fiction, but you know there are others?'

'Yes, I remember my mum mentioning that she'd seen a legless woman haunting the riverbank behind the old forge.'

'I've heard that story as well, and the story that goes along with it.'

'Really? Wait, before you do your listen with Jock bit, where's the loo?'

'Through that door,' he said. pointing to a door marked private. 'You want another coffee?'

'Yes, please.'

'You want a top-up in your coffee?' asked Jock, as Buchanan shut the toilet door behind him.

'Just a splash,' replied Buchanan, as he looked at the bottle of Lagavulin Jock was holding.

'You wanted to know about the legless woman?'

'Yes.'

'The story is, that the ghost was of Mary McLaughlin. She and her daughter worked in the dye mill. One Saturday, as they were leaving to walk home, while Mary's daughter was leaning over the parapet to look at the raging winter water, she overbalanced and fell in. Her mother refused to leave the area, believing her daughter would be found alive. Mary was so grief-stricken she threw herself into the raging water screaming if no-one else could find her daughter she would. Both mother and daughter drowned, their bodies were never recovered. Those who believe in such things say Mary is still looking.'

'A tragic story.

'Yes, it is.'

'As I passed Busby House, I noticed security has been stepped up. When were the security gates installed to the entrance?'

'A few months ago, I saw them being installed when I was leading a couple of horses across to the other side of the river. Our access road to the stables isn't wide enough for the larger horseboxes so we have them come along Field Road.'

'Any idea why the sudden need for security gates?'

'There have been some strange goings on over the river.'

'Such as?'

'A couple of months ago, Sally, she's one of the riders who keeps her horse here, heard a commotion coming from across the river. At first none of us could see anything, but the shouting got louder, sounded like someone was lost and others were looking for them. We were just about to get back to work when a young woman, still in her pyjamas, climbed over the fence and stood on the small stone wall, the one where the previous residents of Busby House used to fish from. Well, she just stood there, staring at the river. A couple of minutes later two men climbed over the fence. One grabbed the girl, the other helped them over the fence.'

'That is weird,

'You said earlier, you used to swim in that part of the river by the wall?'

'Yes, and I seem to remember there was a rope tied to the tree so we could swing out and drop into the deepest part.'

'The rope was still there the next time the girl showed up. Same scenario as the previous episode, loud voices then the girl, once more in her pyjamas, climbed over the fence. This time she was resolute. We watched in horror as she grabbed the rope and tied it round her neck and was about to leap off the wall when the same two men climbed over the fence. One grabbed the girl and the other cut the rope free, then they dragged her back over the fence.'

'Could you put an age to the young girl?'

'Early twenties, maybe.'

'Any idea who she was?'

'Maxwell's daughter?'

'No, she couldn't be. Maxwell's daughter is a singer on a cruise ship, last known location somewhere in the South Pacific, and certainly not in her twenties.'

'How about the daughter of a friend of the family? Mentally unstable and could be an embarrassment if seen in public. Busby House is a big place. It was used as a nursing home in the fifties, maybe Maxwell is expanding his empire and going into the care home business.'

'That would sort of make sense of the security gates, the CCTV and the two individuals you saw restraining the girl. Were they wearing white coats, or anything that would make you think they were nurses?'

'No, just two blokes wearing ordinary jackets.'

'Could you describe them?'

'One looked about your age and size. The other was over six feet and had the physique of a wrestler.'

'If the house was going to become a nursing home again, it would give reason to the fact he is selling up and moving down south to Eastbourne.'

'Yes, it would.'

'All this talk about selling up. Are you going to start from scratch again?'

'Not quite. I told you I've purchased a couple of fields, well, the fields come with farm buildings. The farm used to be a dairy farm so there are three large milking sheds that are ideal for conversion to horse stalls. The architect reckons that I should be able to take in at least forty horses, three times my present number. As I get settled, I will convert the farmhouse into accommodation for visitors.'

'And here's me thinking you were going to retire.'

'Oh, I will someday, but not just yet.'

'Jock, it's been great catching up,' said Buchanan, getting up to leave. 'If anything should happen across the river, would you give me a shout on the phone? I'll call you, then you will have my new number.'

'Thanks. You will come back before you return south?'

'Will do, bye for now.'

Buchanan closed the office door behind him and started his return walk back to his hotel. As he passed the entrance gates to Busby House, a gust of wind blew a pile of leaves into his face. He pulled his collar up round his neck and the brim of his hat down and kept on walking.

As he continued along Field Road, he kept thinking about the mystery girl that lived in what appeared to be nothing other than an open prison. If Maxwell was indeed turning Busby House into a nursing home with security gates on the road, why no proper fences alongside the river?

The welcoming warmth of the hotel greeted him as he stepped into the lobby. He went up the stairs to his room and hung up his coat and hat to dry. He looked at the time and saw it was a little early for dinner, but not too early for a drink in the bar and maybe to catch a game on the television.

There were several people sitting at the bar when he entered so he ordered a double whisky and took a seat at an empty table by the window to think. He was staring out at the rain-soaked road when a loud voice had him look up at the reflected image of the bar in the window. It was Maxwell and his wife, Sheila.

'Hi Rab,' greeted one of the men at the bar, 'what'll it be?'

'I'll have a whisky, Toni.'

Toni, thought Buchanan, could he be Toni Benatti, Maxwell's lawyer?

'Sheila, are you drinking?'

'Gin and tonic, but not too much tonic.'

'Sure. You both here for dinner?'

'No, we're meeting Andy and his wife in town for a drink, then going on to see a movie.'

Andy, mused Buchanan, could that be Andy Jameson, father to Steve Jameson, car thief, double-murderer and who knew what else?

'What are you going to see?'

'A movie called *Where the Crawdads Sing*,' said Maxwell. 'Sheila said she wanted to see it.'

'Strange title for a movie, what's it about, Sheila?'

'It's the story of Kya, an abandoned girl who raised herself to adulthood in the dangerous marshlands of North Carolina, and then gets accused of murdering someone.'

'Oh,' said Benatti, nodding, 'I can see you being interested in that. How is she today?'

'The doctor has put her on a different medicine, still too early to tell if it is working the way it should.'

'Well, I hope for your sakes it does the job.'

'Toni, a word,' said Maxwell, tilting his head and nodding to the lobby.

'Well, if you two are going to have a quiet word, I need another drink,' said Sheila.

Whatever Maxwell and Benatti had to discuss didn't take long. By the time they returned Sheila had finished her drink and was staring at her phone. Buchanan was staring out the window wondering if the person requiring a doctor and new medicine was the girl Jock was talking about.

Maxwell didn't sit but instead said, 'Ready, Sheila? Time to go.'

'I've been ready since the day I was born.'

Buchanan watched as Maxwell and Sheila left the bar and walked out, leaving Benatti staring at the ice cubes in his empty glass.

This gave Buchanan an idea. He left his table and walked up to the bar with his empty glass.

'Could I have another whisky, and would you make it a double? It's not every evening you get good news.'

'Good news?' said the barman.'

'Wife just called to say she just won two hundred pounds on a scratch card.'

'Lucky you,' said the barman.

Buchanan turned to Benatti and said, 'Buy you a drink, I'm celebrating?'

'Why not? I'll have a vodka and lime.'

'Miserable weather we're having,' said Buchanan.

'Yeah, what else can you expect in December?'

'How's the food here? I've just arrived.'

'For a hotel it's quite good.'

'That's what I heard. I remember it from before it was refurbished. We used to live in Busby. Company sent me down south a few years ago. Building the extension has certainly improved the restaurant.'

'Thanks for the drink.'

'No problem. Jack Buchanan.'

'Toni Benatti.'

'You live around here?'

'Yeah.'

'The town have much of a night life, these days?'

'A few bars, a couple of hotels and various takeaways.'

'Sounds like my town down south. You're not from around here,' said Buchanan, 'I'm pretty good with accents and I'd say you were from somewhere in Italy, am I correct?'

Benatti shook his head and said, 'Close, I was born on Sicily. My parents came here when I was three.'

'I was born in Greenock. My dad worked in the yards till he retired.'

'What do you do?'

'Me, I'm a security advisor, I work for a company that provides protection services, and you?'

'I'm a lawyer. You say you're in the protection business, what sort of protection?'

Buchanan smiled to himself, Benatti thinks we're both in the same business and he's checking to see if I am a threat to him. 'We keep undesirable elements away from where they don't belong.'

'You use force to provide this service?'

'When necessary.'

'Ever had to use this force yourself?'

'That was part of the reason I got sent down south. An altercation in a bar, this scar on my face,' said Buchanan, pointing to the scar left when Maxwell's former lawyer, Randal, slashed him across the face with his ring. 'Two men died; I was hospitalised. I'd become an embarrassment to the organisation. To keep the peace, I was relocated.'

'Who do you work for?'

'I'd rather not say, don't want to cause a fuss. You see, I'm not supposed to be back up here. If word got out, things could turn real nasty for a few people I could name but chose not to. The incident is still under investigation, so I'm quite shy about attracting the attention of the police.'

'I understand. I've represented a few men in similar circumstances.'

'I've just thought of something, maybe you could represent me? Do you have a card so I could call you if I get picked up?'

'Ah, I don't think that would be possible. You see, I'm not that kind of lawyer.'

'I thought all lawyers were just that. Lawyers?'

'I specialise in company law, not criminal law.'

'Now there's a pity, and me thinking you'd look good in court.'

Benatti looked at Buchanan, was about to say something, then thought better of it.

'Yes?'

'It was nothing. Thanks for the drink, enjoy your winnings, see you around,' he said, throwing back the last of his drink and walking out of the bar.

See you around indeed, thought Buchanan. He picked up his drink and returned to his table, it was time for dinner and afterwards, a council of war with Gus and Bull.

He looked at the menu, and as much as he would have liked to try it, he decided to put off the haggis, neeps and tatties till later in the week, tonight it was going to be salmon fillet. He'd think about dessert after the main course.

♦

The first to arrive was Gus.

'Jack, you haven't changed a bit since I saw you last.'

'I don't know about that,' replied Buchanan, patting his waist. 'You're looking fit.'

'Thanks, I play squash twice a week, got to keep up with Harriet. Having a wife who's ten years younger does that. How's Karen?'

'She's fine. Since I'm not there to get in the way, she's probably enjoying the opportunity to get on with projects around the house.'

'I saw George Bull on Friday; he says he is really looking forward to going up against Maxwell and his evil crew.'

'I just hope that Bull's muscle power won't be needed. This operation is supposed to be just an evidence-gathering endeavour.'

'Then let's hope it bears fruit. Maxwell's tentacles reach into just about all areas of society. Did you hear about what happened to Jeffrey Moran?'

'Jeffrey Moran? Isn't he the loudmouth politician shouting for Independence?'

'That's the one.'

'What happened to him? Did the *wee lassie* tell him to belt up?'

'No, nothing like that. He got busted at the airport with a kilo of raw cocaine in his luggage.'

'Not very smart, was he?'

'Word on the street is he was doing Maxwell a favour in exchange for Maxwell helping get the word out to vote for Moran at the upcoming election. Plus, he was to get a cut on the sale of the cocaine.'

'Do you think he was shopped? Or did his reputation cloud the public rhetoric?'

'If he was, I wonder who would have done that? Unlikely to be Maxwell.'

'Unlikely for Maxwell to do what?' asked George Bull, as he sat and put his beer on the table.

'George,' said Buchanan, 'glad you were able to make it.'

'I take it as an honour to be here and have this opportunity to put Maxwell out of business once and for all.'

'We're sort of the three musketeers going up against Cardinal Richelieu,' said Gus. 'Except in this case the enemy's name is Maxwell.'

'Actually, there are four of us,' said Buchanan.

'Who's the fourth?' asked Gus.

'PC Graham Bull.'

'My nephew?' asked Bull.

'The very same.'

'He's not bad,' said Gus, 'I've been on jobs with him, he's smart in the right sort of way, knows how to handle himself when in a tight spot.'

'Right,' said Buchanan, 'down to business, and let's keep our voices low. This may be a busy restaurant, and bar, so we wouldn't want to burden the hotel guests with things they don't need to know. I don't intend to get into deep details at this meeting, just go over the background as to why we are all here.'

An hour later, Buchanan had detailed the events of the previous week.

'Sounds like a workable plan,' said Gus. 'But what makes you think we will be able to succeed where others who went before us have failed?'

'We weren't working on the case, that's the difference. Whereas before, all investigations were done as part of the regular working week and had to be fitted in as and when time permitted. This time, we will each be focusing our efforts on Maxwell and his organisation. We will be looking for Maxwell's Achilles' heel, we find that, and we get Maxwell where we want him.

'I would like all of you to act normally at work. Gus, I would like you to be busy on some old case that requires you to be in and out of the office sporadically, any ideas?'

'Yes, there was a robbery and assault at a mini market about eighteen months ago, suspicion pointed to the Smith brothers, and although there were witnesses, no one was prepared to talk. The Smith brothers are hated by just about everyone on the streets, so I will just say that since time has passed, witnesses may be more forthcoming.'

'Excellent. Bull, what about you, what sort of cover are we going to concoct for you?'

'That's easy. I'm no longer in the force, I'm a contractor, so I can come and go as it pleases my boss. I've got some leave due, so I will arrange my schedule to suit what's going on.'

'In that case, could we meet at the office tomorrow morning at nine?' said Buchanan.

'The office?' queried Gus.

'Sorry, should have told you, I've rented a small office on Buchanan Street, number sixty-nine. The entrance is next to a Ted Baker shop. I'll WhatsApp you the details and see you both tomorrow at nine.'

'What about Gray?' queried Bull.

'Good point, would you like to call him and give him the good news?'

'I'd be delighted, see you tomorrow.'

That went well Buchanan thought, as he closed the bedroom door. He undressed and climbed into bed to call Karen.

'How is the room?'

'Perfect, it's on the first floor so I can sleep with the window open.'

'Have you met with Gus and Bull?'

'Yep, just said goodnight to them. We're all ready to go to work tomorrow.'

'Jock, did you get chance to talk to him?'

'Yes, and he told me he's moving the stables. His present one has been compulsory purchased for a housing estate.'

'That's sad.'

'He's OK with it. He's been able to buy the old farm on Eaglesham Road.'

'Which old farm?'

'I don't remember its name, but it's only a couple of miles from Clarkston.'

'And Maxwell, any word on his doings?'

'While there, Jock told me a strange story about a young woman, you remember Maxwell's house is just across the river from his stables?'

'Yes.'

'Well, he said he saw a young woman climb over the fence and tried to hang herself on the rope swing that kids used to swing from into the river.'

'What happened? Did he manage to stop her?'

'He didn't need to. No sooner had she tied the rope round her neck when two men, he assumed to be security guards, climbed over the fence, cut her free, then carried her – screaming obscenities – back into the grounds of the house.'

'That is strange. Has Maxwell turned the house into a sanatorium?'

'I'm not sure. It once was a nursing home.'

'Sounds like you three have your work cut out for you.'

'There's actually four of us. You remember the young man who broke into our house while we were away in Dallas?'

'Yes?'

'You remember George Bull?'

'Yes.'

'That young lad is his nephew.'

'You will feel right at home in a busy office.'

'I think you're right on that, though I hope they are kept busy discovering evidence that will finally put Maxwell and his thugs out of business.'

'Then I'll not keep you and say goodnight.'

'Night-night, I'll call you again tomorrow.'

'Love you.'

'Love you too, good night.'

17
Buchanan Street

What a difference a week makes, thought Buchanan, as the train rumbled into Glasgow Central station. This time last week he was only a few hours away from getting into Lazarus's patrol car, full of the latest technology, for a day on the beat in Dallas.

Now, a week, later here he was heading for his ten by twelve meter rented office and the only technology he had at his disposal were his laptop and mobile phone. The office did have twenty-four-hour access with CCTV monitoring, a lift, secure underground parking, voicemail and vending machines. Everything a modern office needed. There were larger meeting rooms he could book if required, but he reasoned the fewer people visiting him the better.

There was one item that really pleased him, on his short walk from the station to his office, he passed his favourite watering hole, a Starbucks on Buchanan Street.

He pushed the office door open and walked along the narrow entrance hall to the lift and on up his second-floor office.

As he exited the lift he was met by a well-dressed young woman. 'Mr Buchanan?'

'Yes.'

'I'm Fiona, I have your keys, will four be enough?'

'Yes, thanks. Four will be fine.'

'I would show you round your office,' she said, opening the door, 'but as you can see it's quite self-explanatory.'

Buchanan walked into his office and looked at the arrangements. Two desks facing each other in front of a large window looking out onto Buchanan Street. On the right were two small comfortable-looking chairs and a low round coffee table. In front, fastened to the wall between and slightly above was a large whiteboard.

Buchanan nodded his approval and said, 'This office is perfect, just what I need.'

'Toilets and vending machines are in the lobby by the lift. If you require anything else, the office number is in the brochure on the desk, WIFI log-in details are printed on the card beside the phone.'

'Thank you, Fiona, this will do very nicely.'

'Then I'll leave you to your business, good day.'

The door closed and Buchanan was left to his thoughts. He placed his laptop bag on the desk then walked over to the window while sipping on his coffee. Below him people were going about their business. He wondered what they would think if they knew, two floors above, he was plotting a war that could either be over in days; or rumble on for years and affect the lives of many innocent people.

But first, there was a phone call to make.

'Good morning, Jill, how are things in the office this morning?'

'Fine, it's been a quiet weekend. How is your new office?'

'Perfectly formed. Two desks, a couple of chairs and WIFI.'

'Got your coffee? I Googled the address and see you have a Starbucks up the street.'

'Yes, indeed there is, and you are correct, I already have my coffee.'

'So, what's first?'

'Would you keep an eye on my email account and let me know if any important emails come in? I don't want to log in from here. This investigation is about gathering information surrounding the Maxwell operation, so what I'd like you to do is see what you can find out from the Air Traffic Control about the flight patterns of Julian Du Marchon.'

'But he died in the channel when his plane crashed, what good will that do?'

'I was wondering if there was any connection between his drug-smuggling operation between Amsterdam and Sussex and that of

Maxwell's drug dealing in Glasgow. Maxwell has to get his drug supplies from somewhere.'

'Anything else?'

'No, that should keep you busy for a while.'

'OK. What's on the agenda for you and the boys?'

'Gus called us the three musketeers last night, I mentioned there was a fourth, Bull's nephew, Graham. He was a cadet the first time I met him, he's now a PC and on his way up the greasy pole.'

'The four musketeers? You know what, considering your proclivity to secrecy, maybe you should be giving yourselves aliases.'

'That might be a good plot line for a Peter James novel, but I think we're too far into this investigation to try something like that now.'

'OK, it was just an idea.'

'And a good one, in the right circumstances. Remember, if you need to chat, I'm always here.'

'OK, 'bye for now.'

Buchanan turned on his laptop, logged in to the internet and looked at the world news. There was an item that intrigued him from the Al Jazeera news network. It read that it was suspected that the long arm of the Ukrainian special services had reached out as far as Moscow in an attempt to relieve the Russian leader of one of his main supporters. The article was accompanied with a photo showing the mangled wreck of an SUV that had been destroyed in an apparent bomb blast.

He scrolled away from the news to listen to music while thinking the news was nothing but stories about wars and rumours of wars. Why do the nations rage, he wondered?

Then he thought, should his team have a name? The Buchanan Gang – now why did he think of that? A gang is an organised group of criminals. No, he couldn't call his group a gang, they were the *posse comitatus*, and he was the sheriff of the posse. As a DCI he even had a badge, maybe he should wear it like the cowboy sheriffs in the movies did. To bear no malice towards anyone, but to do one's duty as prescribed in the law.

As he mused, the office door opened, and Gray walked in.

'Oh, I see you already have your coffee. I passed a Starbucks on the way and read somewhere you always started your week with a copy of the *Herald* and a cup of Americano, so I brought you a coffee and a copy of the *Glasgow Herald*.'

'Thanks for thinking of me. As you rise through the ranks and put the years of graft as a policeman behind you, you will come to realise you can never have too much coffee.'

'Oh, OK. Gus and Uncle Bull said for me to go on up and let you know they won't be long; they are talking to someone.'

'Thanks. Take a seat, you don't need to stand, you're not on parade.'

'Oh, OK.'

'Gray, you being the youngest member of the team I will be pairing you with your uncle, just till you get your feet wet. I had a look at your record, and I see you are not afraid to get stuck in. A black belt in Judo, a gold medallist in Taekwondo, and qualified as a self-defence instructor at the Carswell academy. That I admire in a person, but I must warn you that you will be dealing with people who will stop at nothing to get their way. The only rules they know are the rules of the street, they fight dirty, and if that means ending your career with a bullet to the head or knife to the throat, they won't even bat an eyelid. Do you understand?'

'Yes, and I can't wait to get started. I've seen your reports and there is one individual I wouldn't mind getting in the ring with and showing him a thing or two.'

'Which one is that?'

'Steve Jameson.'

'Why him?'

'He was in the same class as me at school. He was a real bully, got into a few fights with him. See this?' said Gray, opening his shirt to show a scar running across his chest. 'He did it with a knife.'

'What happened?'

'I was going out with a lass called Dora and Steve Jameson claimed she was his girl.'

'What did you do?'

'I told him to get stuffed, and that was when he knifed me. From that moment on I decided I'd never let anyone get the better of me in a fight. As you can see, bodily I'm not equipped to punch my way out of trouble, but I am quick with my arms and legs.'

'I almost pity the thug that thinks they can get the better of you. Oh, what happened to Jameson after he cut you?'

'Probation.'

'Morning boss,' said Gus, as he entered the office, followed by Bull.

'Morning guys.'

'Sorry we're a bit late,' said Gus. 'Stopped to chat with Sneaky Pete.'

'Someone we need to know?' asked Buchanan.

'Maybe,' replied Gus. 'He used to be helpful for titbits of news about what was happening on the streets.'

'Is he reliable?'

'If he's paid enough.'

'Is he registered?'

'Yes.'

'Before we get started, Bull, since you are probably well-versed in the state of play here on the streets, could you give us a rundown on what's bothering the populace of this fair city?'

'Certainly, but instead of me telling you what I think, let me read a couple of lines from an article in today's newspaper. I get a daily feed on my phone. The reporter was doing an on-going article about the public perception of how well the police and politicians are coping under the unprecedented demands on their services.

'One local resident who worked as social worker had scalding words for city officials who had lined up behind the city police, saying they were out of touch with local communities.'

'A common complaint in many communities,' said Gus. 'A large segment of the local population is frustrated by what they see as the authority's inability to deal with the recent crime-wave of stabbings, shootings, and assaults.'

'That's quite true, Jack,' said Bull. 'For my part I can't remember when I've booked in so many suspected villains for knife and gun crimes.'

'The public see the police and courts as being ineffectual,' said Gus, 'I met a local politician a couple of weeks ago and she said with the current atmosphere being so toxic it's anyone's guess which party will get in at the next election. But she did say that, in the meantime, her efforts were being directed to healing the wounds caused by the years of mistrust created by the misconception that the police were just turning a blind eye to what the public saw as a crime pandemic.'

'People are fed up,' said Bull. 'I was at a local community meeting a few weeks ago and Dan Pasquale, president of the local Merchants' Association, said he and his neighbours and the shop owners he represents had voted for change after watching crime surge on city streets. Businesses that had long struggled with robberies and burglaries were suddenly contending with more serious incidents, including assaults and arson. I tell you; I was glad I wasn't in uniform that night, the meeting was getting really ugly.

'In one instance Pasquale said a vandal set fire to a parked taxi in broad daylight, right outside his favourite coffee shop. He said he'd seen businesses moving out, unable to bear the escalating crime and the cratering economy. As a result, some of the city's most vibrant retail arteries are pocked with vacant shopfronts.'

'I read in an NCA report that perceptions of crime, however, may be disconnected from reality in Glasgow,' said Buchanan. 'In the NCA report it showed that although some violent crime continued trending downwards, in the previous year, unfortunately, homicides, shootings and burglaries were once more on the rise, largely in part due to the activities of the likes of Rab Maxwell and other like-minded groups.'

'It's the city's renewed obsession with quality-of-life issues and your brother's intervention, that has created an opening between various criminal agencies that long have had a stranglehold on business and placed them squarely in confrontation with the police,' said Bull.

'Matthew? Are you sure you have the correct Matthew Buchanan?'

'I'm sorry to say, yes, your brother,' replied Bull. 'He's taken it upon himself to defend the weak against those in society who seek to keep them in servitude to the way things have always been. I recently heard him speak at a meeting where he proposed what was needed was a more traditional approach to law and order, he went on to say that the police should focus on enforcing the law and leave policy decisions to the elected politicians.'

'That's my brother for you, always chasing the windmills of justice.'

'I thought your brother was a company lawyer?' said Gray.

'He is, but that doesn't stop him from sticking his nose into social issues.'

'Are we using HOLMES?' asked Bull.

'Not quite,' replied Buchanan, 'until we know who all the players in this game are, we will do things the old-fashioned way. White board with coloured pens, index cards, and of course photos. Until we go public, I'd like to keep as much information as we can in-house.'

'Are you really that worried that, if we were connected to HOLMES, someone may try and hack into the file and find out what we are up to? asked Gus.

'Someone spilled the beans on Gallagher and McDermott's location, what's to prevent them accessing our file in HOLMES and where we have got to in the investigation?'

'What about this office? It isn't exactly Riverside House.'

'If you mean the MI6 building, no, I must agree with you, this building certainly is not that. But if you consider the calibre of Maxwell's cohorts, breaking into this office is probably beyond the best of them. Beside this building and the offices contained in it are monitored twenty-four hours of the day.'

'All the same, you think there's a rotten apple in the barrel?' asked Bull.

'Until we know differently, that is what we must assume. You know what Karen said to me before I left? '

'No, I do not.'

'She said trust no one.'

'Not even us?' asked Gray,

'Not even the person I see in the mirror.'

'That's going to make it a bit awkward, isn't it?'

'Gray, in this line of work, trust is earned, not assumed. Remember the old maxim, to assume is to make an ass out of you and me.'

'Oh, I see. I think.'

'Right,' said Buchanan. 'Our task isn't to arrest Maxwell, it's just to collect information on his activities. Bull, do you still have your uniform?'

'Of course.'

'Gray, I know you will have a uniform.'

'Indeed, I do.'

'So, this is what I'd like the two of you to do. I want you to hit all the known Maxwell venues. The bars, the betting offices, mini-markets, taxi ranks, anywhere and everywhere Maxwell has placed his marker. I want you to take the mugshots of Volente and Jameson junior with you and make it known we are looking for them. You can say they are not suspects in a crime but may be in possession of information that could be of help in our investigation into the deaths of two men.'

'Sounds like old-fashioned police work,' said Bull. 'I'm really looking forward to that. I've been behind a desk for too long, it will be great to get out on the beat again.'

'Won't word get back that we are looking for them?' said Gray.

'I hope it does,' replied Buchanan. 'Trying to set up surveillance on Field Road won't work, and there aren't enough of us to do a 24-7 tail on them. So, I figure if we let them know we are looking for them, they will more likely stay put at Maxwell's place.'

'Oh, I hadn't thought of that.'

'That's why you are a PC and Jack is a DCI, Gray,' said Bull, giving Gray a cheeky punch in the arm.

'What about me, Jack? What's my role in this escapade?' asked Gus.

'Gus, I would like you to go to work as usual and pull all the records you can find on Maxwell's affairs. Not the originals of course, copies will do. If you use your phone to photograph the documents, you can then WhatsApp them to me on this phone.'

'Not your company phone?'

'No, that may already be compromised. This one is from the evidence room back in Eastbourne. Don't worry, it's one of the many destined for the recycle bin. You know, the irony of the matter is the phone that used to belong to Gallagher.'

'Was it locked?'

'Yes, I had the station techie unlock it for me, and before you ask the password has been changed and I now have full access to the phone.'

'Have you looked at the memory yet?'

'While the techie was unlocking the phone, I had the call log printed, along with the contact list, and the phone's search history.'

'Learn much?'

'Haven't had time to read through it yet, I'll do that later after I've got the office set up.'

'It's going to be a bit of a squeeze having four of us in here,' said Gray.

'Not really,' said Buchanan. 'I'm hoping we will be so busy that none of you will have the time or reason to spend much time in here.'

'Suits me,' said Bull.

'As for technology, I'm going to purchase a decent computer, printer with a scanner, and other basic office materials. All the necessities of a busy office.'

'I suppose you want all communication via our mobile phones?' said Gus.

'Yes, probably for the best.'

'And you really think someone could be listening in on our conversations?'

'I honestly don't know, Gus. Jill said I'm being paranoid; and she may be correct.'

'OK, that works for me. I'd better get going, being late on a Monday morning is never a good thing. Oh, should we have a scheduled time for me to send you stuff? If we are supposed to be working a low profile, it wouldn't be too smart to be popping in and out of here willy-nilly?'

'Unless it is urgent, I'll leave timing to your discretion and see you three back here in the morning for a briefing.'

'We'll see you later, Jack,' said Bull, 'just popping home for the uniform. C'mon, Gray, we can't stand here jawing, we have some serious business to conduct, and I can't wait to get stuck in. Today you will see how a real bobby does his job.'

'That I do want to see,' said Gray.

As the door shut behind them, Buchanan went behind his desk and sat. This was the moment of truth, the general has sent his troops out into the battlefield, would they be mowed down as they crossed no-mans-land, or would they survive the crossing and crawl into the enemy lines unscathed and unnoticed? Only time would tell.

While on the train he had wondered if his plan to setup an investigation outside the regular method was a sound one. If he couldn't trust his own people, how was he ever going to get at the truth?

He googled office suppliers and decided Rymans on Union Street would fit the bill, especially since they would deliver free if he spent more than fifty pounds, which he was sure he was likely to do. Next was to locate a nearby computer store. His first choice, Curry's, was too far out of town. So, he chose from the closest as it seemed to have just what he wanted and would also deliver.

Three hours and several hundred pounds later on his credit card, he stood back and looked at the results of his afternoon's purchases. It wouldn't impress any of the management back in Eastbourne, but it was perfect for his present purpose. At least the white board was of a substantial size.

He began by creating a Maxwell hierarchy tree, with Rab Maxwell's name central, and on top. Below he wrote the names: Andy Jameson – Banker, Toni Benatti – Lawyer. On the row below that he wrote: Steve Jameson – Enforcer, Dino Volente – Enforcer, Frank Laidlow – Enforcer, Reg Wardlow – Enforcer.

Buchanan stood back and looked at the skeletal framework that was the Maxwell fiefdom. Of course, there would additionally be any number of nameless soldiers paid to do the bidding of their master. These cretins probably owed little obedience to their paymaster, and would, given the right financial inducement, change ships at the flutter of a suitable bank note.

It was still too early to close shop for the day, so he turned on his laptop and opened the report on McDermott's phone. The outgoing calls were mostly to Eastbourne numbers, there were a couple to 0800 numbers and the remainder to a few regular mobile numbers. He decided he would email the file to Jill and get her to run the numbers, just in case something surfaced to help in his present investigation. Then he had a thought, if McDermott's phone had been put in the recycle bin, would Gallagher's be there as well? And if so, who deemed them to be of no further use? After all, Buchanan was the SIO in the investigations of the deaths of McDermott and Gallagher. But there was an issue with his thinking: Gallagher's death was ruled an accident as was McDermott's, so why should their phones not be discarded and recycled? It was a problem for another day.

Although he had nothing other than the office to show for his day's endeavours, he felt they had made an excellent beginning, and as such he felt justified at five-forty to shut up shop and head home to the hotel, a shower and dinner.

He exited the lift and walked through into the restaurant and ordered a whisky and water before sitting for dinner. His table of the previous evening was available, so he nodded to the waiter and went over and sat. Instead of sitting with his back to the room like he had the previous evening, he sat in the opposite seat and waited.

He picked up the menu to see what he fancied for dinner. He was mulling over whether to have the salmon or steak when the receptionist appeared in front of him.

'Excuse me, Mr Buchanan, sorry I missed you when you came in, I have a note for you,' she said, handing Buchanan a small white envelope. 'The gentleman left it for you this afternoon.'

'Thank you,' he said, taking it and wondering who could be sending him handwritten notes.

He sniffed the envelope, no scent, so not from a female. He picked up the knife, slid it under the flap and opened the envelope.

He removed the contents and saw it was a simple piece of paper folded twice.

The handwriting was unfamiliar, but the author was not, it was from Jock.

You asked me to let you know if anything out of the ordinary happened. The girl reappeared this afternoon, and as happened previously she managed to climb over the fence, she stood for a while, just staring into the river, then was grabbed by the security guard, and hauled back into the grounds. Just thought you'd like to know. Jock.

Who was the mystery girl, wondered Buchanan? Unlikely to be someone who worked at Busby House, though it could be the child of one of the workers, but if that was the case, why bring her to work? Unless of course the parent was a live-in worker. But given Maxwell's proclivity to destroying life, why would he put up with the situation? Buchanan's thoughts reverted to an earlier idea that Maxwell was indeed turning the house and grounds into a sanatorium prior to his departure for Eastbourne.

If that was the case, there would have to be a planning application somewhere in the City Hall planning department. A job for Gus in the morning.

18
Maxwell

That night Buchanan dreamt of falling out of a tree into a river and trying to lift a heavy weight up from the bottom while desperately holding his breath. This time it was the corner of the bedsheet in his mouth. He looked at his watch and saw it was time for breakfast.

He had a shower to wake up, dressed and went downstairs. The news on the television was just as depressing as the headlines in his newspaper. The war still raged in the Ukraine; North Korea and China were involved in joint military exercises. The Palestinians in the so-called occupied west were firing missiles into Israel, China was conducting live-round exercises in the sea beside Taiwan, Iran was eager to get the proliferation treaty signed so they could get on with enriching uranium for the bomb they say they won't build. Where would it all end, he wondered?

Breakfast over he got on the train into Glasgow and the office. First thing was to check in with Jill.

'Good morning, Jack, sleep well?'

'Sort of, maybe I should be drinking Horlicks before bed.'

'Well, this news should cheer you up. You asked me to dig into Maxwell's background, and I think I may have found something that may interest you.'

'And that is?'

'Maxwell and Anderson went to the same high school, they were class-mates.'

'How did you manage to discover that fact?'

'Three broken fingernails and four cups of strong coffee, I worked late last night while Stephen was out on patrol. I began by looking at Maxwell's history – did you know he was quite an athlete at high school? Won quite a few cups for boxing and athletics. He met his wife, Sheila, one night when he was competing at an interschool boxing match at Kelvin Hall.'

'Where did you come up with that bit of news about the relationship between Anderson and Maxwell?'

'It was getting late, and I was tired. So, as a random act, I googled the combination of words, Maxwell, Anderson, boxing, high school, Glasgow, and that was when I found out that their paths have crossed in the past.'

'Well done, what did you find out?'

'Thanks. Their meeting happened one night when Anderson and a group of friends went to watch a boxing match at Kelvin Hall. The main bout was between Maxwell, and someone called Spenser. It was a vicious fight that went the distance. Maxwell won by a knockout in the final round. With it being a title fight, it was well covered by the newspapers and since Maxwell's fight was the main bout for the evening, the papers all wanted an interview with him afterwards.

'Anderson was there at the match with a group from school. Being underage for drinking, didn't stop them from acquiring a bottle or two. They were trying to be discrete with their drinking and had crossed the road to the bridge where they could drink unobserved. That was when Anderson got a bit too friendly with one of the girls and tried to entice her away from her friend and go with him into the bushes. She wasn't interested, and in an attempt to get away from Anderson she fell in the river.

'Anderson's friends were in no condition to go in after her, so one of them went for help. Maxwell, who was standing outside the Hall being interviewed, heard the shouts, and ran across the road and was just in time to see the girl go down for the third time. Without thinking he jumped into the river and pulled the now incapacitated girl out. Of course, the photographer and reporter had run after Maxwell and managed to get the story in the next day's paper.'

'So, Maxwell saved the girl's life? I wonder if Anderson is under some sort of honour debt to Maxwell. Anything else?'

'Yes, that young girl later in life became Maxwell's wife, her name is Sheila.'

'I wasn't aware of the background, well done for discovering those facts. 'Maxwell probably used the incident to promote his career as a boxer, all the same, good work, Jill. I tell you what, since you've been so successful finding a link between Maxwell and Anderson, I have a slightly more nebulaaic connection for you to look at. While visiting my friend Jock at his stables on Saturday he told me a story that I could only describe as a bizarre occurrence.'

'What was that?'

'Jock's stables nestle in the bend in the River Cart and Maxwell's house sits on its own ground directly opposite. The river is quite deep at that point, a fact I know from personal experience. Well, while there, Jock told me a story about a young girl who climbed over the fence and took the rope we used to swing from, tied it round her neck and would have jumped into the river if it hadn't been for two security guards that jumped the fence, cut her free, and took her back into the grounds.'

'You would like me to see if I can find out who she is?'

'If you could, it might help to make sense of what's going on. Oh, one more thing to consider. Maxwell's house used to be a nursing home; it is possible he has begun the transition back from a private residence to that of a nursing home. Don't spend too much time finding out about Maxwell's plans for the house, I'll have Gus work on that.'

'Anything else?'

'No, that is all for now. If you would WhatsApp me the details to my alternate phone, please

'OK, will do. Talk to you tomorrow.'

'Was that your partner, Jill?' asked Gray, who'd just entered the office with Bull.

'Yes, and she's discovered something very interesting. I'll wait till Gus shows up before revealing all.'

'He shouldn't be long,' said Bull, 'I saw him walking up from Argyle Street.'

'Good, we've got a lot of ground to cover today.'

'Morning boss,' said Gus, as he closed the office door behind him.

'Right,' said Buchanan. 'Before you tell me how you got on yesterday, I have something that may shine a light on our investigations. Jill, back in the office in Eastbourne, has uncovered an interesting fact. Back when Maxwell was at high school, he was into boxing. One evening he was competing in a match at Kelvin Hall. Afterwards he was outside being interviewed and was just in time to save the life of a young girl who had been pestered by Anderson and as a result had just fallen in the river Kelvin. That young girl has since become the wife of Rab Maxwell.'

'Is it possible that Maxwell holds that over Anderson?' asked Gray.

'Very unlikely, Gray. That incident took place at least fifty years ago – if he was being controlled by Maxwell, do you think he would have risen to where he is today? I don't think so, but I will keep it in mind. So, what did you two find out yesterday?'

'The Maxwell name is more feared than respected,' said Bull. 'We began by doing a tour of the taxi ranks, there aren't that many, so it didn't take too long. When shown Jameson's photo a look of fear and dread came upon most drivers' faces. Volente was hardly recognised, and it was much the same wherever we went.'

'We really shook up a couple of employees in one of the mini-markets we went into,' said Gray. 'As Bull was showing the photos of Jameson and Volente to the manager, one of the other staff snuck behind an aisle and made a phone call. I've no idea who he called, but he certainly was worried about something we said.'

'Good. Word will soon filter back to Maxwell that we are on his tail. Any leads on the deaths of McDermott and Gallagher?'

'Remember I mentioned the name, Sneaky Pete? Well, he was in one of the betting offices,' said Bull. 'I pulled him to one side while Gray showed the photos round. Sneaky Pete said there is a story going round that Jameson took a contract to find and kill McDermott and Gallagher and an unnamed DCI.'

'What was in it for him?' asked Buchanan.

'Pete didn't know. All he said was Jameson was going for the gold, whatever that meant.'

'Did he say who put out the contract?'

'That's the strange bit, although we were able to find several people willing to talk about the deaths, no one wanted to mention any names. It seems that there is a certain amount of honour amongst thieves. They all thought that McDermott and Gallagher got what they deserved for grassing on Maxwell.'

'Anyone offer suggestions on how the location and identities of McDermott and Gallagher were revealed?'

'One smartass suggested that the killer simply googled their names and addresses.'

'These days with technology I wouldn't be surprised if that were the case. How about you, Gus, how was your day?'

'Interesting is how I would describe it. I checked with the planning department and there are no planning applications lodged to turn the Field Road dwellings into a nursing home. But there are plans submitted by Maxwell's construction firm to demolish the house and construct an estate consisting of two and three-bedroom flats. I'm surprised he expends so much effort in criminal enterprises, he could be very wealthy running his legitimate businesses.'

'What businesses does he currently run? My experience of him was as a gangster and drug lord.'

'Maxwell also owns a couple of night clubs outright, has a share in one of the taxi firms that plies the station, owns the franchise for several mini-markets, and of course his construction firm.'

'The bit about the construction firm lines up with what Anderson told me about Maxwell purchasing the run-down Governor bar from the widow of the owner. Maxwell was supposedly going to refurbish the bar and turn it into a modern bistro-bar, yet a few weeks later it mysteriously caught fire.'

'Like a lot of buildings in Glasgow these days,' said Gus. 'That fate recently befell a bar which was reputed to be one of the oldest bars in the city. Apparently, a developer wanted to knock it down to build university accommodation but was refused due to the historical importance of the bar. Unfortunately for the bar, it mysteriously caught fire and had to be demolished.'

'Anderson said intelligence thought it was where Maxwell stored a lot of his drugs. It was also where Beckerman was found with a syringe full of smack sticking out of his arm.'

'Did you go into Porters' bar?'

'Yes, and you will be pleased to know that it is still a hub for criminality.'

'I'm glad to hear that; I'd be so disappointed if it had become respectable. Anderson also said Maxwell has two legitimate children, both adults, and not living in the country. Is that information current?'

'As far as I know it is,' said Gus. 'There was a rumour about another child, but nothing definite.'

'Now that is interesting,' said Buchanan, 'tell me about the rumour.'

'This was about fifteen to twenty or so years ago. From what I remember, Maxwell's wife was at a party, had a bit too much to drink and had a one-night drunken stand with an Italian gangster who was visiting Glasgow. She fell pregnant. At first Maxwell was livid but eventually accepted the situation.'

'What about the other man, the one Maxwell's wife had the affair with, is he still around?'

'He was told to leave the country if he valued his life.'

'He was lucky.'

Gus shook his head, 'His body was found on the beach down by Port Glasgow, it was missing its manhood.'

'What about the child?'

'Nobody knows, it's never been seen. Probably put the kid up for adoption, or had an abortion, who knows?'

'Can you do me a favour, Gus? Would you check the dates on that? I have an idea; my niggler is niggling.'

'Sure, it should only take a few minutes.'

'Bull,' said Buchanan, 'you ever hear anything about a Maxwell love child?'

'No, I dealt mainly with street crime. The extra-marital affairs of gang bosses' wives were well out of my remit.'

'Not to worry.'

'Thanks,' said Gus, putting his phone back in his pocket. 'If the Maxwell girl is alive, Jack, she would be seventeen.'

'Now that is interesting.'

'Why is that?'

'I've been thinking. Point one. The Busby House, where Maxwell and his wife live, once was a nursing home. Point two. Yesterday I witnessed a young woman climb over the fence by the swimming hole in the river, grab the rope swing and try to hang herself from the tree at the side of the river. She was prevented from doing so by two males who had probably been following her. I assumed they were security guards who untied her and dragged her away from the edge and back into the grounds. Point three. I was thinking that if Maxwell was turning the Busby House back into a nursing home, the young woman could have been one of the inmates. Point four. We now know that Maxwell is buying a house in Eastbourne and has put up the Busby House estate for redevelopment. Conclusion, the young woman in the house is either an inmate of the yet to be opened nursing home, or Maxwell's wife's daughter.'

'But why keep her a prisoner all these years?' asked Gray.

'That we must find out, but not quite yet. If we were to force an entry into the house it might fare badly for her.'

'You think she might be harmed?'

'Yes, Gray, I do think that is a possibility.'

'But why?'

'You're not married, are you?'

'No, not yet,' he said, blushing.

'Children?'

'No, of course not, I told you I'm not married.'

'Well, when a married woman has a child that is not her husband's, it can cause a great deal of trouble for the woman. So, even if the husband eventually forgives the wife and agrees to her keeping the child, it takes a very special relationship for the husband to forgive the wife's indiscretion and accept the child as his own.'

'But if that is the case with Maxwell and his wife, why is their daughter trying to hang herself? It's just terrible, Jack, we have to help her.'

'Don't you worry, Gray; we will do all we can to get to the bottom of the matter.'

'Good, she sure sounds like she needs help.'

'So, boss, what mischief shall we get up to today?' asked Bull.

'Do you have access to the carpool?'

'Yes.'

'Good. I'd like the two of you to book out one of the unmarked cars and spend the day sitting outside Maxwell's house.'

'Won't that be a bit obvious?' said Gray.

'That's the whole point of it. I want Maxwell to know we are watching him. I want him looking over his shoulder wondering if we are behind him, and, Gray, do you know what happens when you spend all day looking over your shoulder?'

'If I was doing that, I'd probably fall flat on my face at the first obstacle.'

'Precisely. As far as I know, I don't think Maxwell has ever been targeted in this way before. I want to know every step he takes.'

'C'mon, Gray, this is going to be fun.'

'What do you want me to do?' asked Gus.

'I'm still worried about the fact that all the way through this investigation, there has been someone going ahead of me sweeping up the detritus of the evidence.'

'Such as?' said Gus.

'For a start. The body of Gallagher was collected by someone posing as his sister. The body was duly released and cremated within twenty-four hours.'

'He might have been a Muslim; they are very strict about burial procedures.'

'Can you imagine Gallagher having any sort of faith?'

'No, not with his record. Were there any other factors that made you suspicious?'

'His tools and clothes also disappeared.'

'I suppose under the circumstances that could be legitimate.'

'C'mon, Gus. You checked the home address he and Jameson gave – an abattoir? No one lives in an abattoir, at least not while they are alive, and this is just the beginning. The car Jameson was driving was sold off as scrap, along with all its contents. Then a few days later when I went to view the barn where Gallagher died, there was a NCA surveillance operation going on. I tell you, Gus, something is rotten in Denmark.'

'The NCA are a law unto themselves. You say the barn is out in the marshes?'

'Yes.'

'Lots of sheep around?'

'Yes, but we have already discounted the idea of sheep rustling.'

'How about illegal immigration? I read in the press that hundreds of illegal immigrants cross the channel almost every day.'

'That is true and could be the reason for the NCA being out on the marshes. Though, it just seems too pat an idea.'

'So, back to the question of the moment, what do you want me to do today?'

'I've got Jill digging for information on the Maxwell baby, would you like to dig into Anderson's past? There will be plenty of public domain stuff to get you started, so once you've exhausted that avenue, see if there are any skeletons in cupboards that are willing to talk to you. Pretend you are arranging some sort of surprise event to honour his years in public service.'

'You suspect him of something nefarious?'

'Gus, are you a freemason?'

'No, are you?'

'Me? Not on your nelly. There's no way I'm going to roll up a trouser leg.'

'OK, just wondering. I suppose Anderson is one?'

'I believe he may be.'

'Then I won't get very far with my enquiries, will I?'

'I don't see why not. Anderson is quite a vain person, and I'm sure his friends look up to him and will only be too eager to talk to you about him. Give it a go, see what turns up.'

'You still think there may be a link between Anderson and Maxwell beyond the river Kelvin incident?'

'Right now, I have only random thoughts.'

'OK, I'll get on it right away. How about you, got anything planned?'

'I thought I'd go visit Maxwell; see how he's getting on.'

'On your own?'

'Why not.'

'Is that wise?'

'Probably not.'

'But you're going anyway?'

'Yep.'

'Want company?'

'No. thanks, I think this is best done alone.'

'Like Daniel going into the lion's den?'

'I won't be alone.'

'How's that?'

'I don't know, I have no idea why I said that, but it just feels right to make a personal call on Maxwell. I see it as a sort of boxer's handshake before the bout.'

'That makes Bull and Gray your seconds. They will be right outside the gate; you can call them to rescue you if needed.'

'I doubt I will need their help.'

'Well, it's your neck you are sticking out.'

'Don't worry about me, I'll be fine.'

'Will you go now?'

'No. I need to set the scene first.'

'As I said, it's your neck, hope all goes as expected.'

Why had he said he wouldn't be alone? Then he remembered Stanley had mentioned the Daniel in the lion's den story. In a way that was a good analogy, but he wasn't really going into the lion's den, instead, he was going into the Maxwell den, so would there really be someone with him, some unseen friend?

He shook his head, he must get a grip on himself, this investigation wasn't some scripted television show where the hero came through unscathed in the last segment before the ten o'clock news. This was real life, how many deaths or maimings had Maxwell been responsible for during his career as a criminal?' Only God knew the answer to that question.

He decided to start the process by talking with Maxwell. He looked in the file for the home number for Maxwell. He dialled it not knowing what to expect.

'Maxwell residence,' said a polite foreign-sounding voice.

'Yes, could I speak with Mr Maxwell?'

'I'm sorry, he doesn't take phone calls, would you like to leave a message?'

'Yes. Would you tell Mr Maxwell that Jack Buchanan will be calling on him this afternoon about two o'clock?'

'I am sorry, sir, but his diary may be full. If you leave your number, I will pass the message on to his secretary who may return your call.'

'You do that, I'll be there at two o'clock.'

'But, sir, you have no appointment.'

'Two o'clock,' said Buchanan, hanging up. He didn't like being so rude to staff, after all they were only doing what they were instructed to do. He could imagine Maxwell's reaction when he heard that a Jack Buchanan was going to be visiting at two o'clock. Would he immediately realise that it was DCI Jack Buchanan? Probably. Word would have got back to him by now that there was a police investigation team going round the district asking questions. A visit from their leader was to be expected.

♦

As he reached the end of Field Road and approached the gates to the Maxwell residence, he could see the conspicuous presence of Bull and Gray in their unmarked dark-blue BMW police car. He waved at them and pressed the call button on the gate phone.

'Yes?'

'Jack Buchanan to see Mr Maxwell.'

'I'm sorry, but Mr Maxwell doesn't see tradesmen without an appointment.'

'How about telling him Jack Buchanan is here for afternoon tea, and I like mine without milk and strawberry jam on my scone.'

'You want me to tell him that? Do you have any idea who you are wanting to talk to?'

'Listen, lad. Run along and tell your boss Jack Buchanan is here.'

There was an audible hum as the call went on hold. Buchanan thought the lad will be surprised when Maxwell tells him just who Jack Buchanan was. Two minutes later the hum stopped, and the voice returned.

'Why didn't you say you were the police? Do you have a search warrant?'

'No, I really am here for afternoon tea.'

'Wait.'

The hum returned, but this time not for so long.

'The boss said you can come in.'

The hum returned and was joined by the sound of a side gate opening. Buchanan turned and waved at Bull and Gray then stepped through the fortified entrance to the Maxell estate. The gate arrangement wouldn't look out of place at any modern prison he thought.

Before he could take a step further, he was stopped by the two individuals he'd seen on Sunday afternoon. The same two that had saved the young woman from hanging herself.

'Stand still, arms out, shoulders high,' said the shorter of the two, who produced a metal detector wand similar to that used at airports. Satisfied Buchanan was ready, the guard proceeded to scan Buchanan's body.

'You wearing a wire?' the other one said, as he frisked Buchanan's body thoroughly.

'You tell me, you seem to know what you are doing.'

'Looks like you are clear, follow.'

Like a prisoner being admitted into a prison, Buchanan was marched, sandwiched between the guards, along the gravel driveway, past the large conservatory, and up to the main entrance. As they got closer, he looked at the house and wondered once more about why Scottish architectural heritage was being allowed to be vandalised in the name of profit. He could see Busby House, with the secluded grounds alongside the river, making an exceptional hotel retreat.

'Wait here,' said the short one. who walked up to the door and pressed a call button. He muttered something into an intercom, nodded and returned to Buchanan.

'You can go in; Carl will show you through to Mr Maxwell.'

Something wasn't right thought Buchanan as he followed the diminutive Carl along the corridor.

Carl stopped at the entrance to one of the rooms on the right and knocked on the door. He opened it, stepped in and said, 'Your visitor, boss.'

'Send him in.'

'Go on in, he's waiting for you.'

For just a fleeting moment Buchanan thought, this is it, I'm going into the lion's den. He shook his head and said to himself, you're not alone, the boys are waiting outside.

'You must excuse me if I don't get up,' said Maxwell, from a wheelchair in front of the blazing fire. 'Got in a fight with a bullet, I think I came off worse.'

'What happened?' asked Buchanan, as he advanced into the room.

'It's just a flesh wound, isn't that what all the tough guys say in the movies?'

Buchanan shrugged and said, 'Does it hurt?'

'Not at the moment.'

'What happened?'

'Come, sit in front of the fire with me, the doctor said I should keep warm.'

This wasn't going the way he intended, thought Buchanan, as he crossed the room followed by Carl. Here was Glasgow's most feared gangster sitting in a wheelchair, blanket over his shoulders, trying to keep warm in front of the fire. So much for the tough cop routine.

'You ask what happened, but first, what would you like to drink? Or are you on duty?'

'Lagavulin with water.'

'Carl, whisky for the inspector, and I'll have my usual, and put another log on the fire, it's got quite chilly in here, the atmosphere needs warming up. Then, when you've done that, go across the road and ask old Bull and his partner if they want a coffee? Also, tell Bull his boss is OK and doesn't need babysitting.'

'Sure thing, boss.'

'You ask what happened, Jack. Last night, I'd just finished working and stepped out of the site office, it's in the basement and leads out onto the alleyway at the side of the building. I locked the door behind me, started to walk up the alley, I was in the dark at this point.

'I had walked three paces when the PIR turned on the security lights and that was when the first shot was fired. I took the first one in the briefcase that was across my chest, the bullet deflected off my laptop and went through my shoulder. If I hadn't been holding the briefcase across my chest, the bullet would have gone straight through my heart. As I fell forward the second went across my face and in doing so destroyed a perfectly good set of dentures.'

'How bad are the injuries? You're in a wheelchair, shouldn't you be in bed, resting?'

'I'm fine. It's like they say in the movies, it's just a flesh wound, I'll be back at work tomorrow.'

'Did you manage to get a description of your attacker?'

'No, as I said he had the light behind him. He was a pro.'

'Why do you think that?'

'He was standing just inside the entrance to the alley, legs apart, two hands on the gun, that was all I could see, his outline.'

'If it was dark, how did you see him?'

'He was illuminated from behind by the streetlights on Hope Street.'

'How tall was he?'

'I don't know – maybe about five foot nine.'

'Fat, slim, bald, wearing a hat?'

'He looked fit, I think he had dark hair, and no hat.'

'How do you know it was a male gunman?'

'The shrapnel of the bullet the doctor removed from my shoulder; it was a 9mm hollow point, designed to do maximum damage. I suppose it could have been a female, they have been known to be killers.'

'Where is the bullet now?'

'I imagine the police have it.'

'What did the police do?'

'Do? I suppose they were angry.'

'Angry?'

'Because the gunman failed in his attempt. You really have been away a long time, Jack. To every straight cop in Glasgow, I'm public enemy number one.'

'Are you saying they did nothing?'

'Oh, they showed up at the hospital, took statements, then said to get well soon and left while laughing their heads off.'

'Were you alone?'

'Yes, I was the last one out, and before you change from being a sick man's visitor to that of a policeman, let me say you don't have to worry, I will take care of it in my own way.'

'Are you sure that's wise? Glasgow has enough stabbings and shootings already.'

'You should know that is the way it is and has always been done. We take care of issues in-house.'

'How did you get to the hospital?'

'Jack, stop being a policeman and tell me the real reason you are here?'

'I came up to see the family. I heard you were still living here in Busby House, so since I'm staying at the other end of Field Road, I thought I'd drop in and say hello.'

'Really, do I look like I was born yesterday? You're here to clean out the stables, am I correct?'

'You could say that.'

'Am I a candidate to be on the muck pile?'

'That depends on what I find.'

'And if you do think I am, what will you do that many others have failed to do?'

'Rab, can we get one thing straight? First and foremost, I am a policeman. I've sworn to serve with fairness, integrity, diligence, and impartiality, and that I will to the best of my power. To cause the peace to be kept and preserved and prevent all offences against people and property. Other than that, I keep an allotment.'

'Is that the oath they make you take at college?'

'Yes.'

'I suppose that is one answer – what's the real reason you are here?'

'Two names, McDermott and Gallagher, your boys, they died on my patch.'

'I'd heard they had an accident, but I can assure you they were not my boys. I did hear they weren't very good with heights. Gallagher came off his ladder and landed on his chisel, McDermott stepped back to admire his work and a gust of wind blew him over the rail. Did I hear that correctly?'

'Who told you that story?'

'A little bird told me.'

'Did the little bird tell you I was almost run down by a speeding car?'

'No, it did not.'

'And that the driver of that car speaks with a Scottish accent?'

'You speak with a Scottish accent.'

215

'By any chance, has one of your boys been practising a bit of private enterprise?'

'I've told you I don't have any boys, and those who work for me would never do anything like that, they don't need to. I can assure you they are totally loyal.'

'Talking of boys, how is your son, keeping well is he?'

'Yes, as a matter of fact, he is about to make me a grandfather once more. Carl, another whisky for my friend, leave the bottle on the table and you can leave us, and get Ivan to go across the road and let Mr Bull and his nephew know they can go home for the day.'

'Yes boss,' replied Carl, as he stepped out of the shadows of the far end of the room, placed the whisky bottle and water jug on the coffee table and departed.

'I'm also going to be a grandfather,' said Buchanan, as he poured a liberal amount of whisky into their glasses while wondering just what sort of intelligence gathering abilities Maxwell's organisation had.

'I never knew you had children.'

'It's my partner at work, Jill. She lost her parents when she was very young. We have sort of adopted each other. Her baby is due in early spring.'

Buchanan picked up his glass, held it to his lips and looked at Maxwell. He was staring into the fire. He slowly took his unsipped drink away from his lips and was about to ask who the young woman was who lived in the house. But as quick as the thought came into his mind, he discarded it. That question was for another time and situation. Right now, he was dealing with the question of why the police hadn't pursued the attempted murder of Maxwell.

'So, you are saying that the police have dropped the case?'

'They never picked it up.'

'Was the crime scene inspected?'

'Not as far as I know.'

'How can you be sure they haven't been on site and left?'

'The site is behind locked and alarmed steel doors, they would have had to smash their way in to gain access, and for that they would require a search warrant.'

'I thought you were shot in the alley?'

'I was.'

'So, the CSI investigators don't need to get into the site office?'

'You have a point there. If they need to look inside, the site foreman will have a key.'

'How do you know they didn't have a warrant and have already searched the premises?'

'I would know, Jack. There's not much goes on in Glasgow that I don't know about.'

'Why all the security? Are you storing items other than building materials?'

Maxwell smiled and said, 'Jack, this is Glasgow, not your genteel town of Eastbourne.'

'Suppose I had a look at the scene? It is possible the gunman left incriminating evidence behind.'

Maxwell thought for a moment, nodded, and said, 'What if you did? That would one in the eye for the boys in the blue-serge suits.'

'Have things got that bad? Is it open war between you and the police?'

'They haven't started shooting at us – oh, you don't think it was of your lot who took a pot shot at me the other night?'

Buchanan shook his head. 'Things may have got bad, but Glasgow of today certainly isn't Chicago of the thirties. The guys in the blue-serge suits aren't out to gun you down in the streets.'

'I'll take that grain of salt with my porridge in the morning.'

'I'll see if I can arrange for a CSI team to give the area a once-over tomorrow, you never know what might turn up. I will bring Gus with me, be better if two sets of eyes are looking at the scene. Would that cause you any discomfort?'

'Be my guest, they won't find anything that would compromise me.'

'You enjoy the conflict, don't you?'

'It can be fun.'

'Was it fun ten years ago when you were lifted for the bonded warehouse robbery?'

'You know, that really was very stupid of Anderson. Was it his idea to put the grass in the same cell as me? I had to put up with that fawning prat for days, "Oh, Rab, tell me about the time you did this, or robbed that place, had so and so killed," I almost strangled the jerk with my bare hands to make him shut up.'

'That was nothing to do with me.'

'It just didn't make sense to me or my lawyer. Why was Anderson so desperate to get me put away for life?'

'Two security guards died that night.'

'Sad that, especially since I was putting one of their kids through university. I had at least twenty witnesses say they saw me in Porters drinking that night, and I couldn't possibly have been at the warehouse when it was done over.'

'You say Anderson was the SIO for the case?'

'Yes, he was only an inspector at the time. The pompous ass, how he ever made Chief Constable is anyone's business. You should have seen his face when I walked out of court, a free man. He had it in for me from there on out.'

'You've just said it yourself; he was after promotion and the bright lights of being a Chief Constable.'

'I've been clean for the last seven years.'

'That's not what your reputation on the street says.'

'People can say what they like, I've had enough and have retired from my previous occupation.'

'So, let me get this straight, are you saying Anderson stitched you up and since he failed with the bonded store robbery, he is still out to get you?'

'That's the way it looks to me, Jack. I bet he's sent you up here to get me on his behalf. You're his designated hit man. Carry a gun?'

'You should know, of all people, I never carry a gun.'

'I know that, and I know you are a fair man when it comes to the law and justice.'

Buchanan picked up his glass, took a sip, and as he put the glass down, said, 'This is a nice house, Rab, how many bedrooms?'

'You never switch off, do you? For your information, the house has seven bedrooms, five with en-suites, this living room, a formal day room and formal dining room. There is a kitchen and a large conservatory.'

'I was told it was once a nursing home.'

Maxwell shook his head. 'That was the other Busby House, it was further up the river and no longer in existence. Enough of that, now, it is my turn to ask questions.'

'Go ahead. As long as it doesn't involve cases I am working on, I'll do my best to answer them.'

'Fine. Tell me all about Eastbourne, I am thinking of retiring down there.'

♦

Two hours later Buchanan stepped through the gate of the Maxwell estate and pondered the situation. He'd gone in to see one of Glasgow's most feared gangsters and left having had a relaxed and sometimes humorous chat with what to all appearances was a grandfather talking about retiring to Eastbourne. But where was Maxwell's wife, Sheila? Why hadn't she come in to see how her injured husband was doing?' Another question for another time.

He looked across the road at the BMW: they had disregarded Ivan's instructions and had waited for him. As he crossed the road, Buchanan could see Gus sitting in the back seat.

Bull wound down the window and said, 'You know what that cheeky so and so said?'

'I believe the message was something like, *tell Bull his boss is OK and doesn't need babysitting.*'

'Got it in one.'

'What did you say?'

'I told him we're not on the Maxwell payroll and he could go boil his head.'

'Well said. Any sign of Tweedledum and Tweedledee?'

'Not a sausage. Are we sure they are still in the house?'

Buchanan shook his head. 'That is the question of the hour. Unfortunately, no one thought to put a watch on the house when they arrived.'

'So, they could be anywhere.'

'I could freeze to death out here, how about we stop in at the hotel and warm up?'

'Sounds fine to me, jump in.'

♦

Buchanan bought a round of drinks and joined Bull, Gus and Gray in one of the empty booths.

'How was the conversation with Maxwell?' asked Bull.

'Interesting, he said someone took a pot shot at him when he was leaving the building site.'

'When was this?'

'Monday evening, about six o'clock, it was dark by then. Maxwell had finished for the day and was the last to leave. He shut the door to the site office and went down the stairs to his car. As he reached to open the car door someone standing at the top of the alleyway shot him twice then disappeared.'

'Did he get a description of the gunman?' asked Gus.

'A vague one that would fit half of the Glasgow male population. The gunman was in the dark and Maxwell was illuminated by the site security floodlights.'

'I wonder why I never heard about it. Usually, news of a shooting incident goes round the station like a wildfire,' said Gus.

'Maxwell seemed to think the police were taking the shooting like it was a joke.'

'No investigation, no CSI?'

'Nope.'

'We can't let that be, even if it was Maxwell who was shot.'

'Then what we are doing is not quite legal, is it? We're being used,' said Gray.

'No, I think we are in the clear, Gray. If Anderson has convinced my ACC that this caper is above board, then we have nothing to worry about, especially if Maxwell has something to answer for.'

'So, where do we go from here?' asked Bull.

'I think we'll pick up on the shooting and see if we can tie it in with Volente and Jameson. They were tracked all the way from Eastbourne on Friday evening to Busby on Saturday morning. They had plenty of time to figure out Maxwell's routine and set up an ambush on Monday evening.'

'So, where do we start?' asked Bull.

'Tomorrow, I would like you and Gray to canvas the shops on Hope Street and see if anyone saw or heard anything. Check CCTV cameras for anything that stands out.

'Gus, would you ask around the station and see if you can pick up on any reasons for why the shooting wasn't investigated? I'd like us to meet at the building site about nine o'clock. Maxwell says the site has been in lockdown since Monday evening when he was shot. There's also the matter of the bullet taken out of Maxwell's shoulder, see if you can track it down. I hope it's tagged and in a forensics lab.'

'How will we get in?' asked Gray.

'Maxwell says the site will be open again as normal today,' said Buchanan.

'This is not good, a very unprofessional way to go about business,' said Gus. 'We all know that the first sixty minutes after an incident is the most crucial time for investigating a crime. By now witnesses will have fuzzy memories, perpetrators will have solidified their alibis, and evidence contaminated.'

'All the same, Gus, we cannot let a shooting crime go without investigating it. If we did, gun crime would be rife in a matter of months, and we would have life on the streets like you see on the streets of many American cities.'

'That's a good enough reason for me,' said Gus.'

'Gus,' said Buchanan, 'would you arrange for a CSI team to meet us tomorrow morning, as early as possible at the building site? I think it's time we got off the back foot in this investigation.'

'I'll see what I can do.'

'Let them think we are going after Maxwell, that might make them a bit more amenable.'

'Good point. I'll say I've had a tipoff there may be drugs hidden on-site.'

'That should get them interested. Right, I think we've done enough for one day, I'll see you at the Maxwell site tomorrow at nine, I've got to go into the office first.'

'OK, see you tomorrow.'

19
Anderson

Wednesday morning, Buchanan climbed out of bed and as had become a habit, looked out the bedroom window. It was raining. He shrugged, after all it was Glasgow and it was December, three weeks till Christmas.

He was beginning to get used to the routine of getting dressed, going downstairs for his breakfast then catching the train into Glasgow and his Starbucks coffee. He had tried other coffees over the years, but his tastebuds refused to accept them.

'Good morning, Jill, how are you today?' he asked, when she answered the phone.

'I'm fine, though it's taking a bit of getting used to Stephen working the late shifts again. With you being away, I have been contemplating shifting my day to start later.'

'If it works for you, try it. I can always call you later in the day if that helps.'

'Oh, I'll be fine. May as well get used to it, when the baby gets here who knows when I'll get time to sleep.'

'I remember the late shifts only too well. Have anything for me this morning?'

'Yes and no. Nothing exciting, just been looking into Anderson's background.'

'Turn up anything interesting?'

'Our James Rennie Anderson was a born climber of the proverbial greasy pole. He was born on the 4th of August 1956. He is the son of Alasdair Anderson, who at the time of his son's birth was an officer in Glasgow City Police. James Anderson married Alison Demonte on the 20th of June 1974, they have two children.

'As for his school career, he attended a local high school, went on to a secondary where he received five A's. He attended Glasgow

University where he got a degree in accountancy & finance. His career began as a junior working in an accounting firm called Fairmile in Aberdeen. They went out of business not long after he left. From there he changed careers and joined the police force in Aberdeen. Five years later he moved from Aberdeen police to Edinburgh. He worked his way up through the ranks of Edinburgh City Police to Inspector before transferring to Glasgow three years later. He finally made Chief Constable in 2014 and continued in that rank till he retired in 2018. He is currently working as a consultant to the law enforcement industry as a police advisor.'

'Sounds quite basic, anything else?'

'Remember I said not to trust any of your team?'

'Yes, and I remember thinking you were out of line.'

'Well, you may not be correct in that.'

'You've found something?'

'What I have been able to find out is this. Three of the main protagonists in this scenario have history with each other. It's not just Anderson and Maxwell who have met before.'

'Which three?'

'Maxwell, Anderson and Bull.'

'What about Gus, is he in the clear?'

'So far I've found nothing to link him to the other three.'

'How did you come across the bits of news about the three?'

'Another late night in front of the computer.'

'Are you sure you are not overdoing things?'

'I'm fine.'

'So, what did you do?'

'I did a search on each of the team on Facebook, and found all three, four, if you include young Gray. I began by looking to see if they have any friends in common, no match except for Gray and Bull. Then I looked at their posts to see if they had anything in common, such as hobbies, food likes, similar tastes in music, that sort of thing. I went back at least five years.'

'And you found, what?'

'For a start, I looked at Anderson. Has quite an eclectic taste in hobbies. He likes the opera, theatre, and fine dining as well as horse-riding. I read between the lines and assume he is also a practising mason.'

'What you just said matches what I know of Anderson. I suppose Maxwell's hobbies are guns, and gangster history?'

'No, and I was really surprised about this, he is a bit of a gardening guru. He posts loads of photos of his plants and shares tips with those who comment on his posts. He is also a bit of an animal lover, has two cats and an orphan fox.'

'That surprises me, a fox did you say?'

'Yes. He says it was rescued several years ago from a fox hunt and he volunteered to look after it until it could be returned to the wild. Apparently, it became too domesticated for that, so it now lives with the family and runs wild on the Maxwell estate.'

'What about Bull, is he in the clear?'

'Yes, I would say he is in the clear. He's not one for posting much. There are a few posts about going on holiday to Skye. There's not much else, other than the fact he is mad about rugby. Oh, I did find a photo of him, in uniform on a police horse. It was taken at Murrayfield at a rugby match. There was also one poignant photo. It was of a lovely young woman at a table smiling up at the camera.'

'Ah, yes. That would be his cousin, he really misses her.'

'Do you know the story behind the photo?'

'The only details I know are she died in a horse-riding accident a few years ago, Bull never talked much about it. Anything else catch your attention?'

'Just photos of dinners out, the usual stuff people post on Facebook. Oh, I looked for the girl at Maxwell's house and nothing came up on the search.'

'Thanks, I've been told she may in fact be the daughter of Maxwell's wife, but not his. The story is the wife had a one-night stand, and the girl was the result.'

'That happens. Anything for me today?'

'Could you have a search for local hunts and see if either the name of Anderson or Maxwell shows up?'

'Maxwell been behaving himself?'

'I had afternoon tea with him this afternoon.'

'You what?'

'I called the Maxwell house and said I'd be round for tea at two.'

'Was that wise?'

'Maybe not, but it felt right, and after my visit I'm sure it was the correct thing to do.'

'Why do you think that?'

'He told me a very interesting story about the time he was arrested and tried for a robbery on a bonded store.'

'Oh, I came across that story, cost the taxpayer a fortune with little to show for it.'

'Yes, it was one of the cases I missed, I was stuck on a missing person investigation on the Isle of Skye.'

'You'll have to tell me about it when this case is over.'

'I will, it was quite unique.'

'From what I've been able to read, Anderson was an Inspector at the time and the SIO on the case. He pushed to get Maxwell convicted. As you are aware, in the Maxwell case, in the end he was found not guilty and walked free. Could that be what is driving Anderson? He has carried this grudge against Maxwell all these years and is still out for vengeance?'

'Could be. In Maxwell's case it's difficult to say, he's very good at hiding his nefarious activities behind a cloak of respectability, namely the building company that he runs.'

'What are you guys doing today?'

'I'm hoping that Gus has been able to organise a CSI team to meet us at the site where Maxwell's company are refurbishing the old Governor bar and the apartments above.'

'Why do you need a CSI team?'

'Someone took a pot shot at Maxwell on Monday evening.'

'How is Maxwell?'

'The first bullet deflected off his laptop and went through his shoulder, the second destroyed his dentures.'

'Ouch, how is he?'

'Arm in a sling and resting in a wheelchair. He had a good surgeon and should make a complete recovery and be back at work today or tomorrow.'

'What do you hope to find at the building site?'

'The bullet was a 9mm, so there may be shell casings on the ground.'

'After two days?'

'You never know, stranger things have happened in the past.'

'OK, it's time for me to get to work, good luck with the search.'

'Thanks, somehow I think we will need it.'

♦

Buchanan left his office, turned left, and headed up Buchanan Street. As he approached St Vincent Street, instead of turning left, he crossed over and made his way to Starbucks.

Coffee in hand he set off along St Vincent Street, past Five Guys burgers and eventually reached Hope Street, where he turned right and headed up it towards Maxwell's site office.

Gus and the others were already there waiting for him, along with a group of tradesmen, coffee cups in one hand, tool bags on the ground at their feet. Parked across the street was a familiar blue and yellow-striped, white police van. A police cordon had been erected at the entrance to the alley where Maxwell had been shot and the two policemen who had arrived in the van were deep in conversation with Bull and Gray.

'No joy with the CSI team?' Buchanan asked Gus.

'They said they'd meet us here at ten-thirty.'

'Good, hope they are on time.'

As he spoke, the CSI van drove slowly down Hope Street and pulled up beside the police cordon. A tall blonde woman climbed out of the passenger side and said, 'I'm looking for DI Fergusson.'

'That's me.'

'Good. We were told to attend a shooting and possible drug den?'

'Yes, that's correct. Could we deal with the shooting first?'

'Fine with me. Do you have the details?'

'I don't, but DCI Buchanan interviewed the victim and does have the information.'

'That's me,' said Buchanan.

'That name sounds familiar,' she said.

'Buchanan Street, a familiar shopping district perhaps?'

'No, it's not that. Weren't you involved in the Argyll Arcade jewel heist?'

'Yes, but that was quite a few years ago.'

'That's it. The teacher at college used it as an example when talking about crime scene procedures.'

'I hope is was a positive example.'

'Oh, yes, it was.'

'Good, I'm glad to have made a positive impression.'

'So, where shall we begin?'

'The victim said he stepped out of the door, that one just down the alley, it was dark and as he turned to walk up to the street, the gunman fired from up here,' said Buchanan, pointing to the Hope Street pavement behind the police cordon tape.

'When did this happen?'

'Monday evening, about seven pm.'

'And you've just now thought to get us here?'

'Not I,' said Buchanan. 'I didn't know about the shooting till late yesterday afternoon. Gus arranged the CSI callout last night.'

'Oh well, better now than never, though with this being a busy street and alley, who knows how many feet have trodden their way through the crime scene. I understand there is the possibility of drugs being found?'

'Inside, the building is being renovated.'

'Is this the building where the young lad died from an overdose?'

'Yes,' said Gus. 'A lad called Hanse Beckerman. He was found with a syringe of smack in his arm, and when toxicology tests were done, there was enough heroin in his bloodstream to make half of Glasgow high. Yet when his background was checked there was no record of him ever talking heroin.'

'Sounds like someone wanted him dead.'

'Precisely so'.

Buchanan turned to the group of tradesmen. 'Right, you guys can stand out of the way while we get on with our work, I'll let you know when we require entrance to the building.'

'What about us?' said one 'We don't get paid if we don't work.'

'When we've done what we're here for, then you can get to work, but not before.'

'I'd suggest you go get a coffee somewhere,' said Gus. 'This may take a while.'

'Who's going to watch our tools? You can't be too careful round here.'

'We're the police – if you can't trust us, who can you trust?'

'I suppose so. Do you know if there's anywhere to get something to eat around here?'

'No,' said Gray.

'Pity, we missed breakfast this morning.'

'So, why did you go to see Maxwell, Jack?' asked Gray, as they watched the CSI team begin their search.

'I thought it would help to clear the air.'

'He must be getting on a bit.'

'Yes. He's seventy at his next birthday.'

'Do you know how long he's lived in that old mansion on Field Lane?'

'I'm not sure, I think it must be somewhere in the region of twenty years.'

'I seem to remember hearing something about you being involved in an altercation with a couple of his thugs?'

'That was with Randal, the gang's lawyer, and Shelton, the gang's banker.'

'Didn't Randal and Shelton die under a police car?'

'Yes, they didn't appreciate being questioned on their taste in photographs and decided to do a runner when they heard the sound of police sirens.'

'What about the two who died recently in Eastbourne? Where did they fit in?'

'Gallagher and McDermott were enforcers. Maxwell had a myriad of enforcers disguised as security officers. They do the dirty work of collecting money and enforcing the law of Maxwell.'

'I remember reading about that case at college. Where does Steve Jameson fit in?'

'He's the son of Andy Jameson, one of Maxwell's enforcers.'

'Found something,' said the shorter of the two CSI's, 'trapped in a crack in the wall.'

'What is it?' asked Gus.

'Shell casing from what looks like a 9mm bullet.'

'Just one?' asked Buchanan.

'Greedy. We'll keep searching.

Thirty minutes later, two 9mm shell casings had been bagged and tagged and the CSIs were making their way to the door of the site office. After twenty minutes of searching, the tall one came back up the lane and said, 'Nothing down there except for what looks like the aftermath of someone being treated for an injury. You can come down and look if you like, we're ready to do the drug search if you still need us.'

'Unlikely,' said Buchanan, 'but since you are here, maybe you could do a cursory look around.'

'Fine by us, that's why we're here.'

'What about us,' said the lead carpenter.'

'Would you guys wait a few minutes while I check out the alleyway with the CSIs? Oh, which one of you carpenters has the key for the door?'

'I do, but you will need the code for the alarm. It's fifteen fifty-one,' one said, handing a brass secure key to Buchanan.

'Thanks. It shouldn't take long,

Buchanan walked the short distance to the site office entrance. 'This must be where the paramedics treated the victim prior to transporting him to the hospital,' he said, looking at the gunshot medical detritus.

He stood for a moment looking at the ground, then asked the CSI, 'You take plaster casts of the footprints?'

'No. Only the paramedics' and the victim's footprints would be here.'

'Well, I think there may just be one more. If I was the gunman, paid to kill the godfather of Glasgow crime, I'd want to make sure I'd completed my task, wouldn't you?'

'I suppose so.'

'In that case, humour me,' said Buchanan, crouching down at the place where Maxwell had been treated. 'Right, imagine you were standing at the top of the alley, staring down into the dark, waiting for your quarry to come out through that door.' He pointed to the site office door. 'You fired twice, and as a competent marksman, you saw your target wince with the first shot and hit the ground with the second. What would you do?'

'Me, I'd run a mile. I wouldn't want to get caught.'

'The victim told me he clearly saw the gunman standing at the top of the alley, legs apart, both hands on the gun. To me those are the actions of a professional gunman. Someone who knows exactly what they are doing.'

'So, what's your point?'

'If I were the gunman, immediately after firing the second shot and seeing the victim fall, I'd make my way down the alley to make sure that the victim was in fact dead.'

'That makes sense, I think.'

'So, I bet there are footprints in the dirt on the side of the alley. Shall we have a look?'

'Why not?'

Buchanan and the two CSIs walked back up the middle of the alley to Hope Street.

'The victim said he saw the gunman standing about here,' said Buchanan, 'his legs apart, arms outstretched, hands clasped as though he was holding a gun. *Blam, blam*, victim falls, gunman steps sideways against the wall and using the gloom of the building he carefully, gun arm outstretched, ready to fire again, if necessary, carefully makes his way down to the victim.

'Victim is lying on the ground, but not dead. Question – did the gunman check to see if his target is dead, or just pretending? What would you do?'

'Sorry, that line of questioning is out of my area of expertise,' said the shorter of the two CSI's.

'You, what would you do?' asked Buchanan, of the other CSI.

'I'd probably circumscribe the scene and approach the victim from his blind spot, from behind.'

'Remember,' said Buchanan, 'you've just fired two gunshots in quick succession, and the site security floodlight is on.'

'I'd have one eye on the victim and another on the ends of the alley, just in case someone heard the gunshots and had come out to see what was going on.'

'Suppose the victim wasn't working alone and there was a person who opened the door to see what was happening?'

'I'd get the hell out of here.'

'Which direction?'

'Not up the hill, because that would mean passing the victim and whoever had opened the door. I'd make a beeline down the alley.'

'That's what I surmised. Probably past those rubbish bins down there. Shall we have a look inside them just in case the gunman decided to get rid of his gun?'

Still scanning the ground for articles of interest, they arrived at the first bin. The lid was locked, the second bin was more accommodating.

Buchanan swung the heavy lid up while the CSI looked inside.

'They said you were good at your job,' she said, reaching into the bin with her gloved hand, 'now I know where your reputation comes from. This, I presume will be the weapon.' She carefully lifted the 9mm automatic from its position on top of an empty shoe box.

'Thanks, it's mostly luck.'

'Luck, my backside. I'd say you were spot-on with your summation of the facts. The gunman must have been spooked by something or someone and ran down the alley, tried the first bin, found it locked, so tried the other, dumped the gun, then ran off down the alley and out onto West George Street.'

'Excellent, now all we have to do is match the gun with the bullet and we begin to sort out the mystery. Would you take a cast from the footsteps we saw coming down the alley, plus whatever you can get from the scene outside the site office door?'

'OK, and then do you want us to have a look inside the building?'

'Yes, please, but I doubt if you will find much, the building is undergoing a refurbishment following a fire.'

'You know, that probably will have to be another team. The shooting is a case on its own, searching for drugs might jeopardise your case as some smart-ass lawyer might be able to convince the judge and jury that the evidence is contaminated.'

'An excellent point, I should have thought of that. Yes, you are quite correct, we'll have a cursory search and, if we find anything, I'll call in the specialist drug team.'

'In that case, we'll say goodbye. I'll get ballistics to have a look at the gun, where is the bullet?'

'A good question, we need to ask Gus, he was looking after that item.'

They walked back up the alley to where the group of disgruntled carpenters, plumbers and electricians were standing.

'You in charge?' asked one of the carpenters.

'Yes,' replied Buchanan.

'We need to get to work, how long will you be?'

'Not long, just need to have a quick look inside the building.'

'Hmm, it's all right for you, you get paid if you work or not, some of have to earn a living.'

'I tell you what.' said Buchanan, 'why don't you come with me? You can show me round the building.'

'Just me?'

'Yes, shouldn't take us long.'

'What's your name?' asked Buchanan, as they walked down the alley.

'Joseph, I'm the site foreman.'

As Buchanan inserted the key into the lock, he resisted the urge to ask the foreman if his wife's name was Mary.

'You always enter through the site office?' asked Buchanan.

'Just the men, we sign in on that board,' he said, pointing to a list of names on an in-and-out board fastened to the wall beside the outside door. 'Materials go in through the yard at the back.'

The room looked and smelt like a brewery. Plastic pipes of various colours and wires hung from a cable tray fastened to the ceiling. In the middle of the room was a large table with ten chairs and some upturned plastic milk crates with folded sacks acting as cushions.

'This is our mess room, it's where we take our meals and change into our working clothes.'

'How many on site?'

'Six carpenters, three electricians and, depending what is going on, four plumbers.'

'What about bricklayers and plasterers?'

'We don't need them very often, most of the structural work is complete, we're getting into the final fixing stage.'

Forty-five minutes later, Buchanan and Joseph returned to the police cordon.

'Constable, you can take the cordon tape down and these men can all get to work.'

'What now?' asked Gus, as the police and CSI van departed.

'Lunch, I saw a Five Guys down on St Vincent Street as I walked up here this morning.' Buchanan looked at Gray's face, 'Don't worry, Gray, I'm buying.'

'Thanks, I'm a bit skint this month.'

'Thanks, Jack,' said Gray, as he wiped the last of the melted cheese from his mouth. 'I don't remember the last time I had a real burger. I don't know why people buy McDonalds when they could have burgers like these.'

'Price, perhaps?' said Bull.

'You have a point there.'

'Right,' said Buchanan, 'this is not the place to discuss work, so let's grab a coffee and reconvene back in the office.'

♦

'OK, down to business,' said Buchanan, shutting the office door. 'I'll start. What was supposed to be a simple task of investigating the workings of Maxwell's criminal enterprise has turned into a major mess. For a start we have the death of Gallagher, supposedly died of self-inflicted wounds when he fell off his ladder and impaled himself on his chisel. Next, we have the death of McDermott, who according to what Maxwell said to me, stepped back to admire his work and fell seven floors from the scaffolding he was working on and went headfirst through a garage roof. Both deaths were ruled accidental, but my suspicious mind says both were killed by Steve Jameson.

'Next is yours truly, I was almost rundown in my own village, the car driven by Steve Jameson, who, as I said, is also the number one suspect in the deaths of Gallagher and McDermott.

'Then there is the existence of a stepdaughter of Maxwell who is trying to exit this world by hanging herself and then, someone tried to top Maxwell with two 9mm bullets.

'To complicate matters there appears to be some sort of vendetta being carried out on Maxwell by Chief Constable James Anderson, retired.'

'What's that?' asked Gray.

'It was back when Anderson was a DI. He arrested Maxwell for a bonded warehouse robbery where two guards were killed.'

'And did he do the robbery?'

'No, he was in Porters drinking with friends.'

'A perfect alibi,' said Gray.

'Bull, you're tied up in this mess as well.'

'Me, how do you figure that?'

'Your cousin?'

'What's she got to do with this? Wait a minute, are you inferring it was me who took the pot shot at Maxwell? Because let me tell you, if it was me, I'd have made sure the shite was dead.'

'Relax, I'm not inferring anything. I just want all facts to be out on the table.'

'Could Jameson be the gunman who shot Maxwell?' asked Gray.

'I don't think so. His MO is to use a knife, or whatever pointed object comes to hand.'

'So that means there are two killers out there. Who is the second, do you have a suspect?' asked Bull, who by now had cooled down and stopped grinding his teeth.

'Yes, a Dino Volente. He had a record as a teen but cleared off to Spain where he reappeared as a Mafia hitman. His preferred choice of weapon is a gun, he's since been booted out of Spain and come home to cause mayhem here.'

'Disposing of the weapon directly after the hit is typical of how they operate,' said Gus.

'There's one additional person you haven't mentioned that has something against Maxwell,' said Bull.

'Oh, and who might that be?'

'How about yourself? It's common knowledge that you and he have been at odds for years.'

'A good point, but sorry to say, not I.'

'Could it be that Jameson and Volente are working together to oust Maxwell?' asked Gray.

'That, in absence of any other theory, is my impression.'

'Do you think Maxwell knows what is going on, Jack?'

'I'm not sure. When I talked to him yesterday, he gave me the impression he is trying to change direction in life and settle down. He's bought a house in Eastbourne.'

'This doesn't quite make sense to me,' said Gray.

'Welcome to the club,' said Gus.

'Do you have any ideas about what's going on, Jack?' said Bull. 'You've known Maxwell better than any of us.'

'Yes, but I'd like to keep them to myself for now. What I'd like the three of you to do, is to start at the gunshot incident on Hope

Street. It's my gut feeling that someone disturbed the gunman and may be able to give us a description that is more detailed than the one Maxwell gave me.

'Maxwell was shot sometime about seven pm, so it will mean a late night for the three of you. Call me if you uncover anything, otherwise, I'll see you back here in the morning.'

On the way back to the hotel, Buchanan kept going over what Maxwell had said on Tuesday. Did Maxwell know who the gunman was? Would it result in a revenge shooting? If so, who would be on the receiving end, and why hadn't the police properly investigated the shooting? Were they content to leave Maxwell to sort out the problem? After all, what would one more dead gunman matter?

That could be a scenario, it would save the police money and time, and as long as it ended there, the powers that be could just write it down to another random gang death.

What would Joe Jackson do, Buchanan wondered? He'd gone face to face with Arthur Thompson and survived. So, was Buchanan in a similar situation? Maybe not, there was a difference with this situation. Maxwell gave all the impressions of being a spent man. Gone was the arrogance and anger of his earlier years, in fact, he said he was buying a house in Eastbourne. What could be more retiring than that?

20
Bullets and Bombs

Buchanan threw back the bedclothes, got out of bed and glanced out of his bedroom window —it was still raining. He looked over the houses and saw the recent rain had swollen the Cart from a gentle stream to a raging torrent. He'd dropped into bed exhausted the previous evening without calling Karen.

It was then he realised it had been three days since he had talked to Karen. So, before he began his day, he thought he should call her. She answered right away.

'I've been wondering when you were going to call, Everything all right?'

'Yes, except for one particular incident.'

'What's that? Greggs run out of Scots pies, or Starbucks run out of coffee?'

'Now that would be a problem. No, nothing as tragic as that. What happened was someone took a pot-shot at Maxwell on Monday evening.'

'He was shot?'

'Yes, with a 9mm automatic.'

'Is he OK?'

'Yes. I think it would take a greater tragedy than a gunshot to bring him down.'

'What are the local police doing about it?'

'According to Maxwell, not much. He said, as they left the hospital, he could hear them laughing.'

'Really? That doesn't sound like the police I remember from the days when you worked in Glasgow.'

'I've only heard the story from Maxwell.'

'You talked to him?'

'Yes, I had tea with him on Tuesday afternoon.'

'You had someone with you, didn't you?'

'I suppose I did,' he said, remembering the thought he'd had about Daniel in the lion's den. Who'd put that thought in his mind?

'What do you mean by that?'

'Bull and Gray were outside in an unmarked car.'

'Better than nothing I suppose. What will your team be doing today?'

'I sent them out yesterday to look for witnesses to the shooting, hopefully there will be some leads drawn from that to follow up on.'

'Well, I won't keep you from your labours, and next time, don't take three days to call me.'

'I love you, Mrs Buchanan.'

'Love you too, now go get dressed and have your breakfast.'

◆

Buchanan was the first one in the office, he checked the letterbox, there were no messages. He took off his jacket and hung it on the back of the chair, then sat at his desk to read the morning papers and drink his morning Starbucks. Something was odd, there was no mention of the shooting on Hope Street. Surely Maxell being shot didn't warrant a "D" notice, though the alternative didn't make sense either. Maxwell being shot would normally be the headline in the *Daily Record*. Had someone had a quiet word in the *Record's* editor's ear?

He turned to the *Herald* and read about the spiralling list of faults on the two new ferries that were being built at the Ferguson Marine yard on the Clyde in Port Glasgow. The article said that fears had been raised that due to this the two vessels, now overdue for delivery, may never go into service. The article said there still were unresolved problems, and the cost had soared to approximately £240 million pounds, about £40 million over the previous estimate.

He put down the paper, thinking how times had changed. He remembered his father once saying that at its height, the Clyde shipyards employed tens of thousands of workers who made some of the world's fastest, and largest ships, including two Queen Marys, one still sailing, the other now a hotel and conference centre in Long Beach, California.

The shipbuilding industry on the river Clyde had truly been the envy of the world and during the early 1900s it was constructing around a fifth of all ships launched.

He sighed, took a last sip of his coffee, and called Jill.

'Morning boss, how are things in Glasgow?'

'Cold and wet. Have you been able to find out information on Du Marchon's flight schedules?'

'It was quite a task, but yes, I managed to discover he did make regular trips between Headcorn and Strathaven Airfield, that's a small airfield near East Kilbride.'

'So, it is possible he was ferrying drugs from Amsterdam to Maxwell up in Scotland. Well done, Jill.'

'Bit of old news though, since Du Marchon is dead.'

'Nonetheless, it's another piece in the jigsaw that is Maxwell.'

'How is Maxwell today?'

'Not sure yet. When I talked to him on Tuesday, he said he would be back at work this morning.'

'That says something for the man, shot on Monday, back at work on Thursday. Not many people would be prepared to do that.'

'He made light of it, said it was only a flesh wound and was nothing that a glass of whisky and a double dose of paracetamol couldn't take care of. Any joy on your search on local hunts?'

'There are a couple, but due to the issues saboteurs cause, I think they are reticent in putting any real information online.'

'That makes sense.'

'What are you and the boys working on today?'

'Gus, Bull and Gray are out trying to find witnesses to the Maxwell shooting.'

'And you?'

'I'm going to pay a visit to Maxwell at the job site. Hopefully I will be able to appraise him of his situation and get him to realise the danger he is in.'

'I hope you don't mind me saying this, but you sound like you are going a bit soft on him.'

'That could be possible. When I talked to him on Tuesday, I got the impression something had changed in him. I'm not sure what, but he was different, more reflective, not so aggressive as he was the last time, I met him.'

'When was that?'

'That was several years before I came down south. Maxwell had been implicated in the hijacking of a distillery delivery lorry; it had been fully loaded with whisky bound for the bonded warehouse.'

'Is that the case where Anderson was the SIO?'

'Yes. I'd been investigating the Howard clan, as I suspected it was them who did the robbery. But I don't remember meeting Anderson. I had just returned from the Isle of Skye at the time of Maxwell's arrest and only dropped into the station to see if he would assist with information on the Howard clan.'

'Was he forthcoming?'

'What do you think? He would rather be found guilty of a crime he didn't commit than squeal on anyone.'

'The criminal code of honour.'

'Yes, it is what the Mafia call Omertà.'

'What a crazy world we live in. So, what will you say to Maxwell?'

'I will try and impress on him the gunman is a professional and will want to make sure his reputation remains intact.'

'You think the gunman will have another go at killing Maxwell?'

'More than likely.'

'Well, my advice to you is, don't stand too close to Maxwell.'

'Good advice, and I will take it. I've got to go; I hear the boys' voices.'

'Bye, talk to you tomorrow.'

'Morning boss,' said Gus.

'Morning all, how did you do yesterday?'

'We began by going door to door on both sides of Hope Street as far as Renfrew Street,' said Gus. 'Then in the opposite direction to St Vincent Street.'

'Anything to report?' asked Buchanan.

'Nothing of any interest on Hope Street other than a couple of people heard the gunshots, but no sight of the gunman. On St Vincent Street we fared better. Gray, you're on.'

'We found several people who heard the gunshot and one person who saw the gunman.'

'Did he actually see the shooting?'

'No. The witness said he heard the gunshot, went to investigate and as he turned the corner into the alley, he walked straight into the gunman running down it.'

'Description?'

'Unfortunately, not great. It was dark and due to the fact, they were both on the ground in a heap, the description is rather basic. The gunman was described to be Caucasian, about five feet ten in height, slight build, dark straight hair, and clean shaven, wearing tight blue jeans, dark shirt and black hoodie.'

'That could describe half of Glasgow's young men,' said Buchanan. 'Any scars or identifying mannerisms observed?'

'Nope.'

'We scoured the area and didn't find anything of interest,' added Bull.

'That's expected. The gunman is a professional, he would have empty pockets. I expect the clothes he was wearing are now somewhere in a dustbin or charity shop. Did you get the witness's details?'

'Yes, shall I put them in the file?'

'Please.'

'What do you want us to do today?' asked Bull.

'We need to know where young Steve Jameson and Dino Volente have gone to earth. He and Volente were tracked by ANPR all the way from Eastbourne to the East Kilbride Road in Busby. But there has been no sign of them since. What I'd like you and Gray to do, Bull, is to spend the day asking around the Busby and Clarkston area to see if anyone has seen an abandoned car.'

'Sounds like basic police work.'

'You could say the car was stolen and there is a briefcase with important documents in the boot that the owner is desperate to recover. You could hint that the owner is prepared to make a large cash reward for the return of the car and documents.'

'That might work,' said Gray, 'do we have the registration of the car?'

'I don't remember it, but you will find all the car's details in the file.'

'And for me?' said Gus.

'What I'd like you to do is to go through the records and make up a list of known associates of Jameson senior and junior, and their addresses. I doubt if you'll find much on Volente, his record was sealed when he was a teenager.'

'OK, see you later. Oh, where will you be if we need you?'

'I'm going to have a word with Maxwell at his site office on Hope Street.'

Buchanan finished his coffee and picked up his jacket. He was about to open the office door when his phone rang. He looked at the number on the phone's display and grinned, he'd wondered how long it would be before Anderson called.

'Good morning, James, how are you?'

'I'm fine, how is the investigation going? Are you ready to hand over the file to the Procurator Fiscal?'

'Not quite, we're still investigating Maxwell and his associates.'

'What's the issue? I thought you would have enough evidence by now to hang the man. Surely you of all people must realise that Maxwell is guilty of just about every crime under the sun?'

'It's not quite that simple.'

'Simple? What do you mean? All you had to do was watch him and his cronies for a few days and you would have enough evidence to put him away for life.'

'I have competition.'

'You have what?'

'Someone tried to kill Maxwell on Monday evening.'

'They missed, I heard, more's the pity. If they'd succeeded it would have saved us a lot of trouble and the courts the expense of a long and complicated trial, not to mention money.'

'It was a professional hit.'

'I realise that, but never mind, the next time they may be more successful.'

'Do you know something about the shooting that you should be telling me?'

'No, I just heard it through chatter at the club that someone had taken a shot at Maxwell and had missed.'

'Would you mind telling me just who told you?'

'Sorry, the whisky was running a bit freely, someone said something and before I could see who it was, the bar had cleared.'

'Where are you, James?'

'I'm at my club; the Carrick on Wellington Street.'

'If you heard that someone had taken a pot shot at Maxwell, did they happen to say anything else?'

'Such as?'

'A name perhaps?'

'No, no names.'

'You said the killer might try again, why would you say that?'

'The gunman was a professional, he wouldn't want his reputation to be sullied, besides if he's already been paid for the job, whoever contracted him will want value for money spent.'

'That makes sense.'

'Are you actively looking for the gunman?'

'Yes, attempted murder is a crime, no matter who the victim is.'

'Are you going soft, Jack? Why don't you just let the gunman do his job and you can go back to your wife in Eastbourne, and I can go back to life as normal?'

'That is condoning murder.'

'He'd only get what he deserves.'

'I've already started the investigation and I intend to finish it, even if it is the last thing I do.'

'Be careful of what you wish, Jack. That sort of statement would look good on a tombstone. What are you going to do next?'

'I'm going to pay a visit to Maxwell at his building site. When I talked to him on Tuesday, he said he intended to be back at work today, there was a project meeting he had to attend.'

'As I said, be very careful, they may say that lightning doesn't strike the same place twice, but that didn't take into consideration the entity that is Maxwell. How did you find out he'd been shot, Jack?'

'I met with Maxwell on Tuesday; he told me all about the shooting.'

'Was it under caution?'

'No, it was in front of the fire in his living room. Did you know we have similar tastes in whisky?'

'Be careful, Jack. Remember what I said about lightning.'

♦

Buchanan retraced his steps of the previous day and arrived at the Hope Street site office at eleven o'clock. The door was open, and he could hear voices. He knocked and stepped inside.

'Ah, the horse comes to the trough to drink, but will he?' said Maxwell. 'Gentlemen, let me introduce you to Detective Chief Inspector Jack Buchanan, protector of the weak and enforcer of justice. If he ever invites you down a dark alleyway for a quiet chat, make sure your life insurance policy is up to date.'

'That's stretching it a bit, Rab.'

'Really, what about my friends Randal and Shelton? Because of you and you poking your nose into other's business, I lost an excellent lawyer and accountant.'

'They had assaulted a policeman and were attempting to flee the scene of a crime; it was their own stupid fault for running.'

'That is not the story I heard.'

'You weren't there, and I was lying on the floor, unconscious at the time.'

'You want coffee? There's fresh in the pot.'

'Thanks,' he said, holding up his Starbucks cup, 'but I already have one.'

'The eternal Boy Scout, prepared for all eventualities.'

'Aren't you going to introduce me to your friends?'

'Ah, yes. Let me put a face to the names for you. On my left is Toni Benatti, my lawyer, and on my right, someone I think you already know, Andy Jameson, my very able accountant.'

'Andy,' said Buchanan, 'when was the last time you saw young Steve?'

'Weeks ago, why you ask?'

'Just wondering if he's been driving any Golfs lately?'

'No idea what you are talking about.'

'A Golf, little steel box with four wheels and an engine.'

'You're mad, don't you have something more pressing to take care of instead of wasting our time with riddles?'

'Never mind, I'll catch up with him sooner or later.'

'So, Jack, what brings you here?' asked Benatti.

'Just thought I'd see how the patient is doing.'

'I'm doing fine,' said Maxwell. 'Why are you really here?'

Before Maxwell could reply, they were interrupted by a parcel delivery driver.

'Parcel for Maxwell?'

'Drop it by the door,' said Benatti.

Buchanan turned to look and as the driver went to step out of the room, something wasn't right, the hair, the beard, they looked false. Buchanan was troubled, the face, no, it was the eyes, he'd seen them before. Then he remembered the mugshot he'd seen the previous week; it was Volente.

'Quick, get out!' said Buchanan.

'Why?'

'Bomb, that parcel has a bomb in it, don't waste time, get out of here!'

They were twenty feet up the alley when the parcel exploded. Buchanan turned to see the carnage, the wall where the door had stood was now a pile of rubble, and the office door was now implanted in the wall of the building opposite.'

'You saved our lives, said Benatti. 'How can we ever repay you?'

'I'm sure I can think of something, Toni. Everyone OK?'

'I've gone deaf!' shouted Jameson.

'If that's all that happened to you, you got off lightly,' said Buchanan. 'Rab, how are you, how's the shoulder?'

'Shoulder's fine. If I ever get my hands on that shite, he'll wish he had never been born.'

'I suggest the three of you wait up on Hope Street,' said Buchanan. 'How many people working in the building, Rab?'

'Very few if any, it's lunchtime, they're probably all in the bar.'

'Good. Head up to Hope Street, I'll get the emergency services and bomb squad here.'

'Leave it to the police,' said Maxwell. 'They're used to that sort of thing.'

'But I am the police,' said Buchanan.

'Then why didn't you stop the bombing? It could have cost us our lives,' muttered Benatti.

Before Buchanan could dial the emergency services, the wail of approaching fire engines could be heard. Instead of calling the emergency services, Buchanan called Gus.

'Gus, there's a bit of an issue developing here on Hope Street, someone, namely Volente, has just tried to blow up Maxwell and everyone in the building, including me.'

'You, OK?'

'Yes, I'm fine, just a bit of ringing in the ears.'

'What do you want me to do?'

'Would you call Bull and Gray and ask them to join me at Hope Street? The bombing is going to attract all sorts of people and I think we will be quite busy.

He returned his phone to his pocket and walked up the alley to Hope Street to wait the arrival of the others. By the time he reached the top a crowd had begun the congregate and were being herded away by a harried constable.

'Thanks, Constable. DCI Buchanan,' he said, showing his warrant card.

'Are there any injuries, sir?'

'No, thank God. All safe and accounted for, just a few bricks out of place.'

'Is that Rab Maxwell?' he said, nodding to the group of three who moments before had been discussing the work being done on the building.'

'It is indeed.'

'I've heard of him, but never met him. I hear he's a very dangerous man.'

'That's what I've heard. But right now, I think he has more pressing items on his agenda than planning his next piece of skulduggery.'

'Jack,' said Gus as he made his way through the crowd, 'are you all right?'

'I'm fine, we got out minutes before it blew.'

'What happened? I know a bomb went off, but you were there, did you see anything?'

'I saw Dino Volente place the bomb on the table by the door. I was too busy getting everyone out of the building to see which way he went.'

'You are sure it was Volente?'

'Absolutely. He was wearing a wig and false beard but couldn't disguise his eyes.'

'Probably be miles away by now.'

'What happened?' Asked Bull, who had just arrived with Gray.

'Someone tried to blow Maxwell into the next world.'

'Any injuries?'

'Just a bit of earache for Benatti.'

'Any suspicions as to who did it?'

'I don't need a suspicion; I saw Volente plant the bomb.'

Further discussion was prevented by the arrival of the bomb squad. The leader walked over to the uniformed constable to enquire what had taken place. The constable shook his head and pointed at Buchanan.

'Excuse me, sir, the constable said you know what happened?'

'Yes, a bomb was placed in the room on the left down the alley and detonated within two minutes of being placed.'

'Any injuries?'

'No, just ringing in the ears.'

'And you saw the bomb being planted?'

'Yes.'

'We'll need your details for the investigation.'

'That's fine. But I am already in charge of the investigation. I was questioning the occupants of the room prior to the bomb exploding.'

'You were very fortunate you got out in time.'

'That's what I thought; that bomb was meant to kill.'

'Thank you, sir. If you wouldn't mind staying up here while we check out the damage?'

'Jack,' said Gus. 'Just had a thought, do you think the bombing was meant to include you?'

'That is a possibility if my movements were known.'

'Who knew you would be here this morning?'

'Jill, my partner back in Eastbourne, then there are the three of you, and Anderson.'

'How did Anderson know you would be there?'

'I told him. He called earlier; he even warned me about getting too close to Maxwell.'

'There he is again, back in the limelight. Are you sure we can trust Anderson?'

'I'm beginning to wonder.'

'What do you want to do with the three stooges?'

'Where did you hear that name?'

'That was my granddad. When I used to stay with my grandparents, I'd spend hours watching the movies with him.'

'I think we should have them down at the station to give statements. I doubt the station is a foreign land to any of them.'

♦

'I expect you may be finding this a bit strange, Mr Bonetti,' said Buchanan. 'I'll bet it's not every day you are in a police station making a statement.'

'Are you trying to be funny?'

'No, just making a comment.'

'Well, get on with it, I don't have all day.'

'Tell me what happened today in the office?'

'Why ask me? You were there, you saw it all.'

'For the record, would you tell me what caused you to be distracted from what you were doing at that moment?'

'A delivery driver stepped into the office and said he had a package for Rab.'

'Rab being Robert Maxwell?'

'Yes.'

'Did you recognise the delivery driver?'

'No.'

'How would you describe the driver?'

'White, about five feet nine, slight build, dark curly hair, ugly beard, wearing jeans, dark shirt and yellow site coat.'

'Was there anything written on the coat?'

'Don't remember.'

'Did he say anything?'

'Something about a delivery, don't remember exactly what he said.'

'What about his voice, anything of note, like his accent?'

'Sounded sort of foreign, yet it was definitely a Glasgow accent.'

'Was there anything else that stood out about the driver?'

'No.'

'Thank you, Mr Benatti. Would you ask Mr Jameson to come in now, please?'

'Toni said you wanted to talk to me,' said Andy Jameson, holding a tobacco pouch in readiness to roll a cigarette.

'Please sit, Mr Jameson. And, ah, you aren't allowed to smoke in here.'

Jameson finished rolling his cigarette and placed it behind his ear.

'So, what do you want to know?'

'Tell me what you can recall about the events in the office today?'

'You were there, why are you asking me?'

'For the record, would you tell me what caused you to be distracted from what you were doing at that moment?'

'I was looking at our financial spreadsheets when a delivery driver entered the office.'

'Did you recognise him?'

'No.'

'How would you describe the driver?'

'White, about five feet nine, wiry build, dark curly hair, scraggy beard, wearing jeans, and yellow site coat.'

'Was there anything written on the coat?'

'Ah, that was odd, it said Taggarts.'

'Was there something significant about that?'

'Yes, Taggarts are our competition. I thought it was some sort of ruse to see what we were up to. Then you shouted to us to get out of the office.'

'Do you remember the driver saying anything?'

'Something about a delivery for Rab.'

'What about an accent.'

'A mix of Scots and Italian.'

'Would you say it was more Italian or Scottish?'

'Couldn't say.'

'Was there anything else that stood out about the driver?'

'Yes, I didn't hear any vehicle pass the door.'

'Maybe he walked down the alley, like I presume you did.'

'Ah, yes, that makes sense. We always have that issue with deliveries.'

'Thank you, Mr Jameson. Would you ask Mr Maxwell to come in now, please? And if you still wish to smoke, I believe there is an area set aside for that purpose just outside the entrance.'

'Thanks.'

'Good morning, Mr Maxwell.'

'What's all this mister stuff, Buchanan?'

'A formality when taking witness statements, Mr Maxwell.'

'Well, get on with it. Who knows how much this morning's incident will set the project back.'

'I'm sorry to say that until the site investigation is complete, the area will remain a crime scene and be out of bounds to you and your men.'

'How long will that take? I have deadlines to meet, wages to pay and the bank to keep off my back.'

'I'm sorry, I am unable to answer that question.'

'What's your first query?'

'Tell me what happened in the office today?'

'Why are you asking me that? You were there, you saw what we all saw.'

'For the record, would you tell me what you were doing at the moment you were distracted?'

'I was talking to you.'

'And what caused you to interrupt your conversation?'

'A delivery driver stepped into the office and said he had a package for me.'

'Did you recognise him?'

'No.'

'How would you describe the driver?'

'White, about five feet nine, slight build, dark curly hair, straggly beard, jeans, dark shirt and yellow site coat.'

'Was there anything written on the coat?'

'Taggarts.'

'Is there any significance in the driver wearing a site coat with the word Taggart on the back?'

'I thought the shites were snooping on us.'

'Why would you think that?'

'We're in direct competition with them for government contracts.'

'Do you think they would go as far as planting a bomb in your office?'

Maxwell shook his head. 'No, I've known old Jamie Taggart for thirty years, he'd never do a thing like that.'

'That's good to know.'

'Is that all?'

'Yes, thank you.'

'So, who was the shite that tried to wipe us out of existence today?'

'I'm sorry, I'm not at liberty to discuss the case with you at this time.'

'But you do know who he is, don't you? I can see it in your face.'

'I'm sorry, Rab, I can't say anything that might jeopardise the investigation. What I can say is if you wish we can provide police protection for you. I can arrange for a patrol car to be outside your gate till the matter is resolved.'

'I'd be a prisoner in my own house, humph, how ironic is that?'

'You, Mr Bonetti, and Mr Jameson are free to go, thank you for your cooperation.'

'Just a whisper, no one will know you said anything. You know who it is, I can see it in your face. Give me the name and he won't be placing bombs anymore.'

'You know I can't do that. To do as you suggest would be tantamount to signing his death warrant.'

'He's a dead man walking. I'll find him and if it's the last thing I do, he will live long enough to regret it.'

'Good day, Rab, take care.'

♦

'What do you think, Jack?' asked Gus. 'The gunman and the bomber the same person?'

'I'd say that's most likely.'

'But what do you think is really going on?

'I've been giving a great deal of thought to that. As I see it, there are two strands to what is happening. Strand one is someone is trying to even a score with Maxwell, a personal vendetta.'

'And the other scenario?'

'A palace coup. Someone within the organisation is trying to take over the reins.'

'And do you have a suspect in the first scenario?'

'The obvious one is Anderson, but I don't quite see him as the head of an assassination squad, so why would he be behind the attempts? Don't forget we have the deaths of Gallagher and McDermott in this equation. Also, remember the failed attempt to convict Maxwell on trumped-up charges, and the subsequent embarrassment of Maxwell going free.'

'But why would Anderson have you investigate Maxwell? What possible motive could he have? Maybe he had some sort of emotional connection with Randal and Shelton, and he is trying to kill two birds with one stone, or could it be three birds? What have you done to cause him to want you included in the mess?'

'I do remember something. Back a few years ago, just after the Randal and Shelton incident, I was recovering in hospital and Anderson came to see me and went on about his so-called unblemished record and his imminent retirement.'

'That's reason enough in some people's eyes.'

'That is creating more questions and is taking us away from what we're supposed to be working on, Gus.'

'The second scenario, who could be behind that?'

'The obvious ones would be Steve Jameson and Dino Volente.'

21

Maxine

'Good morning, how are you, sleep well?'

'What do you think? A huge bed and only me in it.'

'I'll be home soon, just as soon as this case is over.'

'Are you getting anywhere with it?'

'It's still a mess, too many questions without answers.'

'Will you still be able to go and see your parents tomorrow?'

'Yes, as long as nothing else blows up.'

'Anything else? Jack, just what do you mean by, *as long as nothing else blows up?*'

'Yesterday, someone tried to blow Maxwell up with a parcel bomb.'

'At least you were nowhere near when it happened.'

'Well …'

'Well, what? Are you about to say you were there when the explosion happened?'

'Not quite, we were all outside in the alley before the bomb went off.'

'Was anyone hurt?'

'No. I got them all out before the bomb went off.'

'OK, I'm sitting down, what exactly happened?'

'I went to the site where Maxwell was working and went into the building site office. The site office is off an alley in the basement of a bar on Hope Street. Maxwell was holding a project meeting, or so he said, with his lawyer, Toni Benatti, and Andy Jameson, the accountant. I had barely been introduced when we were interrupted by the delivery of a parcel. Benatti said to place it on the table by the door. I turned to look and immediately recognised the delivery man.'

'Did anyone else recognise him?'

'No, he was wearing a bright yellow work coat, wig and false beard.'

'So how did you recognise him?'

'The eyes, no matter what you do with the face and hair, the eyes are very difficult to disguise.'

'And you're all, right?'

'Yes, I'm perfectly all right.'

'I do wish…'

'That I was retired?'

'I'm sorry, I shouldn't burden you with my fears when you are involved in a case.'

'I'll be fine. I've got Gus, Bull and Gray looking after me.'

'How is Gray working out?'

'Fine. He and his uncle work well together.'

'Bull and Gray, sounds like the title of a television detective show. You know, you should write your autobiography, lots of retired policemen write their autobiographies. Just think of all those cases you've worked on and all those interesting people you have worked with.'

'Don't forget the ones I put away.'

'Of course, they would also have to be included.'

'I'll think about it. But, in the meantime, I have this case to resolve. There's still the forensic evidence to review. We're also still looking for Steve Jameson and Dino Volente.'

'Is Jameson the one who tried to run you down on the Westham High Street?'

'That's the rascal.'

'So, there's been no sight of him?'

'Not Jameson, but I did meet Volente yesterday.'

'Where?'

'In Maxwell's office. Volente delivered the package that contained the bomb. Pity he managed to get away down the alley.'

'Jack, please be careful, you're the only husband I have.'

'That, my lovely wife, I am eternally grateful for.'

'Now you're making fun of me.'

'I love you, Mrs Buchanan, but I do have to get to work.'

'Will you still have time to see your mum and dad tomorrow?'

'Yes, Mum is expecting me for lunch.'

'Church on Sunday, you know how your dad feels?'

'As long as I'm not busy.'

'Will Matthew be there?'

'More than likely. I'll give you a call tomorrow morning.'

'Please, I miss you.'

'Miss you too, bye for now.'

◆

Coffee in hand, Buchanan walked down Buchanan Street towards the office. He was trying to make sense of what was going on. Was Anderson really behind the shooting and bombing? If he was, what exactly did he stand to gain from his actions? Taking over the Maxwell enterprise would certainly bring him riches beyond his pension and whatever else he derived income from. It would also bring him notoriety and he would probably be ostracised by his friends and family. It would also mean always looking over his shoulder to see whether it was another gang or the authorities out to get him.

On the other hand, if he was on the side of the angels, and Buchanan was able to finally get Maxwell put away, and his gang out of business, it would certainly be a feather in Anderson's cap, it might even lead to a knighthood.

Buchanan could see it now, Anderson at six feet two, kneeling in front of the King and hearing the words, "Rise, Sir James Anderson". What a farce this whole business was. But there was an air of reality to this scenario.

As he got closer to the office, he came to the conclusion that Jameson and Volente were the real issue. In Buchanan's mind he had Volente as the gunman and the bomber. So, if Jameson and

Volente were out to take the reins of the Maxwell fiefdom, would Jameson senior and Benatti go along with the plan?

No, probably not. The issue would be with Jameson senior, he probably wouldn't think much of the idea of his son's partner blowing them into kingdom come. This definitely would be something to be discussed at the morning briefing.

As had become part of his morning ritual, Buchanan checked the post box, no post. He parked himself at his desk and called Jill.

'Morning Jack, much going on?' asked Street.

'Not much, unless you consider the fact that someone tried to blow Maxwell to pieces yesterday.'

'You're, OK?'

'Yes, I'm fine.'

'That's good to hear, what about Maxwell, did he get hurt?'

'No, that man leads a charmed life. Shot at and bombed all in a week.'

'So, do you believe that Jameson and Volente are out to take over the Maxwell empire?'

'Yes, but there may be another twist to the tale that we're have not yet considered.'

'What's that?'

'It's possible what we are looking at is an old-fashioned turf war between the Howard clan and Maxwell's gang. The Howard clan has been in competition with Maxwell for years. They've had run-ins with each other many times.'

'Could it be that Jameson and Volente are working with the Howard clan to get rid of Maxwell?'

'That is one scenario we so far haven't considered, and it does have an element of sense when you consider all that is going on.'

'What about the deaths of Gallagher and McDermott?'

'They're still pieces of the jigsaw that we need to find a place for.'

'What do you want me to do today?'

'How are your fingers?'

'They were fine this morning when I rubbed in my hand lotion, why?'

'Would you like to do some random searches on the internet for me?'

'Yes, anything in particular?'

'Could you run a search on all the names in involved in this case? You could also try the PNC and see what comes up. Let your imagination run wild. If anything, major pops up, call me, otherwise I'll talk to you in the morning.'

'Er, Stephen and I are spending the day with his parents tomorrow, then we're going to go to Brighton and shop for the baby.'

'Oh, in that case, I'll talk to you this evening.'

'Bye for now.'

While he waited for his team to arrive, he let his mind run wild with the idea of Jameson and Volente being hit men for the Howard clan. Of all the ideas that they had considered, this one had never come up for consideration. It did make some sense, though the deaths of Gallagher and McDermott didn't quite fit the scenario. Also, the fact Jameson had tried to run Buchanan down on Westham High Street was something that required further thought.

'Morning, boss,' said Bull, as he and Gray walked into the office and closed the door behind them.

Buchanan looked up and smiled, it looked like they had picked up his morning habit of stopping at Starbucks for a coffee.

'Morning, guys. As soon as Gus gets here, there is something I would like to put to you for your consideration.'

'You're not giving up on the case, are you?' asked Gray.

'Certainly not. It's just I think I've finally figured out what is going on and I would like to run my ideas past you.'

'What's going on?' asked Gus who, like the other two, sported a large Starbucks coffee in his hand.

'Right, now we're all here, why don't you sit, and I will go over my ideas. Up to now we've been looking in the wrong place for the wrong thing.'

'Shouldn't that be, the right thing in the wrong place?' said Gray.

'Good try, Gray. But, no, I think we've been looking for the wrong motives in the wrong places.'

'Does that mean we have to start from the beginning again?' asked Bull.

'Any of you do jigsaw puzzles?' asked Buchanan.

'I do with my gran,' said Gray.

'What's the first thing you do when doing a jigsaw puzzle?'

'Empty the pieces out and look for all the edges, and more importantly, first find the corner pieces.'

'But, before you do any of that, what do you do?'

'Look at the picture to see if it looks interesting.'

'Ever start a puzzle and realise the picture on the box isn't the same as the puzzle you are working on?'

'Now I get you. We have all the correct pieces but the wrong picture.'

'Give that man a banana.'

'I like bananas,' said Gray, smiling while pulling his shoulders back and sitting up straight.

'We've been doing the right puzzle with the wrong picture. We've been trying to connect Anderson to Maxwell and this I believe is a red herring. I've given a lot of thought to Anderson's involvement and I think he's just out to put a feather in his cap, cement his legacy as a successful law enforcer. I imagine getting Maxwell put away for a long time would add substantially to his legacy. It will be his valedictorian. Anderson will be able to crow about it and I'm sure he imagines that a knighthood will be in the works.'

'That shite,' said Bull. 'He is asking us to risk a midnight swim in the Clyde, just for his vanity. As far as I'm concerned, he can go and…'

'Calm down, Bull, no one is going for a midnight swim in the Clyde.'

'So, if this is all about Anderson, what about the deaths of Gallagher and McDermott? Where do they fit in to this scenario?'

'That is the last piece of the jigsaw that needs to be placed. It is my belief that, as I just said, Anderson wants us to put Maxwell away. What he didn't figure on was a growing turf war between the Howard clan and Maxwell. I believe that Steve Jameson and Dino Volente are the key to understanding this mystery.'

'That makes sense, now you put it that way,' said Gus. 'Other than the bit about Gallagher and McDermott, they must fit in somewhere, but where? That is the question.'

'Good, then I think we'll take this as our working hypothesis. To that end, Gus, you still working unhindered? No one leaning on you to break off your enquiries?'

'Not so far. I think upstairs will be quite happy if we can manage to bag Maxwell and his cohorts.'

'In that case, Gus, would you check with forensics and see if they have anything for us on the shooting and bombing?'

'Will do.'

'Bull and Gray. I would like you to do the rounds of the Howard bars. See if anyone is willing to talk. While you are doing that, I'm going to have a word with Maxwell, maybe now he will show me the last piece of the jigsaw.'

'That might be awkward,' said Bull. 'We don't usually drink in bars that are frequented by gang members, just in case some enterprising thug decides to take a swing at us to prove a point.'

'You're retired, you could say you wanted to show your young nephew round your old hunting grounds.'

'That sort of works. C'mon Gray, it's not every day you get paid to go on a bar crawl.'

Buchanan sat for a moment and thought about what he was about to do. Should he call first or just show up at the Maxwell residence? Calling first made more sense.

♦

'Maxwell residence, how can I help?'

'Yes, could I speak to Mr Maxwell, please?'

'I'm sorry, Mr Maxwell isn't taking calls just now. Would you like to leave a message?'

'Yes, would you say that Jack Buchanan called, and would like to talk to Mr Maxwell at his earliest convenience?'

'Thank you, Mr Buchanan. I'll see that Mr Maxwell gets your message. Does he have your phone number?'

'Yes, I'm sure he has my number, but just in case he doesn't, let me give you it again.'

Does he have my number, mused Buchanan as he hung up. He was sure every thug and cutthroat and criminal had his number. It must have taken all of three minutes to relay the message to Maxwell for as Buchanan took the last sip of his coffee, his phone rang.

'You wanted to talk to me?'

'Good morning, Rab. How are you today? No ill effects from yesterday?'

'What are you after?'

'Some of your time. I thought I would just like to stop in after work this evening.'

'What time?'

'Say about six-thirty.'

'Here at the house?'

'Might be better for my reputation and yours.'

'OK. When you get here, ring the bell and Carl will let you in.'

'See you this evening,' replied Buchanan.

He hung up from the call with a smile on his face. That was easier than he'd thought, and it was the right thing to do because to meet at the Busby Hotel would be out of Maxwell's safe environment, he would stand out like a spare bride at a wedding. While at home, he would be more inclined to talk without fear of being overheard, and any indiscretions would be denied –with witnesses if necessary.

Buchanan looked at the time: 11:30. Plenty of time to walk up to Hope Street and see if the search of Maxwell's site office was ongoing or now complete; and of course, on the way back, he could stop at Five Guys for a burger for lunch.

As can happen sometimes in life, events can be stranger than fiction. The blue and white tape was still in place across the alley leading to where the bomb had blown up. Two policemen were currently standing guard outside where the door had once been.

Buchanan looked down the alley, then turned to two men standing by the tape.

'What's happened?'

'Did ye no hear? It was a bomb.'

'I thought the *Record* said it was a gas leak?'

'The *Record* ? What does the shite newspaper know? I was in the army, and I say it was a bomb that did that. If it was gas, where's the gas board engineers?

'You have a point there.'

'I'll see you doon the *Grouse an Pheasant*, Tam, remember you owe me a pint?' said one of the men.

Being in civilian clothes Buchanan thought he'd not introduce himself, instead he began by asking if the remaining man knew what had happened.

'Someone tried to send Maxwell into the next world.'

'I've been away from Glasgow for a while, which Maxwell are you referring to?'

'You have not heard of Rab Maxwell? He practically runs Glasgow.'

'Is he the mayor?'

'You really have been away, and you've never heard of Rab Maxwell?'

'If he's he the gangster, I've heard of him.'

'If he's the gangster? If you really knew him, you wouldn't call him that.'

'What should I call him? That is if I ever get to meet him.'

'Depends on why you are meeting him in the first place.'

'Suppose I was looking for a job and wasn't concerned what I had to do to get paid?'

'What are you good at?'

'Depends what sort of work is going on, I'm quite handy with my hands,' said Buchanan, showing his palms.'

'Boxing?'

'I've done a bit.'

'Enjoy it?'

Buchanan grinned and said, 'Only when I win the fight.'

'What do you do?'

'Me, I'm a security advisor, I work for a company that provides protection services, and you?'

'I fix things before they are broken. You say you're in the protection business, what sort of protection?'

Buchanan smiled to himself, he thinks we're both in the same business and he's checking to see if I am a threat to him.

'We keep undesirable elements away from where they don't belong.'

'You use force to provide this service?'

'When necessary.'

'Ever had to use this force yourself?'

'That was part of the reason I got sent down south. An altercation in a bar, this scar on my face,' said Buchanan, pointing to the scar left when Maxwell's former lawyer, Randal, slashed him across the face with his ring. 'Two men died; I was hospitalised. I'd become an embarrassment to the organisation. To keep the peace, I was relocated.'

'Who do you work for?'

'I'd rather not say, don't want to cause a fuss. You see, I'm not supposed to be back up here. If word got out, things could turn real nasty for a few people I could name but chose not to. The incident is still under investigation, so I'm quite shy about attracting the attention of the police.'

'I understand. You been inside?'

'Barlinnie to Parkhurst, only the finest.'

'Aren't you worried about being lifted for breaking your parole?'

'I've done my time, I'm a free man.'

'Well, you're too late if you are looking for work here.'

'Why?'

'That was Maxwell's office down there. I hear he's really angry, the explosion was the final straw.'

'I heard the Howard clan were behind it.'

The man shook his head. 'Not their style. They spit in your face as they stick the knife in your guts, never bombs.'

'Then who's behind the bombing? And I hear there was a shooting earlier in the week?'

The man looked around, leaned forward and almost whispered, 'The word on the street is that the Mafia are trying to takeover.'

'Really? I thought that sort of thing only happened in the movies?'

'You've been away too long, man. If I was you, I'd go back to where you came from.'

'Thanks, I'll think I'll take your advice.'

Interesting, thought Buchanan as he made his way along Hope Street. The local underworld sees the shooting and bombing as the work of the Mafia, could there be anything in that story?

Shootings and bombings were certainly trademarks of the Mafia, but in Glasgow that was stretching things a bit far, but interesting, nonetheless.

♦

Buchanan returned to the office to find Gus was on the phone.

'Will do, he's just come in, goodbye.'

'Tell me what?' asked Buchanan.

'That was forensics, they found the detonator for the bomb. Said it was a typical Mafia device.'

'That is worrying. It's something we hadn't considered. If their Mafia are involved, it would be like rats invading the hen house. What do you think of that, Gus, Mafia involvement?'

Gus shook his head. 'I doubt they'd be involved directly, what we have seen and experienced is more like a contract killing with materials and logistics provided by the Mafia or a similar organisation.'

'So, we're back to local actors in this charade, with possible support from the Mafia?'

'Looks that way,' said Gus.

'Anything else from forensics?'

'No prints on the gun as expected, but they did manage to get a DNA sample from the gloves.'

'How did they link the gloves with the shooting? There must be many of those blue work gloves in the bin from the building works?'

'Not so, apparently all the site rubbish is in different bins round the back of the building. There was also matching oil from the gun found on the gloves.'

'So, we have a DNA sample of the gunman, any match with records?'

'No, but there is a DNA match with a sample found on the detonator of the bomb.'

'Excellent, it's just as we surmised, gunman and bomber are the same individual.'

'Then we are back looking for Jameson and Volente as the main suspects, but are they working for the Howard group against Maxwell, or is it a bit of private enterprise?'

'There is still the possibility they are working for Anderson,' said Gus.

Buchanan shook his head. 'I'm starting to think that scenario is the least of the options. Anything else from forensics?'

'They said the bomb was meant to maim and kill, not intended to blow the doors off the office.'

'Very good, but a misquote. I think the Michael Caine line in the movie called *The Italian Job* was "you were only supposed to blow the doors off".'

'Yeah, now that you mention it, that's how I remembered it too.'

'Shall we get back to work?'

'Yes, certainly. I was going to add that the CSI's, along with forensics, were able to identify several sets of fingerprints on various items in the site office. When checked they were able to identify those of Maxwell, Jameson senior, Benatti, Jameson junior and one other. Those fingerprints were found on a flick knife. The prints didn't belong to any of the others in the office.'

'Could they be Jameson's?'

'Possibly, the initials on the wooden handle of the knife say DV4SJ.'

'Could it be a present from Dino Volente to Steve Jameson?'

'Most likely. That's what I thought.'

'Doesn't prove anything though. Jameson may have borrowed it and left it behind.'

'There were blood traces on the blade and when checked the blood matched the DNA of the bomber and gunman.'

'I don't see Jameson junior being the bomber. I distinctly recognised Volente when he placed the bomb, and if that is the case, we can safely assume they are working together.'

'But for who?'

'Maybe I will ask that question when I go to see Maxwell this afternoon. We've agreed I will stop in on the way home this evening.'

'Will you tell him about your suspicions?'

'No, I don't think that will be helpful, especially if he gets his hands on either Jameson or Volente before we do.'

'Makes sense.'

'Have you heard from Bull and Gray yet?'

'No, have you?'

'No, nothing.

'Anything new?'

'Yes, when I went to look at Maxwell site office there was a police presence guarding the site, and I got talking to one of the lookers on. I didn't say I was the police but let them believe I was a recent resident of Parkhurst. He gave me the impression he was either a Maxwell or Howard supporter, and in a whisper confided in me he thought it was most likely a Mafia hit as the Howard clan would rather stick you with a knife than blow you up.'

'Interesting, shall I call Bull and see if he's got anywhere with their bar crawl?'

Buchanan stood by the window while Gus called Bull.

'Alright see you in a minute.'

'They're coming here?' asked Buchanan.

'Yes. Bull sounded a bit pissed.'

'I'm not surprised, it's not every day you get paid to go on a bar crawl.'

Ten minutes later the office door opened, and a rather happy Bull and Gray stumbled into the office.

'I hope neither of you are driving home this evening?' said Buchanan.

'No, no driving,' said Bull.

'We're taking the train,' said Gray.

'Well, if you're sober enough to speak, what did you find out?'

'Mostly ill-informed nonsense about how Jack Howard is out to take over the Maxwell empire. One said Maxwell is getting soft, another person even said Maxwell had cancer and was dying. All beer-fogged thinking,' said Bull.

'Thanks, and it might be better if the two of you went off home and sobered up a bit. I'm off to see Maxwell.'

♦

Buchanan stepped off the train at Busby, pulled his collar up, and his hat brim down against the late afternoon drizzle and began his walk towards Field Road, Busby House and his nemesis, Rab Maxwell.

Buchanan rang the bell and waited in the drizzle, hoping his wait wouldn't be long.

'Maxwell residence.'

'Yes, Jack Buchanan to see Rab Maxwell.'

'One moment, Mr Buchanan.'

The main gate lock buzzed, a black Audi drove slowly out and down Field Road. Buchanan shrugged and stepped through the open gate and waited for the arrival of his escort, Ivan.

He didn't have to wait long for just as the Audi's taillights disappeared into the evening gloom, the bulk that was Ivan appeared.

'Good afternoon, Mr Buchanan, if you wouldn't mind?'

Buchanan spread his arms and permitted Ivan to pat him down,

'Thank you. Now, if you will accompany me, I'll take you to Mr Maxwell.'

As he walked in silence alongside Ivan, Buchanan tried to puzzle out why this charade was going on. Why not meet in the back room of Porters bar? That was where Maxwell usually conducted his business. Why the pleasantries, the escort, just what was going on?

They were met at the door by Carl. 'Good evening, Mr Buchanan, Mr Maxwell is waiting for you in the sitting room. If you will follow me, please?'

If this was a windup thought Buchanan, it was one magnificent one.

'In here, Mr Buchanan,' said Carl, opening the door. 'Mr Buchanan, sir.'

Maxwell was standing in front of the sideboard.' Ah, Jack, glad you were able to make it. A drink before dinner?'

'Thanks, Rab, whisky please. I hadn't realised I was invited to dinner.'

'Sheila's out this evening, and I don't like eating alone.'

'I'd be delighted, thanks,' replied Buchanan, enjoying the madness of the moment.

'I hope you like fish, Carl is preparing a particularly fine line-caught salmon for us.'

'Salmon will be fine.'

'Shall we sit by the fire? The two of us standing in the middle of the room is a bit too formal; dinner will be served at seven.'

'OK.'

Buchanan watched as Maxwell sat and adjusted the pillows behind his back.

'The doctor said it would hurt for a while; he certainly wasn't wrong. Now, what do I owe to the pleasure of your visit?'

'You've got me there, Rab. I just wanted to have a chat and see how you were doing.'

'As an opening gambit, I'll concede a piece to you.'

'I didn't know you played chess.'

'There's probably a great deal you don't know about me, in spite of our run-ins over the years. How many has it been?'

'I've been a cop for the last thirty-five or so, and our first encounter was the off-licence in Cathcart.'

'Hmm, I remember that one, what a screw-up that was. Jimmy was supposed to be waiting round in the lane with the van, only he was waiting on the other side of the station. I had to drop the lot and high tail it through the tenement close and out into the yard. If it wasn't for the washing line catching me under the chin, I would have got clean away on that caper.'

'You were more successful with the cinema takings. If I remember correctly, you robbed the office just before the end of the movie and handed the takings out through the lavatory window to, who was it, Danny Samson?'

'It turned out it was only pennies. The manager was skimming the till and had already pocketed most of the money.'

'Not a very successful thief in those days, were you?'

'I was only in my early twenties then.'

'So you were, but that didn't stop you from moving on to jewel robberies. Remember the one you pulled off in the Argyle Arcade? If my memory serves me well, you got away with fifteen grand's worth of jewels.'

'We only got half the value, and once again the jeweller was on the take, he pocketed two rings and a brooch that we dropped on the way out. The reason I know that was because he fenced them with Tommy the Greek, the same fence we used. I got my own back though.'

'How did you do that? I never heard that story.'

'Another whisky?'

'Yes, please,' said Buchanan. As he waited for Maxwell to pour his drink, he took out his phone and put it on silent. This evening of all, he didn't want to be disturbed.

Maxwell got up from his chair, grimaced, then walked over to the sideboard and returned with the bottle of whisky and jug of water. He sat, adjusted the pillow, poured Buchanan and himself a large whisky and water, then continued with his story.

'You ask how I got revenge on the jeweller; well, I did a deal with Tommy. I made him tell the jeweller that the rings and brooch only made a few hundred as they were too hot to put out onto the market.'

'Was that when you began your, what shall I call it, building and contents insurance service?'

'That's good, I should have thought of calling it that. Yes, that's when I went into the protection service.'

The conversation was interrupted by Carl coming into the room. 'Excuse me sir, but dinner is ready to be served in the dining room.'

'Thank you, Carl, we'll be right through. Ready, Jack? Bring your glass, I'll bring the bottle.'

Buchanan wasn't prepared for what he was about to partake in. He had imagined a typical family table setting. What he saw was a table set for two and as he sat, he saw his place setting was for a four-course meal.

'Do you always eat this grandly?'

'Today is Sheila's birthday, but she had to rush off to the hospital to be with her mother, so you were the ideal candidate to share dinner with.'

'In some circumstances it could be quite a humorous event, me sharing your wife's dinner with you. How is Sheila's mother?'

'It's her knees, she was waiting for a surgery date to have new knees, but she fell over last week and broke her hip. The surgeon was having difficulties making up his mind whether to do the hip or the knees first.'

'The hip makes the most sense to me.'

'That's what the surgeon finally agreed, he's doing the operation this evening. Sheila's gone to be there for her mother when she comes out of the operation.'

'Aging parents can be a worry. Thankfully mine are still fit and mobile.'

'Will you visit them while you are here?'

'Yes. As long as nothing blows up this evening, I'll be spending the day with them tomorrow.'

'Then let's drink to you spending the day with your parents and I with my wife.'

'Soup this evening is Mediterranean vegetable,' interrupted Carl. 'Soup OK for you, Jack?'

'Sounds fine to me,' said Buchanan, as he buttered his bread.

'You missed me on the train robbery,' said Maxwell, as he put down his soup spoon.

'That was your foray into the adult crime world. I seem to remember the *Herald* said forty thousand pounds was taken.'

'Thirty-nine thousand. We thought there would only be about fifteen, had a nightmare trying to hide the stuff. Thankfully it was all used notes bound for the incinerator so there was no record of the serial numbers.'

'You pulled that job more than once if I remember.'

'Only once more, Jack Howard got wind of what we were doing and decided to copycat us.'

'That was most unfortunate for him. We had anticipated there was going to be a robbery and he and his cohorts got caught on his first attempt,' said Buchanan.

'I decided robbing mail trains was getting too risky, so I diversified into running off-licences.'

'With the proceeds of lorry hijackings, if my memory serves me well. We busted three of your off-licences.'

'Yes, but I still had four running, you never got them, did you?'

'No, but we did get you in your betting scams when you paid certain jockeys not to win when they should have.'

'That's not true, it was the dog racing we fixed.'

'When did you get into money laundering?'

'It was an idea I got when we had so much untraceable cash. At first, we operated quietly under the radar. We had someone who travelled regularly to the continent, he would take the UK cash with him and return with franks, marks, kroner, whatever he could change without attracting to much interest from the excise man.'

'Why did you become involved in drugs?'

'Ah, the coup de grâce question. I'll tell you. At first it was quite a harmless enterprise. We sold pot in clubs and bars. As far as we knew, it was harming no one. Hell, I even tried it myself. When cocaine appeared, I just thought it was like pot, and when I saw the money to be made supplying the high earners, I jumped in with both feet.'

'Did you get supplies flown in?'

'Yes.'

'By someone called Du Marchon?'

'How the hell did you know that?'

'I saw his body after it was dredged up from the English Channel.'

'So that's what happened to him.'

'Was he also involved in the money laundering?'

'Yes.'

'How about smack, you deal in that?'

'For a while, but we made more from cocaine.'

'I'm getting the impression you no longer deal in drugs.'

'When fentanyl became widely available, and I saw what it did to people, I got out of drugs completely and moved into legitimate business enterprises.'

'When was this?'

'About eleven years ago. Jack, you do realise that everything we are discussing this evening will be vehemently denied and backed up with as many witnesses as I require if you decide to try and use it to incriminate me?'

'Rab, this evening is strictly a social call, and as far as I am concerned, we are just strolling down memory lane.'

'Good, just you remember that.'

'Are you ready for the fish?' said Carl, as he removed the soup plates.

'Yes, I do believe we are.'

Buchanan sat quietly and thought about how he was to bring up the subject he wanted to ask Maxwell about.

In the end it was Maxwell who broke the ice. 'Jack, I've been around the police for many years, and I've come to learn that you bunch can be circumspect in all manner of things. How about we clear the air, and you tell me what's on your mind?'

'This salmon is excellent, my compliments to Carl for cooking it to perfection.'

'You can tell him yourself; he'll be here in a minute to ask about dessert. He's a cordon blue pastry chef, did you know that?'

'No, I did not. You ask what's on my mind, well I've been wondering who the young lady is who put on a show of hanging herself from the rope swing by the river?'

'Ah, that young lady is a member of the family. Due to an unfortunate incident a few years ago, she now lives here under our doctor's care.'

'Was she one of those unfortunates that tried your wares?'

'Yes, and that is the one thing I will regret till the day I die. Does that answer your question?'

'I suppose it does.'

'Anything else bothering you?'

'I've been trying to figure out why Jamie Gallagher died the way he did. Do you have any ideas on that?'

'Dessert this evening,' said Carl, as he cleared away the main course plates and silverware, 'is a choice of caramel crème brûlée or rhubarb and strawberry tarte tatin.'

'Jack, what will it be?'

'Rhubarb and strawberry tart.'

'Will that be with cream or ice cream?'

'Cream, please.'

'I'll have the same, Carl, and would you bring the coffee and cheese board at the same time? Then you can knock off for the evening. Any word from Mrs Maxwell?'

'No, sir.'

'Thanks, Carl.'

'Jack, you asked about the late Jamie Gallagher, well, from what I've been told, he stepped off the third rung of his ladder thinking he was on the ground and fell on his chisel and bled to death.'

'And John McDermott?'

'I heard he stepped back to admire his work and went over the railings of the scaffolding.'

'You know they were on the witness protection programme?'

'Of course, I do. Their testimony put me in jail for twelve years.'

'Of which you only served seven.'

'I shouldn't have served any. You know if I'd been able to get my hands on them at the time, I'd have choked the shit out of them both.'

'But you didn't, yet they both died under suspicious circumstances.'

'As I said, both were accidents.'

'Rab, now it's my turn to tell secrets. I know from forensic and witness evidence that they were both murdered.'

'Really, by who?'

'Desserts and coffee, sir,' said Carl, lifting their desserts off the serving cart. 'Shall I put the coffee and cheese board on the coffee table in the living room?'

'Yes, thanks,'

'Then I'll bid you a good night. Oh, Mrs Maxwell just called to say her mother's operation went well and she is now resting. Mrs

Maxwell will be staying at the Glynhill this evening, she wants to be there for her mother when she wakes in the morning.'

'Thank you, Carl. I'll see you at breakfast.'

'Good night, Mr Buchanan.'

'Good night, Carl, and thank you for such a marvellous meal.'

'It was my pleasure.'

As Carl closed the door, Maxwell said, 'You were telling me the deaths of Gallagher and McDermott were not accidents?'

'Gallagher was stabbed to death; he was almost gutted with his chisel as he came down the ladder.'

'And McDermott?'

'Once again, we have forensics to thank. They found strands of McDermott's hair on the rim of an unopened paint tin. Someone hit him over the head then chucked his body off the seventh lift of the scaffolding he was working on.'

'Sad, isn't it? Shall we go through to the living room and have our coffee?'

For the third time that evening, Buchanan watched as Maxwell carefully sat in his chair and adjusted the pillow.

'Would you pour? My shoulder doesn't take kindly to leaning forward at the moment.'

'Cream?'

'Please.'

'Gallagher and McDermott weren't the only ones involved in this scenario.'

'Someone else is involved, who?'

'Me, someone tried to run me down on my own High Street.'

'If that's the case, and if you think that Gallagher and McDermott were killed, do you have any ideas as to who might have been behind these events?'

'This morning, I went for a walk up to Hope Street. While there I had a chat with someone, who I assume has been one of your supporters.'

'Has been?'

'Yes, he expressed a view that you have gone soft.'

'Probably someone who no longer sups at the Maxwell trough. Did he offer any other thoughts?'

'He said something about the Mafia trying to muscle in.'

Maxwell shook his head. 'I've heard those stories as well. In London and Liverpool maybe, not Glasgow.'

'He also said it was rumoured that Jack Howard was trying to take over your territory.'

'He said that, did he? I'll give Jack a call tomorrow and ask him. It's unlikely though, he's got enough on his hands right now keeping the new-style gangs from messing up his operation.'

'When was the last time you saw Steve Jameson?'

'Steve Jameson, not for a while, why do you ask?'

'How about a Toni Volente?'

'Name's familiar, but that's all.'

'What about Steve Jameson?'

'I've known him since he was pooping in his nappies.'

'And you don't know where either of them are hiding?'

'No, I don't.'

'Could they be hiding somewhere in the estate?'

'No, definitely not. I'll have Ivan drive you home, it's late.'

'Thanks, but I would like to walk, you've given me a lot to think about and the evening air, cold as it is, will do me the world of good.'

He stepped out onto Field Road and turned his phone back on. It immediately dinged to say he'd had a message. He looked at the display and saw he'd missed Jill's phone call.

As he walked, he listened to her message,

'Evening Jack, I guess you are busy or have decided to have an early night. I did as you asked and went for a ramble through the internet. I only found two interesting items. The first is I found a school photo of Steve Jameson and Toni Volente – they were in the same class. The other item is more interesting. Maxwell's lawyer, Benatti, deals in company acquisitions and sales. But his speciality is setting up and managing charities and trusts.'

When she said charities and trusts, Buchanan could see a hand holding a sword rising in the mist. The mystery was beginning to make sense, thank you, Jill.

He entered his room and as he undressed, he turned on the news. The headline caught his attention, Vladimir Putin was missing and hadn't been seen for two days.

22
Dinner with Mum and Dad

Buchanan woke, and he'd had no dreams that night. He felt rested, life was good. It was Saturday morning and he'd given the team the day of. Sitting up he glanced out the window, it was still dark but no clouds. He dressed and went down for a leisurely breakfast and a slow read-through of the Saturday newspapers.

He was in a happy mood. The Maxwell case was beginning to make sense and it looked like he would be home for Christmas after all. He ordered a full Scottish breakfast with coffee and opened the *Herald*. The headline statement had him reading it twice to make sure he'd read it correctly. The body of Vladimir Putin had been found floating in the Moskva River. The article speculated that Putin, worried that the war in Ukraine was going so badly, had gone for a late-night walk, suffered a heart attack and fallen into the river. More likely his oligarch friends had taken him for the walk and pushed him in the river. Now there was a death he wouldn't mind investigating.

He wasn't due at his parents till lunchtime, so he moved into the bar, taking his coffee with him. Today was going to be a three-cup morning.

By ten o'clock he'd read all he wanted and returned to his room for his jacket and coat. He left the hotel and turned left at East Kilbride Road. He stopped on the middle of the bridge and looked down at the river. Could Putin really have suffered a heart attack and fallen in the Moskva River and drowned? Or was it more likely a case of his oligarch friends realising that continued support for Putin and the war was not only bad for the country, but it was also very bad for them and their bank accounts?

They had become international pariahs, their funds in foreign banks had been frozen and there had even been talk of confiscating them to aid in the rebuilding of the war damage in Ukraine. Their luxury homes, cars and yachts had all been seized and were in danger of being sold. On top of that, they dare not move outside Russia without the threat of being arrested for their involvement in the reported war crimes committed in Ukraine.

It was probably for the best that Putin's body had been found. For now there could be a state funeral for the fallen hero, something to bring the country together, though definitely not as grand, or as meaningful, as the funeral for the Queen.

Now that Putin was dead, a new leader could be appointed and decisions could be made whether to continue the fruitless war, withdraw their troops and attempt to establish a peaceful working relationship with their neighbours. Or continue till the populace of Russia finally said enough was enough and rose in anger, repeating the mistake of the eighth of March 1917.'

At least the River Cart was at peace and had settled back to its gentle flow down to the river Clyde.

Buchanan had chosen to walk the long way round to his parents' house on Eaglesham Road. Not because he was reticent in joining them for lunch, he just missed his old stomping grounds and wanted to see what remained from his childhood memories.

He was greeted at the door by his father.

'Jack, come in! Your mother is in the kitchen.'

'Is Matthew here yet?'

'No, he rang to say he would be late. Let me have your coat, you go say hello to your mother.'

'Hi, Mum.'

'Jack, how lovely to see you! Why has it taken so long? We miss you.'

'I've been busy, it's not that easy to just come up and visit,' he said, giving his mother a hug.

'You found time to go to Dallas.'

'Guilty as charged, but it sort of was business.'

'I'm sorry, it's just I miss my boy,' she said, with a tear running down her cheek.

'I'll try to find time, I promise.'

'How's Jill, and the baby?'

'Mother and son are doing fine.'

'You're not working her too hard, are you?'

'No, I've put her on light duties till she goes off on maternity leave.'

'I should think so. Here, you can give me a hand. Would you peel the potatoes? Don't cut the skin too thick, make sure you leave enough potato to roast, and when you've done them, would you start on the carrots?'

He'd just finished peeling and chopping the carrots when Matthew arrived.

'Not much has changed,' he said, from the kitchen door, 'I see Mum has you working.'

'I enjoy it.'

'Glad to see you were able to join us, Mum has really been looking forward to you being here.'

'I do have a job to do.'

'Incarcerating those unfortunate enough to fall into your net?'

'Boys, if you're not going to help, go join your father in the living room.'

Pleased to be freed from domestic duties, Buchanan followed his brother through to the living room.'

'Hello, Dad.'

'Hello, Matt, how's the family?'

'All well.'

'It's good you are able to visit, Jack,' said his dad. 'You must find it quite different living in Eastbourne.'

'Yes,' interrupted Matthew, 'chasing all those Zimmer frame thefts.'

'Matthew, you promised to behave,' said their mum.

'Sorry, Jack, just a bit of Saturday mischief.'

'That's all right, but I might say that we have had a spate of bike thefts lately.'

'The thieves given up on stealing car radios?'

'I'll have you know that bike thefts are a big business for the criminals. In one recent robbery, thirty-five thousand pounds of top-end bikes were stolen from a local shop.'

'I didn't think bikes were that expensive.'

'Just wait till Sandy and Elizabeth want bikes, then you'll see.'

'I'll leave you boys to catch up, I'll go and help your mother in the kitchen.'

'How is Jill, Jack?' asked Matthew, as their dad made a diplomatic retreat to the kitchen.

'She and the baby are well and on schedule for a spring delivery.'

'I'm taking Sandy for his swimming lesson tomorrow afternoon.'

'How's he doing?'

'His swimming teacher says if he keeps practising, he could be an Olympic champion.'

'That is impressive, please tell him we're rooting for him.'

'I will.'

'And Elizabeth?'

'She's moving up a grade in her piano lessons.'

'That is impressive, she'll be performing on stage next.'

'She already has.'

'Oh, been a bit busy to keep up on family news.'

'How was Dallas?'

'Fascinating. As a visitor it was breath-taking, the food and entertainment just simply were marvellous.'

'And as a policeman, how did you find it?'

'A very sad experience. I felt there was a constant war going on between civil society and the criminals, with the police stuck in the middle. I came away with the impression society wants the police to lock up all the criminals, yet at the same time police budgets get cut, veteran policemen retire and move away. All because they see the traditional, good relationships with the public being eroded by the woke brigade that say the police are nothing other than gun-toting racist thugs and bullies.'

'I didn't realise things were that bad in in the country. But what about the George Floyd death? I've seen the video. A policeman was convicted and jailed for killing Floyd, wasn't that a racist act?'

'I'm not a judge or lawyer, Matt. I'm employed to investigate crimes against society, uphold the law, and not judge those who I arrest, or make comments about on-line videos.'

'Do you think these people you come in contact with are born criminal?'

'No, of course not.'

'When I was studying for my law degree, the professor told us about an account given by a notable American lawyer in which he said he didn't believe there was such a thing as a crime, as the word is generally thought of. He even went as far as postulating there wasn't any difference between the moral conditions of the people in or out of jail. He said the people in prisons could no more be responsible for being in jail as those who weren't. They were merely in jail because they were not responsible or in control of the circumstances that put them there.'

'I'm sorry, Matt. But your example describes just what is wrong with society, no one wants to take responsibility for their own actions, it's always someone else's fault.'

'No, that's not the case, it is society that makes them the way they are.'

'Are you saying it should be society that should be in jail?'

'Jack, we live in a fallen society, no longer is right or wrong taught at school. God and the bible are just some sort of fairy tale that Hollywood makes movies out of, and comedians make jokes about. In the media, the Lord's name is constantly taken in vain, and used in a derogatory way. Alcohol abuse, drugs, and sexual immorality has become the norm. Children no longer respect their elders.'

'Matt, you should be in a pulpit preaching, you're a natural.'

'That's it, go on, make fun of me. But let me make one thing clear, unless society repents of its wicked ways, God will give over to its debauchery and stand back and watch with tears in his eyes while society consumes itself.'

'Matt, you must realise that if you go making a public spectacle of yourself, you will be the laughingstock of every court in the City. Especially with those who you wish to impress, namely the very people you want to be on your side, the judge and jury that sits in judgement on your client's innocence or guilt.'

'I don't agree.'

'Illuminate me. then.'

'The bible says to trust in the Lord with all your heart and lean not on your own understanding; but in all your ways acknowledge Him, and He shall direct your paths.'

'You're really serious about this, aren't you?'

'Of course, I am, Jack.'

'When did this remarkable transition take place?'

Matt shrugged. 'Who knows? I seem to have been around a bunch of bible bashers recently.'

'Well, it's a side of you that is going to take some learning to understand. You certainly have changed from your earlier bolshie self. Just imagine, my little brother, Matthew Buchanan, defender of the faith and friend of the weak.'

'Someone has to take a stand. Early in the 1800's William Booth tried to get society to understand the desperation of its ways. Cities were full of gin shops, prostitution was rife, cut-throats roamed the streets while the gentry turned a blind eye to what was going on under their very noses. He was ridiculed for his beliefs and look what grew out of his heart-felt convictions. Hundreds of thousands of lost souls rescued from certain eternal damnation'

'And you see yourself as a latter-day William Booth?'

'If that is the way society sees me, I'd feel honoured.'

The door opened and Mrs Buchanan popped her head round the door and said, 'Boys, come and get your dinner before it gets cold.'

Matt and Jack burst into laughter. 'Here we are,' said Matt, 'two grown men arguing like a couple of school kids grousing over whose turn it was for the playground swing.'

'Matt,' said his brother, following him through to the dining room, 'I disagree with how you are going about what you believe, but I have to admit, I admire your sincerity.'

'Well, thank you, big brother, I appreciate those words of encouragement very much. Fancy a walk after lunch? We could go and say goodbye to your friend, Jock, I hear the stables are closing.'

'I'd like that very much, Matt.'

23
Going for a swim

'Mum still knows how to cook, that roast took me back to our childhood,' said Matthew as they made their way down to the river and Jock's stables.

'It truly was excellent,' said Buchanan.

'It's been a long time since we walked along the riverbank,' said Matthew, as they approached Jock's stables. 'I wonder what this is doing here?' he said, pointing at a bright yellow Volvo excavator sitting in the brush.

'Probably belongs to the building contractor.'

'Didn't expect to see you here today,' said Jock.

'I was having lunch with the family and Matthew said he'd like to see the stables one last time.'

'Welcome Matthew, would either of you like a coffee? Sorry, it will have to be instant.'

'Sounds fine to me,' said Buchanan.

'I thought you'd be taking it easy, Jack,' said Jock, as he poured the boiling water into the cups.

'I'll take it easy when they lay me down in the long wooden box.'

'What's the matter, Jack? Why such gloom?'

'I guess I'm missing home and Karen. For most of my working life I've been able to be home each evening. With this case, I'm at a bit of a loss. If I was back home, I could at least bounce ideas off Karen, or my partner, Jill.'

'Is there anything I can do?'

'Not really, I'll just have to work it out by myself.'

'I thought you had help?'

'I do, but there are aspects of the case I need to work out myself.'

'If I still had horses, you could have gone for a ride, I seem to remember that used to work for you.'

'Yes, I remember those days, pity we can't go back and relive some of them.'

'Well, at least it's stopped raining. You two want to follow me round the stables? I just can't walk away and leave it to that monstrosity over there,' he said, pointing at the Volvo excavator.

'I understand your feelings. When I left Glasgow, I took with me a photo of the Carrick and left behind a shadow on the wall. You should take something from the stables with you to remind you of the past years.'

'An excellent idea, I'll have a think as we walk the stalls.'

'When do you close?' asked Matthew, as Jock closed the office door.

'To all intents, we are already closed. All the horses and ponies have either gone to new accommodation or are wintering in the old barns where the new stables are to be built.'

'Where will that be?'

'Not far from here, just off Eaglesham Road.'

'That's not so bad then.'

'I'll miss the river, and the peace and quiet down here. I never realised I'd do this, bolting the stable doors after the last horse has left.'

'Your horses haven't bolted; they've just gone on to their new homes,' said Matthew.

'I suppose you are right in that. Want to follow me as I walk down memory lane?'

'Certainly, lead on.'

'OK, bring your coffee if you wish. This is where it all began, remember Prince, Jack?'

'Your first resident horse, I only remember him when he was getting too old to ride, though he still had fire in his belly. I remember one winter when the ground was frozen solid, I took him for a walk. He must have been really pissed to be kept in as when he thought I wasn't watching, he pitched forward and kicked me in the back with his hind legs.'

'Regardless of his idiosyncrasies he was loved by the children and would never act up when they rode him. There are many riders today who owe their love of being on horseback to that silly pony.

'Box two, if I remember correctly, that was Ashokan. I remember him so well, also his ability to find the strangest things to be spooked by. I remember once when riding up the lane to Newford Farm, he spooked himself when the tractor in the adjacent field drove past the hedge. He wouldn't move till I got off his back and led him, on foot, well past the tractor.

'Then there is box three,' said Jock. 'Do you remember Admiral, Henry Wood's horse? He never really did get on with the animal. Threw him three times in one day when he was out with the hunt. Anyway, I'm having the shoe that is nailed to the wall. It was from Wingate, remember her, Jack?'

'Before my time, Jock, pity all those memories are going to get buried.'

'Yes, it will be a sad day on Monday. Oh, now what's up? She's at it again.'

'Who's at it again?'

'Over there, on the diving step by the rope swing.'

Buchanan turned to see what Jock was looking at. It was the young girl from the Maxwell estate he'd seen earlier when she made it look like she was going to hang herself with the rope swing.

They stood and waited for the inevitable appearance of Ivan and the other guard.

'Something's different this time,' said Jock, 'maybe she was just joking and trying to wind us up the last time.'

'I'm not so sure,' said Buchanan, 'look at her face, she's just staring off into the distance, and her hands, look at her hands, clenching then releasing, she's in trouble of some sort.'

'What's she doing?' asked Matthew. 'Is she mad, or more likely she's on something? When I've been the on-call duty solicitor I've gone into cells to take statements and I've seen that sort of behaviour.'

'She's thinking,' said Buchanan

'What do you think she's thinking about?'

'I'm not sure, but I may have an idea.'

'A lost love, perhaps?'

'No,' said Buchanan, 'it's something more sinister. A few days ago, Jock and I watched her tie the rope swing round her neck as though she was about to jump off the diving step and hang herself.'

'She was probably just play-acting.'

'I don't think so, Matthew,' said Jock. 'Over the years 'I've seen many young people abuse their horses and take out their frustration on their mounts, and looking at her, she puts me in mind of one of them.'

'But she's just standing there, she'll probably turn round and go back in the house.'

'I don't think so, watch, see what she's doing, bending down and picking up rocks,' said Buchanan.

'Lots of people do that,' said Matthew, 'I've done it at the beach.'

'Have you filled your pockets with the stones?' said Buchanan, as he undid his shoelaces.

'No.'

'What are you doing, Jack?' asked Jock.

'Taking off my shoes.'

'Why on earth are you doing that? You'll get your feet wet and muddy.'

'I don't think this young woman is seeking attention,' Buchanan replied. 'I do think she is very disturbed by someone or something. Watch her hands, see how she keeps clenching them then relaxing, little fists of frustration. I'd say she is fighting some internal demon and is unfortunately losing the battle.'

'Are you all right?' shouted Matthew. 'Do you need help?'

'She can't hear you, Matthew, she's in another world,' said Buchanan, as the girl continued to pick up rocks and stuff them in her coat pockets.

'Now what's she doing?' said Jock.

'She's made up her mind,' said Buchanan, taking off his jacket and handing it to Matthew. 'Look at her face, she's smiling, she's made up her mind.'

'About what, Jack? Where are you going?' asked Matthew, as Buchanan climbed over the carpark fence.

'Hopefully where I'm needed,' replied Buchanan, as the girl screamed an obscenity and jumped into the river.

Buchanan didn't wait any longer. He stumbled his way down the riverbank, across the narrow beach and waded into the river.

'Can you see her? Has she surfaced?' Buchanan shouted, as the river reached his shoulders.

'No, she hasn't surfaced,' replied Jock. 'Be careful, the river is very deep out there.'

What the hell are you doing, Buchanan asked himself as he took a deep breath of air, ducked under the surface and began to grope in the murky river water for what he hoped would be the girl's puffer jacket. Seconds passed, nothing, he swam further and deeper, still nothing. He was getting concerned, it had been a long time since he'd tried to hold his breath under water and even then it had been in a swimming pool where the water was crystal clear.

Still nothing, further and deeper he went. Lord, if you are real, now would be a good time to show up, I'm about out of air and the girl may be seconds away from drowning. Swim to the right, came the words in his mind. No, left, he reasoned, the current would be carrying her down river. No, I said to the right, came the thought in his head again. *Lean not on your own understanding.* Why was he thinking that now? Those were the words that Matt had used earlier.

He needed to concentrate, any moment now he would have to surface for air and the girl would be lost. He groped his way to the right along the bottom and that was when he felt clothing. But not a puffer jacket like the girl was wearing, this was the collar of a man's suit, and protruding from the collar was a bearded face. He pulled back his hand and while trying to fathom why a man's fully dressed body was lying on the river bottom, he felt another horror, this was the curly head of what Buchanan reasoned was another male. Jock had told him the tale of Andy's Hole, could it be a regular occurrence where men regularly drowned in the river?

So, where was the girl? It was no good, he'd have to surface otherwise he would be joining the two unfortunates already lying in the mud at the bottom of the river. He felt for something to push himself to the surface and came into contact with what he'd been looking for, the girl's puffer jacket. Grabbing it, he kicked off curly hair and swam to the surface hoping he wasn't too late.

'Is she alive?' shouted a female voice from above.

Good heavens, thought Buchanan, even the angels are out this afternoon.

'I said is she alive?'

He glanced up to see Maxwell and presumably the girl's mother staring down at the spectacle. Buchanan didn't waste time, within seconds of surfacing he reached solid footing and, with his left arm behind the floating victim, using his first aid training, he began mouth to mouth resuscitation.

As Buchanan breathed for the girl, willing her to be alive, he was aware of someone climbing down the riverbank and standing on the edge.

'How is she?' asked Ivan.

Buchanan shook his head and continued with the mouth-to-mouth resuscitation. God must have plans for you, young lady, he thought, as she spluttered, coughed. then vomited river water.

'Oh, thank God,' came the cry from the girl's mother on the diving step above.

'Here, let me help,' said Ivan, as Buchanan carried the girl out of the water and into Ivan's waiting arms.

'Is she all right?' asked Maxwell, from above.

'Have you called the emergency service?' asked Buchanan, as he dripped river water from his clothes.

'They're on their way. Come up, Jack, you'll get your death of cold standing there.'

Buchanan waved to Jock and Matthew who'd watched the spectacle then made his way up the embankment to the diving step under the tree.

'I don't know what to say, Jack,' said Maxwell, 'except thanks and come with me. We have a guest room where you can shower and dry off while Carl washes and dries your clothes. I've motioned your brother to bring your jacket and shoes around to the house.'

24
Heart to Heart

'Feeling better, Jack?' asked Maxwell, as Buchanan, dressed in a guest bathrobe and slippers, entered the living room. 'Come, sit in front of the fire. Carl, a whisky for my friend.'

Matthew was seated in an armchair, glass in hand. 'How are you, big brother?'

'I'm fine, Matt, thank you.'

Buchanan was a little confused. Here was the godfather of Glasgow crime asking after his welfare, and Buchanan's brother sitting with Maxwell chatting as though they were at the brandy and cigar stage after a luxurious dinner.

'Thank you, Carl,' said Buchanan, taking his large whisky and placing it on the coffee table in front of him.

'That was a very gallant thing to do, Jack. You could have drowned in the river.'

'I didn't realise the river was that cold or deep. When we were kids, we never gave it a thought. We'd just strip off, swim across, climb up the bank, jump in from the diving step and swim around.'

'Nonetheless, I thank you.'

'Jock, who owns the stables across from Busby House called it Andy's Hole?'

'I've heard that story.'

'Jock said sometimes his horses would be allowed to drink from the river and even go in to cool off.'

'How is she?' asked Maxwell, as the door opened to reveal his wife.

'Dr Findley has given her something to help her sleep. He says she should be fine in the morning. Mr Buchanan, we don't know how we can ever thank you for what you did.'

'There's nothing to thank me for, it's part of who I am.'

'Nonetheless, you are a hero.'

Buchanan lifted his glass to his lips to avoid showing his embarrassment.

'Will you join us, dear? I think we owe Jack an explanation,' said Maxwell.

'In a minute, I want to say goodbye to Doctor Findley.'

'OK, see you in a minute.'

'I think I have outstayed my welcome,' said Matthew, as he stood to leave.

'No, please stay. I think you, as a lawyer, would want to know the story behind what has been going on.'

'If you are sure.'

'I am,' said Maxwell. as his wife came back into the room. 'Ah, Sheila, come and join us. I've told Jack that we will explain everything.'

'This whole saga is my fault,' said Sheila, as she sat beside her husband.

Buchanan nodded.

'You know?'

'Not all, and probably half of what I know comes from ignorant gossip.'

Sheila looked at her husband who nodded his assent.

'This whole sorry affair began seventeen years ago next week,' said Sheila. 'We were having a birthday party here at the house for my son. Our children are the result of my previous marriage, I was married before and had two children. Robert and I have no children from our marriage.'

'An accident in my youth, Jack. I'm sterile.'

'It was a night of madness, Jack. I'd been drinking, and taking whatever pills were being handed round. Robert was busy playing snooker and I felt left alone, a recipe for disaster. Being out of control, I fell under the charms of one of the guests. Well, one thing led to another, and before I realised what I was doing – well, I don't have to go into details, I'm sure you can use your imagination.

'In the morning, Robert slept late, and I tried to put the event out of my mind. Unfortunately, mother nature had other ideas and two months later my one-night stand was there for all to see, I couldn't say I had eaten too much anymore.'

'How did you take the news of Sheila's pregnancy, Rab?'

'What do you think?'

'I heard a body, minus its genitals, was found in Port Glasgow on a river Clyde, beach.'

Maxwell nodded. 'Some Clydeside ship-worker probably, an industrial accident perhaps?'

'Maxine was born nine months later,' said Sheila, 'a happy, smiling, perfect bundle of joy.'

'It took all of those nine months for me to come to terms with the fact that my wife was pregnant with another man's child,' said Maxwell, patting Sheila on the knee, 'and to eventually accept that there was no going back. And, before you ask, an abortion was never on the cards. By the time that Maxine was born, I'd come to accept the situation and believed the birth was a gift from Him up above.'

'Do you have any idea why Maxine tried to take her own life?'

Sheila looked at Maxwell, who nodded silent assent.

'I had arranged a sixteenth birthday party for Maxine and, unknown to us, someone gave her ecstasy, of which she almost died as a result. The doctors have said her condition is partly chemical reaction and partially psychological.

'We thought she was coping with the treatment she had been prescribed. We'd believed and hoped. that one day our smiling, happy, daughter would come back to us. But now – who knows? Dr Findley says she hasn't suffered from falling in the river and she should be fine in the morning with no aftereffects.'

'I never knew,' said Buchanan.

'Very few do. Other than a close circle of business acquaintances, the doctor and staff here at the house, you and your brother are the only outsiders who know,'

'Rab, I'm duty bound to ask you, do you know what two male bodies are doing stuck in the mud of the riverbed on the other side of your property?'

'Rotting, I hope,' said Sheila.

'Are you responsible for their presence in the river?'

'Jack, you're here as our guest after saving our daughter from drowning, much whisky has been consumed in the celebration, stories were told, memories of the evening's discussions became confused. Do you hear where I'm coming from, for if you don't, I will produce at least ten witnesses who will say they heard differently what I am about to tell you and Matthew. Am I making myself clear?'

'I understand what you are saying, but I must remind you of the fact that I may not be the one doing the investigation. Forensic pathology has come a long way from the days of Joseph Bell.'

'Who's he?'

'The doctor that Conan Doyle used as his model for Sherlock Holmes.'

'And I thought my wife could be vague. Carl, more whisky for our guests. Are you sitting comfortably, then I will tell you a story.

'Jack, we will ever be thankful for you saving the life of Maxine, but I hope you realise that Sheila and I desperately love our daughter, regardless of her condition. As such, as I just said, anything we say, or have said, will be vehemently denied by the two of us and a host of witnesses.'

'I understand.'

'I took on Maxine as my own flesh and have loved her every moment of her tragic life. I have taken her care as my responsibility. I have to look after her no matter what, her care is my penance as long as I live.'

'I understand that, Rab, and I honour your dedication to your daughter's care. But I must repeat, the bodies of two men in the river can't just be explained away as an accident. I will have to report their presence.'

'Do what you must.'

'So, before I make the phone call, tell us the story that you and your witnesses will later deny you ever said.'

'It was at a party for a friend's birthday here at the house a few months ago,' said Sheila, 'Robert was away on business, and I was hosting the event, even Maxine was in one of her more compliant moods and was being helpful. The doctor had put her on a new medication, and she was dealing quite well with it.

'Next morning, I was sleeping late when Ivan knocked on my door. He said he'd been doing his morning rounds of the grounds and had caught Maxine trying to go for a swim in the river. He thought something wasn't right, so he picked her up, you've met Ivan, he could pick you and your brother up at the same time and not miss a beat. So, he picked her up and returned her to her room. I didn't think much of the situation, Maxine can be a bit headstrong if she wants to be.'

'Like my kids,' said Matthew.

'Two days later I noticed the injuries on her wrists, and I was going to say something to Ivan about being a little more careful when he is dealing with Maxine. But next morning, there were more injuries on her wrists, not just scratches, but actual cuts. Years ago, we'd made sure she didn't have access to anything sharp, but she'd managed to find an old knife in the potting shed, thankfully it was so rusty it wouldn't cut anything.

'This sort of behaviour went on for weeks till a few days ago, she tried to hang herself on the old swing attached to the tree over the river. If it weren't for Ivan, she might have succeeded.'

'I saw that happen when I was visiting Jock at his stables,' said Buchanan.

'That wasn't the first time', said Maxwell. 'I had the fence strengthened but that didn't stop her.'

'After the last time,' said Sheila, 'I went to her room and when I looked into her eyes, what I saw frightened me. I saw not the eyes of our beautiful daughter, but the eyes of a mad woman hell bent on destroying herself.'

'What did you do?' asked Buchanan.

'I called Dr Findley. He looked at Maxine and immediately had her committed for observation to a psychiatric unit in a private hospital.'

'Do you know what happened to have caused the change in her demeanour?'

'We did a search of her room while she was in hospital,' said Maxwell 'and that was when we found it.'

'Found what?'

'Her diary.'

'We never knew she kept a diary,' said Sheila.

'In the diary she described what the two shites Wardlow, and Laidlow did to her on the night of the party. I won't describe these details, but suffice it to say I saw red,' said Sheila. No woman should ever have to suffer that sort of depravity.'

'I take it that the names of the two dead men in the river are Laidlow and Wardlow?' said Buchanan.

'Yes,' said Maxwell.

'How did they die?' asked Buchanan.

'Very slowly and in great pain,' said Sheila.

'I've done some dreadful things in my life, Jack, and yes I have taken the lives of those who crossed me, but never have I felt so justified in meting out punishment as I did that evening.'

'So, you killed them?' asked Matthew.

301

'The courts would only have given them, what, six or seven years for sexual assault. With good behaviour they would be out in three and ready to look for other victims. Maxine will have to live with the memories of that evening for the rest of her life.'

'But surely there are places that can help Maxine to deal with her trauma?'

'Possibly, Matthew, but Sheila and I think, and rightly so, that it is our fault that Maxine has suffered, and it is our responsibility to look after her as long as she lives.'

'A life sentence, the punishment suiting the crime,' said Matthew. 'A very strange form of justice.'

> There was a man,
> Of stout years and heart,
> Who from want of nothing
> Should break the necks
> Of those who erred
> To set one free
> From her past
> Her life of slavery

'I didn't know you were a poet, Jack,' said Maxwell

'I'm not really, it sort of comes on like a sneeze does.'

'Is it about me?'

Buchanan smiled.

'All the same,' said Matthew, 'there must be something that can be done for Maxine?'

'Matthew, I thank you for your concern, but Maxine is our responsibility. Jack, the ball's in your court. You say you will have to report your finding the two bodies in the river, that is your prerogative, but no matter what the outcome, the sentence Sheila and I will serve looking after Maxine will be for the rest of our natural lives. A sentence longer than any court would pass on us.'

'Nonetheless,' said Buchanan, 'it is my duty to report the deaths.'

'I understand, do you need the phone? I suspect yours was ruined when you went in the river.'

'I have it,' said Matthew. 'I brought it over with your shoes and jacket.'

'Excellent.' said Maxwell. 'Carl, would you get Ivan to go over the bridge to the stables and let the stable owner know that his stables are about to be overrun by the police?'

'Certainly.'

25

A Question of Duty

Buchanan, now dressed in dry clothes, hung up from calling in his report of the two bodies he'd found in the river.

'Rab, Sheila, thank you for your hospitality and honesty, but I must go, duty calls and I think I need to explain a little of what has been going on to my friend Jock.'

'Certainly, would you like Ivan to accompany you?'

'No, I think the less he's involved, the better.'

'What will you do?' Matthew asked, as they walked across the bridge on their way back to Jock's stables.'

'I plan to do what anyone would do. I will let the evidence speak for itself.'

'You won't report what Maxwell and his wife just told us?'

'Nope.'

'But, Jack, it's your sworn duty to report the facts.'

'Matt, for years, you and I have argued the merits of law and order, and we've never quite understood each other, have we?'

'No. I've always seen you as someone whose whole career was all about locking up the criminals for as long as the law would allow.'

'And I always saw you as someone who felt society was to blame for the crime we suffer from and not the criminal's actions.'

'And that is what most criminals deserve. Jack, let me pose you a question, do you think Maxwell deserves to go to jail for killing those two men who abused his daughter?'

'Anger is no replacement for the rule of law, Matt, you must know that.'

'True, but would the law adequately punish them for what they did?'

'Probably not.'

'There are extenuating circumstances certainly, but even so, Maxwell didn't have the right to act as prosecutor, judge, jury and execute the two men, despite what they did to his daughter.'

'So, Matt, you are saying that if the two men were set an indeterminate sentence, justice would be served?'

'No, you can't look at it that way. If everyone took the law into their own hands, we would have anarchy, the rule of law would be meaningless.

'Matthew, sometimes we have to bow to a higher authority and not lean on our own understanding.'

'Have you been reading the bible, because let me tell you there is another verse which says, "Vengeance is mine, sayeth the Lord".'

'Matt, it just popped into my head, like …'

'Like what?'

'Oh, nothing, just something that came to mind while I was swimming in the river.'

'I was wondering where you two had got to,' said Jock, as the brothers walked over to the office. 'And what's this about the police are on their way to drag the river?'

'Yes,' said Buchanan, 'while looking for the girl, I came across two bodies.'

'In that case, I suppose they'll all want tea and coffee, just as well I bought some extra milk yesterday.'

'Jack, it's been good to have chatted with you today, Jock, thanks for the offer of coffee, but if you two don't mind, I'll give it a miss, I need to be getting home, the children will want their bedtime story.'

'Fine, Matt, said Jock. 'I should be open for business in the spring if you want lessons for the kids.'

'Thanks, I'll bear that in mind.'

'Jack, I've really enjoyed our day together,' said Matthew, 'you've shown me a different Jack to the one I grew up with.'

'You still want coffee, Jack?' asked Jock.

'Please, no milk.'

While he waited for Jock to make his coffee, Buchanan called Gus.

'Gus, it's me, sorry to interrupt your evening, but I'm waiting for the police diving team, I've found two bodies in the river at the back of the Maxwell place, yes, at the back of Busby House. I'll probably be with the diving team when you get here, OK, thanks.'

'Let's stand outside and wait for your colleagues,' said Jock. handing Buchanan his coffee.

'Did a lot of this when I was a constable, standing, drinking coffee, waiting for something to kick-off,' said Buchanan.

'And did it?'

'Chucking out time was the worst. Men who worked in the yards earned their pay by pure physical work, drinking solid for three to four hours, hating life, themselves for living the way they did, hating you because you represented all they despised. Sober, they were the salt of the earth, drunk, they were nothing but demons in human flesh.'

'You're a bit morbid, is everything all right with you?'

'Then drugs moved in, whisky chasers were no longer good enough to help them forget who and where they were. First it was dope, then came cocaine and heroin. Now it's fentanyl, where will it all end?'

'Some people say it's the end of the world, Jesus is coming back. Remember the sandwich board men, Jack?'

'Yes, repent for the end is nigh, used to laugh at them.'

'The end happened for those two out there. What could they have done to end up in the mud at the bottom of the river? Do you know who was responsible for their deaths?'

'Responsible, where do you begin with that? Was it when their fathers got their mothers pregnant, or back a generation? Where does anything begin, or more importantly where will it all end?'

'Maybe these chaps will be able to answer your question about why they are in the river.'

Buchanan looked away from the river to the large police diving team van that pulled up beside Jock's Land Rover.

'That will be the diving team,' said Buchanan. 'I suppose I should go and introduce myself.

Cup in hand, Buchanan made his way alongside the exercise ring and over to the group of divers who were donning their wetsuits.

'Are you the person who called in the report?' asked one of the uniformed officers.

'Yes, DCI Buchanan, Sussex CID.'

'Sussex CID? Don't you people have enough crime on your own patch, that you have to come up here and cause trouble?'

'We have plenty, thank you. This is a case that accidentally spilled over.'

'What do we have?'

'Two bodies, both male, somewhere in the river.'

'Whereabouts?' he asked, looking at the wide expanse of brown murky water.

'I waded in from where that rock is,' Buchanan said, pointing to a large smooth rock sticking out of the riverbank.

'You waded in and found the bodies?'

'Yes.'

'How deep is the river?

'I don't know, I didn't have a tape measure with me, but I can assure you it is deep enough to hide three bodies.'

'Three? We were only told two.'

'I pulled one out with me.'

'Where is it now?' he asked, looking around for a body.

'This one was alive, the doctor checked her out and put her to bed.'

'Can you be more specific as to the locations of the remaining bodies?'

'Not sure if I can. As I said, I waded in here and went under about three meters out. I swam straight across to where I saw the live victim go in. Initially I couldn't find her then figured the current had carried her downstream. That was when the voice said to try to the right, I thought that advice didn't make sense, but when I couldn't find her to the left, I swam upriver to the right, and that was when I found all three of them.'

'You had a voice line? Who was giving the advice?'

'I have no idea. I asked Matt and Jock who were standing on the bank watching, and they said they hadn't said anything.'

'I've heard of divers hearing fish noise, but never voices while under water. Are you sure it was a voice?'

'Strangely enough, whether it was a voice or some extraneous sound, the bodies were there where it said they would be, and I'm glad I responded. Not only did I discover the two corpses, but the young girl survived.'

'You went in without air?'

'If you mean by that, was I wearing a scuba outfit, the answer is, no, I was only wearing my shirt and trousers. I did take my shoes and jacket off first.'

'Not a very wise thing to do, but I suppose under the circumstances a natural reaction. Unfortunately for many people that sort of action results in the rescuer perishing due to the shock of entering cold water.'

'Stupid it might have been, but after 35 years as a policeman, you don't tend to think of your own wellbeing in times of an emergency.'

'Thirty-five years, shouldn't you have retired by now?'

'That's what my boss and wife say.'

'Well, well done for trying, I like that sort of news. Now if you'll excuse me, we have work to do.'

'Zac, Henry, the DCI says to search up from a line between that rock and the tree on the opposite bank. You'll be looking for two bodies, both male.'

Jock and Buchanan stood on the riverbank and watched the trials of bubbles as the divers made their way slowly up the river, till one diver surfaced and said he'd found a body.

Twenty minutes later, two body bags containing the remains of Wardlow and Laidlow lay on the beach awaiting the arrival of the mortuary ambulance.

'Do you know who we have just brought up?' asked the lead diver.

'I have been given names but until forensics has confirmed, I'd rather not say.'

'Having broom poles shoved up their arses must have caused them a great deal of pain,' said the shorter of the two divers with a smile on his face.

'Yes. But the bullet through the brain probably stopped the pain,' said the other, smirking at his attempt at dark humour.

'Gentlemen,' said Buchanan, 'please do not repeat any of that in front of the press.'

'Wouldn't dream of it,' said the taller diver.

♦

Jock, Gus, and Buchanan stood on the riverbank and watched as the coroner's ambulance drove off with the two unfortunate bodies in the back, destined for the mortuary table.

'Quite a collection of detritus,' said Jock, looking down at the debris removed from the riverbed. Alongside the three rusty shopping carts were two bicycles, and an equally rusty safe whose door had obviously been blown open and contents removed many years prior.

'I'll arrange for the safe to be recovered,' said Gus, 'but looking at its condition I think the scrap heap, along with the shopping carts and bicycles, would be the best solution.'

'I could call the local scrap man,' said Jock, 'save you and the police the bother.'

'I think we should hold on to the safe, just in case it's got history,' said Buchanan.

'Anything else?' asked Gus.

'No, that will do for now. Jock, I'll try and catchup before I head back down south.'

'In that case, Jack, don't be such a stranger, I'll send you and Nathan the stables new address when we get settled,' he said, as he headed back to his stable for one last time.

'Fine, Jock.'

'Well, Jack, what will you do now?' asked Gus.

'I think I will make another visit to see Rab Maxwell.'

'Do you think Maxwell expects there to be two bodies in the river?'

'I will answer that question after I have talked to him.'

'I see. What do you want me to do?'

'Would you start the paperwork for the two bodies and make arrangements for the safe to be recovered?'

'Do the two stiffs have names?'

'Wardlow and Laidlow, I've no idea which is which.'

'Maybe Maxwell can tell you when you have your chat. Jack, this may come out the wrong way, but…'

'You're worried Maxwell is pulling the wool over my eyes?'

'Yes, that's one way of putting it. It could look like you have lost your objectivity in this investigation.'

'I realise that, but I can assure you all is well.'

'In that case, I'll see you in the office in the morning?'

'Yes.'

◆

Buchanan pressed the doorbell and waited for Carl to answer.

'Carl, It's Jack Buchanan.'

The gate swung open and this time, Buchanan walked unaccompanied down the driveway and up to the open front door where Sheila was waiting.

'Is it all over?' she asked.

'Act one is. The curtain will go up on act two in the morning. Just as well the house is secluded from the road.'

'Toni Benatti is here with Robert.'

'Good, I wanted to have a word with Toni Benatti.'

'I'd hoped you would come back. What do you think will happen?' she asked, as they walked along the hallway to the living room.

'I don't know at the moment,' replied Buchanan.

'All over?' asked Maxwell.

'No, just the opposite. This is just the beginning. Gus, the DI who will be in charge of the investigation, will open a case file, an autopsy will be undertaken, the identities ascertained, and witnesses sought. Depending on what evidence he discovers, a file will go to the Procurator Fiscal's office. From there, it will be up to the PF's office to decide what, if any, charges will be filed.'

'How long will that take?' asked Sheila.

'I imagine I'll have the initial cause of death report sometime tomorrow, their identities could take longer, unless you were willing to make a statement, Rab?'

'I would need to talk to Toni first.'

'Toni, good to be able to talk to you. I wanted to talk to you about something we found while doing a background check.'

'All above board, I assume?'

'Yes, what we discovered was you specialise in wills, trusts, and company acquisitions, is that a fair description?'

'Before any of us answer your questions, I would like to ask is this meeting on, or off the record?'

'I will answer that if you answer me one question.'

'Fair enough, as long as your questions don't require me to break client-lawyer confidentiality.'

'I think we are on safe ground here. My question is, are you arranging for Rab's business interests to be placed into a trust?'

'Now, that is an interesting question,' he said, turning to look at Maxwell.

'I'll answer that,' said Maxwell. 'Last night, or was it this afternoon? I don't remember. I told you about Maxine and how I feel it is my fault she has ended up where she is. I've seen the devastation that illicit drugs are causing in Glasgow and elsewhere in the world. That was when I realised some of that devastation is my doing. Seeing daily what effect it has on Maxine, I decided to take all my ill-gotten gains and put them into a trust to look after Maxine and others who may have fallen foul of illicit drugs.'

'Is moving to Eastbourne part of that decision?'

'Yes. We needed to get completely away from this environment. Maybe walking on the Downs, out in country lanes, will be part of the medication that will help Maxine to deal with the trauma she lives with daily.'

'You see,' said Sheila, 'we owe it to Maxine to look after her.'

'Jack,' said Toni, 'the ball's in your court. You could make it all go away, you're a DCI, you know how to do it. You must have connections.'

'Toni, my heart goes out to Maxine and her situation. If it were up to me, I would do what I could to make it just go away. But I'm a sworn officer of the law. For me to turn a blind eye to what I've seen and heard, I would be just heaping more wrong on top of the existing midden of wrongdoing.'

'But you will think about what I, Sheila and Robert have said to you?'

'Toni, someone recently said to me to trust in the Lord with all my heart and not lean on my own understanding.'

'And will you?' asked Sheila.

'I'll let you know, first I need to pray about this affair.'

'You, a policeman, are going to pray about it?' said Benatti.

'What is prayer, Toni? An acquaintance of mine once told me that prayer is nothing other than having a chat to God about what's on your mind.'

'You really are an enigma, Jack,' said Maxwell. 'It's late, I'll get Ivan to drive you to your hotel.'

'Thanks, but there are things I need to think about and the walk along Field Road is just what I need.'

'Will we see you again?' asked Sheila.

'I expect so.'

♦

He'd never quite been in this situation before, Buchanan thought as he walked along Field Road.

What was going on? He had definitely heard a voice, not once, but twice. Was there really a creator God? And if so, did the creator of the universe care enough about His creation that he would talk directly to individuals like Buchanan?

Buchanan had always thought if there was a God, he would have looked at what He'd made, then go off and do something else and leave the world to get on with what they were doing without interfering. So, if there really was a God, why then was He interested in Buchanan so much? After all, there must be thousands of detectives like him, all over the world, working on difficult cases at that same moment. But why would He be listening to Buchanan? That was a puzzle.

If God could hear him while swimming in the river, was He listening now? Was He reading Buchanan's mind? A distant memory came to him, it was at Sunday school many years ago, a song they sang. All he could remember were a couple of lines:

Have we trials and temptations?
Is there trouble anywhere?
We should never be discouraged,
Take it to the Lord in prayer.

Is there trouble anywhere? Of course, there was. He had Volente on the loose and if that was the case Buchanan decided he needed all the help he could get.

So, Lord, if it was You with me in the river this morning, maybe You could find time to help me sort out what to do? I realise I could just pull the rug out from Maxwell, make a full statement of facts, and add that Maxwell had threatened me. Even though Maxwell could produce many witnesses to deny what was said, Buchanan still had his squeaky-clean lawyer brother, Matthew, to corroborate what was said that evening at Maxwell's. On top of that, his team had had amassed plenty of evidence that the procurator fiscal could use to put a case together which would probably put Maxwell away for the rest of his life.

But Buchanan had seen the look on Sheila's face when they talked about Maxine. Maxwell had admitted he'd made mistakes in life and was worried sick what was to become of Maxine. He was making amends by turning his empire into a trust dedicated to the lifetime care of Maxine and others like her.

Should Buchanan turn it over to the procurator fiscal and let justice take its course? Or should he put it to the test? Maybe if things weren't resolved by close of business on Monday in

Maxwell's favour, he, Buchanan would push the investigation to its natural conclusion.

If that's OK with You, Lord, some sort of sign would be helpful. Buchanan looked up expecting a bolt of lightning to strike him, instead all we got was the hoot of an owl.

Nonetheless, deep inside he wished he didn't have to do what duty commanded. The look on Maxine's face the moment before she leapt into the river would be with him forever. He just couldn't get rid of the look of absolute despair on her face and not do something to help.

If You are still listening Lord, I'm going to need to know if You have any ideas, and now is the time to make them obvious to this tired old Glasgow cop.

26
Setting the Trap

Even though he'd only had five hours' sleep, Buchanan rose at seven, dressed and went down for his breakfast. He glanced at the newspapers and saw, not unexpectedly. that the *Record* was the only paper where its front page had the story with the photo taken from the bridge of two police divers carrying what looked to be a body out of the river.

The story said that several years ago, two men had been attempting to open a safe, the explosion duly opening the door and throwing the safe and the two men into the river, where the men drowned.

Well, that was better than expected, thought Buchanan wondering if Benatti had called in a favour of the newspaper's editor. At least Maxwell's name wasn't mentioned. Next on the morning's list of things to do was to call Jill.

'Morning, Jill, hope I'm not too early?'

'No, we're just getting ready to go to church, Karen is meeting us there, then after the service we're off out to lunch.'

'Where are you going for lunch?'

'Back to the Sundial in Herstmonceux.'

'I thought you said you went there recently?'

'We did. Stephen's dad can't get enough of the food, says it reminds him of the time they lived in Paris.'

'Well, enjoy your meal.'

'How are things in the Maxwell play?'

'Just added two dead bodies to the cast.'

'Is Maxwell involved?'

'There is a connection is all I can say at the moment.'

'That sounds strange coming from you.'

'It's a delicate matter. There are some people involved in this story that may be severely traumatised if things don't go the way I hope they do.'

'Is there anything I can do from this end?'

'Not at this moment. You go and enjoy yourself, and if you think about it, say a prayer for me, would you?'

'Certainly. Are you sure you are OK?'

'Yes, I'm absolutely sure.'

Buchanan sat back, looked at the time. and had an idea. For years his dad had wanted him to attend church on Sunday with the family, but he'd always been too busy. Today his dad would get his wish. Buchanan picked up his phone and called the family number. As usual his dad answered.

'Ah it's Jack, just a minute I'll get your mum.'

'No Dad, it is you I want to talk to.'

'Oh, what is it, son?'

'Are you and Mum going to church this morning?'

'Yes, we always do, why?'

'I'd like to come along with you – Dad, are you still there?'

'Yes, it's just I thought you and church didn't go together, any time in the past when we asked, you were always too busy.'

'Well, this morning I'm not too busy. What time is the service?'

'Ten o'clock.'

'Is it still the church on Eaglesham Road?'

'Yes, Greenbank Parish Church.'

'Good, I'll see you both at 9:45 at the front door.'

'I'm surprised to see you here, Jack,' said Matthew.

'Life's full of surprises, Matt.'

'Nice to see you here anyway. According to Mum, Dad's been singing to himself ever since you called.'

'Happy tunes, I hope?'

'Oh yes. Listen, if you're free this evening, fancy going out for a pint?'

'That sounds like a fine idea, whereabouts?'

'How about your hotel? I hear the bar has been refurbished and is becoming the place to be.'

'OK, what time?'

'Say seven o'clock?'

'Seven it is.'

'Look smart, the family are here.'

♦

'What's an Alpha course?' Buchanan asked his dad, as they were leaving after the service.

'I think it's where you have an opportunity to explore the basics of Christianity in a welcoming atmosphere, usually with a meal and short video. Why, are you wanting to sign up to one?'

'Karen's church runs one, I never knew what it was, that's all.'

'What will you do with your day?' his mother asked.

'I might visit a friend at his club, there is something I need to discuss, and a face-to-face in private is the only way to do it.'

'Do you have time for lunch, Jack?'

'Sorry, not today, I need to call on a person who is involved in the case I am working on and see if he is available to answer some pertinent questions.'

'You work too hard, Jack.'

'I know that Mother, Karen says the same thing.'

♦

Buchanan returned to the hotel and dialled the number for James Anderson, a recorded message replied, 'James Anderson is busy, but if you care to leave a message, he will return your call at the earliest convenience.

'James, it's Jack, I need a word with you, It's urgent.'

♦

While he waited for Anderson to reply, Buchanan called Sir Nathan Greyspear.

'Jack, how are you?'

'I'm fine.'

'Are you still in Glasgow?'

'Yes.'

'Have you been to see Jock at his stables, or what is left of them?'

'Yes, talked to him yesterday. I think the stables are due for demolition on Monday.'

'Pity about the stables, but he seemed to be happy enough about the new ones, more space and more horse stalls. So, you didn't just call to talk about horses, what's up?'

'I have a question to ask you, and you are quite at liberty to refuse my request.'

'Oh, one of those is it?'

'Sort of.'

'Well, ask away, though by the sounds of it, I may have to say no.'

'How well do you know James Anderson?'

'The Anderson who was here at the club with you and your boss the other week?'

'Yes, that's him.'

'Very little. why?'

'This is the cheeky part. Do you know anyone who might know if Anderson's name is going to be appearing on the coming New Year's Honours List?'

'Jack, that information is a closely guarded secret. May I ask why you want to know?'

'Because the answer will depend on whether someone goes to jail for life and two other lives will be subsequently destroyed.'

'Like that is it? Since it is you who is asking, and I trust your integrity, I just may know someone.'

'A text will do, Nathan. Just the word yes or no. You don't have to say anything else, but Nathan, I can't impress on you enough how urgent your response is.'

'I'll see what I can do, bye for now.'

Buchanan hung up, let out his breath, wondering if what he was about to do was ethical.

He had just hung up from Nathan when his phone rang.

'Jack, it's James, Your message said it was urgent.'

'Thanks for returning my call, James. I need to run something by you, and it needs to be done in person.'

'When? I'm going to be out this evening.'

'How about this afternoon – now?'

'Are you in Glasgow?'

'Not quite. I am in my hotel.'

'Forty minutes, at my club, the Carrick.'

'I'll be there.'

As his train rumbled into Glasgow Central, Buchanan wondered why train journeys were sometimes so frustrating. If the journey was a pleasant one, like the trip up from London, the time passes so quickly, yet on a commuter train they seem to go so slowly.

He left the train station and hurried his way over to Wellington Street and Anderson's club. the Carrick.

'Good afternoon, sir, are you a member?' asked the uniformed commissionaire.

'Jack Buchanan, sorry, no, I'm not a member, but I do have a meeting booked with James Anderson.'

'I see, if you follow me, I'll take you through.'

As they walked along the carpeted hall to the members' bar, Buchanan said, 'Have we met before?'

The commissionaire turned to look at Buchanan and replied, 'I thought your face was familiar, and the name Buchanan certainly rang a bell.'

'How are you, Andrew?'

'Retired three years ago, couldn't give up wearing uniform.'

'At least the only collars you now feel are the collars on guests' coats.'

'Too true. In here please, you'll find James Anderson is in the corner seat by the window.'

'Thanks, George.'

Anderson looked up and waved Buchanan over. As he walked between the chair and tables on the plush carpet, Buchan realised that the future of Maxine and Sheila's sanity and of Maxwell's freedom, all depended on the conversation he was about to have.

As he approached, Anderson stood and reached out to shake Buchanan's hand.

'Jack, it's so good to see you again. You have good news for me? We can go to the Procurator Fiscals office. Maxwell's heading for jail?'

'One thing at a time, James.'

'Something to drink?' asked Anderson, as a waiter arrived at their table..

'I'll have a Lagavulin and water,' said Buchanan.

'Excellent. Terry, a Lagavulin and water for my guest, and I'll have the same again. Oh, make mine a double, I feel a I'm going to be celebrating when my friend tells me the good news.'

'I wouldn't get too excited, James.'

'Yes, I see, still much water to run under the bridge, that sort of thing? I can't wait to finally see the back of Maxwell and his gang. I have to tell you, Jack; I've had a few sleepless nights over this case.'

'Well, I hope I can help put your mind to rest.'

'Really, we have him?'

'Well, maybe not quite as you imagine.'

'Why? What's happened?'

'Nothing in particular.'

'You're giving up the case? Oh, please don't tell me that!'

'Oh, no,' said Buchanan, shaking his head. 'Definitely not. My inquiries are just coming to a head.'

'Good. You had me worried for a moment. Another whiskey?' said Anderson, as he drained his glass

'No thanks, I'm fine.'

'Well, I certainly could do with another one,' he said, nodding to the waiter.

'Yes, Mr. Anderson?'

'Could I have another and make it a double, I feel my friend here is becoming the harbinger of dark news.'

Interesting comment thought Buchanan, who as yet hadn't touched his drink.

'Are you sure you don't want another, Jack?'

'Need to keep the head clear, James.'

Anderson nodded. 'Good idea. I understand, you're getting close to your quarry, don't want to scare it off, is that the case?'

Never a truer word spoken, thought Buchanan.

Buchanan waited for the waiter to deliver Anderson's drink. 'Well, Jack, if you are not quite ready to fire the torpedoes at Maxwell's ship and sink it, where exactly have you got to?'

'Well, we began by checking on his known associates, his haunts, and even made enquiries with his enemies. We have amassed a great deal of information on Maxwell.'

'Anything further on who took a pot shot at him and missed.'

'They didn't miss, the bullet ricocheted off his laptop and went through his shoulder.'

'Pity about that. It would have saved as a heap of trouble if the gunman hadn't missed. There was also a bombing I heard?'

'Yes, destroyed his site office while he, his lawyer and accountant were having a meeting, and, if I hadn't recognised the bomber, the bomb would also have got me.'

'You were there? What for?'

'I wanted to talk to him about something he mentioned the last time we talked.'

'How often do you two have these little tête-à-têtes?'

'As and when necessary.'

'Not at his bar, Porters, I hope? Remember what happened the last time you were there? If I remember correctly someone tried to knife you?'

'I remember only too well, still have the scar on my face to prove it.'

'So, where did you meet?'

Why was Anderson looking so worried wondered Buchanan? What did it matter where and when he talked to Maxwell? Then a thought came into him his mind, was Anderson concerned that Maxwell may have paid Buchanan off to drop the investigation? Time to put Anderson off guard.'

'I had tea with him at Busby House last Tuesday.'

'Just the two of you?'

'No, his manservant, Carl, was there as well.'

'You want to be careful, Buchanan. You don't know how a jury and judge would look at fraternising with the enemy. You did have witnesses with you, didn't you?'

'No, not that time. I'm staying at the Busby Hotel and thought I'd just go for a walk along Field Road and just drop in for afternoon tea.'

'How was he, worried I hope?'

'His doctor said as long as he rested there would be no long-term effects from the gunshot.'

'That's not what I meant, did he show any signs he was worried that you were investigating him, did he threaten you if you didn't back off?'

'No, we just talked about family matters.'

'This is not good, Buchanan. I chose you to head up this investigation because I felt of all the people I could have chosen, you had the grit and tenacity to get under Maxwell' skin and find his Achilles heel. You were to gather evidence that we could use to finally bring him down, not have afternoon tea.'

There it was again, thought Buchanan, the "we" word, just who were the "we" in this scenario?

'Do you have any idea who took a shot at him?'

'Yes, I have a pretty good idea who the gunman is.'

'How about the bombing?'

'It was the same person.'

'Do you have a name?'

'Yes, but I'd rather not reveal it at this time. I'd rather keep that confidential for now.'

'Do you know where he — and I'm presuming it is a he – is hiding?'

'Not at the moment, we're still looking for him and his accomplice. The car they were driving was traced from Eastbourne area all the way up to the Busby, where it appears to have vanished into thin air.'

'There are two of them?'

'That's the way it looks.'

'This is not good, Buchanan; we have enough trigger-happy thugs loose on the streets as it is. To hear that a gunman who also uses bombs to commit their crimes is bad news. What do you and your team plan to do about it?'

Before he could answer, Buchanan's phone buzzed. He quickly glanced at the screen and smiled.

Anderson waited for Buchanan to put down his phone before resuming. 'We know he runs a very successful construction company amongst other businesses,' continued Anderson.

'Sounds like he's going straight to me,' said Buchanan.

'Leopards never change their spots; Maxwell needs to pay for the damage his drugs have done to the unsuspecting youth of Glasgow.'

'Just suppose for a minute that Maxwell has fact gone legitimate, is giving up his nefarious affairs and is handing all over his businesses over to a charity to fight drug addiction, what would you say to that?'

'I'd say you were writing a fairy-tale.'

'Thank you, James, I'll keep you appraised of anything that happens.'

'You do that.'

27
Curtains

As Buchanan walked back to Central Station and his train back to Busby, he thought about Greyspear's message, it simply said "Yes". So that was what all this was about. A complete charade for Anderson's benefit. If Anderson could convince his backers that using Buchanan as a front man to put the godfather of Glasgow crime in jail; it wouldn't just be James Anderson, it would be Sir James Anderson.

As the train rumbled out of Glasgow Central, Buchanan reflected on the day. Church with the family in the morning. Did he miss living in Glasgow, being far away from the immediate family? He supposed he did in a way. But he and Karen had made a new life for themselves down south. They now had a new family, though not connected by birth. Jill and Stephen were as much family as anyone could wish for, and there was the bonus of Jill's baby, affectionately known in the family as Buchanan's grandson, also to be called Jack.

♦

He opened his bedroom door and saw someone had slipped an envelope underneath. He bent down, picked it up and opened it.

It was a short message that read: *Jack, would you stop by Busby House this evening, urgent, M.*

Buchanan surmised the initial M was for Maxwell. He looked at the time, five forty-seven, what should he do? Would he be able to get to Maxwell's house, discuss what Maxwell wanted and still get back to the hotel by seven? It was a tricky one. He decided to have a shower and a change of clothes while thinking about his response.

As he brushed his hair, he decided to call Matthew and apologise and say that work had to come first.

'Matt, sorry to do this to you, but Maxwell has just sent a message saying it's urgent and would I stop by his house this evening.'

'Not a problem, big brother, would you like me to come along for support? Then afterwards, as long as it's not too late, we could go and have a beer.'

'Perfect idea, when can you get here?'

'Twenty minutes, that do you?'

'I'll be waiting in the lobby.'

♦

'That was quick, did you drive?' said Buchanan.

'No, took the bus.'

'Good idea to take the bus, pity there aren't any along Field Road, it will be a walk to Maxwell's house.'

Buchanan pressed the gate doorbell and waited.

This time, no audio inquiring who was there, just the groan as the hydraulic ram pulled the gate open.

'Don't think much of their security,' said Matthew.

'Up there, and over there,' said Buchanan, pointing at CCTV cameras high up on top of the gate posts. 'They knew we were here.'

Buchanan didn't have to knock; Carl was there to open the door for them.

'This way, Mr Buchanan.'

'Thanks,' said the brothers, in unison.

'They are waiting for you in the sitting room.'

They, wondered Buchanan? Who are 'they'?'

He entered the room, and his question was answered. Standing at full height in front of the fireplace, arm still in a sling, was Maxwell, beside him, his wife Sheila. Seated in the armchair on Maxwell's left was Andy Jameson, in the other chair was Toni

Benatti, the settee was empty as were the two armchairs on the right of the fireplace.

'Jack, I see you've brought reinforcements, welcome Matt. Carl, drinks for our guests.'

'We were going out for a beer before I read your message, Rab.'

'McEwan's do?'

'Perfect.'

'Why don't you take a seat?' said Maxwell.

Jack and Matthew sat in the two available armchairs, Maxwell and Shelia on the long settee.

'Now that you are all seated, I'm sure Jack would like to know why he has been summoned, wouldn't you, Jack?'

'Yes, I must admit to having those exact thoughts.'

'Well, hold on to your horses, Andy here would like to say something. Andy, the floor's all yours.'

'I would like to begin by apologising to you, Jack, for what happened.'

'What for, we were on two sides doing what came naturally. I nicked you and you got what you deserved.'

'I'm not referring to that past, what I am referring to is what my son, Steve has been up to. Please, let me continue. I hadn't heard from him for several months, so when I heard he was around, I put out a message that I would like to see him, just like any father would when his son has been out of touch for several months. Eventually I heard he was down south, in your neck of the woods, Jack. I managed to get in touch with him through the place he was staying. He told me he was working as a labourer for a couple of Glaswegians that he knew from the days up here. I asked him who they were, and he told me Jamie Gallagher and John McDermott. I enquired how they were doing, and he said they were very busy. That was the last I heard from him till yesterday.'

'Excuse me for interrupting, Andy, but did he say where he was staying?'

'With a friend from his school days, he wouldn't say where, that was on account that you lot were looking for him.'

'Go on.'

'Well, he said he was worried because the police were getting close, and he needed money to get out of the country. He said he'd got in with the wrong people and he's killed twice.'

'Why doesn't he turn himself in and take what is coming to him? Surely that would be better than a life on the run?' said Matthew.

'And who are you to give me advice on what to do with my kid?'

'Matthew Buchanan, barrister.'

'Oh, one of them.'

'Careful with what you say,' said Benatti, 'I'm one as well.'

'Sorry, that kid has me all wound up.'

'Did he say who he's killed?' asked Buchanan.

'The two guys he was working with. He said it was easy, just make it look like an accident he was told, no one would know the truth.'

'Who hired him?'

'The guy he's been hanging out with took the contract and paid Steve to do the job.'

'Who was that?' asked Buchanan.

'Someone he went to school with, first name Dino, don't know the surname, has a Glasgow accent. He just got kicked out of Spain.'

'Why are you just now telling Rab about this?' asked Buchanan.

'Because, bad as he is, he's still my son, my only son. I don't want him to end up being killed. Twenty-five years inside would be preferable. At least I could go and visit him.'

'So, what do you want me to do about it?'

'I said to him I would talk to you and see if it could be arranged for him to give himself up.'

'Why doesn't he just walk into any police station and say who he is, and he wants to give himself up?'

'He's afraid you lot will fix him proper, prisoners still die in police custody, especially those who kill cops.'

'He's killed a cop?' said Buchanan.

'Yes. It was where they were working, Dino saw a detective crossing the road and made Steve run him over.'

'He didn't succeed.'

'How do you know?'

'That cop was me. If it wasn't for my neighbour pulling me back in time, he might have succeeded in his quest.'

'He said if he gives himself up, you'll make it look like suicide.'

'You said he was sharing his digs with a school chum?'

'Yes, and that's another issue, Dino is watching him, thinks he's going to rat on them both for a more lenient sentence if they are caught.'

'Did he say why Gallagher and McDermott were killed?'

'He didn't know but when he asked Dino, he said it was something to do with a new supply of drugs that were about to come into the country, and they were going to tell their handlers about it.'

'Where is Steve?' asked Buchanan.

'I wish I knew. If I did, I would go get him myself.'

'Is there anything else you haven't told us?'

'Yes, he said Dino was mad and wanted to start a turf war so he could take over Rab's operation. I told him Rab was winding it up and giving it all to charity.'

'How as Dino going to start this turf war?'

'He was going to kill Rab and blame it on the Howard clan, and we know he almost succeeded.'

'Did you tell Steve that he almost killed you?'

'Yes.'

'What did he say?'

'It's not worth repeating.'

'Now you know all, Jack,' said Maxwell, 'what do you advise?'

'Not knowing what Dino will do next is a problem, Rab. Will he have a go at the Howard clan and blame it on you? That is the question, and issue. With you being public enemy number one, the authorities might just believe it was you. No matter what, we have to get Dino off the street before he has a chance to do worse.'

'So, what will we do?'

'I suggest we first take stock of all of what is involved. We have Maxine's future to consider, the transfer of the company assets to the trust, amnesty for Rab so he and Sheila can continue to look after Maxine, Steve Jameson wants to give himself up and face the music, Dino Volente needs to be neutralised before he starts a turf war, and then there are the two stiffs pulled from the river and finally, there is the issue of Anderson.'

'What's that buffoon got to do with this?' asked Maxwell.

'He may just be the key that unlocks this tangled web of deceit and treachery.'

'Waxing lyrical, brother?' said Matthew.

'Just mangling Walter Scott. What we need to do is to create a scenario that resolves all the issues I laid out.'

'How?' said Benatti.

'I had a drink with Anderson this afternoon where he remarked that the two bodies removed from the river were victims of a caper that went wrong, I didn't dissuade him of that idea, especially since it was headline news in the *Record*.'

'That trash,' said Maxwell.

'Nonetheless, it could be your way out of a very difficult matter.'

'What about forensics?' asked Matthew. 'Won't forensics be able to determine how and when the men died?'

'Yes, but that is a problem further down the road. As long as we can keep Rab and Sheila out of the line of investigation about the two men found in the river, it should clear the way for the main issue of Dino Volente.'

'Do you have any ideas, Rab?'

'If we knew where he was, we could just knock on the door and when he answered blow his head off."

'No, that just wouldn't do,' said Buchanan. 'Andy, how do you get in touch with Steve?'

'Mobile phone.'

'Do you know where he is right now?'

'Yes.'

'Is he free to come and go?'

'Yes.'

'Does he have transport, Andy?'

'No, and neither does his friend he s staying with, and he doesn't want the police at the door. He won't come out if the police are there.'

'How about I go?' said Matthew. 'I'm a lawyer. He doesn't know me, but I'm used to dealing with prisoners, I know how nervous they can be.'

'How will you get there? You came by bus.'

'I'll have Ivor drive him,' said Maxwell.

'I'll need the address,' said Matthew.

'It's 105 Cartside Road,' said Andy.

'Carl,' said Maxwell, 'would you tell Ivan he is required?'

'Yes, boss.'

'Matthew, make sure you bring him here first,' said Maxwell, 'I want to have a word with the little shite before the police get their hands on him.'

'How about Dino? Is he there with Steve?' asked Buchanan.

'No,' said Andy. 'Steve said Dino went to stay with someone called Sean Feeney.'

'You wanted me, boss?' said Ivan.

'Yes, would you drive Andy and Matt to pick up Steve, Andy's son? Use the Audi.'

'Sure thing, boss.'

'Feeney?' said Benatti, 'He's one of Howard's men.'

'Where's my phone?' said Maxwell. 'I need to have a word with Jack Howard.'

All eyes stared at Maxwell as he called Jack Howard, boss of the Howard clan.

'Jack, it's Rab Maxwell … never mind the pleasantries. You've got a fox in the henhouse… what I'm saying is your man Feeney is harbouring someone who is detrimental to both our interests. What's his name? Dino Volente. The shite tried to gun me down on Monday then when he failed, he came back on Wednesday and tried to blow me and my friends to kingdom come. What do I want you to do about it? I don't give a shite what you do about it except I don't want to hear about him walking the streets. Yes, a midnight swim in the Clyde would be fine.'

'You've just signed his death warrant,' said Benatti.

'That's life on the streets,' said Maxwell.

'I have a phone call to make,' said Buchanan, 'I'll put it on speaker.' He scrolled through his phone directory and pressed the phone for James Anderson's number.

'Good evening, James, Jack Buchanan.'

'Hello, Jack. Would it be possible for you to call back later? I'm in a meeting.'

'Could that be with those who wish peace to prevail on the streets of Glasgow?'

'As a matter of fact, it is.'

'Good, they will need to hear what I have to say as well.'

'Are you sure?'

'Absolutely. James, I've been giving consideration to our conversation this afternoon. Do you recall saying something about the two bodies removed from the River Cart yesterday?'

'Yes.'

'I won't ask you to confirm or deny, but it looks like someone has got to the editor of the *Record* and told the editor to print the story about the two men being killed in a botched robbery.'

'No one here has talked to any newspaper editor.'

'Well, I think for once, the *Record* has published the facts correctly and those two men actually were killed over a botched robbery.'

'Jack, I don't quite understand where you are going with this fabrication. We all know it was Maxwell who killed them. The resultant publicity around their gruesome deaths will put to death any chance Maxwell has for exonerating his past'

'James, I will say this only once. Men who get drunk and push young girls into rivers, leaving them to drown, never, ever, make it on the list of names published in the New Year. Do you hear me?'

'Yes, Jack, I hear you loud and clear. Those two men died as a result of a botched robbery by persons unknown.'

'Does that mean we can still move to Eastbourne and begin life again?' said Sheila, as Buchanan hung up from talking to Anderson.

'Yes, you are free to sell up here and take Maxine away from this house and its memories.'

As Buchanan put his phone away, Matthew, Ivan and Steve Jameson entered the room.

'You're a short little shite, aren't you?' said Buchanan.

'Before you get arrested,' said Maxwell, 'I would like to ask you a question.'

'Rab, sorry, but duty must come first. Steve Jameson, I am Detective Chief Inspector Buchanan of Sussex Police, I arrest you for the murder of Jamie Gallagher and John McDermott, you do not have to say anything, but it may harm your defence if you do not mention when questioned something which you later rely on in court. Do you understand?'

'Yes.'

'You have the right to a court appointed solicitor if you cannot afford one.'

'Are you done?'

'Yes.'

'What about when I tried to run you down, aren't you going to charge me with that?'

'No. I should have been looking where I was going.'

'Do you need legal support?' asked Matthew.

'You a lawyer?'

'Yes. Would you like me to represent you in court?'

'Why not?'

'Now it's my turn,' said Maxwell.

'Rab,' interrupted Buchanan, 'Steve is under caution, anything he says can be used against him. If you want to talk to Steve, you will need to do it down at the police station.'

'That's all right Mr Buchanan, I'm done for anyway.'

'I'm not here,' said Buchanan.

'Steve. I sent you down to Eastbourne to look after a house that I was buying. What happed?'

Steve looked at Buchanan, who nodded and said, Go, ahead and answer Rab. I'm not in the room so can't hear what you are saying.'

'It was all going fine, I found somewhere to stay near the pier. One Friday night I was in the bar drinking and that was when I met Gallagher. He remembered me from the days in Glasgow and asked me if I was looking for work. Well, you hadn't found a house yet and I was bored, so I went to work with him. Two nights later I met up with Dino, we went to school together. He and I had a few drinks together, went back to his place and that was when asked me if I wanted to try some skunk. I said why not. By the end of the week, I was on pills that made me weird. He asked me if I wanted to make some real money and I said yes. That was when he told me to do Gallagher.'

'How much did he offer you?' asked Maxwell

'A monkey.'

'Five hundred pounds,' said Buchanan. 'Is that all life is worth these days?'

'He doubled it for McDermott.'

'Did he say why he wanted them dead?'

'Something about them getting involved in a new line of drugs that would put everyone out of business. I'm ready, Mr Buchanan.'

♦

'Thanks for the beer, Jack. You know you truly are an enigma,' said Matt, as Buchanan placed his beer on the table.

'I'll take that as a compliment, thanks.'

'I just don't understand how you, as a dedicated policeman, would conspire to see that a known killer and drug dealer was just simply told to get on his way and not do it again. He deserves to be in prison for the rest of his life for what he's done.'

'That's where grace triumphs over the law, Matt. I thought you of all people could see that.'

Matt put his beer down and leaned back in his chair, smiled, and slowly shook his head. 'You're quoting scripture, aren't you? If I understand you correctly, what you are saying is Maxwell didn't get what he deserved, instead he got what he didn't deserve.'

'Got it in one, Matt, the definition of grace. Whereas he should be spending the rest of his natural life in prison of the State's making, he will be dedicating the rest of his natural life, twenty-four-seven, to looking after his daughter, Maxine, a voluntary task of his own making.'

The End

Lightning Source UK Ltd.
Milton Keynes UK
UKHW051512161122
412249UK00002BA/2

Bear the Burn

(Fire Bears, Book 2)

T. S. JOYCE